# HEART BLOCK

# What Reviewers Say About
# Melissa Brayden's Work

"This was an engaging book with believable characters and story development. It's always a pleasure to read a book set in a world like theater/film that gets it right...a thoroughly enjoyable read."
—*Lez Books*

"This is Brayden's first novel, but we wouldn't notice if she hadn't told us. The book is well put together and more complex than most authors' second or third books. The characters have chemistry; you want them to get together in the end. The book is light, frothy, and fun to read. And the sex is hot without being too explicit—not an easy trick to pull off."—*Liberty Press*

**Visit us at www.boldstrokesbooks.com**

# By the Author

Waiting in the Wings

Heart Block

# HEART BLOCK

*by*

Melissa Brayden

2012

**HEART BLOCK**
© 2012 By Melissa Brayden. All Rights Reserved.

ISBN 10: 1-60282-758-3
ISBN 13: 978-1-60282-758-5

This Trade Paperback Original Is Published By
Bold Strokes Books, Inc.
P.O. Box 249
Valley Falls, NY 12185

First Edition: November 2012

---

**Credits**
Editor: Cindy Cresap
Production Design: Susan Ramundo
Cover Design By Sheri (graphicartist2020@hotmail.com)

# Acknowledgments

First of all, I have to share with you how much I enjoyed working with the characters in Heart Block and how much I will miss them now that our journey together is complete. But I know without a doubt that I'll carry a little piece of each one of them along with me as I go. I wouldn't want it any other way.

But down to serious business. There were numerous people who contributed to making this story happen, and I would be remiss in not offering them my gratitude.

Many heartfelt thanks to the following people:

Len Barot and the well-oiled machine of creativity that is Bold Strokes Books. I feel supported, nurtured, and cheered on in all the right moments, and that's pretty cool. It's my hope that we have many more stories to tell together.

Sheri. You turn out amazing covers and this one brings me great happiness.

The great writers I'm now happy to call my friends. That's been the best surprise of all. The publishing world can feel scary at times, and I'm beyond grateful for the advice, laughs, and heartfelt conversations we've had over the past year. How lucky I feel to know you.

My editor, Cindy Cresap, who is smarter than me. Thank you for catching my errors and thinking of things that would never occur to me in a million years. You're also always right and thereby valuable beyond measure. You made this book stronger and are the voice of reason to my Hail Mary attempts at writing. Thank goodness for that.

The "Core Five" and the "New Additions." You made me who I am and taught me what I know. Thank you for wine nights on the patio. Game nights around the table. And memories to last a lifetime. You keep me going. You're my safe place to fall.

The readers who have sent me notes, e-mails, and Facebook messages that keep me smiling. You make a difference.

# Dedication

Love to A, T, & B

# CHAPTER ONE

L aundry had never been sassier. Sarah clutched the basket of clothes to her side with her right hand and freed her hair from the ponytail holder with her left. Giving her curly hair an effective shake so it fell in haphazard waves down her back, she proceeded to dance down the hallway of her two-bedroom apartment for all she was worth. It was mid morning, she had the place to herself, and damn if she wasn't going to work it for the length of the song. She sashayed aggressively on the downbeat of the chorus to "Brick House" and shimmied forward then backward through the second verse, adding her own Latin flair. She full-on rocked out the remaining distance before jumping onto the couch, discarding the laundry basket, and falling to her knees, finishing the number like the champ she knew she was. She internally applauded herself, not necessarily for skill, but for serious commitment. Finally, she picked up the laundry basket and calmly completed her walk to the washing machine.

It was a good day, and Sarah was enjoying the leisurely pace she'd established for completing the mundane chores on her to-do list. Just outside her petite laundry room, she straightened Grace's second grade school picture on the wall and smiled as the image of her daughter, two years younger then, grinned back at her.

Sarah made a mental checklist of all the things she needed to accomplish before the day was out and groaned inwardly when she recognized the tap-tap-tap of small raindrops on the laundry room window. Okay, she'd have to make a few adjustments to her day. Luckily, there were still several more around-the-house chores she could knock off the list, followed by a short trip to the grocery store. She sighed deeply, deciding that in order to be practical, she should probably pick up the pace a tad. *Less dancing, more working.*

She hit the start button on the washer, mamboed her way into the kitchen, and poured her second cup of coffee that morning. There could never be too much coffee. Somewhere in the back of her mind, it registered that the phone was ringing. She turned absently in its direction, interrupting her enjoyment of the warm, caffeinated pick-me-up.

"Hello," she answered cheerfully. She was always a morning person.

"Yes. Hello. May I speak with Sarah Matamoros please?"

"This is Sarah." She glanced at the caller ID readout. It was Grace's school calling, which gave her minor pause. She'd dropped her off at school nearly two hours ago. "Is everything okay with Grace?"

The calm female voice hesitated. "That's what I'm calling about, Ms. Matamoros. Grace had an incident in her classroom this morning and lost consciousness for several minutes."

Sarah stood up straight, her hand fluttering to her heart, her stomach dropping as if on cue. "What happened?"

"We're not exactly sure. Her teacher mentioned she'd been quieter than usual most of the morning, but she assumed Grace was just tired. Just as the students were beginning work on their science assignment, Grace got up to sharpen her pencil and collapsed in front of the sharpener. She didn't strike anything as she fell, but it took a couple of minutes to revive her and EMS was called. She's alert now and communicative but still somewhat confused about what happened. The paramedics have expressed concern and would like to transport her to Mercy General for further evaluation. Can you meet them there?"

"Of course." Sarah looked around the room wildly for her purse. "I'm leaving now. Thank you." She hung up the phone just as her once-stable world seemed to tilt on its axis. She gripped the countertop tightly to steady herself against the onslaught, her heart ready to jump from her chest. After a few purposeful deep breaths, her vision once again cleared and the room righted itself.

As she made her way through the door of her apartment, she thought back to earlier in the day, scrutinizing Grace's every move with new perspective. She'd been just fine a few hours before in the car on the way to school. They'd talked about their plans for the summer and the possibility of Grace attending the YMCA's day camp now that she would be in the fourth grade and showing signs of responsibility. She'd been so excited. The image of Grace's face lighting up at the news played like a movie in Sarah's mind. So what had gone wrong? Her rational side understood that Grace could have fainted from something as simple as not having eaten a decent breakfast. They had been in a hurry and she hadn't examined whether Grace had actually eaten the cereal and juice she'd set out for her. But the mother in Sarah feared the worst, conjuring up all sorts of terrifying scenarios. She put her key in the ignition and gunned the engine, doing eighty-five easy on the freeway.

It was raining outside. Hard. Emory Owen could hear it mercilessly pelt the roof and see the thick drops as they raced past the somewhat smudged window she stared out. It was the kind of rain that made her want to stay inside, snuggled up under the comfort of her favorite chenille blanket, a cup of hot mint tea in her hand. Instead, she sat amidst uncomfortable blue plastic chairs, harsh fluorescent lighting, and year-old magazines in the waiting room of Mercy General.

"Miss Owen?" A pause. "Excuse me, Miss Owen; did you hear what I said?"

She did and she didn't. Emory turned fully to the older woman in the white coat who'd said her name. She blinked, trying in vain to clear her head. "I'm sorry. Would you mind repeating that?" Numb. With very good reason, she felt numb.

The woman's tone softened. "My name is Dr. Turner and I'm in charge of your mother's case." Emory accepted the extended hand and stared at the woman, randomly noticing the patches of gray at her temples. "Why don't we sit down?" Emory nodded her agreement, trying to read the doctor's face. "We've run some tests on your mother."

It was a massive stroke, just as we originally thought. Unfortunately, Ms. Owen, her prognosis at this point is not very promising and there are some things we need to discuss."

Emory nodded her understanding, suddenly acutely aware of the sounds in the room—the hum of the lights overhead, the steady beep of an unidentified machine behind the nurse's station, the squeak of the custodian's sneaker on the vinyl floor just feet away. Everything seemed so much louder. Why?

"The stroke has caused her brain a great deal of trauma. What this comes down to, Ms. Owen, is a profound loss of brain function."

"She's brain dead? Is that what you're saying?"

The doctor nodded. "It is. Her heart and lungs are currently sustained by artificial means, but—"

"I understand. Can I see her?" Emory asked.

"Of course. Is there someone we can call for you?"

"No, there's no one. I'll handle it." And she would.

❖

"A heart block?" Sarah repeated. "I'm not sure I understand. What does that mean, Doctor…?"

"Turner," the woman supplied. She had kind eyes. "A heart block occurs when the electrical impulses that tell the heart to beat do not transmit properly. The EKG showed that the heart block in Grace's case is producing a bradycardia, or very slow rhythm, which we believe was the cause of her loss of consciousness this morning."

Sarah leaned against the wall for support. She didn't like the implications of what she was hearing. "Is this a life-threatening condition?"

"No, not usually. Grace is lucky. She's not dealing with a complete block but rather a block of the second degree. The impulses in her heart are delayed, slowing her rhythm, but they're not blocked entirely."

Sarah shook her head slowly. "Why didn't I pick up that something was wrong?"

Dr. Turner placed a reassuring hand on Sarah's shoulder, dipping her head to meet her eyes. "Don't beat yourself up. Without an episode like this one to prompt an EKG, the block wouldn't have presented itself on a normal checkup. Most likely, Grace was born with this condition. Often times with symptoms like fatigue, shortness of breath, a fluttering feeling in the chest, children don't know how to describe what they're feeling and assume they're simply tired."

It did make sense, but Sarah still felt as if her mother's intuition had somehow failed her. She should have known something was wrong, should have picked up on the problem. "What do we do now?"

"Well, the first step is to get you set up with a pediatric cardiologist, who I imagine will want to run a few more tests. There's a chance that Grace may require a pacemaker at some point, but that might be something the doctor will want to hold off on, as Grace hasn't exhibited many symptoms up until this point."

"What does she need in the meantime? Medication? How do we stop this from happening again?"

"For now, continue to monitor her physical activity. Children with heart blocks can still lead physically active lives, but their endurance is generally weaker. Grace informed me she had been running on the playground before school, and that could have contributed to the collapse during class. She may have to pull back a little."

"You haven't spent much time with my daughter."

"I'll leave the hard work to you then." Dr. Turner patted Sarah's shoulder and began walking down the hall. "The nurse will bring you some literature along with her discharge paperwork, and I'll get you a list of referring cardiologists. Be back in a little while. And, Ms. Matamoros?"

Sarah straightened. "Yes."

"Try not to worry."

Sarah swallowed hard and nodded politely, knowing the impossibility of that request.

Once alone, she took a moment in the hallway and exhaled slowly before pushing open the door to the small hospital room. Grace turned her head on the pillow and smiled up at her. She'd worn her hair in a ponytail to school that day, but it was down now and framing her delicate face with soft waves. "So what's going on in here, monster? Have you run the nurses ragged since I last saw you?"

"Nope. A perfect angel." But the smile didn't reach her eyes.

Sarah sat next to Grace and leaned across the space between them, kissing her forehead and smoothing her hair. "It was scary today, wasn't it? When the paramedics came?"

Grace met her eyes. "A little. I didn't know what had happened and I was confused. But…"

"But what, mija?"

"I just don't want you to be upset anymore. You were crying when you came in before, and I hate it when I make you sad."

Sarah's heart ached at just the thought of Grace thinking more about her feelings in this scenario. She'd always been a sensitive, caring kid, and for that, Sarah was grateful. She didn't know what she would do without Grace. The thought ran her over like a Mack truck. She pushed the gathering emotion aside, however, and focused on putting on a brave face. She was the adult, and it was up to her to get them through whatever might be ahead. "Well, I'm not upset anymore. See?" She crossed her eyes playfully and Grace giggled. "I talked to Dr. Turner and she says you're going to be fine. You just have to take it easy until we sort this whole thing out. Deal?" Sarah extended her hand.

"Deal." Grace accepted the handshake, her smile genuine this time.

Sarah stood. "Hungry?"

"Thirsty. Can I have a Sprite?"

"I'll see what I can dig up. I think I saw a vending machine on the next hall."

As she walked, she reminded herself of Dr. Turner's comforting words. This diagnosis did not mean Grace wouldn't go on to live a normal, healthy life. They were just going to have to be a little more cautious and follow whatever orders the cardiologist laid out for them.

She paused at the vending machine, waiting her turn behind a well-dressed woman attempting to get the machine to accept her dollar bill. On her fifth unsuccessful attempt, the woman swore under her breath. On her sixth, she launched a physical assault against the machine, hitting it repeatedly with her open hand and kicking it simultaneously. Sarah watched in surprise before tentatively stepping in. "Excuse me?" Whether the woman didn't hear her over the banging or was choosing not to acknowledge her was unclear, but Sarah pressed on. She took a step forward, now standing next to the machine and its attacker. "Hey, hey, take it easy," and then finally, "STOP!"

The woman turned and looked at Sarah, blinking in surprise. She took a look around her, seeming to take stock. Her hands fell dejectedly to her side and she took a pointed step back from the machine, shaking her head once. "I'm sorry," she said quietly. "It's been a rough day."

She turned to go, but Sarah put a hand on her forearm, stopping her. The look in the woman's striking blue eyes was hauntingly empty. It registered deeply in Sarah, and she wondered what the woman must be going through. "Wait," she said gently. "I have some extra quarters." She stepped up to the machine and deposited three coins into the slot. "What would you like?"

"A Diet Coke would be great."

"Coming right up."

The woman accepted the cold drink and held it up weakly. "Thanks." She then extended her dollar bill to Sarah in payment.

"Not necessary," Sarah answered, purchasing the Sprite Grace had asked for. "I hope your day gets better."

Sarah thought of the woman and the look of profound loss in her eyes as she walked back to Grace's room and realized how lucky she was. She vowed then and there that she would treasure every moment she had with her loved ones and count each one of her blessings from this moment forward. Life was too precious not to.

## CHAPTER TWO

Trevor, do you have the agency packet ready for my presentation with 3M?" Emory asked. It should have been on her desk hours ago.

"I thought your appointment with 3M was next week," her assistant said. He looked a lot like Bambi in headlights, but she didn't care.

"They moved it up earlier today. I put it on my Outlook calendar. Didn't you see it?" Emory dropped the 3M file on his desk with a thud. "I need you to keep up."

He reached for the file. "I can have it ready for you in thirty minutes."

"Don't let this happen again. I don't have time for your mistakes." With that, she made her way back into her office and closed the door, hard. She felt a twinge of guilt for snapping at Trevor. She had high standards for her employees, yes, but it wasn't her nature to level them so overtly. She brushed off her behavior as a symptom of the stress she was under and turned back to her monitor to strategize for her impending presentation.

Lucy Danaher entered her office at a quarter after twelve and perched on the side of her desk. "Hey, there. How's that presentation coming?"

"It'll get there."

"Em. Em? Hello, I'm over here. Can we talk for a second?"

Emory paused, hating to kill the flow of her creative energy, but turned to face her friend and vice president of her company. "What can I do for you, Luce?

"You can tell me how you're doing, to start."

Emory shrugged nonchalantly and smiled. "I'm fine. If I could just close this deal, I'd be better."

Lucy narrowed her eyes and stood, folding her arms and coming around the desk. "You know that's not what I'm talking about. Emory, you just lost your mother. Are you sure you should be back at work so soon, guns blazing? This has been a difficult two weeks for you, and I know no one would think less of you for stepping away for a while. I can handle the 3M deal and we can filter down some of your smaller clients to the senior account execs."

"Thank you, but really, I'm good. Getting back into the regular swing of things is what I need. I know you're more than capable, but this one's mine." Emory relaxed into her chair then, a thought occurring to her. "There is one thing. Can you recommend a company to help with the house? You know, go through everything, box it up, and ship it out, that kind of thing? It's going to be kind of a big undertaking, and I'm not up for it."

"No problem. Let's see…" Lucy thought for a minute, biting her bottom lip in a way Emory used to find very attractive when they were together. "My mother uses a company to clean her house twice a week, and I know they offer a lot of different around-the-house services. She thinks they're amazing. I'll give Trevor their number and he can set something up."

"You're a lifesaver, Luce," Emory mumbled absently. She'd already swiveled back to her computer monitor, wasting no time refocusing on her project.

Lucy sighed in defeat. "Don't I know it."

It was eight a.m. on Tuesday morning, and Sarah managed to push open the glass door of the office with her foot, frustrated to hear the phone ringing and see the reception area empty once again. "Clarice, the phone is ringing!" In one hand, Sarah balanced a box of cleaning supplies and in the other a newly repaired vacuum cleaner to return to the supply closet. "Clarice! My hands are full. Can you answer the phone, por favor?" Realizing that Clarice was nowhere to be found,

Sarah set the vacuum down, leapt across the counter, and answered the phone breathlessly. "Immaculate Home. How may I help you?" Dial tone. She sighed deeply at the thought of the lost opportunity. It was then that Clarice puttered in from the small kitchen adjacent to the reception desk, carrying a pint of ice cream, and licking the spoon.

"Good morning, Sarah, how are you today?"

"I'm great, Clarice, but I'd be doing better if we hadn't missed a call. Try not to wander too far, okay?" She smiled at the elderly receptionist, who didn't seem too concerned.

"Mija, is that you?"

Sarah smiled at her mother's voice as she made her way down the short hallway to her office. "Hi, Mama." She kissed her cheek before settling into the empty chair across the desk. "I picked up the extra supplies and had the sputtering vacuum repaired. How are things today?"

"Swamped." Yolanda Matamoros gestured at the appointment book in front of her and sighed. "We're completely booked, but I can't stand the thought of turning away business. I think I might go out to Mrs. Jeffries's myself and do her Thursday cleaning."

Sarah nodded, not at all surprised by her mother's dedication. It's what had made the business what it was today, successful. This was her mother's company and she was in charge, but that didn't preclude her from rolling up her sleeves and going to work in the field whenever necessary. Sarah had worked for Immaculate Home since she was sixteen years old and took pride in the company and her mother's leadership of it. "What can I do?"

"Let's see." She scanned the spreadsheet on her computer. "We did get a request for a home organization and clean out. You could take this one, mija. You're incredibly good at organizing. It may take several days, though."

"That's okay. Grace has summer camp all week. My schedule's free."

"I guess with you gone, Clarice will have to cover the office alone. Lord help us. Here is the address." She scribbled onto a Post-it. "The house is on Banning Street in La Jolla. The appointment is set for four this afternoon."

Sarah raised her eyebrows and whistled low as she studied the address. "Nice neighborhood."

❖

Emory pulled into her mother's driveway at 4:17 p.m. and stared up at the sprawling home before her. She hadn't been back to the house since the day of the funeral, and then it had been full of people. It felt strange knowing that when she entered the home this time, there would be no Catherine Owen to greet her with an air kiss to either cheek or chat with her about the latest charity auction or eventful women's brunch. The realization left her flat. She'd never been close with her mother, that much was true, but she never imagined a world without her either.

Further up the driveway, Emory spotted a red VW Beetle and assumed it must belong to the worker the service had sent over to assess the job. As she approached, a Hispanic woman exited the car and waited expectantly for her at the top of the drive. She had her hair pulled into a ponytail and wore jeans and a light blue cotton T-shirt. "Miss Owen?"

"Emory, please. And you are?"

The woman extended her hand and smiled. "Sarah Matamoros. I'm very sorry to hear about your mother. I hope we'll be able to help."

"Thank you. I hope so too."

As they walked the long sidewalk leading up to the front door, Emory tried to get a feel for the kind of service the company could provide, and more importantly, their competence level. She had high standards. "So do you take on this sort of thing often?"

"On occasion," Sarah answered. "It's certainly something we're capable of handling, but I have to be honest with you, Ms. Owen, this looks to be a rather large house. I hadn't anticipated—"

"Where are you from?" Emory interrupted her.

"Um, Logan Heights."

"No, I mean you have a very slight accent. Where are you from originally?"

"Oh. My family immigrated from Guadalajara when I was nine. English is my second language."

"Well, you speak it marvelously. I didn't mean to imply otherwise. Let's go inside."

When they entered the home, Sarah's eyes widened in surprise. The house was beyond lavish. The entryway towered three stories in the air, and a grand staircase opened before them winding languidly up and away. An expansive living room lay ahead, decorated impeccably with fabrics, tapestry, and very expensive looking furniture. There were chandeliers, French doors, and all sorts of things she would tell Grace were on the do-not-touch list.

"I'm not sure how much your agency told you, but I'd like to have the house empty and on the market next month. That means there's a lot of work to do here."

"I'd have to spend some time looking around before I could give you a quote, Ms. Owen. This seems like it could take some time. A month is—"

"Again, please call me Emory and money is not a problem. Send me your bill when you finish. How is this kind of thing usually handled anyway?" She strolled further into the house. "Do you just box it up and send it away?"

Sarah couldn't help but notice the removed look in Emory's eyes when she turned back to face her. Geez, didn't she care at all? "The items you plan to get rid of, yes, but the things you choose to keep, we arrange to have picked up and then delivered to a storage unit or your home."

"I can't imagine there will be much like that. Family photos and an occasional piece of art, perhaps. The rest I plan to donate. I'll try to stop by each day after work to check in with you." She glanced at her watch. "I hate to cut this short, but I have a conference call at five. When can you start?"

Sarah shrugged. "Now?"

"Perfect. Here's a key. I'll have boxes delivered tomorrow. See you soon." And with that, the attractive blonde in the perfectly tailored business suit was gone. Sarah found herself alone in what she could only describe as an honest-to-goodness mansion. Her first impression was how cold it felt in comparison to her parents' small home. She wondered if Emory Owen had grown up here and if perhaps that accounted for the cool, aloof persona that seemed to match that of the house so perfectly. Sad, if that was the case. She rolled up her sleeves, smiled, and set out to explore her new project. She loved a challenge.

❖

After work the next day, Emory opened the door to her mother's house and was greeted by a sound she'd never heard in there before—rock music. Was that U2?

"Hello? Um?" *Damn, what was the woman's name? Sarah.* "Hello, Sarah?" Emory called above the cacophony. "Hello?" When she wasn't greeted in return, she dropped her attaché case at the door and followed the sounds of Bono to the kitchen where she found every cabinet standing open and packing supplies across the floor. In the midst of it all, there was Sarah, dancing around wildly with the freedom one only has when they're alone. Her eyes were closed as she jumped up and down, shook her hips, and mouthed the lyrics of the song along with the radio. Emory was stunned by the display and all she could do was stare, unsure how to proceed. Eventually, as the dancing continued, a small smile crept onto her lips. The first smile in quite a while.

Sarah opened her eyes and nearly dropped dead at the sight before her. Ms. Owen—Emory—she mentally corrected herself, was standing right there in the kitchen, a perfect witness to her booty poppin'. If she could have paid the floor to swallow her up, she would have mortgaged her life away in a heartbeat. Her first action was to race to the portable boom box she'd brought with her and silence the blaring music. Next, she thought she'd better find a way to explain her behavior to her seemingly amused client. Wait, amused was good. So playing that card, she flashed her most winsome smile. "Sorry you had to see that. Sometimes after a long day, I cut loose for a minute. A dance break, I guess some might call it."

"Not a problem," Emory answered. The smile still touched the corners of her mouth. "I think I needed that, actually. How are things here?"

Sarah took this opportunity to dust off her clothes and moved quickly to the sink to wash her hands. Somehow, the visual of this perfectly pressed woman reminded her of the fact that she probably looked like a wild person after her day. It wasn't so much that she was embarrassed. She was pleased with her work and the progress she'd made, but she could at least go to the trouble of making the effort. "It's been a very productive day. Your mother must have been a very fascinating woman. I've come across some exotic pieces of china I thought you should take a look at, and there's a crystal bowl in here that I thought you might also like me to set aside for you."

Emory rubbed the back of her neck. "No, uh-uh. All of that can go. I told you, unless it looks like it has some family connection, you can get rid of it. It doesn't matter how exotic or expensive. This whole house is exotic and expensive. If we played that game, we'd never finish."

Emory's frustration was apparent and Sarah felt the smile fall right off her face. "I'm sorry. I just thought when I—"

"It's fine. I'm the one who should apologize. I've just had a rough day." She turned then and made a beeline for the one cabinet that wasn't open. The one that contained the liquor. "I'm going to have a drink. Join me?"

"Oh, no, thank you. I don't think so."

"Suit yourself."

As Emory mixed herself a drink, Sarah caught the creases in her brow and could tell Emory was indeed upset, which was understandable given the month she'd had. "Is there anything I can, um…do? Do you want to talk about it?" It was incredibly forward of her and not at all her place, but Emory was a human being who was dealing with a significant loss, and she should be sensitive to that.

"I lost an account at work today. It was a project I'd been working on night and day for weeks, and it didn't go through. It's just…frustrating as hell."

Sarah tilted her head to the side, understanding curiously that Emory was not upset about the loss of her mother, but instead about an issue at work. It didn't compute, but she pressed forward. "What is it you do for a living, if you don't mind me asking?"

Emory leaned her hip against the counter and sipped her dry martini. "I own a newswire agency."

"Like the Associated Press, you mean?"

"Kind of. We're more of a wire for hire. Companies use our services to send out their press releases. Plus, the Securities and Exchange Commission requires all public companies achieve something called 'simultaneous disclosure,' which means any and all investor announcements must be sent out to a variety of news sources at the exact same moment. We're able to satisfy that need at Global Newswire with a fleet of high-powered satellites."

Sarah was intrigued. "So if AT&T lays off two thousand employees…"

"They're required by law to report that to the public, and more importantly, their investors, all at the exact same moment. We make that happen."

"I had no idea a company like that existed."

"Most people don't, but without us, the stock market would be a very different place."

"Wow. Impressive. Maybe you can tell me more about it sometime." She inclined her head to the door. "For now, I better head out. It's time to pick up my daughter."

"Oh, you have a child?"

"An eight-year-old, yes. She's in summer camp and my father picks her up for me when I'm working."

"You didn't mention that when I hired you."

"Is it a problem? I can have them send someone else if—"

"No, of course not. I'm sorry." Emory straightened. "I didn't mean to keep you."

"No, I don't mind." She casually touched Emory's arm as she made her way out of the kitchen. "I enjoyed hearing about your work. It sounds exciting." And she genuinely meant it. She liked meeting new people and had a habit of making friends with the clients she worked for. It was yet another trait she'd inherited from her gregarious mother, an outwardly friendly disposition. Emory Owen, however, was an interesting departure from the upper middle class families that typically hired the agency. Her high-powered corporate lifestyle was fascinating, if not a little intimidating.

Sarah shrugged off thoughts of Emory as she opened the door to her apartment in the southern part of San Diego. Time to leave work at work.

"Mama!" Grace rounded the corner carrying with her a small shiny blue bowl. "Today at camp we made pottery and guess what?"

"What?" Sarah wrapped her up in a warm greeting and kissed her cheek about three dozen times before examining the bowl with exaggerated appreciation.

"We baked it in the oven to make it hard as a rock."

"Wow, little monster, that's crazy good. From the looks of this masterpiece, you might be a real-life artist." Sarah held the bowl up in appreciation and watched as Grace's eyes shone brightly at the thought.

"Do you think I could be an artist, Papi?" Grace raced back into the kitchen to get her grandfather's opinion. Sarah followed just in time to hear her father's response as he laid down the newspaper in contemplation.

"No question, Graciela. You could do it, if anyone could. You're destined for great things."

Sarah placed a kiss on his expectant cheek. "I agree. Now, if we can just get the aspiring artist to keep her room clean, we'll be in business. Thank you for picking her up today. This job is going to take a little longer than Mama initially thought. You wouldn't believe this place if I told you. It's humongous."

"Maybe your mother should send you some help," he said.

"No, I can do it. Mama's overloaded as is. What she really needs is to hire more workers, but she's so particular about who's good enough. It's a losing battle with her."

"She's a stubborn woman. Just like her own mama and just like someone else I know, carita. See you tomorrow." He bopped her on the head with his newspaper as he passed.

Emory sat in the darkness of her mother's kitchen, nursing her second dry martini. The alcohol had loosened the pent up thoughts in her head. Alone in the house, she could feel the memories, or ironically, lack thereof, swirl all around her, and it was proving too hard to push them aside.

She'd not allowed herself to think much about her mother, not fully, and it had been a good decision. It was best to just move forward. If her mother were here, that's what she would tell her, just as she'd told her when her father died sixteen years earlier. All emotion should be controlled, managed, minimized. But it felt increasingly like the night was closing in on her, and Emory finally gave in.

Her mind drifted to the Christmases her family shared together when she and Vanessa returned home from boarding school. She thought of the designer sweaters she'd received at seven years old in place of the frivolous items like paints and brushes she'd begged her parents for. Then there were the "family" vacations from which her on-site nannies appear in more photos than her parents do. She shook her head at how desperately she'd wanted to be noticed by her parents, and how she would have given anything to make them happy, proud of her just a little.

Emory stood and wandered to one of the pristine couches in the living room, intent on sleeping off some of the Grey Goose before driving home. And then it hit her. Here she was, thirty-two years old, and she would never have that chance now. They were gone. It was over. She closed her eyes, understanding fully that she would forever remain a disappointment. The thought was sobering.

## Chapter Three

Y ou know, I don't think there's a drink in the entire world I'd like better than raspberry iced tea. It's what heaven must be like." Sarah glanced down at the tall, glistening glass in her hand and turned to face Carmen. "It really is the most remarkable beverage."

Her childhood friend shook her head in amusement. "It doesn't take a lot to make you happy, you know that?"

"Not true. I'll get back to you when I win the lottery and move to Hawaii." She punctuated the last word with a raising of her eyebrows and a deep pull on her straw as she stared dreamily into the sky. It was Saturday and Grace was spending the night with her cousins. Sarah welcomed the opportunity for a little girl talk with Carmen at Sabro's, the little outdoor café they frequented.

"Anything else I can get for you, ladies?" the waitress asked as she cleared the dinner dishes from their table.

"I think we're going to need another round, if I know my thirsty friend here." Carmen angled her thumb at Sarah who nodded happily.

"So what else is new with you?" Carmen asked, turning her attention back to Sarah fully. "We haven't talked in over a week. It feels weird not to see my best friend for days on end. I'm neglected."

"I know, and I'm sorry. We picked up kind of a big job and Mama was shorthanded, so I took it." Carmen Alcocer had been Sarah's best friend since she'd moved to San Diego as a child. They'd lived two doors down from each other through the entirety of their growing up years, and there was no one closer to her in the world. "You know something, it's actually kind of nice to be out in the field. You should see this place, Carmen. You would die."

"It's in bad shape?" She played with her straw.

"Not even close. It's a mansion, at least, and in absolutely pristine condition. It's like no one ever really lived there. They just came by to take tours and snap photos. The warmth is completely absent. No family photographs on the wall, no greeting cards tucked away or messages on the refrigerator. It's completely presentational." Sarah shrugged, mystified.

"I don't think I could be comfortable in a place like that. I don't care how luxurious it was."

"Me neither. I don't see the appeal of having nice things if you never use them. I kind of feel sorry for the woman in a way and her daughters too."

"Her daughters?"

"Yeah, she apparently has two. Her younger daughter is the one who hired me."

"What's she like?"

"Beautiful, successful, rich, and she knows it. Outside of that, I can't tell you much. It must have been a cold place to grow up though. You can't fault her for how she turned out."

"Well," Carmen began, tossing her napkin onto the table, "as much as I'd like to stay and talk with you for another hour or five, Roman, lord of the manor, will be home soon and complaining obnoxiously about the whereabouts of his dinner. If I didn't love him, I'd kill him."

Sarah laughed. "Geez, another reason I long desperately to be married again."

"Oh, you'll get your turn. In fact, I've been waiting for the right moment to mention this. I have someone who I think would be perfect for you. Before you say anything, hear me out."

Sarah groaned loudly and nudged Carmen's shoulder with her own as they walked down the sidewalk to their cars. "No, Carmen, no more setups. Absolutely not. They never work out, and I always wind up feeling like a failure." So she sounded like a petulant child, that's how she felt. She had her daughter to consider, and maybe that made her standards way too high. At any rate, she was exhausted from Carmen's endless setups and was coming to the conclusion that she was best on her own. She and Grace against the world. That's how it should be. End of story.

"Before you hang up your little black cocktail dress for life, just go out with this last one. His name is James and he's an architect who works on the job site with Roman."

"An architect?" Sarah couldn't help but perk up a tad. An architect did sound promising—a steady job, an education—maybe one date wouldn't hurt. "All right, all right. I can get behind one date, but don't get your hopes up." She sighed. "Is he free Friday?"

"I'll check," Carmen practically sang. "Did I mention he's an architect?" Her eyes sparkled in matchmaker victory.

Emory didn't make it to her mother's house the next day or the two days after that. She had meetings late into each evening and was still playing catch-up from the days she'd been out the two weeks prior.

She decided to check in with Lucy on her way out for the day, knowing she'd be working late on the sales kit redesign and going over the mock-ups with a fine tooth comb. She stuck her head into Lucy's office and smiled. "I guess you win tonight. I'm out."

Lucy swiveled around in her chair and jokingly patted herself on the back. "It's rare that I outlast the boss. I accept the victory proudly. I would like to thank God and Red Bull." Her light brown hair was pulled back loosely into a clasp at the back of her neck, and she'd already removed the designer jacket and heels she'd worn to work that day. Emory knew her well enough to tell that she was settling in. "I've got at least another hour, maybe two, probably three. I'm proud of you for breaking away though. You've been working like a crazy person."

Emory shot Lucy a wry look, smiling internally at the irony. "Says the girl who has at least another hour, probably three."

"Hey, that's why you pay me the big bucks. Plans for tonight? Hot date? Please say no. I haven't had a date in months and I'll die."

"Nope. You're destined to survive. I need to head over to Mother's and see how it's coming. I think I'll pick up a pizza first.

Starving. Today got away from me and I never caught up." She rubbed the back of her neck in defeat.

"Did you use the service I suggested?"

"Yeah. They sent someone over. She seems competent enough. She dances." Emory smiled as she thought back to the scene she'd interrupted earlier in the week.

"I'm sorry. She dances?"

"Never mind." She waved off the comment. "I'll see you in the morning."

When she arrived at the house this time, she considered knocking so as not to startle Sarah. Exhaustion precluded those plans, however, and Emory opened the door with purpose. Hunger trumps manners, she thought. Everyone knows that.

She was impressed actually, to see Sarah's car still parked out front. She thought there was a strong chance she would have left for the day. Apparently, Sarah shared Emory's strong work ethic. She wasn't in the least bit prepared, however, for the mountainous display of boxes that greeted her in the entryway. Emory gazed in amazement at nearly one hundred tightly packed boxes, stacked systematically along each wall. Upon further examination, Emory could see that affixed to each box was a typed up label detailing each and every item the box contained. As she studied one of the labels, still in amazement at the organization she was witnessing, Sarah appeared carrying yet another labeled box.

"Oh, hey, Emory," she said cheerfully. "Better day at work today?"

"A little, thank you," she answered absently. Her mind was still focused on the overwhelming progress Sarah had made in just the few days since she'd been to the house. "Did the agency send you help?" She set the pizza on the small table.

Sarah glanced at the boxes and then back to Emory. "No, still just me. But not to worry, I'm getting there little by little."

"I'll say. I can't believe you've done all of this. I'm utterly shocked."

Sarah, who now seemed to understand that Emory was impressed and not concerned, smiled. And it was a nice smile. Warm. "I just try to stay systematic with my approach so as to not overwhelm myself. One room at a time."

"And the labels?"

"Right. I hope it was okay that I used the PC in the office to print them out. I thought it would make it easier if I cataloged each item for you, just in case. There's a master list of everything I've packed and that can be cross-referenced with the box numbers located on the upper right hand corner of each label. The boxes are stacked in order as well, so if there was an item or keepsake I didn't know to set aside for you, it could be easily located and retrieved."

Emory didn't know what to say.

"I'm sorry. Should I have checked with you first?"

"No, no. This is just more than I had imagined. I have to admit, I'm beyond impressed." And she was. She liked the way Sarah had come in and taken it upon herself to organize such a detailed system. This woman was a go-getter.

Sarah beamed even brighter at Emory. "Thank you." And then she appeared to relax a little. "I was worried you'd be upset. You seem like someone who likes things done a certain way." She turned then moved back into the living room and began taping up yet another box.

Emory was intrigued by the comment and couldn't resist following Sarah into the next room. "What makes you say that?"

Sarah gestured to Emory's designer suit. "You run a very successful company and didn't get there by accident."

"True. But I could never have implemented all this. I'm the least organized person you'll ever meet. That's what I have assistants for." As the comment left her mouth, she heard how arrogant it sounded. For some reason, the idea of hurting Sarah's feelings didn't sit well with her and she scrambled to take back her words. "What I mean is—"

Sarah looked up and offered a tilt of her head, accompanied by a soft smile. "It's okay to have assistants who do things for you. If you didn't, you'd never be able to focus on your job and run your company."

Emory nodded once, and stared at her shoes, a little off-kilter in a very strange way. She felt like she'd drawn a line in the sand between her and Sarah, and she didn't like it. Why in the hell she cared what Sarah thought of her, she had no idea. Shaking it off, she lifted the box in an offering of peace. "Pizza?"

Sarah hesitated, but her eyes gave her away. She was starving, Emory could tell.

"Go ahead, please. You're bound to be hungry. It's close to seven." Sarah still seemed reluctant. "Tell you what. I'm going to sit on the patio and enjoy the view while I eat. Why don't you fix a plate and join me? That way you can fill me in on your progress and I can answer any questions you have. It'll be a working dinner."

"All right. Thanks."

"Perfect."

Emory made her way out onto her mother's deck and looked out over the lush lawns kept green for decades by the family's hired landscaping service. At the far portion of the yard stood a bubbling brook, manmade of course, capped off with a lazy waterfall. She'd always enjoyed spending time in the backyard growing up. It was her favorite spot on the property.

Sarah joined her on the deck then, pulling her from her thoughts. She had taken the ponytail down and her thick, dark hair now fell around her shoulders in generous waves. Catching her curious look, Sarah glanced upward, signaling her new hairstyle. "Sorry if it's crazy. I keep it pulled back while I work."

Emory nodded, but was keenly aware of the fact that she hadn't actually taken the time to look at Sarah, or at least *really* look at her. Until now. Suddenly, that's all she wanted to do. Sarah's skin was a very smooth olive, and her eyelashes were long and dark and really just pointlessly attractive. And was she mistaken, or were her eyes a combination of light hazel and possibly a little bit of green? Unusual…pretty. How had she missed this before?

"What?" Sarah asked. "Do I have sauce on my face?"

"Not at all. Sorry, I was just…nothing."

They ate their pizza in companionable silence for a few moments, Emory savoring the warm mozzarella and melt in your mouth crust as the fatigue of the day seemed to fall away with the re-nourishment process.

"It's beautiful out here," Sarah finally said. "Did you spend much time out here when you were young?"

Emory nodded. "I did. It was one of my favorite places to be actually. I used to paint." Before the words even left her mouth, Emory was shocked she'd said them. Where had that come from exactly? She hadn't talked with anyone about her painting in years.

"You did?" Sarah sat up straighter. "That's awesome. Are you any good?"

Emory laughed at the question and tenacity of the woman asking it. "Some of my instructors used to think so. They said I had a rare talent. I'm not sure if that's true or not. But it doesn't matter. I don't paint anymore."

"And why is that?" Sarah asked.

Emory sat forward and removed her gray suit jacket, leaving her clad in her gray slacks and short sleeve white dress shirt. She slipped out of her heels and pulled her legs beneath her. She used the movement to stall, realizing this wasn't a topic she wanted to delve into. The past was the past. Yet, somehow Sarah put her at ease. Her presence was nonthreatening. "It wasn't practical. You have to understand, I come from a family where success is measured in dollar signs within the confines of a world in which societal perception is everything. Art is for people like us to admire, not create. That's a direct quote from my mother, by the way. It didn't matter how much I wanted to be an artist. It was a nonissue. So after some crying, some soul-searching, and a few deep breaths, I grew up and joined the real world. I applied to Stanford the next week and never looked back. I haven't picked up a brush since."

Sarah looked at her with sadness and maybe a little bit of shock. "You must have cared *a lot* about what your parents thought of you to give up something you were so passionate about."

Emory smiled wryly and took another bite of her pizza. "Unfortunately, I did. My father died of a heart attack when I was a teenager so my focus fell squarely on my mother's attention. I guess you could say I failed miserably from her vantage point at pretty much everything. We never really saw eye to eye."

"I'm sure that's not true." Sarah reached across the space between them and placed a reassuring hand on Emory's arm. Emory studied the hand and smiled, again surprised at herself for not pulling away from someone offering comfort. There had been so much of that lately. Maybe, she reasoned, it was because Sarah wasn't directly connected to her everyday life. She was a virtual stranger. And something about her spoke of kindness.

"Thank you for saying that, but it is. I knew my mother well and am very aware of the shortcomings she perceived in me. My older sister, Vanessa, was the golden child, not me. It's a fact of life I've learned to deal with. So the answer to your question, Sarah," she said, standing and taking both of their plates, "is that yes, I spent a great deal of time out here and will remember this view fondly when it's sold. Hopefully, very, very soon." She moved quickly into the house then, sticking her head out the door wearily one last time. "Maybe we can talk about the house tomorrow? I don't think I'm up to it today after all."

"Of course," Sarah answered. "Whatever works best."

Emory had only been home an hour, but she was restless. Her mind was racing, and as much as she tried to concentrate on the sales report in front of her, she simply couldn't focus. The conversation she'd had with Sarah came back to her again and again. She hadn't opened up to anyone about her parents in a long time. Now that the lid had been pulled from the box, it was as if she couldn't get it back into place. She made an impulsive, albeit executive decision. She was going out. She needed to take her mind off all that troubled her, and a dark, overly loud nightclub would suffice. Without allowing herself time to think, she changed into her low-slung faded jeans and purple tank top, grabbed her keys, and drove her Jaguar FX to The Edge.

The club was especially crowded for a Tuesday night. The lights were low, the music was loud, and she could feel the regulars' eyes on her as she casually made her way past them to the bar. Emory was well aware of the fact that she'd been placed at the top of the eligibility list in the San Diego single scene. If she overheard a "damn," as she walked by from some of her more aggressive admirers, she didn't let on and she didn't care. Years ago, comments like that were what fed her, kept her ego afloat, but nowadays they did little more than annoy her. Since the breakup with Lucy, she'd had virtually zero interest in dating, realizing there was no room in her life for someone else, and she was perfectly fine with that. She was better on her own, stronger, and more effective.

She was in another space tonight, however. She ordered a Kentucky mule and made her way to the familiar table to the left of the bar where she'd spent many a night in her more carefree days. Just as she imagined they would be, several friends of hers were chatting animatedly over the thrum of the music. The women in her set weren't your typical club kid fare. Each of them was smart, successful, and from lots and lots of money. Most of the girls knew each other from prep school, with a few connections made at the odd charity event or business luncheon. This was a powerful group of women and they knew it.

"Am I hallucinating, or is Emory Owen making an appearance in the world outside of her office?" Mia feigned shock as Emory closed the gap to their table. Mia Parsons was an up-and-coming attorney at Taylor and Fullbright and the consummate socialite. She worked hard and played hard and everyone liked and feared her equally.

Emory moved into Mia's open arms. "You're hysterical, Mia. So how is everyone tonight?" Emory regarded the table of three women, two of which she hadn't seen in several months.

"Better now that you're here," Barrett said. "We were all so sorry to hear about your mother, Em. We've missed you. I wish you'd come out more often and let us take care of you. You know, be your friends."

Emory smiled in Barrett's direction. Barrett's kind eyes penetrated the bubble she'd placed around herself, and she was genuinely happy to see her. Of all of her friends, Barrett was the most down-to-earth, and she could always count on her. She made a mental note to not let so much time go by without calling her next time. "I got your messages, Barrett, thank you. It's just been a busy time."

"Well, if there's anything I can do, just let me know. When I lost my dad, it took quite a while before I got back in the swing of things."

"I'll keep that in mind."

"Ditto," Christi Ann chimed in. Emory suppressed the urge to roll her eyes. She couldn't think of a single instance when the vapid Christi Ann had been there for anyone. She was more interested in who she could suck up to and who she could tear down behind the scenes. She'd known Christi Ann since the second grade and she had the girl's number.

"Again, thanks, guys, but I think what I need right now is a dance, so if you'll excuse me." Emory noticed the young blonde leaning up against the bar. The one who'd been clearly checking her out since she'd walked in the place. Without a second thought, she took a mollifying swig of her drink and left it on the table, intent on one thing, mindless distraction. She made brief eye contact with the blonde and inclined her head toward the dance floor in silent invitation. She maintained an even pace, confident in every way that the girl was trailing behind her. She felt a hand move down her back and smiled as she turned, pulling the girl tightly up against her body.

They danced, hips pressed together, bodies moving to the techno beat blaring from the club's speakers, hands moving freely across shoulders, stomachs, thighs. Two songs in, Emory slowly began to let herself drift into the unassuming connection she'd created with a nameless, faceless individual on a dance floor—someone she owed nothing to and expected very little from. "I'm Aimee," the woman whispered seductively in her ear once the music shifted to a slower, more sensual ballad. But Emory didn't care and, in fact, would prefer not to know.

"Emory," she answered back out of nothing more than a sense of polite obligation.

"I know exactly who you are." *Well, so much for an anonymous interlude.*

The song ended, but Emory wasn't finished with what she'd started. She allowed the blonde to tug her gently into a darkened corner of the club where they could get better acquainted. Aimee pressed her back up against the brick wall and pulled Emory slowly to her. Emory smiled at her would-be conquest with enough heat to make the girl grip her tightly for support. She was aware of the power she wielded and couldn't help but like it. Her sex appeal had always been a valuable tool in her arsenal, and she wasn't afraid to use it when the time was right. Tonight, she had one goal and one goal only. Total and complete diversion and Allie—or was it Aimee— would fit that bill nicely. She dipped her head in slowly and captured Aimee's lower lip between her own and kissed gently, steadily and then quickened the pace. Aimee reciprocated easily, though it was clear who was in charge. Even though Emory's lips were occupied, the rest of her was having difficulty following suit. She tried hard to free her mind and allow her body to react to the sensations that should be assaulting her in the arms of this ripe and ready twentysomething, but they simply weren't there. Finally, she wrenched her mouth away and stared blankly at the brick wall. "I'm sorry. I have to go."

"Is everything okay? Did I do something wrong?" Aimee asked. Her wide eyes searched Emory's in the dimness of the club.

Emory did her best to smile reassuringly. "Completely me. I think I need some sleep." She took a step back and turned to go.

"Can I get your number then?"

Emory froze and thought carefully about how to handle this situation. She had no intention of seeing Aimee again but also felt no desire to hurt her feelings. "Why don't you give me yours?" She pulled her BlackBerry from her back pocket and obediently typed Aimee-with-two-e's number into her phone, and with a quick good-bye to her friends, was driving home, listening to soft jazz, and thinking fleetingly of a pair of understanding hazel eyes.

## CHAPTER FOUR

So it turned out he was cute, handsome even, and well dressed. Sarah sipped her sangria and watched cautiously as James surveyed the dessert menu. Dinner had gone well. They'd chatted easily about their jobs, families, and even football, a sport Sarah felt beyond passionate about. She smiled to herself and marveled at the fact that one of Carmen's setups might actually pan out.

"Why don't you choose for us?" James said. He handed the small menu to Sarah and smiled. "They all sound wonderful to me."

Sarah certainly had no problem choosing and zeroed in on the warm pecan pie and vanilla ice cream, her mouth already watering. They placed their order with the waiter and settled in for more conversation.

James relaxed easily into the plush chair. "Tell me about your daughter." He seemed genuinely interested, and that scored major points with Sarah. Not many of the men she'd gone out with had so much as mentioned Grace on their own. This was promising, very promising indeed. As long as he didn't live with his mother, they might be in business.

"Well, she's eight years old and about as precocious as they come, interested in everything. Yesterday, she asked me if she could start drinking espresso, because that's what the Italians did. I love her to pieces, but I may have my hands full when she's older." She smiled widely just thinking about Grace and then played back how that must have sounded. Maybe she shouldn't point out that her child was odd.

"She sounds like a lot of fun."

"Oh, she's definitely that and more, a laugh a minute, that kid."

The car ride to her apartment was quiet with the exception of the radio playing softly. Sarah couldn't help but wonder if James would expect to be invited in, and if so, how she would go about explaining to him that she just, well, didn't go there on the first date. Grace was spending the night with her parents, and that left the apartment empty. She didn't want him to get the wrong idea.

As he followed her to her door, her anxiety only grew, and she was already formulating her polite explanation. But to her amazement, he paused on the front step and took her hand in his. "I had a wonderful time with you tonight, Sarah. You're everything Carmen said you would be. I'd love to see you again, that is, if you'd like to."

Sarah blinked once, again surprised by what a charming cutie her date was turning out to be. He actually looked nervous. "Um…I'd love to see you again. Next weekend?"

"Sounds perfect. I'll call you later this week to firm up plans." He leaned in and placed a soft kiss on Sarah's lips. It was simple. It was sweet. And it left her smiling as she watched him walk the length of the sidewalk back to his car. It had been a nice night, she mused as she made her way into the apartment. She was glad that she'd gone.

The next day was Saturday, and though Sarah usually took the day off, setting it aside for spending time with Grace and the rest of her family, today was a no-go. The house on Banning Street demanded her attention, and if she had any hope of finishing before the cows came wandering over, she would have to work overtime. It upset her, however, not to have the time with Grace. They usually spent the day on some sort of joint activity, which allowed them to connect after their mutually busy weeks. She decided to compromise, and after assembling a bag of Grace's favorite "stay busy" activities, she picked up Grace and headed to work.

"Is this place really a mansion?" Grace asked as they turned onto Banning Street. "Like in the movies?"

"Just like in the movies," Sarah assured her. "Which means that everything inside is very expensive and cannot be touched, mija. Do you understand?"

"Yes, Mama. I won't touch anything. I'll just pretend it's all mine and that I'm an orphan adopted by a rich man with no hair."

Sarah took a moment. "Did you and Papi watch *Annie* again last night?"

"How did you know?"

"Lucky guess."

As they pulled into the driveway, Grace's mouth fell open at the expansive home spread out before them. "Wow. I wish we could live here."

"I like where we live just fine. Don't you? It's our home—yours and mine."

Grace returned her smile. "Me too."

After situating Grace with some paper and crayons at the kitchen table, Sarah made her way back to the master bedroom to pack up the final contents of the closet.

There was a sadness that overtook her looking around the empty, dismantled room and understanding that it had been Catherine Owen's sanctuary for so many years. She was in the midst of boxing up the books and casual clothes that were folded neatly in the multiple chests of drawers when there they were, a group of four blue canvas books. Three of the books were tied tightly from each side with twine. A fourth sat on top, unbound. Sarah flipped through the top book, assessing her find, and took a breath at the delicate, cursive handwriting and dated entries that lined the pages. This was her journal, Mrs. Owen's personal journal. And the last entry was dated just over a month ago, not long before her death. The journals were thick and the writing quite small. The four books together could easily chronicle a good portion of the elderly woman's adult life.

She slowly untied the twine that held the bundle and opened the bottom book. On one hand, she felt an enormous amount of guilt for the intrusion into the woman's personal thoughts, but at the same time, something was pushing her to do just that.

She sat on the bed and began to skim the words written in very distinctive formal script. With each sentence, Sarah fell further and further into the world of Catherine Owen. She found herself exchanging one book for another as the entries turned to months and the months moved into years.

❖

Emory pulled onto Banning Street cursing herself for still not having forwarded her mother's mail. She'd not tended to the house as much as she should have and realized that there were still very pressing matters that required her attention. Bills needed to be paid, and there were charitable obligations that still needed to be fulfilled in her mother's name. She was surprised to see the red Beetle in the drive as she pulled in. She hadn't expected Sarah to work on a Saturday.

Emory sorted through the mail on the way into the house, categorizing each envelope into subscriptions to cancel, correspondence to follow up with, and checks to write. She decided in the future to have her assistants help with this process. There was no point in personally tending to these mundane issues. In fact, it was probably better for her to distance herself from the process as much as possible. She stopped abruptly as she entered the kitchen, double taking as she glanced up from the electric bill in her hand. She stared curiously at the strange child sitting at the kitchen table. "Hello?"

"Hi," the child answered cheerfully.

"Um…And who might you be?"

"Graciela. But everyone calls me Grace. It's very nice to meet you. Who might *you* be?"

"Emory. Owen. This is my house." She was still off-balance by this unexpected visitor and didn't know quite where to go. Damn it, she never knew quite how to talk to children. "So I take it you belong to Sarah."

"Sarah's my mom. Do you live here?" she asked.

"Yes. I mean, I used to. I don't anymore. My mother lived here."

"I'm sorry that she died." Grace set down her purple crayon and gave Emory her full attention. "When I'm feeling sad, I like to color. I'm probably too old for it now, but I don't care." Grace extended a green crayon in Emory's direction and tore out a sheet for her from the book she was working in.

When Emory didn't immediately move, Grace re-extended her arm for emphasis. Clearly, she was not taking no for an answer. "You know, I have some bills I need to look through. How about I do that while you color?"

That seemed to be an acceptable solution to Grace who shrugged once and went back to work. Emory threw a glance over her shoulder looking for a possible rescue from Sarah, who had to be somewhere in the house. She could go and look for her, but what would she say when she found her? Your kid makes me uncomfortable? Instead, she reluctantly sat at the table and spread the mail out in front of her, focusing on the task she came to complete. Out of curiosity, she shot an occasional glance in Grace's direction. Watching her color was, she had to admit, relaxing. The way she outlined each bunny before lightly shading in the gaping white portions until they were full of vibrant color. Okay, it was a child's activity, but tempting all the same.

"Are you sure you don't want a page?" Grace asked warily thirty minutes later. The kid was undoubtedly aware of being watched.

"I guess I could take one," Emory replied nonchalantly. "I have a minute now that some of this is out of the way."

Grace regarded her knowingly and nodded before handing over a picture of three small rabbits looking up at a large friendly bird in a tree. She moved the oversized box of crayons to the middle of the table so Emory had easy access to the assortment and went back to her own page, a rabbit curled up for a nap with several other rabbits. They worked in silence for a good forty-five minutes, Grace spending more time watching Emory color than coloring herself. Grace shook her head in awe as the once cartoonish outline turned into an honest to goodness, realistic forest scene. "You're really good. Like *really*."

"Oh, thanks." Emory glanced up for the first time since she started. "You know, this is a lot more fun than I thought it would be." And it was. For the first time in as long as she could remember, she felt calm, relaxed, and free. "I see why you like this."

Grace reached for Emory's page and held it up in front of her face, still shaking her head in astonishment. "It's like the rabbits are real. How did you do that?"

Emory studied the piece of paper Grace held so reverently in the air and smiled at her, noticing how much she resembled Sarah. She didn't have eyes as light, but her brown replicas were close. "It's just a shading technique. Instead of only using one color for the rabbit's fur, I used several to give it texture and layers."

"That's amazing," Grace breathed. She shifted her focus to Emory. "Can I keep this?"

"Sure, go ahead." She was somewhat honored that Grace would want to.

"Wanna color another?"

"Hit me." But it was a foregone conclusion. Emory was already reaching eagerly for a new crayon.

❖

Sarah closed the last and final journal in the stack and blew out a long, emotional breath, brushing a stray tear from the corner of her eye. She glanced at her watch and shook her head. She'd lost two hours of valuable work time reading the words of Catherine Owen, but she didn't regret it for a second. She understood the importance of these journals and what they could mean for those she left behind, one woman in particular.

Sarah bounded down the stairs, hopeful that the silence from Grace was an indication that she'd been on her best behavior, as she'd promised she would be. She hadn't meant to leave her alone so long and realized that it was now well past lunchtime. *I'm a horrible mother, destined for parent jail.* She decided she'd take Grace out for a bite to eat, just the two of them, before dropping her off with her mother, where she could have more fun for the rest of the afternoon. She still had work to get done at the house.

The scene she walked in on in the kitchen was not at all what she expected. There was Grace, munching on a plate of Oreos and coloring alongside none other than Emory Owen herself, who interestingly enough seemed quite content coloring a rabbit of her own. Sarah watched them, shocked but still able to enjoy the serenity of the quiet moment as the two artists concentrated in tandem silence.

"I take it you two have met?" She hated to interrupt their work.

Emory looked up. "We have. Grace was rifling through the china and I walked in just in time." Sarah was horrified, but Emory calmly held up one hand. "Joking. Your daughter has been very polite company and even lent me the use of her crayons. How old are you again?" She turned back to Grace.

"Eight. How old are you?"

"Grace!" Sarah was beyond embarrassed. *Maybe add manners to her motherhood to-do list.*

"It's okay." Emory offered Grace a wink. "I'm thirty-two."

Sarah moved further into the room, stopping behind Grace's chair. "I hope it's okay that I brought her here. No summer camp on Saturdays and I didn't want to get behind."

Emory gestured as if to wave off any of Sarah's concerns. "It's fine. She caught me off guard at first, but it's turned out to be a nice morning." Emory smiled at Grace, who beamed back at her with about as much hero worship as was conceivable.

"Mom," Grace said. She turned around to face Sarah with a tight grip on Emory's first picture. "Emory said I could keep it. Can you believe how real it looks?"

Sarah took the page from Grace's hands and studied it, impressed as Grace was at the intricate detail Emory had added to the once basic outline. "Wow. She's kinda good at this, huh?"

"Yep, she's going to show me how to shade sometime."

Sarah glanced apologetically at Emory, who'd clearly gone above and beyond to be nice when there were surely things she'd rather be doing. "Um, we'll see. Ms. Owen is a very busy woman. Now pack up your backpack and head to the car. We're going to Burger King and then Mami and Papi's. I need to talk to Ms. Owen."

Grace gathered her things together, and with a wholehearted wave to Emory, was out the door.

Emory raised an eyebrow in amusement. "You're sure she won't just drive away?"

"I keep the keys with me."

Emory laughed and Sarah noticed her dimples for the very first time. "She's really something, a likable kid."

"Thank you." Sarah was pleased with the sincerity in Emory's voice. "If you have a minute, before I go, there's something I came across of your mother's that I thought you should see." No, *need* to see, Sarah amended internally.

Emory studied her with a look of restrained annoyance. "I don't feel like going through any of Mother's things today. If you could just place whatever it is in a marked box for me, I'll find time to go through it all at some point."

Sarah held up a hand. "Please just hear me out and take a look. If you're not interested, I'll pack them up."

"Them?"

"Just wait here a moment." Sarah quickly retrieved the journals and returned with the small stack in her hands.

Emory stared at the books, unblinking. "What are those?"

"I came across some writing your mother did, journals she kept over the years. The entries are sometimes frequent and sometimes not. There are months that go by without anything and then weeks where every day is chronicled." Sarah heard the excitement in her voice and commanded herself to slow down. "Please forgive me for this next part, but I did read a portion of what she wrote. At first, I was just curious, but it seemed the more I read, the more I couldn't put them down."

Emory looked back at her dumbfounded, skeptical. "Are you sure that they belonged to my mother? It's more likely that she was keeping them for someone."

"They were hers. Each inside cover contains her name and the year she began the journal."

Emory ran her fingers across her forehead absently. "I just wouldn't have imagined that she…Mother wasn't what I would call a deep person."

Sarah took a step forward feeling the need to defend the woman she had come to know in the past few hours. "That's not true. She had a lot of deep feelings and, I think that maybe you should take a look at what she's written, Emory. I've bookmarked a few sections for you if you don't want to read everything." When Emory didn't respond but instead stared blankly back at her, she placed the books on the counter. "I guess…I'll just leave them there then." As Sarah turned to go, she was stopped cold by the dull, venomous tone of Emory's voice.

"Why would you bring these to me? I specifically informed you when we first met not to bother me with the details of whatever it is you might find. It's not up to you to decide what's in my best interest and what's not. You've overstepped your bounds and it's unacceptable."

Emory's blue eyes were like ice, and Sarah felt as if she'd been slapped as they bore into her. Of course she'd known that she was pushing the envelope with the journals, but she believed in her heart that it was the right thing to do. Emory needed to read what she'd read and maybe it would help her recognize her own grief. But Emory's reaction made her think that perhaps she'd been wrong. She realized now that she should have just stayed out of it. She took a breath and answered simply. "I'm sorry, Ms. Owen. I won't make that mistake in the future." She quickly made her exit.

❖

An hour and a half later, Emory was still glued to the kitchen chair in the midst of paperwork not three feet away from the stack of books that glared back at her. Why was this even an issue? She should pick up her keys and go. She had a mountain of work waiting on her that would keep her busy late into the night. There was no reason to get caught up in whatever the hell was in that bundle of pages. She knew her mother. Hell, she more than knew her, and hearing her voice again from beyond the grave was only going to reiterate what she already knew, that Catherine Owen was a self-involved society woman who cared more about appearances than substance. It was best to put all of that behind her now.

Even though that's what she told herself, that's not what she did. Swearing under her breath, Emory snatched the book on top of the stack, the one Sarah had bookmarked, and made her way onto the patio. She stared at its blue fabric cover for several full minutes before opening to the page Sarah had noted. She scanned the eerily familiar handwriting and a shiver ran down her spine as she began to read silently.

*May 29, 1997*

*I write to you from Wallingford, Connecticut. Today, my younger daughter graduated with honors from the most prestigious preparatory school in the nation. This mother's heart was full as I watched that beautiful young woman, who was once but a helpless infant in my arms, cross the stage and accept her hard-earned diploma.*

*Emory was named salutatorian of her graduating class and was asked to make a speech at commencement. At first, I was nervous for her. I'd never heard her speak publicly, though she'd always been an articulate child. Once she began, however, my fears fled me and I was awestruck at her grace and the wisdom she imparted to her peers. She's grown into such a well-mannered, mature young woman, with much of that credit going directly to her and the admirable life she's led thus far. I was lucky to have brought my handkerchief along with me to the ceremony. I've never been so proud. Grayson, had he lived to see this day, would have been over the moon at his daughter's many achievements.*

Emory stared at the passage, unsure how to feel. The words were so entirely unexpected, especially in comparison to her own recollection of the day of her high school graduation. Her memory was vivid, especially how her mother, whom she hadn't seen in months prior to the commencement, had said very little to her after the ceremony. She'd behaved as if her attendance was a required formality, a box she was there to check on her motherhood to-do list. Catherine Owen had kissed Emory's cheek and embraced her briefly, offering a few short words of congratulations before heading back to her hotel. Emory had been on cloud nine that day, celebrating with Mia and the girls from her hall, but saw none of that same excitement reflected in her mother's eyes.

Yet, here in her lap sat evidence to the contrary and it was hard to take in. She had no idea that on that day, underneath that crisp and polite pretense of conversation, there existed a depth of feeling, actual emotion even, and it had been held back from her. Stolen.

She did the only thing she could think to do. She reread the earmarked passage again and again and again as if it were a drug she couldn't get enough of.

On a mission now, she flipped to the very first page of the journal and settled in. Hours passed as she tore through the pages and read her mother's innermost thoughts, most of which brought about startling revelations for Emory. It turned out that Catherine thought of her twice-a-week tennis match at the club as a necessary evil, while what she really longed to do with her afternoon was curl up with a good book, preferably a classic. She'd read *Pride and Prejudice* seven times. Emory never knew that and shook her head in wonder at the information. Emory loved that book, and if only she'd known, they could have discussed it and a myriad of other Jane Austen works. Other interesting pieces of information included the almost schoolgirl crush Catherine seemed to have developed on Peter Fullbright, their attorney, and the fact that she'd regretted never having a dog as a pet. But most notably, the fact that she thought Emory had amazing talent as an artist.

*June 14, 1994*

*It's hot today in California, and before the afternoon is over, we're expected to break record temperatures. Vanessa and I have taken refuge indoors and spent the afternoon selecting colors for the new furniture in the dining room, but Emory's been with her sketchbook in the backyard since ten this morning. I've stolen glances at her work as I've passed by the window, and each new glimpse impresses me further. Her steady progress on the work was remarkable.*

*The sketch is a very vivid representation of the birdhouse nestled on the back fence, an item I've paid very little attention to until now. The detail she's created is striking, and I marvel at her unique talent. I have no idea where she gets her gift, as neither Grayson nor I have any sort of artistic ability whatsoever. At any rate, it's astounding what Emory's able to produce on a blank canvas. She's presented me with several of her works over the past year and I'm still figuring out the perfect place to showcase them. No location I've come up with seems to do them justice.*

Emory stopped. It was hard to read when she could no longer see the page in front of her. Unexpected tears assaulted her eyes, and large wet drops fell from her cheeks onto the page. She sat there in a helpless sea of emotion that overtook her with a force she couldn't compete with. She hadn't cried once since learning of her mother's death, not at the funeral or even in the quiet solace of her own home. It wasn't that she wasn't sad; she knew inherently that she must have been, but she simply hadn't felt anything at all. But now, as the sun was beginning to set on a Saturday evening in June, Emory cried. She cried for the loss of a parent and all that never was and all that never would be.

She wrapped her arms around herself and held on as one emotional wave after another rolled through her. She didn't hear the back door open, but it must have because as she raised her tear-filled eyes they found Sarah's, who stood motionless on the deck, her lips parted in surprise. A moment later, something in Sarah's eyes softened and the way she looked at her now, with such tenderness and understanding, caused Emory to crumble into herself once again.

Sarah walked slowly to the couch and took the spot next to Emory, letting her hand settle on her back, softly soothing her with gentle circles. It had surprised her to see Emory's Jaguar still in the driveway when she returned to the house, but it was an even bigger shock to find her in shambles on the back porch. She quickly noted the journals next to Emory and understood.

Emory's shoulders shook as the sobs wracked her and Sarah instinctually put her arms around her. As she did, Emory fell into her, settling her head onto Sarah's lap. Sarah didn't mind and held her as she cried quietly. Neither of them said anything, as there was no need. Emory was a person in pain and Sarah would be there for her.

When Emory's sobs quieted, Sarah began to slowly stroke her hair, a gesture that always soothed Grace when she was sad. Minutes passed and though Sarah could not see her face, she could tell Emory was beginning to regain control, her breathing not so ragged. As she watched the sun on its daily descent, just as the oranges changed to pink, Emory stirred, slowly pushing herself into a sitting position. She met Sarah's eyes, but neither spoke for a moment.

"I'm sorry about this," Emory finally managed. "This is ridiculously embarrassing." She gestured in the direction of the journals. "I was reading and it was all just too—" She had to stop then as her eyes once again welled up with tears.

"It's all right. I understand." Sarah covered Emory's hand with her own.

With tears still gathering in her eyes, Emory stood, crossed to the corner of the deck, and gazed across the yard at the sunset. "She was proud of me," she said, half to Sarah and half to herself. "And I went my whole life without knowing."

"Of course she was. Why wouldn't she be?"

Emory laughed sardonically. "I don't even know where to begin. Because I got a B instead of an A. Because I missed being valedictorian by two-tenths of a point. Because I'm a lesbian. Because

I don't support the right charities, or because as a kid, I spent time drawing rather than playing tennis. I could go on and on." She raised her arm and let it drop in punctuation.

"And how do you feel after reading her words?"

"I feel cheated. She had all of these feelings, concerns, opinions, and didn't share any of them with us. She kept herself tucked away. What kind of mother does that? Doesn't mother their children?"

"I don't know. I'm sure she had her reasons." But in all honesty, Sarah couldn't relate. Not a day went by without her telling Grace how much she loved her, how valuable she was.

"Maybe it's just who we are, the Owen family. Not exactly a warm and fuzzy bunch. I shouldn't let this get to me. I hate that I care so much." Emory wiped her eyes and turned back to face Sarah apologetically. "I'm usually a much stronger person than this, I promise."

"Trust me, I get that. But the thing is, you don't have to be strong right now, Emory. You're upset, and you're grieving. Anyone who has ever lost someone knows that grief happens in cycles. Allow yourself the time you need to deal with this."

Emory took one last look at the disappearing sun and ran her hands through her hair. "I'm going to have a beer. I think I've earned it," she half laughed. "Can I bring you one?"

Sarah considered the offer and decided the day's events warranted accepting the invitation. "Sure. A beer would be great."

Emory was gone longer than was necessary, and when she returned Sarah could tell that she'd straightened herself up a bit and washed her face. Gone was the little bit of makeup Emory usually wore, her face now fresh, clean, and sporting just a slight tan. She was maybe even more attractive this way, Sarah thought as Emory handed her a bottle. She probably had no trouble in the man department, or woman department, she mentally corrected herself, recalling the information she'd just learned.

Emory sat. "So I should apologize. I snapped at you earlier about the journals, and that was wrong of me. Somehow, you knew I needed to see what was in them, and as hard as it is to admit, you were right. I'm sorry for speaking to you the way I did."

Sarah lowered the Dos Equis bottle from her lips. "Don't give it another thought." She smiled for a moment before continuing. "I just told myself that was your 'I call all the shots' executive voice."

Emory laughed out loud. "I guess maybe it was." She studied Sarah. "Is that what you get from me? That I need to call all the shots?"

Sarah looked thoughtful for a moment. "Is it wrong of me to say yes?"

Emory laughed again. "No, it's not."

"You're the type of person who is used to having things done a certain way...yours. That's not a bad thing. It's probably why you're so successful. Trust me, I'm taking notes." She smiled then, and took another pull from her beer.

"Why is that? Do you have aspirations in the corporate world? With your organization skills, someone would snatch you right up."

"Yes and no. I graduated with my bachelor's in business administration from UC San Diego two years ago."

Emory sat up a little straighter, seemingly puzzled. "Really? I had no idea. I guess I just assumed—"

"That because I'm Hispanic and work for a cleaning agency I have virtually no education?" Sarah raised her left eyebrow expectantly.

Emory paled a little.

"It's not a big deal. I'm only teasing you. Though I'm sorry to ruin the stereotype. The truth is my mother owns the agency I work for, and I've been working alongside her since I was a teenager. Typically, I handle the books, the marketing, and the outside vendors. Occasionally, during busy seasons like this one, I pick up a job or two to help out."

"What made you decide to go to school?"

"I wanted to learn how to better develop the business. I think we have the potential to grow into something much bigger than what we are right now and I have a lot of ideas. I just have to convince my mother to hear me out. Baby steps."

Emory regarded her skeptically. "The thought is noble, Sarah, and I don't mean to pry here, but you have to think about yourself and what's best for you. You could take your business degree, go out into the corporate world, and ascend the ranks, create a successful career of your own. Your mother will survive without you."

Sarah shook her head, smiling. "My family is everything to me, and the business is where my heart is. I plan to have a very important career, but it will be with Immaculate Home."

Emory didn't seem convinced. "I guess if that's what makes you happy. What does your husband think?"

"Not married," Sarah stated matter-of-factly. "Grace's father and I divorced when I was twenty-one. We were married for exactly eighty-six days. She was still a baby when I kicked him out. Not long after, he got into some trouble, and lucky for me, we haven't heard from him since. It's just Grace and me."

"Then that's all the more reason for you to aim high."

"And that's exactly what I'm doing. I have a list of changes for Immaculate Home that I think could take us to the next level. You're an entrepreneur yourself. Surely you understand what it's like to have a vision."

Emory bowed her head in submission. "Of course I do. I hope it all works out. In fact, I'm sure it will."

It was completely dark an hour later when they finally brought their conversation to a close and headed in separate directions. It had been a welcome evening for Sarah, if not an unexpected one. She and Emory were from two entirely different worlds and with that seemed to come a freedom to speak candidly. Sarah felt more and more comfortable as the conversation went on. Then again, that second beer hadn't hurt matters either.

As they walked out to their cars together, Emory hesitated before looking sideways at Sarah. "Tonight was kind of unscheduled, huh?"

Sarah smiled and leaned against her car. "A little. But I enjoyed seeing you relax some." She gestured to the journals Emory carried with her. "Do you plan to read all of them?"

Emory thought for a moment. "I think I need to. It'll be hard, and it may be something I have to do little by little, but I need to know the real her." Emory started to go before turning back. "I should say thank you. You know, for being there for me tonight."

"No problem. Good night, Emory." Sarah watched Emory descend the steep driveway to her car, somehow unable to turn away until she was inside. She pushed herself off her own car and shook her head at the surprising turn the night had taken.

## Chapter Five

The following Monday morning offered up one of the more beautiful days only Southern California can. It was an even seventy-three degrees without a single cloud marring the crystal blue sky. Sarah blasted the radio, set to Grace's favorite station, as she made her way to drop Grace at day camp. They sang along, enjoying the morning together. They'd spent an extra ten minutes getting the French braid in Grace's hair just right so she'd look as cool as Alyssa Martinez, her new friend and idol at camp. But at last they'd done it, and Grace was now in high spirits. "So will you be spending the day at the mansion again?" Grace asked dramatically over the music.

"Yep, still a lot to do over there, but if I work hard this week, I just might be able to finish up the packing so the movers can come and transport the boxes. And then, my little girl, you and I can spend next week relaxing and doing anything we want." Grace's eyebrows rose in imaginative anticipation. "Within reason," she amended.

"Sounds fun to me. Maybe we can go swimming and I can show you what Miss Kathy taught me. I can do the backstroke," she declared, her eyes wide. "It's amazing."

"Wow, you are really coming along with those swimming lessons. I'm raising a little caballa."

Grace laughed. "A what?"

"It means mackerel in Spanish. It's a type of fish."

"That's me all right!" Grace was clearly proud of herself. "A fish!"

"Are you remembering to pay attention to how tired you feel?"

Grace sighed. "Yes, ma'am. Miss Kathy asks me how I'm doing about a million times a lesson."

"She's just making sure you're okay. Your health is important."

"I know, I know. I just don't want to talk about it all the time. The other kids are going to think I'm weird or something."

"You? Weird?" Sarah asked with mock enthusiasm. "No!"

"Mom!"

As their laughter died down, they drove in silence a little ways, Sarah humming to the radio. "So I heard something about you yesterday," Grace said.

Sarah looked at her suspiciously, wondering what the sly look was all about. "And what's that?"

"That you're going on a date tomorrow night. A *second date* with the same man."

"You heard this from your no-good grandmother who can't keep a secret from a pesky little girl?"

"That's the one." Grace seemed to enjoy the turn the teasing had taken. "So do you loooove him?" She made kissing sounds. "Will there be a wedding?"

Sarah rolled her eyes. "No. But he is a nice man, and I'd like to get to know him better. His name is James." Joking aside, Sarah could've strangled her mother for passing on this information to Grace. Sure, she was eager for Sarah to find a man and settle down, but it was way too early to involve Grace. Her mother should know better.

"Well, don't put all your eggs in one basket," Grace said seriously.

"Where on earth have we picked up this new phrase?" Sarah wasn't exactly surprised. Grace often picked up mannerisms and vocabulary that she'd clearly pilfered from someone she looked up to.

"Miss Kathy."

"Miss Kathy, of course. Well, I'll try not to put all my eggs in one basket if you try to behave yourself today and be the nicest camper this place's ever seen." Sarah put the car in park and leaned into the kiss Grace placed on her cheek. "And don't forget to take it easy. If you feel tired or overrun, be sure to tell Miss Kathy right away and sit down. Remember what Dr. Robles said."

"I will. I promise. Bye, Mama!" Sarah waited until a camp counselor retrieved Grace before pulling away from the curb and heading to the house on Banning Street.

She spent most of the day in the main living room and two guest rooms, cataloguing everything as she went. She'd taken a brief lunch break, eating the sandwich she'd brought with her, before plowing ahead, intent on finishing this project in a timely manner if it killed her. With headphones in her ears as she worked, she about jumped out of her skin when she turned around and saw Emory leaning casually in the doorway of the guest room she was working in, her hip kicked out, her shoulder holding her in place. With a hand to her racing heart, Sarah stood slowly, pulling the headphones from her ears. "I didn't see you there."

"Clearly." A small smile graced Emory's lips. "It's after five and you've, again, done an enormous amount of work." Emory produced two very enticing open bottles of Dos Equis. She dangled the sweaty, sure-to-be-refreshing bottles in front of Sarah and then teasingly backed away, her retreating form enough to garner a laugh from Sarah who only waited a beat before washing her hands and following.

She found Emory on the deck, this time positioned on a cushioned chaise lounge, her long, tanned legs laid out in front of her. She wore athletic attire today, and the shorts she'd selected certainly complimented her toned physique. Sarah scooped up the beer Emory left on the small table for her and took up residence in the chair next to Emory's. "So how was your long day at the office?"

Emory sighed. "Murder. But there's hope on the horizon in the form of some big rollouts that could mean more business in the long run. We need to start interviewing new PR firms to handle our streaming video product launch."

"We?"

"I guess that would be Lucy and me, and the other account executives to a lesser extent. Lucy is my VP and has been with me since the company's inception. We also have kind of a history." She squinted her eyes sheepishly.

"You grew up together?" Sarah immediately thought of the deep history she had with Carmen.

"Not exactly. She's my ex. We lived together for two years."

"Oh." Sarah let the comment land. She knew Emory was gay; she'd said as much the night before, but the idea of Emory with another woman was still surprising to her…and intriguing at the same time. She'd never had a lesbian friend. This was new territory.

"It's nice that you're able to still have a working relationship," Sarah offered politely. She took a drink of her beer.

"That's kind of the point. We're both workaholics, and eventually, I realized I was dating myself. Our relationship became one of convenience, and we rarely did anything but talk about the office. I did learn a valuable lesson, however. I suck at relationships and should avoid them at all costs. Over time, we both came to the understanding that we'd make better friends anyway. Since then, our relationship has only grown stronger. It was the right move."

"Wow," Sarah replied. "That's a very mature way of handling it. When my friends break up, you can generally expect a lot of shouting and crying, sometimes in the street. Maybe it's cultural."

"Trust me, it's not. The lesbian community is nothing if not dramatic. Ours was an ideal breakup, though. We just kind of shifted into new roles and it worked." Emory stared at the label on her beer, wondering why she was *again* divulging so many intimate details of her life. She'd wanted to see Sarah for a purpose, and another conversation full of personal confessions had not been on the books. Emory delicately changed the subject. "So I was thinking a little more about what you were telling me, about your business aspirations."

"Okay," Sarah answered tentatively.

"And I don't know if this is overstepping my bounds, but I might be able to help."

"How do you mean?"

"Well, I was thinking about what you told me about Immaculate Home. You want to grow the company and you mentioned several new ideas. Can you offer me an example?"

"Um, sure." Sarah didn't miss a beat. "We've been cleaning homes in the San Diego area for more than twenty years. Not long ago, we began receiving calls, similar to this one, for home organization, either for a move or a death in the family. What I'd like to see happen, is for us to go one better and open up a separate branch of the company for home management, reorganization, custom closets, custom storage space, the works. We could hire a designer and subcontract with several of the construction companies in the area. The way I see it, we can start transforming space within our existing clients' homes so their lives are less cluttered, more manageable. Once they're sold, word of mouth should bring in more business. There's a real market in our area for this. Our clients would eat it up. I know they would."

Emory had to admit, she was impressed with the pitch, or at least the manner in which it was articulated. Sarah spoke with such passion, such spark, that she believed whole-heartedly that she'd find a way to succeed with the new venture. "That's where I come in. Let me send a press release or two over the wire once you're ready to offer the new services. All it takes is one feature editor to pick up the story of the little company that could, and you'll have more business than you know what to do with."

"Oh, well, I'd have to take a look at our budget. It's possible, but it would depend on what the upstart would—"

"No charge. I'm willing to donate our services temporarily. If it works out and you decide you'd like to continue, which I feel strongly you will, we can set up a formal account and you can become a full-fledged client."

Sarah's eyebrows rose and she seemed to let the full weight of Emory's offer settle in before finally speaking. "That's one of the nicest things anyone's ever offered to do for me, but I'm sorry, I can't accept. It's too generous."

"First of all, it is not. This wouldn't be the first or the last time we've comped a release. You've put a lot of work into this company and obtaining your degree, all the while raising a child on your own. I'm just saying it's impressive, and I'd like to help."

Sarah met her eyes. "I appreciate the offer, but I'll need to take some time and think it over."

Emory was confused. She thought surely Sarah would jump at the opportunity of some free exposure, knowing full well she would have had their roles been reversed. Hell, she'd taken every chance she could to get ahead and didn't for a minute understand Sarah's hesitation. But she had to respect her wishes.

She turned to face her fully, covering the top of Sarah's hand with her own. "Just promise me you really will put some thought into it, and I'll leave you alone." She wasn't sure why she felt the need to push the issue, but she did. "You're talented, Sarah. Just seeing the way you've organized and cataloged and implemented systems— getting this place turned around in record time. That's ingenuity, and it goes a long way. The way you work is indicative of a very clever mind, and if sticking with this business and expanding it is what you want, well, I guess I just want to see you go after it."

Sarah stared at the hand atop hers and then raised her eyes to meet the intense blue ones staring back at her, and she was quite simply, touched. Emory, a highly successful career woman, saw value in her. That meant something, didn't it? Hearing that someone credible believed in her might just be the motivation she needed. She leaned her head against the pillow of the chaise, unable to hide her small smile. "Thank you for saying that," she told Emory softly, holding her gaze. "I promise to give it true thought."

"That's all I'm asking." Emory squeezed her hand softly.

They sipped their beers and watched the sun set, not saying a whole lot. Occasionally, Sarah stole a glance at Emory, careful to turn away before she was caught.

"Oh, wow," Sarah whispered quietly. She closed her eyes and savored the succulent flavor of the light and delectable sea scallop on her fork. "This is amazing." She sank down in her chair in utter surrender. In fact, it was so much more than amazing. It was heavenly. That was it. For a moment, she thought she'd died and gone to heaven.

James chuckled quietly at her response to the dish. "I was hoping you would like it." He leaned a little further into her across the table. "I think that was my exact reaction the first time I ate here. The chef is world-renowned, and when you'd told me on the phone you'd never been here, I knew I had to fix that."

"It's a wonderful restaurant. Thank you for introducing me to it." It was a crazy expensive restaurant is what it was, and Sarah couldn't quite relax. She looked around Fleur de Lys, the French restaurant James had selected for their second date. It was the picture of everything opulent. Everything she wasn't. The dining room was accented with touches of gold, grand bouquets, and votive candles. From the ceiling, patterned fabric tented softly overhead offering the feel of dining under a large canopy. Sarah was a bit shocked when she initially opened the menu and caught the lavish prices, but it was clear to her that James wanted the evening to be special, and to be honest, so did she. So she was willing to ignore the unease that she felt. She was determined to enjoy the evening with this wonderful man and not concentrate on the fact the cost of their dinner would add up to a fourth of her rent for the month.

"So I have a confession to make," James began. Was he actually nervous? Again, cute. "I haven't been able to stop thinking about our date last week. You made quite an impression on me, Sarah."

She smiled. "I had a great time too. I'm so glad we decided to do it again."

"Is it too soon to ask for a third date?" He laughed, yet made it clear he was sincere.

She matched his smile. "I accept." There was something about him that she liked. He was easygoing, kind, and a complete gentleman. Her hopes were high and she was truly having a fantastic evening. The conversation had never lulled, they'd laughed together easily, and as an extra added bonus, he was really good-looking. Yes, sir. Things were looking up indeed. She owed Carmen big time for this.

James picked up his wine glass and offered a toast. "To new beginnings."

She lightly touched her glass to his. "New beginnings. Cheers." She brought the glass to her lips slowly and sipped the sweet red wine, never taking her eyes from his.

"How's work?"

"Busy. I've been working in the field the past couple of weeks to help my mother out, but I'm not complaining. I'm happy to do it."

He shook his head. "I find it admirable that you've been so loyal to your mother. Family is important to me, and it clearly is to you as well. You should be proud of the choices you've made."

"Thanks, that's sweet of you." Sarah reached for her wine then, just in time for her eyes to land on a familiar blonde two tables away. Surely, it couldn't be. But it was. She'd never seen Emory Owen outside of the Banning Street house, and seeing her here, now, in the real world, was surreal, almost like when you see your teacher at the grocery store. She was talking quietly with a striking brunette who delicately sipped from a martini glass. If Emory was surprised to see Sarah, she didn't show it. She nodded her head in silent greeting, a smile eventually making its way onto her lips. Sarah smiled back shyly. The brunette, picking up on some kind of exchange, tossed a quick glance in Sarah's direction before turning back to Emory, who leaned in, probably in explanation.

"You know Emory Owen?" James asked, inclining his head discreetly in Emory's direction.

Sarah nodded, sipping her wine. "She's a client. We've gotten to know each other a little bit over the past couple of weeks. How do you know her?"

"My firm's done work with her company, and of course, I know of her from friends of friends. Nothing against her, but she's one of those trust fund babies who's practically had the world handed to her. Must be nice not to have to work as hard as the rest of us."

Sarah thought of the long hours Emory consistently put in and the careful work she'd done to get her company off the ground. The description didn't seem to match, but she decided not to argue the point.

"And just so you're aware," he lowered his voice. "She's a lesbian. Not that it's a bad thing. I just thought you should know."

"Ah. Yes, I think she mentioned that." But Sarah couldn't help notice the underlying warning in his voice, almost as if Emory were a predator and she the unassuming prey. The idea almost made her laugh out loud. James was a nice guy but clearly not as worldly as he would like to think. Only a minor strike against him.

"Just didn't want it to come as a shock."

She nodded, understanding that James meant no harm. He just didn't have a lot of experience in this department, not that she did either for that matter.

They made small talk as they ate, and occasionally, Sarah's gaze drifted in the direction of the table two away from theirs. She wondered how the two women knew each other. A date, maybe? She couldn't be sure. They seemed very comfortable together, and if they were dating, they certainly made a striking pair. In the course of her ascertainment, she somehow became aware of the fact that James was offering her the details of his recent move from an apartment to a house, and she was also aware of the fact that she wasn't actually listening. She was nodding—she was a great nodder—but her attention was captivated by the activity at the nearby table.

The brunette was laughing at something Emory said, and Emory was shaking her head trying to contain her own laughter.

Damn it, she should stop staring. It was rude and intrusive.

And she would.

She focused on James then and forced herself to ask a question that would bring her back into the fold of the conversation. "Do you feel at home there yet, in your new place?"

"Not quite. But I'm sure with time I'll get there. It's the perfect place for me with room to grow into, you know?"

"I'm sure you will." She nodded again, but her gaze was pulled across the room as if attached to a magnet.

❖

"Oh, and that brings me to my next topic," Lucy said, "which is to congratulate, and at the same time scold you, for your much talked about dalliance at The Edge last week. Mia was all too eager to dish every last detail when I saw her for lunch."

Emory regarded the after-dinner drink in front of her and frowned in annoyance. She hated the way information traveled like wildfire among their group of friends. "It was not, what was the word you just used? A dalliance. I danced with a woman, actually a girl if you want to get technical. Not a big deal, Luce."

"It is a big deal if you took her home with you. It's been a while since you've gotten out there. This is kind of monumental."

Emory couldn't help but laugh then. "I would hardly call whatever *that* was dating, and no, just for the record, she absolutely did not go home with me. I don't think I could stand myself if I slept with a woman who uses five letters to spell Amy."

"Such an elitist bitch," Lucy mused, clearly enjoying it.

"Am I?" Emory laughed along with her. "I wish I wasn't. I don't want to be."

"It's okay, Em. I think it's our lot in life. We were brought up to be selective about who we surround ourselves with. There are worse things in life than good breeding, trust me."

Emory thought about that sentence and the people she did choose to surround herself with. She didn't have a whole lot of family left. There was Vanessa, but she lived in Colorado with her own family, and they'd never been close. She had Lucy, Mia, and their circle of friends, and of course, her assistant, Trevor, and the people she worked with. She also spent time with the co-chairs of the various charities she volunteered with—planning events, galas, and fundraising opportunities. And lately, there had been Sarah. Her gaze moved across the short distance between them and she studied her. When she'd first recognized Sarah in the restaurant, her movement had stilled, and she'd lost the last bit of something Lucy was saying about olives.

Emory had noticed Sarah more and more as they'd gotten to know each other, but seeing her outside of work, wearing a black and blue cocktail dress that hugged her in all the right places was another story. She looked stunning. She'd worn her hair down, and the dress showed just enough to completely entice, yet withhold. Seeing Sarah in this whole new light had Emory's mind in overdrive. Slow down, she reprimanded herself. Sarah is your very straight employee who, as such, needs to remain in the do-not-imagine-naked column.

Lucy shot Emory a questioning look and followed her gaze to the nearby table. "So this woman does work for you?"

Emory accepted the bill from the waiter. "Right, I told you that."

"In what capacity? Your taxes, investments, what are we talking here?"

Emory met her gaze. "She's from the company I hired to sort out Mother's house."

Lucy's eyes widened in shock and she turned around to steal another glance at Sarah. "She's your cleaning woman? *That's* your cleaning woman?"

"Please lower your voice, but yes," Emory answered, somewhat annoyed.

"As in, the *dancing* cleaning woman?"

"Yes."

"Wow. Suddenly, my house could use a little touch up." Lucy stole another glance.

"Shut up. Let's get out of here." Emory signed the slip of paper and returned it to the leather bound book, leaving a generous tip for the superb service.

Sarah watched Emory's retreating form and followed the gentle sway of her hips as she and her companion exited the restaurant. She was curious as to where they'd go next, what the rest of their evening entailed. A moment before they'd disappeared around the corner, Emory turned back and offered her a slight wave, her eyes lingering on Sarah for a moment. It wasn't until they were gone that Sarah remembered she should probably breathe.

James held Sarah's hand as he walked her to the door of her apartment. "I had a great time tonight. If it's possible, I think I enjoyed tonight even more than our first date."

Sarah was feeling bold. "Would you like to come in for a cup of coffee?"

His face lit up. "I'd love a cup, if you're sure you don't mind."

She squeezed his hand. "Of course I don't mind. Come on in."

Sarah didn't invite too many people over outside of Carmen and her family, but you know what, maybe that should change.

"This is a nice space you have here." James looked around while Sarah put the coffee on. The two-bedroom apartment, though small, had been decorated with care. Grace's artwork adorned the refrigerator, and matching sky blue curtains hung serenely from each window. A comfy couch and an overstuffed accent chair made the living room the perfect locale for TV watching and late night reading.

"Thank you. It's home to us."

He picked up a framed photo from the end table. "This must be Graciela."

"Yep. That's my little monster." She came up behind him laughing at the goofy photo of Grace in an oversized business suit and tie, carrying a briefcase. "Her Halloween costume last year. She was a stockbroker." James raised his eyebrows in amused curiosity.

She waved him off. "During her finance phase. She was watching a little too much CNN with my dad that fall. In the past now. You're currently joining us in the midst of a swimming phase for which we blame *The Little Mermaid*, and I do mean blame."

"I see." He chuckled. "I look forward to meeting her one day."

Sarah was warmed. "Me too."

It was a nice moment, and James took hold of the opportunity and leaned down, brushing her lips with his. When she responded, he kissed her harder, and it wasn't long before they eased slowly to the couch. She placed her open palms on his chest, enjoying the warmth beneath her hands. It had, for damn sure, been a while since she'd allowed herself to be kissed. It was nice. Their pace was even, non-threatening, and she liked how comfortable James made her feel. He nudged her ever so gently and Sarah leaned back, her head against the sofa cushion. James followed her down, the coffee forgotten. She closed her eyes giving herself permission to surrender to the moment. She had no intention of sleeping with James so early in their relationship, but a little make out session on the couch certainly couldn't hurt. James seemed to respect her boundaries and didn't push things any further than she was comfortable with, following her cues nicely. Gradually, she pulled her lips from his. "This was nice," she whispered.

He smiled at her through labored breaths. "More than nice."

Pushing herself to a seated position, she straightened her dress and ran a hand through unruly hair. "Can I get you that cup of coffee?"

He stood. "I think I'll pass, if that's all right. You've given me enough to keep me awake tonight as is."

She laughed at the overly tortured look he flashed her.

"I'll call you soon," he said and kissed her gently before heading off into the night. She closed the door and walked back into the room smiling, taking her time getting ready for bed. As she slipped between the cool sheets, she thought back on the evening with James and how enjoyable it had been. She replayed the events of the date over again in her mind. Without warning, her thoughts drifted slowly to Emory, and she wondered what she was doing. Had she and the other woman gone home together? Had Emory kissed that woman just as she had kissed James?

As she faded into slumber, images of her and James kissing passionately on her couch shifted behind her eyelids until they were replaced with images of Emory and the other woman, their lips pressed together, legs intertwined. Her stomach did a series of flip-flops at the thought of Emory kissing that woman, touching her. Those images continued to play out in her mind until eventually, it was no longer the brunette's body pressed up against Emory's, but her own. Sarah bolted upright in bed, startled at her body's overt and powerful reaction to the image. She stared at the black room around her for several minutes, slowly understanding, for the first time, her extreme attraction to Emory Owen.

## Chapter Six

Emory watched the burly moving men hustle about her mother's house carrying furniture and boxes all precisely labeled and tagged with the proper destination. The men seemed organized and on task, another testament to Sarah's supreme direction of the project. Emory leaned against the wall in the living room and watched as her family's life literally passed by in front of her eyes. Sarah stood in front of the house directing traffic. They hadn't spoken since running into each other at the restaurant, other than a polite hello as Emory arrived on site that day. In actuality, she'd wanted to stop by the house several times that week, but work had been insane, and by the time she was free, Sarah had surely already gone home to Grace. However, when Sarah called to inform her that the movers were coming and today would be her last day of work, Emory had taken the afternoon off to be on hand. Everything seemed to be under control, and it was clear Sarah had a much better handle on the situation than she did.

Emory walked slowly from one room to the next, overwhelmed by a profound sense of sadness. While it was true her memories of her childhood home were fairly sterile, it was still the end of an era, and she couldn't help but feel utterly alone in that moment. She stood in what used to be her bedroom, a room she hadn't so much as set foot in since she was maybe nineteen.

"It must be very hard," said a voice from behind.

She turned to find Sarah watching her from the doorway. She brushed a stray tear from her cheek and exhaled slowly. "We have to quit meeting like this. You know, you dancing, me in the midst of my emotional breakdowns. You're never going to believe this, but I am *not* a crier."

Sarah raised a shoulder and let it drop. "Don't be strong on my account. I think crying is healthy, especially in a situation like this one."

Emory pondered the concept. There weren't very many people throughout her life who would have agreed with that sentiment. Crying showed weakness; at least that's what she'd always been taught. Now that she thought about it, she'd never seen Lucy cry in all the years they'd known each other, and she was the closest person to her in the world. The thought made her sad and she now regretted the lack of emotion they'd shown each other.

She moved silently across the room and sat on the floor, her back against the wall of what was once her sanctuary. It didn't take long for Sarah to join her, taking her hand. The simple gesture made such a difference, and just Sarah's presence there next to her provided a real sense of comfort. They sat for several minutes before she turned to Sarah. "Movers gone?"

"Yep. The last truck drove away twenty minutes ago. I'd offer to get you something to drink, but—"

"They took the refrigerator and all of the glasses," Emory finished wryly.

"Bingo."

"That's okay. I think I'm just going to sit here for a few minutes."

"Tell you what. I'll give you some time alone." As Sarah started to get up, Emory squeezed her hand.

"Stay. Please? I mean, if that's—"

"Of course I will," Sarah answered softly, settling back in next to her. Emory held fast to Sarah's hand and now cradled it in her lap.

"You're close with your family, right?"

"Very. I see my parents nearly every day, and we do big family dinners every Sunday with my brothers. I have two, and the older one has a wife and son. I also have a rather large extended family, and while they're a loving group, everyone is a little too involved in everyone else's life. I guess meddlesome is the word I'd use."

Emory smiled at the thought. "They sound fun. I would have liked to have had a family like that I think."

Sarah ran her thumb across the top of Emory's hand, surprised. "Really?"

Emory lifted her eyes slowly to Sarah's and nodded. The wistful sadness Sarah saw there was simply too much. She reached out and wrapped her arms around Emory and held her, resting the bottom of her chin on Emory's shoulder. "Maybe you will one day."

"Thanks, but I don't think so."

"Have you read any more of the journals?"

"Some. It's enlightening and frustrating all wrapped in one. It's like being introduced to a whole new person who never really wanted me to know them. It turns out, unbeknownst to me, that my mother had no problem with the fact that I'm gay." Emory shook her head, still in awe of this reality. "All these years, I thought it was the biggest disappointment of her life. Oh, and she knew all along that Lucy wasn't right for me." Emory laughed sardonically. "I wish she would have clued me in to that fact."

"Lucy's the ex you told me about?"

"That would be her. She was with me at the restaurant the other night. I told you, we're still close."

Not a date, Sarah thought, filing that information away for later.

"By the way, you looked beautiful the other night, Sarah." Emory turned her head against the wall so she was facing her. It occurred to Sarah that their faces were merely inches apart. She stared into Emory's eyes, nearly falling into them. Her gaze dropped then and she studied Emory's lips, full and slightly pink, and a little pouty. She decided then and there that she really liked her mouth. She wondered what it might taste like, which was ridiculous and out of bounds. "Who's the lucky guy?"

"Hmm?" She raised her gaze, forcing herself to focus. She was vaguely aware that she should probably change her expression from *blatant lust* to something closer to *easygoing employee.*

"The dashing gentleman you were having dinner with. Boyfriend?"

"Oh, James. No. I mean yes. It was a date. It was our, um, second date. Not exactly a boyfriend though." *Concentrate.*

"I think I've seen him before. Is he an architect?"

"Yeah, he works for Anders Design. He said your company had done work with his."

"That's where I've seen him. So you like this James?"

"I do. He's sweet."

"So it's Sarah and James sitting in a tree, huh?"

Sarah raised a playful eyebrow. "I know when I'm being mocked."

"I would never."

"You would and you are."

Emory grinned. "I like that I can be playful with you. Is it strange that I feel like I've known you longer than I have?"

"I know what you mean."

"Hey." Emory pushed herself up off of the floor and offered Sarah a hand. "Don't you have something to give me?"

Sarah stood, her face flushed as all sorts of thoughts chased each other around her head. *Stop that.* "What do you mean?"

"Well, this is your last day. I was thinking a bill, perhaps?"

Sarah brightened and smacked herself in the forehead. "Of course. Follow me." As they walked from Emory's second floor bedroom down to the kitchen, Sarah was a little nervous to present Emory with the amount she owed. It had been a large job that entailed lots of coordination and work from external companies. She'd made sure to itemize each and every dollar so Emory could see clearly where each charge came from.

As Emory opened the envelope, her eyebrows rose noticeably, but she didn't say anything, making Sarah all the more uncomfortable.

"Um, Sarah. This is a little crazy."

Sarah leaned in and looked over Emory's shoulder at the itemization. "Is there a problem or a mistake on the detail list?"

"No, it's not that." Emory turned to face her. "This number is way too low. I should be paying you at least three times what this statement says."

Sarah shook her head. "No, this is a fair assessment of our expenses and labor costs."

"Well, it's ridiculous and I'm not paying it. I'll pay what it was worth, and that's the end of it." Emory pulled out her checkbook and filled in three times the amount of the invoice, tore the check out, and handed it to her.

"I can't accept this."

Emory adopted what Sarah was coming to identify as her executive voice. "Yes, you will accept it and hopefully take another look at your prices. You're undercharging. By a lot, Sarah. When was the last time your company raised their rates?"

Sarah thought for a moment. "About two years ago. I've been trying to convince my mother that we're capable of charging more, but she wouldn't hear of it. She likes coming in on the lower end. She says we get more business and referrals that way."

"She's right about the more business part, but you'll take on twice the work for half the pay. Please tell me you'll talk to her again."

Sarah smiled at Emory, grateful she saw the value in the work she'd done. "I'll do my best, but I'm afraid you haven't met Yolanda Matamoros. All the same, thank you for this. It's very generous." She nodded at the check in her hand and put it in her back pocket.

"It was worth every penny. I'm serious. I'm in awe of how quickly and efficiently you got this done."

Sarah blushed, grabbing her bag and walking to the door. "Now I'm the one who's embarrassed."

"Don't be." Emory followed slowly behind her.

As they reached the entryway, she looked at Emory and realized this was good-bye. Without the house as their commonality, they would have no reason to see each other.

"I'm glad I met you, Sarah. You were a friend to me when I needed it."

Sarah nodded. "Well, if we're being sentimental, you did something for me too, you know. It's been a while since someone's given me that extra push to get out there and make something happen for myself."

Emory beamed upon hearing the information, the kind of smile that Sarah couldn't take her eyes from. "Speaking of which, I can't believe I almost forgot." Emory moved quickly to her attaché case and handed Sarah her business card. "I was serious about that press release. Let me know when you're ready."

"I'd be a fool not to take you up on it."

They shared a smile. "I hope everything works out for you, Sarah."

"For you too."

Emory exhaled, wordlessly opening her arms for an embrace that Sarah moved easily into. And there it was, that powerful hum of electricity. They stood there a moment, and Sarah enjoyed the feeling of having Emory's arms around her. She was suddenly very aware of Emory's body up against hers, and her heart rate quickened. And as she stepped back, she felt the loss. Unsure what motivated her but knowing there was no other choice, Sarah acted on impulse. She slowly placed her hands on either side of Emory's face and brushed her lips with her own ever so briefly with a feather light kiss. She pulled back slowly, just enough so she could see Emory's eyes, gauge her reaction, her thoughts.

Emory stared back at her blankly and the moment shifted. She took Sarah's shoulders, pulled her in, and seized her mouth in sizzling answer. Suddenly, what Sarah'd imagined alone in her room several nights ago plunged into her reality. The taste of Emory, the feel of her as she pressed Sarah against the door in an ever-deepening kiss was shockingly potent and very real. In the quiet of the late afternoon, Sarah felt heat rising in her blood. She didn't push Emory away, she didn't stop what was already in motion, and it was all she could do to hold on. Then thinking stopped being an option. She moved her hands from Emory's face, into her hair and gripped softly.

The action seemed to jolt Emory. She straightened and took a step back. Her shocked eyes never left Sarah's. They stared at each other, Sarah doing her best to catch her breath.

Silence reigned.

"I shouldn't have...I think I thought when you...wow. I'm so sorry." Emory fumbled for her keys in her pocket and reached for the door behind Sarah. "I'm gonna go. Really sorry," she said one last time.

Sarah stood in the entryway and listened to the beep of Emory's car unlock and the subsequent start of her engine.

What had just happened? She slid to the floor and moved her hand to her forehead in mystification. She'd just been kissed into next week, that's what had just happened. Who knew a kiss could feel like that? She was still lost in it. She nodded slowly as the puzzle pieces drifted together in her mind. This was what being swept away meant. She'd heard the term before, but never quite thought it was a real thing. She ran a shaky hand through her hair and to her still-swollen lips.

*Swept away.*

❖

Sarah spent the next week doing what she loved most in the world, spending each moment of her day with Grace. It meant taking the week off from work, but between summer camp and the Banning Street house, they hadn't spent enough one-on-one time with each other, and Sarah had every intention of correcting that before school began in just three short weeks.

They spent their mornings at the park, people watching and insect observing, with an occasional game of catch, stopping every so often to make sure Grace wasn't overexerted. In the afternoons, they attended movies, played cards, and spent lots of time at Grace's favorite place in town, The Children's Museum. It felt wonderful to spend so much time with her. She even found out that Grace had moved on to yet another new passion.

"So now you want to be an artist?" Sarah took a lick of her pistachio ice cream cone. They sat at an outdoor table at Baskin Robbins, enjoying the even-keeled seventy-five degree temperatures.

"Mhmm." Grace caught the chocolate running off her chin just in time. Sarah handed her another pile of napkins.

"What happened to being a mermaid?"

Grace giggled and rolled her eyes. "I wasn't exactly serious about that, you know. I hear they're not paid very well."

Sarah shook her head but enjoyed Grace's dry wit, yet another in a long list of traits she'd picked up from her grandfather.

"I've just figured out that I love art. I don't know if I'm good enough, but I'm still learning."

"Well, I happen to think you're really good. I love how colorful your drawings are."

"Emory helped. She says that color choice is a big part of the mood you want to elist."

"Elicit?"

"Yeah, that's what I said. Elicit. We should go see Emory again."

Sarah stared at the table. "I'm not sure about that, mija. I finished up that job, remember?"

"You could always call her."

"Uh, I don't think so." Grace looked sad. "But, hey, I know I'm not as talented as Emory, but I can help a little. We can also stop by the library and see if they have any books about drawing and painting. That could be fun, right?"

Grace smiled, giving in. "Yeah. We could see what they have."

Emory. It had been a full week since they'd parted ways at the Banning Street house. She'd wondered if Emory would call, hoping secretly that she would. She thought about calling herself but didn't quite know what she'd say. *Hi, Emory, have you thought about that kiss as much as I have?* Sarah rolled her eyes at herself. Emory was a gorgeous, successful woman who was quite comfortable with her sexuality. Sarah, and the moment they'd shared, was probably a fleeting blip on her radar and one it was clear she'd regretted as soon as it was over. She probably hadn't thought about Sarah since. No, it was better to push the memory of Emory aside and focus on the here and now. Emory surely wasn't dwelling on it; why should she?

The situation did beg her to ask some difficult questions of herself, however. It was time she took a good hard look in the mirror. She was attracted to Emory; she knew that much. But did that mean she was gay? She wasn't denying the possibility, but she'd never noticed an attraction to women before. But then again, when she thought about it, she'd never actually noticed an overwhelming attraction to men either. She could definitely tell you if she found a man good-looking, as she did James, but did that mean she was *attracted* to him? Sarah was beginning to understand that there might be an important difference. She liked James. He checked all the boxes. But he didn't make her stomach flip-flop the way Emory did. She'd postponed her next date with James, feigning exhaustion, until she could understand things better. It seemed only fair.

Despite whatever had happened between them personally, Emory had given her the extra shove she needed to take Immaculate Home to the next level. She would be stupid not to take Emory up on her offer to help. It was up to her to make the best life for herself and for Grace. No one was going to do it for her.

❖

"Trevor, did you confirm lunch with Veronica from Penino and Partners at one?" Emory stopped next to her assistant's desk.

"Yes, she confirmed an hour ago, and you're all set for your three o'clock with the developers after that. They have new art they want to run by you, and legal wants to touch base at four forty-five about the new language in the proprietary agreements."

"Damn it, I don't have time for legal today. I'm going to be here until midnight tonight as is. See if you can make some time for them tomorrow morning or ask Lucy to meet with them if she has a break in her schedule."

"Will do."

"Also, Trev, make sure the Nashville office is back online. They were having uplink issues with their satellites, and Chicago had to transmit all their releases. If they're not back, let me know so I can rip someone in IT."

It was all Emory could do to not slam the door to her office. Things were beyond hectic and didn't show any sign of letting up. The "to address" pile on her desk was only growing, and she'd like to punch herself in the face for volunteering to be on the committee for the Women's Health Initiative fundraising dinner. It would have been so much easier to just write a check. She dropped into her executive chair and swiveled around to face her monitor. Lots of new e-mails had flooded her inbox in the short time she'd stepped away from her desk, and after a few well-placed curse words, she decided it was best to just dive in.

She scanned the list of bold subject lines with a sigh. She deleted many without reading them, filed others into the appropriate action folders, and typed short and to the point responses to the questions being asked of her internally. The last e-mail snagged her undivided attention, however, and when she read it, the world slowed down for her as if on cue.

*Dear Ms. Owen,*

*Attached is the company profile you requested. Immaculate Home would very much like to take you up on your offer and put out a press release about our (fingers crossed) expansion. Just as soon as I get the go-ahead from management, I'd like to discuss the details of the release with you.*

*Best Regards,*
*Sarah Matamoros*

Emory stared at the screen, her thoughts now free of the work chaos and stress she'd felt just moments earlier. Instead, they were right back in the entryway of her mother's house where she'd last seen Sarah. Correction, kissed Sarah. Sarah, whose enjoyment in the simplest of things was so utterly disarming. Sarah, who saw past all of Emory's bullshit bravado to just…her. Sarah, who had the most kissable lips she'd ever encountered.

This was dangerous territory. She was attracted to Sarah. Of course she was, but it wouldn't be wise to let anything come of that attraction. Sarah was warm, wholesome, and sweet—pretty much everything she wasn't. Anything further would just be a bad idea.

But she had to admit that she was proud of Sarah for following through and taking the much-needed step forward, despite the boundaries she'd stepped over the last time she'd seen her. Emory was confident she could get that little company some attention, maybe even a feature story in some of the smaller papers. She would handle this client personally. She owed her one.

It was after nine p.m. and Sarah settled onto the sofa, exhausted and content from a day at the zoo with Grace. It was the end of their week together, and Sarah would be going back to work at Immaculate Home the following Monday. She'd just tucked Grace into bed, and it wasn't five minutes before she heard the rhythmic, even breathing indicating she was already fast asleep. She gave Grace one last look as she lay in the glow of her Harry Potter nightlight. As it should be, she thought, smiling to herself as she made her way to the living room.

The week had been an active one, and Sarah sent a silent thank-you to the heavens for Grace's continued good health. They'd only had to cut the day short once, and Sarah had been proud of Grace for speaking up about her fatigue. It had been eight weeks since the initial diagnosis, and Sarah was finally starting to trust Grace and the doctors. With careful attention, things were going to be okay. They really were.

She grabbed the remote from her coffee table and set out to find a decent movie on TV to veg out to. She was jazzed to run into one of her favorite movies of all time, *You've Got Mail*. She snuggled up on the couch, eager to settle in to all the film's goodness. But the activity of the day had definitely taken its toll, as twenty minutes later, her eyelids felt like they were weighted down with tiny sandbags and she struggled to keep them open. Just as she gave up the fight, surrendering to the onslaught of slumber, a distinct buzzing sound awakened her from across the room.

"Damn it, Carmen," she muttered irritably as she crossed the room, searching through the overflowing bag for her stupid phone. "This better be good." She glanced down at the phone's readout, blinking several time to find her focus.

"Taken the plunge and talked to the boss yet?" the text message read.

What was she talking about—the boss? She carried the phone back with her to the sofa, racking her brain for understanding. It was as she began to type back her confused and somewhat annoyed response that the sender's name snagged her attention. Emory Owen. She stood and walked the length of her small living room, immediately awake. Her heart rate accelerated at the thought of talking to Emory again, and she was grinning at the phone as she typed.

"Not yet. On my to-do list for tomorrow. Any advice?" She sat down again, waiting for Emory's response, but then changed her mind and went back to walking.

"Go in courageous and with lots of numbers. Hard to argue with evidence."

"Numbers I have. Courage I'm gathering."

"You'll be brilliant."

Sarah smiled as she typed. "Thanks for the confidence booster."

"Not a big deal. It's true."

She hadn't seen or talked to Emory since the Afternoon of Sexy Kissing. But she was feeling bold and decided to shift the conversation a little and ask what she really wanted to know. "So how have you been?" It took several minutes for Emory to answer this time, making Sarah wonder if she should have left it with a polite good night and thanked her again for the well-wishing. The text that arrived, however, stopped her in her tracks and tightened her stomach muscles reflexively.

"Mostly good. Busy. Miss seeing you."

She grinned. "I miss seeing you too."

"How's the little one?"

"Feisty. But at the moment, sleeping." In between text messages, Sarah moved about the room, examining random objects and straightening things as if this were somehow the perfect time to clean up a bit. She shook her head at the nerves that tickled her skin. *This is just Emory, who you've talked to many, many times. Quit being a moron. Get it together.*

"Oh. Hope I didn't wake you."

She decided to be a hardcore liar. "Nope, I was awake. What are you up to tonight?"

"At the office. Contract language review. Beyond boring." Sarah was surprised. She'd pictured Emory at home for the night, settled in, much the way she was. Geez, it was well past ten o'clock.

"Is it possible you work too much?"

"I've heard that before, yes. You?"

"Sofa. Blanket. TV."

"Jealous. Wish I were there instead."

"Me too." Sarah smiled at the idea, enjoying the exchange more than she was willing to admit.

There was another lengthy pause before the next text message came in. "Should we maybe talk about it…?"

There it was. Those three little dots that stood for so much more. She frowned as she pondered how to handle the situation, grateful for the fact that she had time to think before responding. Thank the beautiful universe for the gift of text messaging.

If she wanted to sidestep what could be a complicated situation, this was her opportunity. She could downplay the amazing kissing another woman thing, act like it was no big deal. Happens every day. Safety is your friend, she reminded herself and began to type a conservative albeit cowardly response. After all, this was maybe not something she was ready to deal with.

But her fingers stilled mid stroke.

Nope.

She just couldn't let go of this new, other side of herself. It was scary as hell, and she wasn't sure at all what she was doing or even if she should be doing it, but she had to find out about these feelings that had so boldly interjected themselves into her life. Was that such a horrible thing? Checking out what was behind door number two? She made her decision and hit the backspace, reconstructing her message.

Deep breath. "I was hoping we could."

"Feel like I maybe crossed a line that day. Misinterpreted things. If I did, I'm sorry."

"I'm not." She hit the send button and waited for her phone to vibrate back at her, her heart pounding in her chest at the direction the conversation was heading. She knew she was pushing the envelope, but she couldn't seem to stop. Minutes passed without any response from Emory, and that wasn't a good sign. It was possible she'd made the wrong choice, and now things would be forever awkward between them. The beginnings of regret rippled through her.

Then her phone buzzed.

She closed her eyes momentarily before checking the readout.

"Will I ever see you again?"

She collapsed onto the couch. All was not lost. "I think you will."

"Until then. Sweet dreams, Sarah."

Inexplicable relief laced with adrenaline. That's what she was feeling. She stared mutely at Meg Ryan on the television screen in front of her. She was aware of the fact that she was smiling and shook her head in wonder at whomever this was who'd taken control of her mind and body. She was flirting with another woman via text message for heaven's sake, and for the first time in a long while, she was excited for what life may have in store.

❖

Emory said good night to the building security guard and strolled into the parking lot, peering up at the clear night sky and exhaling. She was exhausted from her long day of work, the muscles in her neck tight, but she didn't care. Her spirits were high.

She'd behaved like a teenager tonight, texting Sarah impulsively when she couldn't get her off her mind. She'd promised herself that she would sidestep the Sarah situation. That would have been the mature thing to do.

So much for maturity.

But Sarah missed her and had confirmed the connection between them at least on some level. Normally, Emory would pursue the other woman for whatever casual enjoyment she could get out of the situation, but with Sarah, it was more complicated. A) Sarah was not a declared lesbian, B) she terrified the hell out of her, and C) had a child, which was pretty much a deal breaker. Though she didn't know exactly how to move forward, or even if they should, the fact that Sarah might be feeling even a little bit of what she was left her with enough to call the night a good one. She decided not to look beyond the here and now and enjoy the small victory. Maybe she would go for a run on the beach when she got home. Suddenly, she didn't feel so tired. Checking the sky one last time, she grinned and was pretty sure the stars were twinkling extra bright.

## Chapter Seven

Sarah popped her head around the corner of her mother's modest office. "Mama, can we talk for few minutes?"

"Sure, sure. Come in, sweetheart. Sit." Her mother took off her reading glasses and gestured her into the small space. "What would you like to talk about?"

Sarah took a seat across from her mother and nervously pulled opened the ledger she carried with her. "Before you say anything, please hear me out."

"What am I looking at, mija?" She regarded Sarah with a mixture of amusement and reservation, turning her attention to the ledger.

"This is a listing of our accounts receivable for the past two months, and as you can see, we did a record number of jobs. So many, in fact, that we didn't have enough workers to fill them all."

"Yes," her mother chimed in. "We all just have to work a little harder. I don't mind cleaning a few houses each week if it means we don't have to turn down work."

"Mama," Sarah began, her tone clear that she meant business, "we have to face facts. It's time to raise our prices, and not just a few percentage points this time. We have an established name and a credible reputation, yet our fees are on the low end of the scale for the market we service. It doesn't add up. We could be doing half the work for twice as much and see a real rise in profits." When her mother began to protest, Sarah politely raised her hand to signal she had more to say. Her mother inclined her head in acquiescence. "You've always instilled in me, Mama, that the quality of the work was more important than anything else. We offer quality work, and we should be paid for it. If we raise our prices, yes, our client list will shrink, but we'll make just as much money and focus our time and energy into continuing to establish ourselves as the best in the business."

Her mother frowned. "Where is this coming from, mija?"

Sarah pulled Emory's check from her pocket. "This is from the Banning Street job."

Her mother reached for the check and placed her glasses back on her nose. She studied it, her eyebrows rising appreciatively at the payment received. "You always do good work, Sarah, and you're a smart girl. I'm not surprised Ms. Owen included a bit more."

"It means more than that. When your *clients* inform you that you're undercharging and insist on paying you more out of principle, it's time to take notice. This came from a successful businesswoman, Mama, who also thinks we should raise our prices. Will you think about it?"

Her mother nodded. "Is there something else you'd like to talk to me about? Is everything okay with Graciela?"

"Grace is fine, but now that you mention it, there is something." Sarah took a breath and decided it was just best to plow forward. "I'd like permission to expand Immaculate Home. I've put a business plan together that I'd like you to look over. It's a little bit of what we've talked about before, but essentially, it's a guaranteed win for us. Our clients have raved about our space reorganization, and if we take it one step further and offer full construction and customization, we can't go wrong. I promise you, Mama, there's money to be made. We have enough capital now to take on a designer, and I've talked to Roman about handling construction contracts for us. Everything's in this folder, every last detail. I've even scouted some office space at the new building across the street. Mama, I'd like to head up the new sector. I know I can do it."

Sarah handed the leather bound folder she'd purchased for her proposal to her mother. "Take your time and see what you think."

Her mother's eyes were guarded and she nodded very slowly as if in thought. Sarah watched patiently. Finally, after flipping casually through the folder, she offered Sarah a small but reassuring smile. "You've put a lot of work into this, haven't you?"

"Yes, I have because I think it's the right thing for us. For me."

"Let's do it."

Sarah's mouth fell open. "What? Just like that? You haven't even read what I've put together. There are projections there and suggested rates and—"

Her mother waved her off and came around the front of the desk and pulled Sarah from her chair into an embrace. "We'll get to all that. I trust you, mija, and believe you're capable of great things. If you think this is the way to go, so do I."

Sarah felt like doing a backflip. More than that. If there were music, she'd have broken it down right there. Her mother pulled back and looked at her. "I'm proud of you. You're the future of this place. I'm just an old woman who's happy to have a job."

Sarah laughed at the silly statement. Her mother had built this company from one client twenty-five years prior. "Thank you, Mama, but I don't know what any of us would do without you."

It was dusk, Emory's favorite time of day, and she decided to enjoy it. It had been several weeks since she'd taken a walk along the shoreline, and she chastised herself for not taking more advantage of living on the beach. She kicked her shoes off, leaving them on her back deck, and made the short walk to the water's edge, savoring the feel of the dry sand on her skin. She rolled up the bottoms of her jeans and made her way a little further out so the tide would just graze the tops of her feet as she walked. It was getting chilly out as the sun made its descent in the sky, and she was grateful for the gray hoodie she'd put on before leaving the house.

It was a quiet evening on her favorite stretch of Mission Beach with just a few joggers and a family trying desperately to save their sand castle from the encroaching tide. She stopped and watched them for a moment. The little boy threw his body in front of the castle, his parents laughing and scrambling to help.

This was a moment for them. A real moment. And she couldn't help the jealousy that crept in.

She'd never spent a day at the beach with her family, even though they lived so close. Her father was perpetually working, and her mother wasn't exactly a fan of sand and water in combination. She'd come with her friends when she was older, and perhaps that's where her love of the ocean had first surfaced.

She made a vow that she would have moments of her own someday.

At least, she hoped she would.

Emory flipped around at her typical halfway point, not too far from the tourist section of Mission Beach, which she tried to avoid. As she walked, she got the distinct impression that she was being followed. A quick glance over her shoulder confirmed her suspicion, and she cursed silently under her breath, hoping her stalker would get the hint when she didn't engage. A few minutes more and still no luck. Why didn't he get the picture? Her walk, which she'd looked forward to, felt intruded upon, and she was growing frustrated. She turned to face him finally. He had dark hair, a seemingly cheerful disposition, and four furry legs. She wasn't the best judge of breed, but he looked to be some sort of chocolate brown retriever. Bottom line, she'd never been much of a dog person, and today was no exception. "What can I do for you, buddy? I don't have any food. Time to find someone else to bother."

Her new friend's answer was to turn in a half dozen or so frenzied circles.

Okay, even the coldest heart couldn't resist that display. She knelt in the sand bringing herself eye level with the culprit who sat back on his hind legs and regarded her with kind brown eyes.

"Very impressive. Four stars. But you should really go find your owner now. I don't feel like playing. Nope."

The dog looked back at her, offering what could only be described as an actual doggy smile that seemed to say *I'm sorry to keep you, but don't I have the most twinkly eyes?* Emory laughed, unable to help herself, and offered the dog a soft pat on the head. Standing, she scanned the beach, looking for someone, anyone who this showman might belong to. There was a couple nearby watching the waves, but that was about it. She pointed to the dog questioningly, but they shook their heads. *Damn.* She looked around one last time, but the stretch of beach was pretty quiet. Out of options, she looked down at the dog. "Stay," she commanded, holding her hand up and backing away. He whined softly but seemed to understand her command, remaining glued to his spot as instructed. She glanced back as she walked and there he sat, watching her move farther and farther away. She was off the hook.

She arrived home and climbed the stairs to her deck, satiated from the little bit of exercise the walk had given her. She typed in her code to let herself in just in time to hear her cell phone buzzing from where she'd left it on the counter. Her first inclination was to ignore it. The last hour had been so peaceful.

But the phone continued its incessant notification.

Deciding reluctantly that it could be work related, she grabbed for it just milliseconds before the call would be forwarded to voice mail.

"Emory Owen," she said.

"She gave me the green light!"

Emory recognized Sarah's voice and a smile broke across her face.

"You got the go-ahead?" She could hear Sarah laughing on the other end of the phone and her heart swelled instantly. "You're kidding." But she knew she wasn't.

"I'm not. I thought the chances of her saying yes were about as plausible as a moose walking through my kitchen, but it happened. My mother, not the moose, but you know what I mean."

Emory laughed as Sarah continued talking.

"I'm interviewing designers on Wednesday and meeting with Roman at the construction company today to finalize the details of an agreement. It's crazy in a really good way."

"What made her sign off on it all?"

"She said she was proud of me, that I'm capable of doing great things. And I think I am."

"Well, of course you are. That's what I'm telling you. You're the real deal, Sarah, and your mom would be blind not to see that."

"Now you're just being nice."

"I'm rarely nice, and today is not an exception."

"Well, I respectfully have to disagree."

There was a noticeable silence then, and Emory did the next thing she knew to do to prolong the exchange. "We should celebrate." Not her best idea, but it was out of her mouth before she could rationalize it.

"We should?" Sarah answered weakly.

"Let's go out somewhere." Alarm bells were sounding, but what the hell. "What about Friday? I have season tickets to the Civic, and I've missed the last few shows that have come through town. I don't know how you feel about theater, but it could be fun."

There was a slight hesitation before Sarah answered. Emory felt her stomach muscles tighten with—what *was* that—nerves? She didn't get nervous. Did she?

"I'd have to get a sitter, but I think my brother could take Grace for the night."

"Great, give me your address. I'll pick you up at seven."

They squared away the details, and Emory congratulated Sarah once again on her great news. She couldn't have been happier if it had been her own monumental achievement. In fact, she knew inherently this felt better. She hung up the phone and returned it to the counter, excited with the prospect of seeing Sarah, talking to Sarah, and going out with Sarah. The report that she skipped her way to the shower instead of walking was completely exaggerated, and the tale of her singing once she got there was probably just rumor.

Four days later, Emory stared at herself in the mirror of the women's restroom at work, running her fingers through her hair to fluff it just a tad. She was scheduled to pick Sarah up for their celebratory night out in less than thirty minutes, which meant she had little time to spare, knowing traffic on the 805. But damn it, she hadn't had more than five minutes to master a quick change at the office, and the results were leaving her underwhelmed. She wore an aquamarine dress and simple heels suitable for the theater, a sharp contrast from the no-nonsense navy business suit and white cuffed shirt she'd sported only moments ago. She applied just a tad of lip gloss and turned for the door where she came face-to-face with Lucy.

"Aha. There you are."

"Very perceptive of you. What do you win?" Emory attempted to sidestep Lucy who, damn it, was blocking the door.

"Not so fast, young lady. You've been acting strange today, hyperactive, some might even say, and now you've changed into a very flattering, somewhat alluring outfit. Spill."

"I have a commitment, if you insist on knowing, and I'm late, so if you'd be so kind as to—"

"Commitment? Is that code for sex? Because if we're using codes now, I need to be updated."

"Not code for anything."

"So then it's business?" Lucy took a step to her left, blocking Emory's path. "Don't try that again. I'm a ninja. You know this."

Emory rolled her eyes.

"Aha. Not business at all." Lucy studied her, smiling, enjoying this way too much. "You look all excited and dreamy. A *date* perhaps? Is Emory Owen going on an honest to goodness, butterflies-in-your-stomach *date*?"

"If I answer your very intrusive question, will you let me leave the restroom without a full-on scuffle? And please don't forget I'm stronger than you."

Lucy considered this. "Deal."

"All right, I'm going to be honest with you."

"I do prefer it to lies."

"It might be a date; it might not be. I'm not exactly sure. Good-bye." She patted Lucy twice on the shoulder and slipped past her, effectively escaping.

Lucy called after her down the hallway. "What does that mean? You're not even going to give me a name?"

She walked backward, smiling. "You're good."

"You're not off the hook, you know. I'm contractually required to be here Monday, and I know where you work."

Emory turned and waved backward over her shoulder, offering nothing further.

❖

Damn San Diego traffic. She was late again. Emory was beginning to think she was incapable of arriving anywhere on time. Couple that with the fact that Sarah was always early, and Emory internally cringed, secondarily taking note of the fact that it was rare that she cared. Interesting.

She double-checked the address of the apartment complex before pulling in. Her passenger was waiting outside and offered a wave and a very genuine smile as she approached the car.

"I'm so sorry I'm late. The 805 was nightmarish."

Sarah hopped easily into the passenger seat. "No problem."

Emory took a moment to catch her breath and took Sarah in. "So, hi."

"Hi."

"You look great." An understatement. Sarah wore a simple off-red cocktail dress. Not too dressy, but just enough. "Ready to celebrate your wild success?"

Sarah grinned like a kid on her way to Disneyland, and Emory's heart did that thing where it tugged pleasantly. "Please, let's. I've always wanted to go for a night at the theater; I've just never gotten around to it. I've also always wanted to say 'night at the theater,' and now I have. Two birds."

"Glad to help."

"I'm glad you invited me."

"Me too." Emory stole another indulgent glance at Sarah before turning her attention to the road.

"How was the world of corporate news today?"

"Not too bad a day. We had some press releases go out for some important clients this morning and no glitches that I've heard about. But then again, we also had two errors on smaller accounts out of the Denver office. Unfortunately, that's fairly normal for them. We're working on their error rate." She winced apologetically. "This is boring. You were probably just being polite."

Sarah laughed. "I've never once thought of you as boring, you know that? Boring is one thing you can cross off the list of adjectives I use to describe you."

"There's a list? Now you tell me."

"I don't have to report everything back to you. It's not like I work for you, you know."

"Touché."

Things felt easy between them and Emory relaxed, content to enjoy the evening for whatever it was. She'd be lying if she told herself she hadn't already noticed how brightly Sarah's eyes shone when she laughed or how her hair, when pulled partially back, was both simple and alluring.

Sarah checked her watch. They'd arrived at the theater with little time to spare before curtain, and they maneuvered the steps as quickly as they could. It was difficult for Sarah to keep pace in her I'm-trying-to-look-nice-tonight shoes. Emory seemed like she was born wearing killer pumps and took the steps like a pro. "Easy now, I don't wear heels ten hours a day." But she was laughing.

Emory reached out. "Take my hand."

So she did, finding the steps infinitely easier now.

Emory smiled. "Better?"

"Much." Sarah liked how vibrant she felt alongside Emory and how much she got a kick out of Emory's smile. She hadn't seen a lot of it up until this point, but it was quite possibly the most striking thing she'd ever seen.

Once they were inside, the house manager greeted them. "Good evening, Ms. Owen. The curtain is just about to rise. Let's get you to your seats. Right this way, ladies." He escorted them quickly down the aisle to their fifth row seats. Sarah sighed with relief that they'd made it on time.

Then she took in the view. "These are amazing seats," she breathed.

"I'm glad you like them. These tickets have been in my family for years. It's a shame I don't get to put them to use more often."

"You really should." Sarah's attention drifted to the patrons around them. Most were in the midst of animated conversations. There was a serious amount of fancy jewelry, shoes, and designer bags on display. And she was pretty sure they were all real. That little annoying voice in the back of her head began its song. *One of these things is not like the others.*

Emory leaned in. "This show, however, I've been interested in checking out. I've met Adrienne Kenyon, the lead actress, a couple of times at various charity functions, and she's always such a good sport about doing whatever we need. She's supposed to be killer in this role."

"I can't wait," Sarah whispered just as the house lights dimmed around them. For the next two and a half hours, Sarah was transported to another world entirely. She was captivated not only by the story that unfolded in front of her, but by all of the dazzling technical aspects of the production as well. By the end, she didn't hesitate to jump to her feet in standing ovation. She knew she'd like the show before she came, but she was moved in a way she wasn't prepared for.

During the standing ovation, Emory watched Sarah rather than the actors onstage, much in the way she'd managed glances at her throughout the show. Sarah was probably the most expressive audience member she'd sat alongside, genuinely laughing on cue and gasping audibly at each shocking revelation along the way. Seeing the show through her eyes made it ten times more enjoyable, and it had already been an exciting night of theater. Sarah, she realized, clearly understood how to enjoy herself, and she'd be lying if she said it wasn't a contagious quality.

As they exited the theater, Sarah was beyond enthusiastic. "I had no idea a musical could be like that! I've seen the movie version of *Oklahoma* and a local production of *Chitty Chitty Bang Bang* when Grace was six, but it was nothing like that. I'm in absolute awe if you can't tell."

Emory liked seeing Sarah so happy. She had to say it was ridiculously attractive on her. "So you didn't like it at all then?"

"Stop it." Sarah laughed and nudged Emory with her shoulder. "It was easily the coolest thing anyone has ever taken me to." And with that, Sarah took Emory's hand in hers in a move that felt so natural it startled Emory. The warmth of that physical connection was motivation to do anything she could think of to prolong the night just a little bit longer.

"Want to take a walk around downtown? We could head over to the Gaslamp District. There's a quaint little wine bar I know. That is unless you need to get home. I mean, if you have to pick up Grace soon, we can always just—"

"No, I'd love to. Take a walk, that is. Grace is fine. I called over to my brother's at intermission, and he said the girls were playing poker with him and his buddies. Apparently, Grace is up eight dollars." Emory raised an amused eyebrow. "I told you I have an unusual child."

"Unusual can be good, I think. It keeps life exciting."

Sarah's eyes darkened and she glanced away. "You know, I think I could do with a little less excitement for a while. Boring would be just fine with me."

Emory inclined her head sideways. "Are you referring to something in particular? What kind of excitement are we talking about?"

Sarah pulled her hand from Emory's and turned to face her. "A story for another time? I'm having too much fun tonight."

"Me too, by the way," Emory answered softly. "And we can talk or not talk about anything you want."

"Anything?"

"Anything."

"In that case, I do have one question for you."

"Ask away."

"Are we on a date tonight?"

"Oh. Hmmm. Well, I didn't exactly…Wow, let me try this again." *Smooth, Emory, so smooth.* Gone was the confidence she'd exuded her entire life and the ease of communication that she'd always relied on. For some reason, Sarah Matamoros had the ability to strip her of that skill set. Left without a witty line or confident declaration, Emory sighed and decided to level with Sarah. She lifted one shoulder weakly. "I didn't know."

"Okay. That's fair."

They walked in silence for a few moments.

"I was just asking because you did kiss my brains out the last time I saw you."

Emory froze, shocked at the blatant declaration. "Is that what I did?"

"I'd say that's an accurate description, yeah."

"Again, sorry for the attack."

"Do you always apologize so much after you kiss someone?"

Emory thought about it. It was a legitimate question. "No. I guess this would be new. A lot of new lately, it seems."

They walked on.

There was a chill in the night air the way there was always a chill in the night air in a typical August in California, but Emory didn't notice. Sideways glances at Sarah left her utterly captivated at the way the moonlight seemed to accentuate the green flecks in her eyes. Sarah looked back at her, seeming to catch her staring, and smiled. Oh, that was dangerous. Emory shook her head in amazement. Who smiles like that? Honestly. She felt that smile all the way down to her toes. "If I'm being forthright, it did cross my mind."

"What?" Sarah seemed puzzled.

"The date."

More silence.

Ouch. Emory felt as if she'd crashed and burned. Not a big deal, she told herself. It was probably better in the scheme of things. She should now do whatever she could to save the evening and enjoy spending time with her friend.

"I'm a little embarrassed," Sarah finally said.

"Don't be. Please."

"Because I thought it was."

Emory stopped walking and blinked as understanding arrived. "And you said yes."

"And I said yes." Sarah started walking again, leaving a pleasantly mystified Emory behind.

"So this is a date?" Emory called after her.

Sarah turned and walked backward, smiling all the way. "No way. You didn't think it was."

"Yes. Yes, I did. I just didn't want to seem too presumptuous." Emory closed the distance between them and arrived on the sidewalk alongside Sarah. "Maybe we should try this again."

Sarah's smile faded and she stared back at her sincerely. "Okay."

"So I was thinking,"

"You were? That's awesome."

"You're so very funny."

"Thank you."

Emory continued. "Well, I thought it might be nice to take you out, on a date, to this little place I know that serves great wine. What do you say?"

"You know, the wine part sounds fun. I think we should go, but the date thing I'm going to have to think about."

Emory nodded, smiling at the irony but catching the playful twinkle in Sarah's eye. "Okay. Take your time. But while you're thinking it over, I'm going to take your hand back as we walk. It's a little chilly out here, and you're nice and warm."

"Well, as long as it's for weather purposes."

"Strictly."

A short walk later, they arrived at the Gaslamp District, an historic section of San Diego that was transformed in the late eighties to an eclectic, hip, urban stomping ground. It offered hundreds of entertainment options and came alive at night when the old-fashioned gas lamps began to glow. They strolled past sidewalk cafes, nightclubs, boutiques, and coffee houses, dodging the throngs of people that crowded the streets. Emory was pleased to find a jazz trio on the corner just adjacent to The Grape House, the wine bar she frequented.

"Inside or out?" Emory asked.

"Outside, definitely. There's something about sitting under the stars with you that I seem to like. Plus, there's music."

"I was hoping you'd say that." Emory arranged for a table outside, and with Sarah's permission, ordered two glasses of her favorite Sangiovese.

Sarah sipped from the oversized glass. "Oh wow, this is smooth."

"I know. I first fell in love with this bottle on a trip to Milan last year. I was surprised to find it right here in San Diego, but that's why I love this little place. They have all the greats."

"I take it you're very well traveled."

"For the most part, yes. What about you?"

"Not as exciting a history, I'm afraid. Mexico, before my father moved us to the U.S. and now California, most of its big cities. I've read about a lot of other places though."

Emory was intrigued. "You're telling me you've never been out of California?"

"Never been on a plane either. Try not to look so shocked over there. I'll do it one day. Maybe when Grace is a little older, we'll head out and see some sights." Sarah's eyes fell to the table then. She seemed to noticeably withdraw, and Emory internally cringed at having been the cause.

"That'll be fun." Emory took a sip of wine. "You mentioned growing up in Mexico. What was that like?"

Sarah sat back in her chair, her eyes reflective. "I don't remember a lot about it. Mainly being around family, my grandparents. Most of my childhood memories center more on making the transition here. Learning the language, the culture at school, I remember being frustrated a lot."

"In what way?" Emory reached across to the center of the table and interlaced her fingers with Sarah's. Sarah stared at their hands, her expression unreadable, before continuing.

"More than anything, I just wanted to fit in, and that meant being American, just like most of the other kids. It didn't exactly go well. But I never stopped trying. I took mental notes on all the cool things the kids from California did, said, and wore and then went home and wrote them down so I'd remember. I actually did that. Then I'd rehearse popular phrases with an American accent alone in my room." She took a sip of wine. "I even went so far as altering my name on the first day of sixth grade. I guess I always felt like an outsider looking in. It wasn't until late in high school that I finally started to accept myself and be okay with my own culture and where I came from. It didn't happen overnight though. It was a process. I guess it still is."

Emory didn't like the story, and the idea of Sarah doing everything in her power to be liked tugged at her heart. "If it's any consolation, I like who you are. A lot."

"Thanks, but you may want to reserve judgment until after football season starts. You haven't met the rabid Chargers fan that lives within."

"I'm afraid already. Wait. Can we backtrack a minute? I'm interested to hear about the name change you mentioned. Is your given name not Sarah?"

"No, it is but without the h, pronounced *Sada*. I always had to correct my teachers on the pronunciation on the first day of school.

Then one year, I stopped doing it and started writing an h after my name on all of my papers. And then magically, I was Sarah. Again, doing everything I could to be on the inside track."

"Sara is a very pretty name. You could always go back to it."

"No, I'm afraid that ship has sailed. I've been Sarah for too long now. Even my parents have adopted it."

They finished the last of their wine while listening to the jazz combo that had recently returned from a break.

Emory couldn't remember the last time she'd enjoyed an evening out so much. She was thoroughly content in this moment and more relaxed than she'd been in a long, long time. The music, the company, and the nice glass of wine were all to thank for that. The waitress politely dropped the leather bound book containing the check onto their table. Emory reached for it casually, but was beaten to the punch.

Sarah hugged the portfolio to her chest. "I'm getting the drinks. You paid for the tickets."

Emory made a grab for the check, but it was easily moved out of her reach. "Come on. I suggested this place and chose the wine. I'll get it."

"Nope. It's only fair and—eighty-four dollars?" Sarah looked up from the open folder. "But we only had a glass each. Do you think they made a mistake?" She raised her hand, looking behind her for a waiter.

Emory winced apologetically and slowly brought Sarah's hand back down. "The vintage is an Italian reserve, so it's a bit pricey, which is why I insist on paying tonight."

Sarah was shocked. The wine had been good, but not that good. She considered next week's trip to the grocery store and inwardly cringed at the implications this would have on the month's budget. Swallowing her pride, she handed the bill to Emory wordlessly, defeated inside and more than a little embarrassed. Emory handed the check and a credit card to the passing waitress and turned back to Sarah. "Really, I'd planned to get this. Money is not an issue for me in the same way it is for most people. It just makes more sense—"

Sarah nodded, the differences in their worlds hitting home. "Well, thank you. But just for the record, I'm not exactly destitute."

"Of course not. I didn't mean to insinuate otherwise, but be honest. If I were the architect you've been seeing, would you have argued over the check with me?"

"I don't know, maybe not. But that's beside the point."

"No, it isn't."

Sarah didn't respond.

They rode back to her apartment in noticeable silence. Alone with her thoughts, Emory tried to see things from Sarah's point of view. Even though she didn't necessarily understand, she knew she should respect Sarah's feelings. The wine had been a little extravagant, but it was something she'd wanted to share with Sarah. Maybe she had been trying to impress her. Was that such a bad thing? Emory switched off the ignition as they pulled into a parking spot in front of Sarah's apartment. She turned to face her, intent on smoothing things over between them.

But for the second time that night, Sarah beat her there. "I'm sorry. I overreacted. It's just tonight, this kind of night, it's not what I'm used to. But what I know for sure is that I don't want to fight with you."

"No, I should apologize. Sometimes I can be a little—" But she didn't get to finish as Sarah's mouth captured hers in a kiss that she would stay up half the night reliving. It was the kind of kiss that meant something, promised something, and made Emory want all kinds of somethings. Sarah was all soft lips and sweet taste, just as she'd remembered, and a jolt of heat shot straight through her in response.

Sarah pulled gently away and said nothing for a moment, just tucked a strand of hair behind Emory's ear and looked softly into her eyes.

Emory swallowed, feeling so much more than she expected to. "I'm bad for you, Sarah," she managed to whisper.

Sarah held her eyes. "You're not good at relationships. I remember."

"I can't be who—"

Sarah placed a finger softly over her lips. "We had a nice time tonight. Why don't we leave it there for now?"

Emory nodded, holding tight to Sarah's words, trying to rationalize more than was probably safe to because falling for her would be colossally stupid.

"Good night, Emory."

"Good night."

Sarah walked into her apartment, closed the door, and leaned against it. Her heart was beating a mile a minute. She'd just gone on a successful date with another woman and boldly kissed her in her car. Who the hell was she exactly? She was beginning to understand that she didn't know the answer to that question anymore, and it was scary and thrilling and scary again for days. While she couldn't deny that she had taken a lot of enjoyment in the kiss itself, her world felt wildly off-kilter. How, exactly, was she planning on fitting whatever this thing was with Emory into her well-established life? Was there even a chance she could?

"Are you going to tell me her name?" Lucy sat opposite Emory on the bench that lined the steam room wall. "I let an entire spin class go by without asking a single question about this mysterious date of yours, just sure you'd think enough of our multi-tiered relationship to tell me yourself, but clearly, I was wrong."

"I think the world of you, Luce. You're the peas to my carrots and the apple of my corporate eye. Why would you think otherwise?"

"The peas to your carrots? Did that just come out of your mouth? Someone is in a good mood and it's definitely not me. I don't know if you've heard, but *my* best friend has completely shut me out." Lucy sulked dramatically, slinking further into the terrycloth towel wrapped around her. "I'm guessing it's something I've done. I can't help but wonder if it's because we were together, and if that's the case, I think we're both way past that, don't you? I mean I have no problem hearing about you with other women. So if you're worried about jealousy, stop because—"

"All right, all right, you win!" Emory took a swallow from her bottle of water and decided it was best just to lay it out for Lucy. "Yes, I went on a date last night with someone I've been getting to know recently. I didn't tell you right off because somehow things feel different with her than I'm used to and I just wanted to have it to myself for a little while so I can figure it out. Come to an understanding of things on my own, privately. Make sense?"

"Her name, Owen."

"Sarah."

Lucy thought on this for a moment, her eyes finally widening in understanding. "Sarah Montgomery, the attorney from Barrett's birthday party? Aha. Okay. She was definitely flirting with you that night."

"What? No. Luce, that woman was predatory. Sarah Matamoros from Immaculate Home."

Lucy stared back at her blankly.

"Sarah," Emory emphasized. "From Fleur de Lys, remember?"

It seemed to hit her then and the expression on her face was the same as if Emory had told her Eskimos had taken over Texas. "The cleaning woman?"

"Can we not call her that? I told you, her name is Sarah."

"Sarah, the *hot* cleaning woman?"

Emory rolled her eyes. "It's not like that. Her family owns the business. She handles marketing and occasionally picks up a job or two when they're busy. You would like her."

"Yeah, I would. I saw her, remember?"

"Knock it off. I'm serious."

Lucy softened. "You are serious, aren't you? You really like her."

Emory nodded solemnly. "I think I do."

"Aww, Em. I think that's great news. I do. If I weren't your smokin' hot ex-girlfriend in a towel, I would grab you and hug you right now, but you get it. So instead, I have an even better idea, why don't you tell me about her?"

Emory couldn't contain the burst of happy energy she got when her thoughts turned to Sarah. "Well, the best part about her is how much fun she has. Seriously, Lucy, she seems to appreciate everything. Things I always take for granted. Plus, she's caring, thoughtful, and smart, really smart. Her daughter is quirky and funny too."

"Whoa. Stop there and rewind. She has a child?"

"Grace. She's eight. I've only met her once, but she's something else."

"Yikes. But a kid, Em? Come on, that changes things. Are you sure you know what you're getting into? Somehow, I just can't see Emory Owen caught up in a world of bedtime stories and sticky fingers. You're a lot of things, but warm and fuzzy isn't at the top of that list. No offense."

The wind fell drastically from her sails. "Geez. I'd like to say none taken, but ouch. Am I that bad?"

Lucy turned on the bench to face her. "You're not bad. You could never be that. You just don't share how you're feeling very often. When we were together, it was very hard to…feel close to you. It was like just when I had the last wall torn down, you'd build another one. Over time, I just had to accept that this was who you were. And I'm not sure that works with a kid."

Emory let the information sink in, and though it was a horrible thing to hear about herself, she knew that every word was sadly true. "I know it's late in coming, Luce, and I don't know if these are even the right words, but I'm sorry."

"I know. You did the best you could, and you know what? I truly believe that we're right where we're supposed to be. And if you're serious about this girl, Sarah, then it's what I want for you too."

"It's not like that. I just like being around her. Instant family is not what I'm projecting here." She sighed. "In fact, I should put a stop to things now, but—"

"You're too far in. You don't want to be, but you are. Just look at you, all conflicted."

"I just don't see where this can go. You said it yourself, Luce, and you were right. I honestly can't see myself being someone's mother."

Lucy scrunched one eye. "The image doesn't come easily, no, but crazier things have happened. I don't think there's anything wrong with testing the waters a bit."

"Testing the waters." Emory let the concept marinate. "I guess."

"Just please go into this with your eyes open."

"Yes, your wiseness."

"See? You're seeing things clearer already." Lucy then looked around helplessly. "The wise one is melting. Let's leave. There's a martini somewhere calling my name and I'm not one to disappoint."

## CHAPTER EIGHT

Hi, Mom," Grace said. She sat atop the small nurse's cot, her eyes filled with sorrow.

"Hi, baby, what happened?" Sarah moved into the tiny room, discarding her purse on the floor as she crossed to Grace. She stroked the back of her hair and wrapped her arms around her, needing to feel for herself that she was okay.

When she'd received the call that Grace was in the nurse's station at camp and she should proceed there right away, she experienced a horrible case of déjà vu. She'd torn out of the office and raced to the campground just as she'd raced to the hospital two months prior. She gripped the steering wheel in utter terror, and even though the nurse had assured her Grace was absolutely fine, there was nothing she could do to quiet her irrational fear. Now that she was here, she glanced expectantly at the faces of the three adults gathered in the room—the nurse; Grace's camp counselor, Miss Kathy; and the camp director, Mr. Ingersol.

"Grace had a fainting spell today," the nurse explained calmly. "She lost consciousness for less than a minute, but given her circumstances and condition, we thought it best you came."

"I'm fine, Mom. I feel normal, I promise. It wasn't as bad as last time. Can I please go back to camp now?" Grace looked up at her and the desperate hope Sarah saw there tugged at her.

Mr. Ingersol cleared his throat. "Miss Kathy, would you take Grace to get a refill on her juice so we can speak with her mother?"

"Of course I will. Come on, kiddo."

Grace shot Sarah a worried glance over her shoulder as she walked quietly from the room with Miss Kathy. Sarah nodded in encouragement and smiled back.

Once the door closed, Sarah turned to Mr. Ingersol and the nurse expectantly. "Tell me the truth. Is she okay? What exactly happened?"

"She was playing volleyball with the other kids and she just went over. Kathy checked in with her throughout the day, and Grace said she felt fine. It's a sand court, so luckily her fall was cushioned. She was out for maybe thirty seconds, and by the time I arrived on the court, she was sitting up and telling everyone not to worry. She's a brave little girl."

"Yes, she is," Sarah said, but only halfheartedly. The fact that this had happened a second time in only two months had her shaken. Without a reoccurrence and with Grace's cardiologist sounding so encouraging, it was easy to slip back into normal life. Today was an unfortunate wake-up call.

"Ms. Matamoros, I think this is something we need to discuss from a safety perspective," Mr. Ingersol said. Sarah tensed, hoping against the worst. "I have very real concerns about our ability to provide Grace with what she needs. I hate to have to do this, but for her own benefit, I think it would be best if Grace did not finish the summer with us."

Sarah felt as if she'd been punched squarely in the stomach. "You're kicking her out for having a heart condition? Can you do that?"

"I'm so sorry, but it's for her own safety. This is a very active camp, and based on what we know of Grace's very recent diagnosis, I'm not confident this is a safe environment for her. There are plenty of camps that cater to children with special needs. Perhaps in the future, you could look into one of them."

"Can we come to some sort of compromise? Maybe limit her participation in the more strenuous activities. Let her watch but still get the chance to be around her friends. It would kill her to not be able to finish."

"I'm sorry, but from a legal perspective, we can't have her return. I had concerns when we agreed to admit her, given her recent medical history, but after consulting briefly with our attorney, this is the best course of action for everyone involved. We'll offer a partial refund, of course, for the remaining two weeks."

"Thank you," Sarah said with icy calm. "If you could just locate her backpack for me, we'll be out of your way."

"Of course. And again, we wish nothing but the best for Grace."

"Clearly."

As they walked to the car, hand in hand, Sarah struggled with how she would possibly explain to Grace that she was no longer allowed to attend camp. Grace loved this place and had blossomed so much that summer with all the new activities she'd been exposed to, not to mention the new group of friends she'd made. The idea alone broke her heart.

"Mama, why can't I stay? I feel fine."

"Well, because I want to make sure you're okay. The doctor said this would happen if you overexert yourself, and so you probably need to rest a little. Lay low."

"But this afternoon we're supposed to do water balloons, and I don't want to miss it. Angela and Brianna asked me to be on their team."

"That sounds like it would have been fun, but don't you think it's more important to make sure you're okay?"

Grace thought on this for a moment. "I guess so. If that's what you want. Maybe they'll have water balloons tomorrow too."

Sarah took a deep breath as they climbed into the car, and then stared at the leather pattern on the steering wheel, hating what she was about to say. "Mija, I have some not so good news."

"What?" Grace's large eyes, already filled with fear, made it even more difficult to deliver what she knew would be a horrible blow.

"We're not coming back to camp anymore. You see, Mr. Ingersol also wants to make sure you're feeling well, and he's afraid that the activities at camp are not good for your heart condition."

"He said I can't come back?" Grace asked in a horrified whisper.

Sarah nodded solemnly. "You know what, though?" She forced herself to brighten. "I think you're going to have more fun this way. Papi was just saying that he didn't get to do enough cool stuff with you this summer. And since I still have to work in the daytime, I have a feeling you two will get into all kinds of trouble together."

Grace nodded almost imperceptibly and stared out the window.

"Sweetheart?" When Grace turned back to her there were tears streaming down her face. At the sight, Sarah felt them spring into her own eyes.

"I want to go back to camp tomorrow," she managed to gulp out. "This is all my fault."

"Of course it's not your fault." Sarah brushed the tears gently from her cheek. "Why would you say that?"

"Because I didn't tell anyone I was feeling tired when I was. I just wanted to keep playing. Our team was winning the volleyball tournament, and I was going to get to serve next. I should have said something." She managed to take a deep, shuddering breath in the midst of her sobs.

"You're right, you should have said something. We've talked about this. But it's not your fault you can't come back to camp. It's not your fault that your heart gets sick sometimes. It's just the way things are, baby. But promise me you won't keep how you're feeling a secret ever again. This is so very important. Do you understand?"

Grace, still crying openly, nodded. "I promise."

Sarah placed her hand gently under Grace's chin and turned her face fully so she could look directly into her eyes. "I love you more than the moon and back, and I know that this must be so hard for you. But things are going to get better. School's about to start and you're going to see all your friends again. Mindy didn't get to go to summer camp at all. Think how she must feel. She'll be so excited to see you again."

"Yeah," Grace said. Her crying was now subsiding into sniffles.

"I have an idea. Why don't we pick up a couple of double chocolate milkshakes, veg out on the couch together, and watch a movie?"

"Don't you have to go back to work?"

"I'd rather spend today with you. You're my favorite."

"Okay, I guess."

Well, that was at least something. They could spend the afternoon together, and she could try her best to make Grace forget about camp. Show her a good time. She absolutely could not stand to see her so dejected, so heartbroken. It was tearing her up inside. What she really wanted to do was punch that Mr. Ingersol square in the face.

When they arrived home, Sarah opened the cabinet next to the television and began listing off potential movies they could watch to Grace, who hadn't moved very far from the entryway. "What about *The Princess Diaries*? You love that one."

Grace took a sip from her milkshake and then placed it on the end table. "I think I'd rather just go to my room for a little while."

"You don't want to watch a movie?"

"I don't think so."

"Okay, baby. Is there anything I can get you?" Sarah plastered a cheerful smile on her face. "Do you want me to sit with you?"

Grace shook her head wordlessly and headed quietly down the hall to her room. Before she turned the corner, Sarah caught a glimpse of fresh tears welling up in Grace's eyes. At the sound of her bedroom door closing, Sarah allowed herself to collapse onto the couch. She covered her face with her hands and realized how completely and utterly helpless she felt. She couldn't overrule nature and take away Grace's heart block, she couldn't protect Grace from the harshness of the outside world, and she couldn't even so much as cheer her up on such a difficult day. What kind of mother was she?

She remained on the couch for the next half hour, sinking further and further into a powerless state. She needed perspective, she realized. She needed to talk this out. She thought briefly of calling Carmen, knowing she would sympathize with her from a mother's point of view, but that wasn't what she needed. Sarah pulled her phone from her back pocket. Emory didn't answer until the fourth ring, but when she did, just the sound of her voice was enough to calm Sarah in a way she wouldn't have thought possible.

"Hey, you."

"Hi," Sarah answered, already finding her footing. "Are you busy?"

"That's a relative question. Not too busy for you. What's up? How are you?"

"Grace and I have had a bit of a bad day. I guess I just need to talk to someone. I thought of you. Is that crazy?"

"I'd be upset if you didn't. What happened?"

"Are you sure you have time, I mean, I can call you later if you have a lot on your plate."

"Do you want me to come over?"

The offer alone stopped Sarah short. "No, absolutely not. It's the middle of your work day."

"Like I said, everything is relative. Tell me what happened."

Sarah sighed and recounted the story to Emory, starting in May with the first diagnosis and concluding with Grace's seclusion in her room. She found herself including even the small details, needing Emory to hear all of it. When she finished, she felt somewhat relieved.

Emory didn't answer for a moment. "Sarah, I had no idea. That's a lot for you to deal with. I mean, we sat on the back patio discussing life in detail and you never said a word."

"I don't think I was ready to let you that far in. You were a client and we became friends, but it's different now. At least I think it is."

"It is."

"I don't know what to do for her, Emory. I have a call in to her cardiologist about today, but it's not just her health. Her spirit has really taken a hit. I've never seen her so desolate."

There was a pause on the other end of the phone. "Didn't you say she likes to swim?"

"Yeah, it's her passion du jour."

"Why don't you guys come to my place in a couple of hours? I can move some things around here and meet you. Grace can swim, I can whip us up something to eat, and we can see if we can't get both of you in better shape."

Sarah blinked several times, considering the idea. She could definitely use someone in her corner today, and seeing Emory would probably be a nice diversion for Grace. She'd asked about visiting Emory endlessly since they initially met. "That might be nice, but I'm not sure that swimming is such a good idea. She should probably take it easy today."

"What if there was no actual swimming? Would she go for floating around in the pool on a raft?"

"Chances are good."

"Great. I'll give you directions."

"Are you sure you don't mind because—"

"Do you have a pen?"

"Right here."

❖

"Where are we going?" Grace sighed in annoyance. Her mood had apparently shifted from sad to angry in the span of two hours.

"I thought it might be fun to get out of the house. Do you remember Emory from the great big house we went to?" At the mention of Emory's name, Grace snapped to attention. Aha, now she had her.

"Yeah, she's the artist."

"Right. Well, she invited us to come over for a swim at her house and then dinner afterward. I told her you'd need to take it easy in the pool, but she has some fancy rafts that might be fun to float around on. Game?"

She answered with noticeably more energy. "Game." Grace turned her attention back to the window but was unable to hide the small smile that crept onto her face. Sarah reached for the radio controls and turned up the volume, catching Grace bobbing her head to the beat of the music. It seemed this had been a good idea after all.

Sarah pulled into the short driveway, parking her car behind the familiar Jaguar, her signal that she had in fact located the correct house. She leaned across the steering wheel and stared up at the two-story, medium sized home in front of her. When Emory informed her that she lived on Mission Beach, it had surprised her. All along, she'd pictured Emory living in more of a hoity-toity neighborhood, more akin to Banning Street, in a large formal home. This funky beach scene, while still high-end, was a much more appealing choice.

"Remember your manners today," she instructed Grace as they made their way from the car. "Please and thank you."

"*Thank you* for reminding me," Grace said.

"That's my girl."

Emory opened the door just moments after the bell chimed and smiled brightly at them. "Hi, you two, come on in. Um, I can take your bag, Grace." Grace gratefully handed her backpack to Emory as she passed. "What have you guys been up to today?"

"Nothing until now. Can I see your pool?" Grace asked.

"Sure, right this way."

Sarah followed Emory from the two-story entryway through a small hallway that opened them up into the living room. Her eyes widened as she took in the sight before her. The interior of the house was damn impressive. Shiny hardwood floors, streamlined bookcases, and hip steel lighting fixtures worked together to give the place an entirely modern look and feel. If the outside was unassuming, the inside of Emory's house was downright stunning. The entire back wall of the house was floor to ceiling windows, with the most beautiful view of the beach Sarah could possibly conceive of. The room itself was very open with a sleek little bar and four tall chairs separating the living room from the contemporary kitchen. Sarah didn't see a lot of places to throw yourself down and lounge comfortably, as the light blue sculpted sectional was a far cry from the worn in, cuddly couch at her own apartment. While it wasn't exactly her style, she had to admit the place was breathtaking.

"How long have you lived here?" Sarah asked, doing her best to mask her amazement.

"Two years. The house was built in eighty-three, and when I bought it I decided to upgrade a few things."

"It's beautiful. This view alone is…wow."

"Thanks, I like it too. I just wish I got to enjoy it a little more. It's nice having company though." Emory must have picked up on Grace's puppy dog eyes as she sat patiently through their conversation. "I have a feeling that the miniature person is ready to get in the pool. Tell you what, Grace, why don't you go get your suit on right through there and I'll open this place up a little bit."

Grace eagerly snatched the backpack from Emory's hands and hurried into the bathroom pointed out to her. Emory moved to a small console in the kitchen and pushed a code into the keypad. The glass wall that separated the kitchen from the outdoors rose upward, completely opening up the room to the refreshing breeze moving in from the beach.

Sarah gaped. "Okay, you just made a wall disappear. What else can you do?"

"Be patient. You never know."

"Will there be a fireworks display later?"

Emory smiled wisely. "Fireworks are strictly for Tuesdays."

"Got it. Presumptuous of me. May I ask if you plan to swim with us?"

"Mhmm. Already set. See?" Emory tugged a red bathing suit strap from underneath her T-shirt. "What about you? Do you need to change?"

"I do." Sarah placed a hand on her bag. "Is there somewhere I can…"

"You can change in my room," Emory offered. "It's the first door on the left, at the top of the stairs."

Sarah followed the lazy spiral staircase that snaked its way to the second story and easily located Emory's bedroom, which seemed to be one of three in the house. The room itself wasn't overly large, but the two glass walls looking over the expanse of the ocean made it feel so much bigger. The elevated second story offered a more expansive view of the Pacific, and she took a moment to watch the waves roll in from as far as the eye could see. A soft beige love seat faced out, overlooking the ocean. Something about this room seemed a little bit more personable, warm. Sarah imagined Emory cuddled up on the small sofa, reading a book, and watching the surf.

Shaking herself from the coziness of her daydream, she undressed and put on her sky blue one piece and surveyed herself in the mirror of the master bathroom. Somehow in these new surroundings, her bathing suit seemed to pale in comparison. So plain. And there it was again. That sinking feeling of doubt. She decided to shake it off. Because, you know what? She wasn't in the fourth grade anymore, struggling to measure up. She was an accomplished single mother who had every reason to hold her head high. At least, that's what she would keep telling herself.

The living room was seemingly empty when she returned so Sarah drifted into the kitchen, pulled along by the wafting aroma of something surely sent from baby Jesus. She peeked in the small oven window and her mouth watered at the sight of bubbling lasagna. Unable to stop herself, she opened the heavy oven door so she could fully appreciate the amazingness of what was before her.

"Freeze, grifter. Back away from the lasagna."

Sarah smiled, stood upright at the sound of Emory's voice, and turned around innocently to plead her case. However, what she found herself faced with was enough to make her mouth water a second time. Emory was standing just beyond the interior of the house clad in a red bikini that complimented her toned physique and, well, curves to complete perfection. She'd taken her blond hair out of the ponytail she'd been wearing earlier and it fell haphazardly around her shoulders. Her very tan shoulders. Sarah tried to swallow and recapture the witty comeback that had been on the tip of her tongue just a moment before, but her brain wasn't exactly cooperating at the moment.

"What is it?" Emory looked at her with concern. When Sarah's only answer was a guilty smile and a sheepish shrug, Emory's expression took on understanding. There was a liquid heat to the gaze they now exchanged, and even though Emory was fifteen feet away, she affected her all over. Immediate warmth started in her stomach and moved rapidly downward. Intensely, achingly so.

"For another time," Sarah offered quietly and inclined her head in Grace's direction.

Emory took a deep breath, blinked several times, and nodded finally as if coming to. "Follow me. Grace is waiting for us."

The pool was grotto style and formed a languid, wandering shape capped off with a small waterfall, originating from a grouping of large boulder styled rocks. Just beyond the pool was a half wall that separated the deck from the beach itself. Grace sat at the edge of the pool, allowing her feet to dangle. Though she'd taken swimming lessons, she'd been taught at an early age to never enter the water unless an adult was present, and Sarah was grateful that she'd always been one to listen. There were two rafts already floating in the pool and a pitcher of lemonade sat enticingly on a small table on the deck.

"Can you believe she lives right next to the beach, Mom? I mean you just step over this little brick wall and you're there, like shazam."

Emory laughed at the description. "That's what I say when I climb over too. Shazam."

"She's pretty lucky, huh?" Sarah said. "It was nice of Emory to invite us over. Did you happen to remember to say thank you?"

"Not yet. Thank you, Emory. I like your house a lot. It's pretty cool."

"You're welcome and that's nice of you to say. Cool is absolutely what I was going for. Ready to get in?"

"Definitely."

"Okay, it may be a little cold at first, but I turned the heater on a tad so it should get more comfortable in about ten minutes."

Grace eagerly made her way down the stairs into the four feet of water and Emory slipped in after her, showing her how the raft worked and all the little features it had attached to it, like a built-in radio. Sarah could tell that Emory was a tad nervous around Grace, but she hid it well. She appreciated the effort Emory was making and enjoyed watching them interact.

Once they settled on a station, Emory took it upon herself to move Grace and the raft around the pool, chatting with her the whole time about the fun she'd had at camp, the start of school in just two weeks, and of course how she'd put Emory's art tips to use as of late. With Grace taking the reins and dominating most of the conversation, Emory seemed to relax.

Throughout her playful conversation with Grace, Emory kept one eye on Sarah. She couldn't help it. Never in her life could she imagine a one-piece bathing suit could be so alluring. Perhaps it was the fact that the suit only offered a glimpse of the body underneath that teased her so mercilessly, but the visual was quite simply doing her in.

She and Grace chatted for a good part of a half hour, while Sarah listened from the far end of the pool, chiming in occasionally. When she did, this generally prompted an embarrassed glance from Grace, which amused Emory. The dynamic between Sarah and Grace was so informal, so everyday, it was intriguing. So different from what she was used to.

But in a surprise turn of events, Emory was having fun, more fun than she thought possible with an eight-year-old. Who knew they could be this smart or this funny? Maybe kids didn't deserve the hard rap she'd given them all these years, or then again, maybe it was just Grace. "So what should we do now, kiddo?"

"Ever played twenty questions?"

"Are you kidding? I'm like the Jedi of twenty questions. Am I guessing or are you?"

Grace thought for a minute. "You."

Seventeen questions later, and Emory was finding her stride. "So the individual in question is a living female government official over the age of fifty. Hmmm. Is she a congresswoman?"

"No, two questions left."

"Has she ever gone to jail?"

"No! One question."

"Is she funny?"

"Yes. What's your guess?"

"Easy. Judge Judy."

Grace stared at her in utter mystification. "How did you do that? How did you know?"

"Well, let's think about it. You're eight. You probably watch TV. We ruled out the legislative branch of the government and no woman has ever been president. What woman judge would you find funny? And there you have it."

Grace couldn't contain her admiration as she stared at Emory as if she'd just cured cancer. Sarah shook her head. She had to hand it to Emory. She was good, and damn it, so incredibly good-looking. Watching Emory move about the pool in her swimsuit like it was made specifically for her body left her feeling a combination of supreme jealousy and plain desire all rolled into one. What a complicated situation this liking another woman thing was. So many new angles to examine.

They'd been in the pool for a little over an hour and the sun was beginning its final descent over the ocean. Emory glanced at the clock on the deck. "Dinner should be ready in just a few minutes. Should we head in?"

"I think so. Grace, why don't you go ahead and get changed? It's getting a little chilly out here."

"Yes, ma'am." As Grace scampered inside, Sarah found herself alone with Emory, who smiled at her from the other side of the pool.

"You're great with her, Emory. She's a different kid from earlier today."

Emory swam the short distance that separated them. "Really? Sometimes I don't know what I should say, what I shouldn't say."

"Stop second-guessing yourself. You're a natural."

"Well, to her credit, she's fun to hang out with. Makes me want to be a kid again." Emory stood in front of Sarah then and placed her hands against the wall of the pool on either side of her. Standing face-to-face, their bodies only a millimeter apart, Sarah offered a slight smile.

"Hi," she whispered.

"Hey. So tell me how you're feeling." Emory moved a strand of Sarah's hair behind her shoulder. "And be honest. I'm worried about you."

Sarah met Emory's eyes and there was that click, that connection, and all at once, she felt safe. Emory had her. She could relax and be truthful. "It's been rough. I just keep telling myself that everything is going to be fine, but I don't know how much I believe that. The doctor said her collapse at school was probably an isolated instance and that her life would be mostly normal. But now she's collapsed a second time in a two-month span. I have an appointment on Monday with her cardiologist to discuss our options. I just want her to be okay, physically and emotionally."

Emory nodded. "You know, you can lean on me. You were there for me in some dark moments, and now I want to be there for you, whatever you need."

Sarah nodded, tears touching her eyes. It was hard to be strong all the time, and with Emory, she somehow knew she didn't have to be. She instinctively wrapped her arms around Emory's waist, pulling her in closer and resting her chin on her shoulder. The closeness was nice.

"Are you guys going to change?" Grace asked from just inside the kitchen.

Emory took a step away, releasing Sarah who turned to face Grace. "Yep, on our way."

After everyone changed, they made their way back to the dining room table. Since it was no longer as warm out, they opted to close the glass and enjoyed dinner with some music Emory pulled up on the intercom system.

"That lasagna was from another planet." Grace placed her napkin on the table. "I've never tasted anything so good. No offense, Mom."

"No, it's fine. I clearly do not possess the culinary genius of this one over here. Where did you learn to make this succulent concoction?"

Emory got up to clear their plates. "I took some cooking classes while I studied art in France. Wait till you taste my chicken carbonara. It'll rock your world."

"Where do we make reservations?" Sarah asked innocently, glancing around the kitchen for an imaginary maitre d'.

"Well, I suppose if it's the two of you we're talking about, there's a standing invitation."

"Cool, then Mom and I will be back soon. Like tomorrow." Grace laughed and handed Emory the salad bowl and returned to the table for the remaining dishes.

Sarah bumped Emory with her hip. "You know what, Julia Child? You've done enough today. Get out of here and let me take care of these dishes."

"Absolutely not. You're a guest in my home, and besides, there's not much here."

"You're right. There isn't, which is the only reason I'm offering." Sarah grinned proudly. "Now get out of this kitchen before I take my business elsewhere." She held up a threatening spatula in Emory's direction.

Emory held up her hands in surrender. "Yes, ma'am." She turned to Grace. "You know your mom can get a little scary when she wants something."

"Tell me about it." Grace shook her head in commiseration. "Try changing the channel when the Chargers are playing and lose that arm in the process."

"Duly noted."

"Out of this kitchen," Sarah chided them. "Go." She shooed them into the living room, which was really just on the other side of the bar, and set to work on the small conglomerate of dishes, just sure she'd figure out the futuristic looking automatic dishwasher.

"Hey, Mom, can I walk down to the beach?" Grace called from somewhere not too far away.

"It's getting dark out. I don't think I want you down there on your own."

"What if Emory took me?"

"Oh." Emory said, pausing momentarily. "I guess I could take her down."

Sarah shot her a questioning look to make sure she was okay with the arrangement.

"Relax. Those child endangerment charges were dropped months ago. But if you'd rather, we could wait for you. Or even better, you could stop being so stubborn and leave those where they are."

Sarah came around the bar to see them fully. "I'm good. You guys have fun while I finish up."

"Do you always get your way?" Emory arched an eyebrow.

"I'm a little strong willed."

"So I'm finding."

Once Grace and Emory were gone, Sarah set back to work.

Realizing after washing the dishes that she didn't have a clue about where each dish lived, she set about doing her best to figure it out. Opening the first cupboard, she was struck with how much its interior looked like a display from Pottery Barn itself. Neat little rows of mugs, all the same color and style, stood at attention like perfect little soldiers, not one out of place. *Whoa.* It was in stark contrast to her motley set comprised of her World's Best Mom cup, Grace's preschool attempt at pottery, and mugs sporting her favorite Far Side jokes. While her own cabinet boasted all sorts of bright colors, some complimentary and some not, Emory's were all light green, in three distinct sizes, handles all facing to the right. *New goal. Don't let Emory see your cabinets. Shouldn't be that hard.*

Emory and Grace strolled along the shoreline at an extra slow, even pace. Emory made sure not to travel too far from the house so as not to tire Grace out. They walked in silence for a bit, letting the tide wash across their bare feet. Emory struggled with what they could talk about. They'd already exhausted twenty questions. What else interested an eight-year-old?

"Do you walk down here every day?" Grace asked.

Saved. "Not every day, but I try to go for a run at least twice a week. Sometimes I get too busy at the office though, and it doesn't work out." Emory brushed the windblown hair from her eyes.

"If I lived this close to the beach, I'd come here every day."

"I guess I take it for granted. I shouldn't do that."

"Well, lesson learned. That's something Mom says to me a lot when I figure out something I could have done better."

"She's a wise one, your mom."

"Yeah."

Slowly easing into the conversation, Emory decided to push further. "So things have been a little rough for you lately, huh?"

Grace shrugged and looked up at her. "Did my mom tell you about what happened today? About my heart condition?"

Emory nodded and turned out to the water, trying to seem as cavalier as possible. It was important she not say the wrong thing here.

"I'm upset that I can't go back to camp, but the worst part is that this was my one chance to get these girls from my school to like me, and now that will never happen."

"Explain. What girls?"

"Angela and Brianna are two girls from my class who were also at summer camp. Everyone wants to be their friend, but they don't like talk to just *anybody*. All last year they ignored me or made mean comments, and I wasn't invited to Brianna's sleepover that all the girls went to. But at *camp*, they started paying attention to me and they didn't say anything mean, at least lately. They asked me to eat lunch with them some days too. But that'll never happen again now. They saw me faint, and when they hear I got kicked out of camp, they'll probably laugh about it and ignore me again."

Emory frowned and faced Grace who looked completely crestfallen. "What do you mean they would laugh about it?"

"They make fun of people a lot."

"They sound like mean girls to me, Grace. Do you like them?" She knew she was pushing, but she didn't like what she was hearing.

"Do I like them?" Grace repeated. She seemed to be asking herself the question for the first time. "Um, I don't know. But I want them to like me."

"Why?"

She thought for a moment. "Because everyone thinks they're cool."

"Everyone but you," Emory pointed out gently.

"Yeah."

"Who do you think is cool, if I may ask?"

Grace shifted her mouth to the side, considering her options. "Mindy. She's my friend from school. She loves to watch movies and then write reviews about them. She's a great writer, so funny."

"She sounds creative."

Grace regarded Emory through thoughtful eyes. "So you're saying I shouldn't care so much about people I don't even like and remember who my real friends are."

Emory shrugged casually. "I didn't say anything. I just asked a few questions. C'mon, let's head back." They walked in silence again, Grace trailing behind Emory a couple of steps until finally she stopped walking entirely.

"Thanks."

Emory turned back and faced Grace, who met her eyes squarely. "For what?"

"Listening and not trying to fix it. Mom always tells me exactly what I should do when something is bothering me. You didn't do that. You just listened and let me figure it out myself."

"No big deal. Plus, I think you probably already knew."

"I guess. Why don't you have any kids? You would be a cool mom."

The comment resonated. "Uh, that's a tricky one. I guess what it comes down to is that I'm really, really busy."

"Too busy for a family?" Grace was clearly shocked.

"Well, I used to think so."

"But not anymore?"

"I guess I have some figuring out to do myself."

"Take your time." Grace patted Emory on the shoulder. "You have to do what's right for you. You may regret it though. You know, never having a family of your own. Lonely life."

"Geez." Emory ran her hand through her hair. "Way to give me a hard time. That's kind of heavy talk from an eight-year-old."

"Mom says I'm going on forty."

"At least."

Just then, Grace's eyes flared at something just past Emory. Curious, Emory turned just in time for two very large paws to land squarely on her chest. "Whoa," she gulped just as Grace managed to call, "Watch out!"

"Too late, I think." Emory stared into the familiar chocolate brown eyes of the offender. "Oh, hell."

Grace inhaled sharply. "That's a bad word."

Emory slid her an apologetic look. "Sorry."

"We don't have to tell Mom."

"I appreciate that."

"He seems to like you." Grace giggled, enjoying the giant doggy kiss the retriever forced on Emory's unwilling cheek.

"It seems so," she agreed dryly. "We've met before." She gently lowered the stray to the ground, and he responded by rolling onto his back and offering up his lonely, unscratched tummy. Grace fell to her knees and set to work, providing him with a good rub and earning a few kisses of her own.

"Aww. He's so cute, Emory. Where are his owners?"

"That, my young friend, is the sixty-four thousand dollar question." She surveyed the expanse of the beach, but there was no one but a couple of guys tossing a football who informed them they weren't familiar with the dog. "I guess he's just a stray that hangs out in this area. Maybe I should call animal control."

"No!" Grace practically shouted. "They may put him to sleep like on *20/20*. Can he come back to your house with us? Please?"

Emory shook her head apologetically. "Sorry, kiddo, I'm not a dog person. Plus, I'm not home enough to take care of him and he'd probably tear up the house." Grace looked crestfallen, and Emory felt the pang of regret in her chest. "But, hey, why don't we just let him hang out on the beach? He seems to like it out here. I won't call anyone if you don't want me to."

"Promise?" Grace offered up her miniature pinky.

"I promise." Emory intertwined the pinky with her own. "Let's head back. Last time he was pretty good about obeying when I told him to stay."

"Wait. He needs a name."

"All right. A name is okay, I guess. What do you want to call him?"

Graced didn't hesitate. "Looks like a Walter to me." She nodded her head in affirmation of her work.

Emory arched an eyebrow. "Walter? Not Ace or Lucky or Bo? You know, something a little more dog friendly?"

"After Walter Cronkite," Grace supplied, as if Emory might have missed something. "My papi and I think he was the greatest newsman in the history of the United States, and this dog looks smart. Like he wouldn't fail you."

Emory had to admit, the kid could back herself up. "All right then. Walter it is."

When they arrived back at the house, the dishes were put away and the kitchen in tiptop shape, much to Emory's delight and regret.

"You truly didn't have to do that, you know," she said to Sarah, who was waiting for them in the living room. While it was a nice gesture, she felt a little guilty about allowing her company to handle the clean up. However, Sarah had been so insistent, and she still wasn't entirely clear on what would or would not upset her. They seemed to be so in tune, yet so different at the same time. It was puzzling.

"I know, I know. I think you've said that a hundred times tonight. You don't want people to start calling you Broken Record do you? Because there are more favorable nicknames I can come up with for you."

Emory frowned. "Well, that's a shame because I happen to like Broken Record."

"Lying is wrong."

"It is," Grace chimed in sincerely.

After much discussion, they decided a movie would be a fun way to cap off the evening, and Emory allowed Grace to select one from her extensive Blu-ray collection. They each took a spot on the spacious sectional, and Sarah watched Emory work her magic with the plethora of foreign looking remote controls until Grace's favorite movie, *Up*, appeared on the large plasma screen on the wall. Thirty minutes later, just as the little boy was annoying the poor old man, Grace was fast asleep.

Sarah surveyed Grace who had managed to curl up on the side of the sectional closest to Emory, her head resting on her shoulder. "They look so peaceful when they're asleep, don't they?"

Emory threw an affectionate glance down at Grace's angelic face. "They really do."

"Don't let it fool you," Sarah whispered dramatically.

"Stop talking about me," Grace mumbled, her eyes still closed. "I'm right here."

"Busted," Emory mouthed. She pointed at Sarah who only shook her head innocently.

"We were just kidding around, monster. But you seem extra tired. We should probably head home now."

"No, you guys finish the movie. I'll just rest."

"Would you rather lay down in the guest room upstairs?" Emory offered. "It might be more comfortable."

The idea caught Grace's attention and she sat upright. "Can you see the beach from up there?"

Emory considered this. "Yeah, really well."

"Can I, Mom? It'd be cool to lie there listening to the waves."

Sarah tilted her head to the side, mulling over the option. "All right, but just for a little while. I want you in your own bed before long. It's been a long day for you. Agreed?"

"Agreed. Just a little while, I promise."

"I'll show you." Emory escorted Grace to the cozy room in the corner of the house, which did have a magnificent view. Grace chose to nestle in on the small blue couch that faced out over the water, rather than the queen-sized bed on the inside corner of the room. Emory provided her with a blanket and watched as she snuggled down into it looking completely content.

"I love your house, Emory. It's so dreamy."

"Dreamy? What do you mean by that?"

"It just seems like a person could come up with a lot of good dreams for themselves if they lived here. It's…what's the word we learned? Inspiring."

Emory was touched by the comment and instantly had a real-life reference for terms like warm and fuzzy because that's exactly how she felt. "Thank you," she murmured. And suddenly, she wished she'd done a little more dreaming of her own inside her "inspiring" walls. Realizing there was still time for that and more, she tousled Grace's hair affectionately and turned to leave. "Let me know if you need anything."

There was no answer, and before Emory reached the doorway, she heard the soft, even breathing indicative of serious slumber. She smiled in response to the peaceful sound, another puzzling surprise in a series of puzzling surprises.

Maybe there was hope for her after all.

She closed the door most of the way, deciding to leave it cracked in case Grace was to call for something.

Sarah waited patiently downstairs on the sectional, worried there was something she would do to get it dirty. The place was just so entirely chic that she found herself intimidated in its mere presence.

Sitting very still on purpose, she reflected on the day's events. It had been such a fun evening for her and Grace, and she felt miles better than earlier that afternoon. Yet for most of the day, it had been the three of them, and with Grace present, she knew exactly what to expect and what tone to set. She was nervous now, realizing that the dynamic was about to shift. Whatever it was she was feeling for Emory brought up more questions than answers and she wasn't sure how to proceed.

It was then that Emory descended the stairs and Sarah couldn't help but admire what she saw. After swimming, Emory had changed into a simple pair of yoga pants and a white cotton T-shirt, and somehow she even managed to rock that outfit.

"She's out like a light."

"One of her many talents. Thanks for being so great with her today. In case you haven't noticed, she's really taken to you."

"Well, I can safely say that the feeling is mutual." Emory hit the bottom step. "How about a glass of wine?"

Sarah narrowed her eyes. "Not if it's eight hundred dollars a bottle."

"Very funny. Seventy-five at most."

"Still high-end. Are you sure you don't mind being seen with me?"

"Listen, you, do you want the wine or not?"

Sarah grinned like a kid. "Please."

Emory returned with two oversized globes, handing one to Sarah and taking a seat on the sectional next to her, curling her legs underneath her. She watched Sarah take a cautious first sip.

"Verdict?"

"Um, pretty amazing."

Emory seemed happy to hear the endorsement and turned to her own glass. Instead of drinking from it, she began by taking a deep inhale and letting the aroma settle. Sarah was intrigued. Next, Emory took a small sip and allowed the wine to roll around in her mouth a moment or two before swallowing. Sarah took another sip from her glass, enjoying the pensive expression on Emory's face as she dissected the flavors. "You're super serious over there. A true aficionado, it would seem."

Emory smiled at her. "Just taking it in. Tell me what you taste."

Sarah cringed. "Oh, no, I couldn't. I don't know anything about wine, except that I mostly enjoy it."

"That's okay. There's no right or wrong answer. Everyone's palate is a little different. I could tell you that I taste Cocoa Puffs and marshmallows in this wine, but if you taste plums and cinnamon, that's what matters. A great wine is very complex...kind of like a woman. Tell me what you taste, Sarah."

It took Sarah a moment to process the question because there was something very alluring about the way Emory described wine. And there was that mouth again. So full and almost heart-shaped. She was going to need oxygen any minute now. Forcing herself to focus, she took another sip and did her best to articulate what she experienced. "Okay. It's got a strong taste of fruit, but it's not sweet."

"Dry," Emory supplied, meeting her eyes.

"But it's more than just the fruit I taste." She grappled for a moment. "It's got an edge, almost a kick at the end."

"A spicy finish."

"Spicy, that's a good word for it." Who knew wine tasting could be so incredibly sensual?

"What else?"

She took another drink. "I like that there's no aspect of it that pulls me too far in one direction. There's a little bit of everything."

Emory nodded in slow agreement. "Balanced, clean." She'd already finished her glass and set it on the table. "You're good at this."

As she looked at Emory, her heart rate escalated. Somewhere in the course of their conversation, they'd moved closer together on the couch. They'd kissed before, but both occasions had been in parting. Yet there was nothing she wanted more in this moment than to kiss Emory again. She was so close, and there was that very appealing mouth again. All she had to do was close the distance and capture it with her own.

"You know, I think I'm going to switch to water now, but can I offer you another glass?" Emory slid away from her and into the kitchen.

"No, I'm fine." *Damn it.*

Alone in the kitchen and out of Sarah's view, Emory grasped the edge of the countertop and let her head fall forward. It had all started so innocently. Okay, not entirely, because there had been some intense kissing in the entryway that last day. But it had been escapable. Something she could have walked away from. *Should* have walked away from.

But there was just something about Sarah. When she was with her she felt good inside. And now, after the time they'd spent together, her heart was turning on her and that hadn't been part of the plan. She liked Sarah, hell, *more* than liked her, and the chemistry between them was somewhere off the charts, but she just couldn't let herself give in to it. Why?

Because it was too big a risk. When she compared what she was feeling for Sarah with what the facts in this scenario were, it was a lose-lose. And she wasn't one to ignore the odds.

But Sarah made her consider things she'd never once considered: love, a family, home. Sarah had broken through a barrier within her that no one else had. And those feelings were starting to invade her life. Damn it.

She straightened. Plain and simple, there were things she needed to say and questions she needed to ask. She stalked back into the living room on a mission now. "Can we talk?"

Sarah looked somewhat startled by what probably sounded like frustration in her voice. "Of course we can. What do you want to talk about?"

"This, I guess. Us. What we're doing here. There are things. Going on in my mind. And I need to talk about them."

Sarah's face softened. "We can talk about anything, Em."

*Em.* The casual use of her name stopped her momentarily. She wished she'd say it again, while looking at her just like that, little flecks of green dancing in the hazel. Stay the course, she reminded herself. Clearing her head, she concentrated firmly on her goal.

"I like you a lot."

Sarah smiled. "I like you too."

"But I'm having trouble seeing where we go from here. I'm not sure I can be who you would need me to be. For Grace. For you."

Sarah took a deep breath, her eyes falling squarely on the coffee table. "I know."

"You should run from me."

Sarah raised her eyes to Emory's and nodded. "I should."

"But you're not?"

Sarah shook her head slowly. "I can't seem to. No matter how many arrow signs are pointing me in the opposite direction. But I could ask you the same question. Why did you invite us over today?"

She thought on this. "Because I care about you more than I ever expected to, and I was worried about you, and I wanted to see you. All of those things."

Sarah lifted one shoulder. "That should count for something."

She had a point. "It does. But there's so much more. Have you ever dated a woman?"

Sarah shook her head. "No."

"Have you been attracted to women before?"

"No."

"But you're attracted to me?"

Sarah smiled. "I can say most certainly, yes."

"So do you consider yourself bisexual?"

Sarah sighed. "Why don't you sit down so we can actually talk about this? Unless you prefer the inquisition you've got going here. I'd like to do my best to explain."

Emory sat, but this time on the opposite end of the couch.

Sarah took a deep breath. "My whole life, I've dated men. That's just how things were. 'Pick a man and get married' was the message

I was sent from the time I was little. I never *considered* the fact that there was another option for me. I've never personally known anyone who's gay."

"Until now."

"Until now." Sarah nervously took the last swallow of wine from her glass. "So to answer your question, no, I've never noticed an attraction to women before this. Maybe this part of me has been there the whole time, just waiting for me to notice it. I don't know." She slid closer to Emory on the couch. "What I do know, Emory, is that since I've met you, I feel like so many things I thought I knew about myself have gone straight out the window. I don't have all the answers because I'm still figuring them out myself." Emory didn't respond. Suddenly, she was very interested in the plastic grooves of her bottled water. "Please say something. Tell me what you're thinking even if it's that you want me to leave."

Emory lifted those sky blue eyes and the raw emotion Sarah saw staring back at her was enough to steal her next breath. "I'm thinking that I don't want to be your experiment in sexuality or your short-lived foray into the land of lesbian before you wake up and realize this isn't what you'd envisioned for yourself or your daughter. The perfect picket fence is a lot to undo. I'm thinking I don't want to disappoint you down the road when you realize that I'm not family material. Because I'm probably not. I don't know anything about kids and what if I—" She turned her head away then.

Something in Emory's words struck a chord with Sarah, and she moved until she sat alongside her, gently placing a hand on her cheek and forcing Emory to look her in the eye. "You're a good person, Emory. I know that or I wouldn't have you around Grace. I would never do anything on a whim where she was concerned. If nothing else, believe that."

"I do," Emory whispered, giving in. "I love that you put her first. You're a wonderful mother. I think my problem is that I don't have a clear idea of where we're headed."

Sarah offered a small smile. "And the lack of control is killing you."

Emory nodded.

"I think we're complicated. But I don't think we have to have it all figured out. Here's my proposition. Let's not make each other any grand promises. I like spending time with you. Let's see where that goes."

Emory nodded. "So, casual?"

"Casual."

"Okay."

"Emory?" Sarah whispered back.

"Yes?"

"If you don't kiss me soon, I don't know what I'm going to do."

Emory stared at her wide-eyed, a soft smile forming on her lips. With slow determination, she ran her fingers through Sarah's hair, lifting it gently away from her face and letting it fall. She cradled Sarah's face in her hands and moved in slowly, brushing Sarah's lips ever so lightly with her own, once, twice, and deepening the kiss on the third go-round. Jesus, her brain staggered at the feel of Sarah's lips on hers, the faint smell of her shampoo, the way her skin felt under Sarah's touch. Emory tentatively swiped Sarah's lower lip with her tongue, encouraged when Sarah parted her lips in response.

Sarah felt lightheaded. She melted as she moved closer into Emory and began to kiss her back with an unfamiliar ferocity. Driven by need, she slipped her hands under the hem of Emory's T-shirt, moving her nails slowly over the skin of her lower back. Before she knew it, they'd sunken into each other and lay on their sides, pressed hip to chest. Sarah was having trouble forming a coherent thought as the heat between them seemed to grow with each passing moment. She was dizzy with desire and knew only one thing, she needed more of this, now.

Emory trailed her lips along Sarah's chin and down the column of her neck stopping there to suck ever so gently. Sarah trembled in her arms, aching, throbbing even, and pulled Emory closer still. Out of sheer desperate need to touch her, Sarah inserted a hand between them to palm Emory's breast through her T-shirt, causing Emory to let out strangled moan of pleasure. Perhaps it was the sound of her own voice breaking through, but Emory went still alongside her. In that moment, Sarah became very aware of their surroundings and how incredibly impractical they were. *Damn it.* Emory took a shuddering breath and pulled her lips away. "We have to stop," she panted in Sarah's ear.

Sarah turned her head and blinked back at her, saying nothing. She wanted to say something; she tried to say something, but found herself in the depths of an Emory-induced fog and her faculties strangely weren't what they should be.

Emory sat up, and with a gentle hand, eased Sarah up with her. Emory faced her, tenderly tracing the line of her jaw as she spoke. "Your daughter's upstairs, and while I'd like nothing more than to continue what we've started here, I don't want to rush you." And then with a mumbled, "Oh, God," she captured Sarah's mouth for a final sensuous, toe-curling kiss. "Sorry, momentary lapse. Had to do that one more time."

Sarah caught Emory's hand and kissed the back of it. "I knew I kept you around for a reason." This got a smile. "And while you're probably right about the timing, you're not off the hook that easily."

"Trust me when I say I don't want to be off the hook."

"Good, because that," Sarah gestured to the couch with her head, "was..."

"I know," Emory finished, because she did know. Hell, she knew.

They sat there, staring at each other, and Emory smiled proudly at this new level of intimacy between them.

Sarah broke the trance. "I should get Grace."

Emory stood. "It's the second door down the hall. I'll find her backpack."

The sight of Sarah carrying her sleeping child, more than half her own size was entirely precious. "Do you need some help?" Emory whispered. "Do you want me to take her?"

"Nope. I'm a pro. Check out the mommy muscles."

"Right." Emory raced around to open the door for Sarah and followed her out to the car. Sarah gently laid Grace in the backseat, taking extra care to buckle her in without waking her. "Wow, she sleeps through a lot."

Sarah ran a hand through her hair. "Always has. When she was a baby, I could blare the TV, vacuum the living room, host a rave, nothing. Oh, I almost forgot. Grace asked me to relay a message to you while we were upstairs, but maybe she was just talking in her sleep, as it doesn't make a lot of sense. Something about someone named Walter needing fresh water. He may get thirsty tonight."

Emory nodded. "Got it. Tell her I took care of it."

Sarah grinned and took a playful step into Emory. "Secrets from me already?"

Emory held her thumb and forefinger very close together in response, which earned her a playful poke in the ribs. "Ow. That hurt," she said, rubbing the spot. "I may file charges."

"I have to go now."

"And if I don't file the charges?"

Sarah squinted apologetically through one eye. "You're very cute, you know, but I still have to go." And after a quick check over her shoulder that Grace was still dead to the world, she leaned in for a kiss good-bye. As she pulled away, she lingered, moving her lips very close to Emory's ear. "Not off the hook," she whispered, sending goose bumps up and down Emory's body.

Moments later, Emory watched as the car turned the corner. She stood in her driveway for several delicious moments, the glow in her chest almost painful. There was a part of her that wished she were going with them. Instead, she made her way back to what now felt like a very empty house. It was with a full heart, however, that she placed a very large dish of water on the dividing wall out back along with a few small cubes of chicken for good measure.

## CHAPTER NINE

It was all very well to make out with another woman on a couch and daydream about it for hours afterward, but quite another to take the first step toward a very big, life-altering declaration to the people she knew and loved. Sarah sat on the corner of her brand new desk, delivered just hours ago to the small office she'd rented for herself across the street from the main office of Immaculate Home.

Three days had passed since she'd seen Emory, and though she should be getting some work done on her new venture, she was desperately preoccupied with thoughts of Emory and dying to share this new development in her life with someone, anyone. While she was never one to keep secrets, the idea of announcing to her parents that she was dating a woman had about as much appeal as an all-night dentist's appointment. She decided to go for the next best thing.

"We need to talk," Sarah stated matter-of-factly into the phone. She could hear crashing and shrieking in the background, a sure sign that the boys were up from their naps. "Bad time?"

"Not at all," Carmen practically shouted with relief. "You're a grown-up, a hot commodity in my world. Hang on. Let me drag this cord into the closet."

Sarah waited patiently while Carmen hid herself from her children in what sounded like a lost scene from *Lord of the Flies*. "Maybe I should call you later," she offered, envisioning one of the boys with blood pouring from his face.

"No need. They're just having fun. They're boys. It's what they do. What's up?"

Sarah stood and walked to the window. "A lot. I think I might be ready."

"All right. Ready for dinner? Ready for some football? To rumble? You're going to have to help me out a little here."

Sarah took a breath. "Ready to tell you that I have feelings for someone. I didn't plan on this happening. In fact, it completely blindsided me. It's not perfect, and there are things still in the way of this being a fully functioning relationship, but it's a step, right? These feelings?"

There was silence on the other end of the phone before Carmen exploded like a Fourth of July firework. "Ahhh! This is the best news I've heard in months! What color should my bridesmaid's dress be? Green? I like green. I can work it in green. I knew you two were perfect for each other! I told you. I told you! Didn't I tell you?"

"Wait, Carmen, let me finish."

"I can't wait to tell Roman. He'll be home any minute. We should all go to dinner together."

"Nope, flag on the play. It's not what you think."

"Are you free this weekend? I could get a sitter."

"Carmen, you're not listening to me. I'm not talking about James."

Another pause. "Well, then who?"

"Someone new."

"What's his name?"

*Here goes nothing.* "Actually, I've been kind of dating a woman."

Silence. "I'll be right over."

❖

Things were hopping at Global Newswire that Wednesday. Emory had personally handled five new client calls (three of which landed them new accounts), hired two new upper level sales people in the southwest region, and outlined a new leadership development track for promising junior account executives. Now she was moments away from concluding her weekly sales meeting and couldn't wait to get home and tend to her real life, a feeling that was entirely new to her.

"So as you can see, our selling strategy is working for the mid-range companies, but the larger, public corporations haven't latched on to the multimedia releases as readily." Emory moved to the last slide of her PowerPoint presentation.

The end of the day was in sight.

"What I'd like to see happen in the next quarter, at least on the West Coast, is more of the services listed here, offered to our top clients, free of charge for five releases. If we give them a taste of the multimedia side of things, they're going to see a huge jump in their stats and inevitably want more. After that, ladies and gentleman, we've got 'em."

Her sales staff answered with a hearty round of applause.

"Thanks, everyone. August was a good month. Let's make September even better."

After some proverbial patting on the back of her upper level staff as they shuffled from the conference room, Emory sank into a black leather conference chair and finally gave her BlackBerry, which had buzzed several times throughout the meeting, her full attention.

Lucy lingered and tidied up the conference table, a job Emory had told her a hundred times could be left to their assistants. But Lucy was the type who liked to have her hands in everything, and eventually, she'd just given up.

"So that went well," Lucy mused. "I think you sufficiently fueled their fire. I like this new motivational side of you. You look good in positive."

Emory stared at her BlackBerry in horror. "Shit."

"No, it was much better than that, trust me."

Emory held her head in her hands. "This is so not what I needed right now."

"It's surely not that bad. What's up?"

"Vanessa's coming."

"Shit."

"Exactly."

"What brings the ice queen to California?"

"Mother's house sold earlier this week, and instead of just signing the papers and making this as quick and seamless as possible, she's insisting on doing it in person. It gets better. She's bringing her Mini-Mes and that robot of a husband along with her."

"Double ouch. My sympathies, Em."

"Want to come to dinner with us this weekend?"

"Ah, gee. So much to do this weekend. So terribly much," Lucy said without a trace of emotion. "I don't think I can swing it. Wow, so disappointed."

"Nicely done."

"Take Sarah."

"In case I haven't made it clear, I actually like Sarah, and it's too early to scare her away entirely. Cruel and unusual punishment does not a good impression make. Vanessa's not only a bitch, but she's a snob and would be about as welcoming to Sarah as a cuddly python."

"Touché."

"Maybe I should start drinking heavily. An alcoholic for the weekend. What do you think?"

"I think I don't envy you when it comes to spending time with Viper Barbie, but I know that you'll handle her with the utmost of class and finesse until the moment you get to gleefully put her back on that plane to Aspen. I'd like to get your cartwheels at the airport on video this time."

Emory sighed dramatically and wondered why in the world God had just slam-dunked her on what had been such a good week, thus far. *Vanessa, really?*

Sarah stared across the red and white checkered tablecloth at a very shell-shocked, wide-eyed Carmen. She'd managed to hold her off until the end of the workday when they could get together for a drink at Sabro's and discuss the newest development in her life.

They sat at a table along the sidewalk so Carmen could keep an eye on her boys, who were busy wreaking havoc on the small playground across the street from the café.

Carmen set down her glass. "So you're serious about this."

"I'm serious."

"I just never would have—you know what? You have a lot of explaining to do," Carmen chastised her, changing directions. "Who is this woman? Are you a lesbian now? Why didn't I know about any of this? That's really my first question, why didn't I know about any of this? I'm your *best friend*." Through the anger, Sarah spotted that earnest quality in Carmen's eyes that signaled she was hurt she'd been left out. Sarah tried to explain as best she could.

"Part of me didn't fully realize I was feeling what I was feeling until it was well underway, and I just needed time on my own to process. I guess there was another part of me that worried about what you, what everyone, would think. This probably seems like it's out of left field."

"It's definitely a lot to take in. I've known you since the fourth grade, and you've never even hinted at anything like this. We've scoped guys together for as long as I can remember. Granted, I did a little more of the scoping, but you were right there with me. A sidekick scoper."

"That's true. I scoped."

"So, yeah, I'm a little shocked here." She paused. "That being said, I might find a way to forgive you, but only after you tell me every last juicy detail, and leave nothing out." Carmen leaned back in her chair and grinned expectantly.

Sarah lifted one shoulder and let it drop. "I'm not exactly sure. It was out of the blue. But now that I think about it, maybe it wasn't. It started with the house. There was coloring at the kitchen table. Then the crying on the patio outside, hers not mine, and then long talks. Mad kissing in the entryway, like socks-knocking caliber, an actual date with way too expensive wine, and then lots more kissing, groping, and pretty much all-around torture on the couch a few days ago. Now I don't know which end is up."

Carmen squinted. "Only because I've known you forever, am I able to translate half of what you just said. This is all so—wow. But it's good? It sounds good."

"It feels good. But the logistics are pretty dicey."

"Okay. Well, start with the good."

Sarah smiled. "It's all so different than with anyone else I've ever dated. It's like I crave being in her presence, and not just physically. She was my friend at first, and I deeply value that side of us too. She's smart and funny and—"

"Rich," Carmen supplied, grinning.

"She is that, but to be honest, that's been more of a hindrance than anything else. There's somewhat of a culture gap because of it."

"But you are attracted to her physically?"

Sarah exhaled deeply and thought about Emory. Even now, with Carmen, that sneaky wave of lust overcame her. "Yeah, I really, really am."

"But there's been no sex."

"Sex has not happened."

"Do you want the sex?"

Sarah regarded Carmen seriously and took a moment to ask herself the question. Easily finding the answer, she nodded slowly.

"Wow."

"I know. As far as sex goes, I think I'm finally starting to understand what all of the fuss is about. Listening to you go on about Roman for years and the guys you dated before him, I thought you were just an overly enthusiastic person, when actually I was the one who was out of touch. I feel this, I don't know, jolt of heat every time I'm around her. Or even when I just think about her."

"So what's the problem, Juliet? There are issues?"

"Well, yeah. Am I ready to change my life this way? It's a big lifestyle shift and not everyone is going to approve. I wish that kind of thing didn't matter to me, but it does. It always has."

Carmen regarded her seriously. "I remember."

"And if it came down to it, I would need to know that she was all in first. And right now, I'm not getting that from her. Family, based on the way she was brought up, almost has a negative connotation, and so she's leery of me, Grace, and the concept of happily ever after. She doesn't trust it."

"So you're in this, but it feels like you may be in this alone?"

Sarah bit her bottom lip as she thought on this. "Yeah, I guess that's it."

Carmen reached across the table and squeezed Sarah's hand. "Are you sure you haven't bitten off more than you can chew?"

"I'm not sure, no. But what I do know is that when I'm around her, I feel more alive than I've ever felt in my life."

Carmen's face lit up listening to Sarah talk. "Aww. It's so cute when you talk like that. Seriously, you're all glowy. I like seeing you happy. It looks good on you."

Tears touched the corners of Sarah's eyes against her wishes. "Thank you. I don't know if there's a future here yet, but for now, it feels right. Is that crazy? Am I crazy? I feel a little crazy."

"To want to be happy? No, Sarah, that's not at all crazy." And then schizophrenically switching gears the way only mothers of young children can, she yelled, "Nicholas, freeze! Put that rock down right now, mister."

Sarah laughed and took a fortifying swig of her beer, waiting out the tongue-lashing. Once Carmen came back to her, she brought up obstacle number two hundred and twelve. "So there's more. I received a delivery of roses from James today."

"Oh shit, I forgot about James, and the fact that Roman introduced him to your father when he stopped by the job site earlier this week. I meant to tell you. I'll do it now. Your father met James."

"Oh God."

"I know. And your mother's already drafting a guest list for the wedding. I don't think they're going to take this well."

"Probably not. Let's not tell them. Ever."

"Just a shot in the dark. Why not bring Emory to your brother's birthday party next weekend? Let them get to know her first. That way, if they already like her when and if you decide to spring the relationship on them, well, that's half the battle." Carmen narrowed her eyes. "She is likable, isn't she?"

Sarah smiled. "Yes, she's very likable." And she was. Usually. "That might not be a bad plan. You're a smart one."

"The smartest." Carmen grinned. "And the cutest. You consist-ently forget the cutest."

James stood as she approached the bar and smiled in that charming way he often smiled. This wasn't going to be easy, but she'd put it off long enough.

Deep breath.

"Hey there, beautiful." He kissed her cheek and pulled out the bar stool across from his. "I ordered myself a drink, but wasn't sure what you'd like."

"Um, a Crown and Coke," she said to the bartender. Stronger stuff than her normal fare, but she'd need it. She turned her attention to James. "Thanks for meeting me. You've been so sweet about giving me time to catch my breath."

He took her hand and held it in his lap. "I'm just glad we're back on track. Speaking of which, how do you feel about the Eagles?"

Slight diversion. "They're my favorite band."

He smiled and pulled the back of her hand up for a kiss that made her discomfort level spike. "Thank God the rumors were true. They're in town on the fifth of next month. I got us tickets."

Her drink arrived and she took the opportunity to not only free her hand but to take a large, fortifying swallow. And then another. "About that. I asked you here because I wanted to talk. Some things have…shifted in my life and, God this is hard to say. I've met someone else. And this person has started to mean a lot to me."

James sat back and studied her. The silence seemed to go on forever. "When did this happen?"

"I guess rather unexpectedly over the past few weeks. And as much as I enjoy your company, James, in light of the circumstances, I don't think I can continue seeing you. At least not in a romantic sense."

He stared into his drink. "Well, I certainly didn't see this coming. Is it serious? With the other guy?"

She considered the question, choosing to ignore the pronoun. "It has the potential to be, I think."

A pause. He raised his eyes to hers and offered a halfhearted smile. "Definitely not what I wanted to hear. But I care about you, Sarah, and want the best for you. Given, I still think that's me, but if it's meant to be between us, it will happen someday. Right?"

She decided not to argue, and to just roll with it. No need to drag out the conversation. "Thank you for understanding and if at all possible, maybe we could be friends." It was generic and lame but all she had.

He nodded, his energy noticeably lower. "Of course. Women like you aren't easy to come by. I don't plan on letting you get away entirely."

She smiled at the compliment, but still felt a little uneasy. "I should go." She took out a ten from her wallet and slid it toward the bartender. "Take care, James."

He nodded. "You too."

❖

It was windy on the beach as the sun made its final descent in the sky and Emory enjoyed the view as she slowed her speed to a moderate walk. The run on the beach had been just what she needed, and she was glad she'd picked up what had at one time been her daily routine. It felt good, she thought, stretching her calves.

As she approached her back door, she saw a familiar face waiting for her, and much to her chagrin, she actually smiled at his unannounced visit.

"Hello, Walter." She stroked him behind his ears. "And how was your day today?" He whined softly and leaned into her hand for more. She knelt and scratched gently under his chin, earning herself a few swipes of his tongue across her face. "All right, all right, that's enough of that. Yuck." She stood and wiped away the dog slobber. "It was nice to see you, Walter. Thanks for stopping by." Emory gave his head a final pat and went inside to set about the task of cooking herself a small dinner.

Deciding on a chef salad, she went to work pulling the ingredients from her fridge. She decided to whip up the dressing herself, as the store-bought stuff never seemed to sparkle. She threw some red wine vinegar, honey, garlic, and rosemary into a small bowl, and set about whisking like there was no tomorrow. She stopped a short time later to sample her work. Nice flavor balance. She offered herself a mental high five and accepted it.

While she ate, she turned on some soft jazz and enjoyed the pairing of her salad with a little Charlie Parker. It was the second chorus before, out of the corner of her eye, she glimpsed none other than Walter himself, still on her deck. He sat at perfect attention and stared at her through the glass, his eyes warm and expressive as if to say, "I'm a very good dog. Give me some salad."

But she was more annoyed by his adorable display than anything else and turned away, taking her dinner to the living room where she could veg out in peace. The DVD case to *Up* was still tucked into the arm of her sectional. She studied it while she ate, letting it mentally take her back to the recent evening she'd spent with Sarah and Grace.

She'd talked to Sarah a couple of times on the phone since then. There had been some mild flirtation, which gave her day an extra added charge, but their schedules, coupled with Grace's, had kept them from actually laying eyes on each other. This was a problem she hoped to remedy soon. She had dinner plans with Vanessa on Saturday after they closed on the house, but she was hopeful she could persuade Sarah to see her Friday. Pulling her cell from her pocket, she decided to try her luck. And after three rings, there she was.

"Hey, you," Sarah said.

"Knock, knock."

Amused chuckling. "All right. Who's there?"

"Wanda"

"Wanda who?"

"Wanda go on a date with me tomorrow night?"

Sarah laughed at her lame attempt at humor. "That was really, really bad. You have to know that was bad."

"I do, which makes it awesome."

"I don't think it gets any worse than that."

"Oh, it can."

Emory heard her laugh again and pause. "And as absolutely horrible as that joke was, I would like nothing better than to say yes."

"Then say yes," Emory said, still playful.

"I would but, um, how should I say this? I already have a date."

Emory took a moment, her heart sinking as the fun fell from her voice. "The architect?"

"Not actively seeing the architect anymore, no. I closed that loop. He accepted my offer of friendship. Kind of."

Emory was confused and still a little deflated. "Okay, then who are you going out with?"

"She's eight years old and a tad on the feisty side. I promised I would take her to the movies tomorrow night. However, I think she would love it if you came with us."

"The movies?" Her spirits were lifting. "That could be fun. There's an art house I like to check out sometimes. I could see if they have anything kid friendly. Sometimes they have subtitles, but—"

"Gonna have to nix the art house this time, Ivy League. We want to see the new *Twilight* flick."

She paused for the punch line. "You're kidding, right?"

"I am most definitely not kidding. Meet us at our place at six thirty?"

"Okay, but I want you to know how much this could damage my reputation if word gets out."

"Blackmail material makes this all the more alluring."

Emory sighed softly. "Okay, well I'm all for alluring. See you at six thirty."

"I can't wait. Bye, Wanda."

Emory grinned to herself as she carried her plate to the kitchen wondering what rabbit hole she'd fallen down. *Twilight*, seriously? Though she had to admit there was something appealing about the sheer whimsy of it.

As she walked past the back door, she was forced into an honest to goodness double take at the newest demonstration just outside. With all four paws standing straight up in the air, she would have thought someone had shot Walter dead if it weren't for those ridiculously earnest eyes blinking back at her from his upside-down position. She tilted her head to the side and held eye contact with him. His eyes seemed so soft, yet so hopeful. She felt her resolve crumbling. "All right! I'm not made of stone. You win."

As she opened the back door, Walter leapt to attention and trotted eagerly into the house. He stopped at her feet and gently pressed his wet nose into her hand, offering a lick. She rolled her eyes and relented, scratching obediently behind his ears. "This doesn't mean anything. You can hang out for a little while, but if you get the furniture dirty, I swear, there's going to be trouble." Her answer was a powerful thwacking of his tail against the back of her legs.

She spent the rest of the night reviewing sales reports for work, her eyes growing hazy from strain, her neck muscles aching from use, and Walter curled warmly into her side, fast asleep.

# CHAPTER TEN

O n Friday night, Sarah entered her kitchen, shrugged into a long cardigan sweater, and found Emory standing in front of her refrigerator, studying the myriad of random snapshots. "Grace should be ready in just a minute. Are you all set?"

Emory looked back at her and nodded happily. "Is this your friend Carmen?"

Sarah leaned in over Emory's shoulder and followed her gaze to the photo in question. "Yep. That was taken right after high school graduation. Please ignore my hair. I hadn't discovered the magical world of hair care products yet."

Emory shook her head in amusement and pointed at a photo near the center of the group held to the fridge by an Immaculate Home magnet. "How old is Grace in this one?"

Sarah frowned in concentration. "She would be four years old there. You can't tell, but she burst into tears moments after that photo was taken. Santa kind of freaked her out until she was about six."

"Her and me both." Emory chuckled, turned around, and took Sarah's hand. "I like that you have all of these photos up here. It just feels so, I don't know, homey."

"Is that a secret word for lame?"

"Nope. I like your place. It feels happy and vibrant, like you." While that was true, Emory was also aware of just how strange it felt to her. She tried to imagine herself living in such a bright little busy world, but she was stalling out. She wouldn't know how to go about creating "homey" if she tried. It was a problem.

"It's excruciatingly small next to yours."

Emory had to agree. The place was tiny. She was guessing less than nine hundred square feet, but Sarah had definitely made use of the space. There were potholders dangling from the oven, magnets of the alphabet on the dishwasher, and framed photos of family and friends all over the place. Organized chaos was a good word for it. "No, it seems perfect for you two."

Sarah beamed back at her. *Her smile could end wars.* Unable to help herself, Emory leaned in for a soft kiss, lingering a bit longer than she meant to and sighing internally at the tingling sensation Sarah always seemed to leave her with.

"You know, I've missed you," Sarah told her quietly. She brushed Emory's cheek ever so softly with the back of her fingertips. "Is it mandatory that we wait a week to see each other? I know you're busy but—"

Emory placed a gentle thumb to Sarah's bottom lip, quieting her. "I can find more time. I'll buy it if I have to." For some reason, when she was with Sarah, the rest of the world seemed less important. It was an illusion, she reminded herself, but lately that was getting harder to remember.

Sarah kissed her thumb. "Good. Now that that's solved, we have some vampires to watch. Let me rustle up my kid."

Once at the theater, Grace bounded to the concession stand. Emory followed casually behind her as Sarah paid for their tickets, a condition she insisted upon. After settling on popcorn and Junior Mints, they found their seats in the theater, Sarah sitting in the middle.

"I guess I should update you on what's happened so far in the series," Sarah said.

Emory stared back at her blandly. "If you feel it's important."

"It is," Grace chimed in. She leaned across Sarah in all seriousness. "Very."

"Got it. Inform away."

As Sarah recounted the trials and tribulations of Edward and Bella in precise detail, Grace waved to a boy a few seats in front of them, who waved enthusiastically back and continued to steal glances at Grace throughout the next few minutes. "I don't mean to interrupt," Emory said. "But I think the child has an admirer."

Grace blushed and shook her head emphatically. "That's just George. He's my friend. Can I go talk to him, Mom?"

"Sure," Sarah answered, seemingly amused at Grace's sudden shade of red. "Be polite to his parents."

Emory watched Grace scamper down to the front of the theater. As soon as Grace was out of earshot, she turned to Sarah. "How's she been?"

"She's had a great week, actually. Hasn't mentioned camp once, and invited Mindy over to play, which from what I hear, I have you to thank for. I'm glad she felt she could talk to you."

"I hope it was all right. I think she just wanted an outside opinion."

"You are the cooler one, after all."

"Well, obviously," Emory replied. "What about the cardiologist? Tell me again what he said."

"He doesn't love that she had a second episode, but thinks it's nothing to get too alarmed about, as fainting can be a symptom of this particular condition. But he did recommend we consider a pacemaker so Grace can live a more active lifestyle without worry of similar spells in the future. He wants to implant it over her Christmas break so she has time off from school to recover."

"That sounds a little scary. Are you going to do it?"

"I think so. I'd be lying if I said it didn't terrify me to have her operated on, but maybe it's for the best when you think about it in the scheme of her entire life. I've talked to Grace and she's all for it, but then she's always been a little too fearless."

"It sounds like you're doing the right thing."

Sarah elbowed Emory softly as the lights in the theater dimmed. "Shhh, vampires are about to make out." Sarah snuggled down into her seat and smiled up at Emory. "Hand me the popcorn."

Grace returned and the screen lit up with action, adventure, and romance. Emory, as hard as she fought, found herself actually sucked into the vampire storyline. About halfway through the movie, Sarah climbed over Emory for a quick trip to the restroom. It was less than a minute before Grace leaned across the empty seat between them.

"Can you keep a secret?" she whispered.

"Usually," Emory whispered back, curious.

"It's important."

"Okay. I'll do my best."

Grace leaned in a little closer. "I think my mom likes you."

"I like her too. I like both of you."

"No. I mean, I think she has a crush on you."

It was all Emory could do to not choke on her mouthful of Diet Coke. She was fairly certain this was not information Sarah would have shared with Grace. "What makes you say that?"

"She smiles a lot more when you're around or when she talks to you on the phone, and it's not like with her other friends. I'm telling you, it might be a crush."

"All right, I'll keep that in mind." She leaned back into her own seat, still trying to process Grace's very surprising revelation.

And then in a much louder whisper, audible to almost the entire theater, Grace asked her final question. "You *are* a lesbian, right?"

Emory didn't have a chance to answer and pretended not to notice the several curious heads that turned her way because luckily, Sarah chose that exact moment to return to her seat, planting herself between them. "What did I miss?" she asked excitedly, looking from one of them to the other.

Emory offered her a wry smile.

"Are you sure she actually used the word lesbian?" Sarah eyed her skeptically two and a half hours later. They sat on the stairs in front of the door to Sarah's apartment so Grace, now asleep for the night, would not overhear.

"I'm fairly certain, yeah."

"Wow. Just when I think she can't surprise me any further."

"She's a very intuitive little person."

"Apparently, more than even I realized."

Emory stood. "I wouldn't worry too much about it. She didn't seem distressed at all. Strangely, quite the opposite. I have a feeling she'll come around and talk to you about it sooner rather than later."

"If she waits too long, I think I'll have to broach the subject with her first. I want to make sure she's not full of some wild notion she saw on television." Standing up and joining Emory, she shook her head. "I could just kill my father, by the way. I'm pretty sure this is straight from their afternoons of CNN."

"Don't be too hard on him. At least he's spending time with her. I can't imagine what it would be like to watch television with my parents growing up, not to mention my grandparents."

Sarah nodded and seemed to study Emory for a moment longer than usual.

"What?"

Sarah shook her head. "You're so beautiful. Sometimes it just hits me."

Emory didn't know what to say. There were times when Sarah rendered her speechless, and this was one of them. All she knew to do was kiss her, Sarah, who could make her feel so many things. And she did just that, leaning in, and then sinking into that wonderful flood of pleasure that kissing Sarah always led her to. But what was meant to be just one kiss turned into much more as the always-present spark between them took hold and caught fire.

Sarah kissed Emory back eagerly until she found herself pressed up against the brick wall of the stoop. Emory was kissing her now with what could only be called skilled precision and she was getting lost in it all. *She must have a master's degree in kissing.* Sarah felt a weakness creep into her body that could only be cured by pulling Emory closer to her, up against her, so she could feel her all over. She allowed her hands to drift lower from around Emory's neck where they rested, until she caressed the small curve of her hips and even lower until she was cupping Emory's ass tightly, all the while their mouths continued to dance.

Sighing deeply, and warring with her body's natural instinct, Sarah reluctantly slowed the pace of the kiss and pulled her mouth begrudgingly from Emory's. She took a moment to catch her breath and right herself.

When she raised her gaze, there was a new look in Emory's eyes. There had been so many times Sarah had asked herself how Emory was feeling, but in this moment, she knew. She could see the sincere emotion clear as day. Sarah lifted her palm to Emory's cheek and caressed it softly.

"I might be in trouble here," Emory finally whispered. "Doesn't feel casual."

Sarah shook her head slowly in agreement. "Maybe trouble's okay."

"I didn't plan on this."

"You're not the only one."

"It's like no matter how many barriers I put up, you're able to decimate each and every one." Emory moved away, and when she did, her eyes flashed a vulnerability Sarah had never seen in her before. It was clear she was uncomfortable and it pulled at Sarah.

"Don't run from me, Emory."

"I'll probably screw up."

"It's possible."

"But I want to try."

Sarah leaned in and kissed her softly. "Then we will."

Emory took a deep breath and smiled. She took Sarah's hand as they walked the short distance to her car. "Let me know how it goes with Grace."

"Okay." And then a terrifying thought occurred to Sarah. "What if she says something to my parents?"

"I get the impression she's protecting you a bit, so I don't think she would do that. But would it be so terrible if she did?" Emory seemed to be testing the waters a bit. "I'm going to take the freaked out expression on your face as a yes."

She should probably explain. "Don't be upset. I think it might be best for them to get to know you a little first before I say anything… about this." Emory didn't respond. Her face was carefully blank. "You know, so they have a real life reference and not just a perceived idea to draw conclusions about. Make sense?"

"I guess so."

"I was actually hoping you'd come to my older brother's birthday party next Sunday. You can meet everyone together, all in one fell swoop."

Emory seemed to brighten at the mention. "Done. I would love to meet your family. I'm actually kind of excited about the idea." She then leaned in for one final toe-curling kiss that left Sarah thinking about so much more. They were one spark away from a fire that wouldn't be so easy to put out, and it was beginning to feel like the worst kind of torture.

"We need to schedule a more adult themed date. Soon. No eight-year-olds allowed. Did I mention the word soon? Because I meant to."

"I think I could be agreeable to soon." Emory raised an eyebrow. "How soon are we talking exactly?"

"Are you free tomorrow?" Sarah feathered her fingers through Emory's hair.

"Damn it, I'm not. My sister's coming into town, and I've agreed to have dinner with her and her family."

"Vanessa? That's great news." Sarah practically bounced with excitement. "I'm happy you'll get to spend time with her. I can't imagine my brothers not living close by."

Emory seemed to mull this over. "I wouldn't go with wonderful. As I've mentioned before, Vanessa and I are very different people, and tomorrow is going to be, what's the word I'm looking for? Hell. Tomorrow is going to be hell."

Sarah rolled her eyes. "Don't you think you're being a little dramatic? I bet you wind up having a great time."

❖

Twenty-two hours later and Emory was not having a great time. She and Vanessa had signed the papers for the sale of the house earlier that day at the realtor's office and decided to meet that evening for dinner.

Traditionally, the day had been a hotbed of passive aggressive comments and thinly veiled judgments from Vanessa, mostly aimed at her. Deciding to be the bigger person, she'd let them all go.

Emory had opted to cook dinner for her sister's family at the beach house, thinking the in-home environment might relax everyone a bit more than the ambiance of an expensive restaurant would. Plus, Vanessa hadn't ever actually been inside her house, as they'd always spent family dinners together at her mother's house. She'd been kind of excited, much to her own chagrin, to show off the place to her older sister, hoping with some strange backward childhood derived reason that she would like it. No such luck.

Vanessa and her minions arrived half an hour late. She breezed in wearing a striking red dress with a wide belt and gorgeous Jimmy Choo pumps. Her twelve-year-old twin nieces, Calie and Chloe, were dressed like miniature trashy pop singers in short-shorts, fishnets, and matching low-cut blouses. She didn't let herself dwell too much on the style of parenting that had allowed for such ensembles. Lastly, her brother-in-law, Lawrence, strode in behind them looking utterly bored with the world and his place in it. Kill me now, she thought to herself.

Vanessa floated casually into the living room and gazed around. "So, little sister, this is where you live. My, my, looks pricey." Was that a backhanded compliment? Emory was pretty sure it was.

"Vanessa, Lawrence, can I offer you a glass of Chardonnay?" She was going to remain super cheerful if it fucking killed her. "Girls, I have several options for you in the fridge if you want to take a look."

Her nieces scurried from the room in search of a fruity drink, as Vanessa seemed to consider her options. "If the Chardonnay is unoaked and at least five years old, I'll take it. If not, some mineral water will suffice."

"Chardonnay coming right up," she sang through gritted teeth.

"Make sure it's from California," Vanessa called after her.

"I'll see what I can do." Luckily, the bottle she'd chilled seemed to fit the very specific bill her sister had laid out for her. She retrieved it from the chiller and set to pouring three glasses.

"What's that smell?" Lawrence asked, seeming to wake up from his trance and join the land of the living.

"Um, dinner, I guess."

"How nice." He seemed unconvinced.

"Not to worry, everyone. I made sure it's vegan. I looked up a few recipes I thought you might like, and I think it all came out nicely." She didn't mention that she'd spent the entire afternoon slaving in the kitchen to make sure every detail of the meal would be to complete and utter perfection. "So tonight we'll be dining on spinach and tofu cannelloni, apple coleslaw, and some tropical sweet potatoes. We'll finish with vegan chocolate cake for dessert." That one had really killed her.

"Oh, didn't I tell you?" Vanessa said. "We're not vegan anymore. It just got to be too hard, and the food never tasted good. But I'm sure your meal will be sublime. Won't it, girls?"

"Sure," Chloe replied with zero enthusiasm.

Calie shrugged. "Want to see our dance routine, Aunt Emory?"

"Um, right now?" She glanced at the waiting meal in the kitchen. She didn't want to hold off too long on serving the cannelloni, but then again, the night was not about the food, she reminded herself.

"Come on, Emory, let the girls show you. They've been working very hard in class the past few weeks."

"All right." Emory sat on the sectional next to Vanessa who pulled out an iPod and plugged it magically into a small set of speakers she apparently carried in her Prada bag for such an occasion. The girls assumed their opening position, which consisted of crisscrossed gangster arms. *Interesting.* The next three minutes flew by in a whirlwind of bumping, grinding, midriff flashing madness of the like Emory would never forget. The idea that this highly provocative routine came from two twelve-year-olds was enough to make her want to scrub the images from her head immediately and for always. She wondered what her mother would write in her journal about this one.

Before she knew it, all eyes were on her and the now silent room waited eagerly for her response to the performance. Time to think quickly. She did the only thing she could think to do. She clapped. She clapped hard, if for no other reason than to buy herself a few extra seconds to think of which words should leave her mouth and which ones should not. "That was a...dance sensation," she finally managed. "A real show of skill and...tenacity. Where did you learn this routine, may I ask?" Big gulp of wine.

Vanessa beamed and answered for them. "The girls are enrolled in a hip-hop dance class at the country club in Vale. It's a great way for them to meet people."

*Who work on the corner?* Emory wanted to ask. "Well, it's clear you girls are committed to your craft. Everyone ready for dinner?"

Fifteen minutes into the meal and Emory couldn't take the inane babbling of her nieces for another minute. They seemed obsessed with three things and three things only. Money, fashion, and how they could topple every kid in their path to social (and probably world) domination. Feeling the need to change the subject, she turned to Vanessa. "How's your End Hunger campaign going this year? Just a few months from your big benefit, right? Christmastime?"

"That's right. I've been killing myself making the arrangements. We've secured Sting to play the event and we're working on a big name to emcee. You'll be there, of course, with a checkbook? It's important that we represent the Owen name the way mother would have."

"Of course, I'll be there. I've never missed it."

"How's work?" Lawrence chimed in.

"It's been a busy quarter, but we're continuing to make strides in the market."

Vanessa frowned. "Truly, Emory, do you really find it fulfilling, bombarding consumers with excessive amounts of corporate news?"

Emory set her fork down. "I personally don't think of it as bombarding anyone. I work in news. My company gets the information in the hands of the people who need it."

Vanessa took a delicate sip of wine. "Chloe, if you could spend your time healing sick people, like your father, or using satellites to transmit stock quotes to newspapers, which would you choose?"

As if channeling Tiny Tim, Chloe regarded Vanessa with solemn eyes. "I would heal sick people, Mommy, because that would make a difference in the world."

Emory fought with everything she had not to roll her eyes and instead smiled at her niece. "I would hope you would do whatever profession made you happy, Chloe."

"What's that?" Calie screamed, pulling her feet into her chair.

Emory followed Calie's gaze through the glass of the back window and couldn't help but relax into a grin. "Don't worry. That's just Walter. He hangs out here sometimes. I think he's just stopping in to say hi."

"A stray dog?" Calie practically shrieked. "He probably has rabies!"

Emory mulled this over. "Highly doubtful, but maybe I should take him in to see a vet for his shots."

"So then he is your dog," Vanessa said, her expression sour.

"Well, not exactly. I feed him and sometimes he comes in and hangs out. He's friendly though. Girls, maybe when we finish eating, I can introduce you. He loves to play."

Calie looked at her as if she'd just suggested they skydive off the second story. "Or not."

Emory looked outside at Walter who regarded her with uncharacteristically sad eyes. She wondered if he somehow understood that he was not welcome among these new guests. Emory offered him a wink in solidarity.

"So how's Lucy?" Vanessa segued.

"She's great."

"I don't know how you work together after a breakup."

"Because we enjoy and respect each other. We just weren't right in a relationship."

"Well, let that be a lesson to you." Vanessa gestured with her fork. "Learn something from the experience."

"I'll try." Though Emory didn't have a clue as to what that meant or what she should learn.

"You should try dating," Calie said. "That way you won't be so alone."

*Ouch*. That stung.

Vanessa picked at her food as if investigating a science project. "Not everyone is meant to settle down. I think what it comes down to, girls, is that your Aunt Emory prefers to be on her own, which is why it didn't work out with her friend Lucy."

Feeling the need to defend herself, Emory spoke up. "Well, first of all, that's not exactly true, and second, I have actually been seeing someone." Damn it, the words were out of her mouth before she had a chance to stop them.

"Really? That's new information. I had no idea."

Might as well, she thought to herself. She'd already come this far. "Her name is Sarah, and things seem to be going well. It's early, but maybe you'll meet her one day."

"We'd like that," Lawrence offered. Emory smiled warmly at him and nodded, grateful for the rare show of support.

"And she has a daughter, Grace. She's eight."

Interestingly enough, the room went quiet. Vanessa frowned at her. "Are you sure that's something you're ready for? You've never wanted kids, Emory, and I always thought that was a very mature outlook given the way you live."

Emory stared at the table. "People change. Maybe my priorities are shifting."

Vanessa squinted in scrutiny. "Uh-huh. Where did you meet her? This woman."

"Well, coincidentally, she works for the company that cleaned and sorted Mother's house."

"So when you went in for a consultation?"

"No, she handled the job herself so we met at the house. She's the daughter of the owner."

Vanessa smiled and stared at her for a beat. "How interesting." And she was instantly very fascinated with her plate.

Emory wanted to let the discussion end there, badly she did. It would have been the smart thing to do, but she couldn't quite get around Vanessa's tone of voice. "What does that mean, *interesting*?"

"It's just not like you, Emory. A cleaning woman?" She laughed then. "What's next, the pool girl? The mail carrier? I mean, even you have to admit, it's a tad cliché. But," she said, regaining composure, "we all have our little dalliances. Heaven knows I did before I met Lawrence. It's probably just something you need to get out of your system. But for the sake of that child, do it soon. It's not fair to either of them to drag it out."

Emory was deeply offended. "I don't think of it as a dalliance, and her job is not that important to me."

"I'm just saying I'm not surprised you didn't bring her up sooner is all. I get it. I'm not judging you, darling."

*Really? Because* I *was just wondering how judgmental one person could be.* Realizing no good could possibly come of this conversation, she stood and cleared the dishes from the table, all the while groping for a more neutral subject matter. "So what time does your plane leave tomorrow?"

"Early," Lawrence answered. "Six a.m. I have a surgical consultation tomorrow afternoon."

"Oh no." Emory did a happy dance inside her head, already planning her cartwheels. "So soon?"

❖

"It was horrible. No, it was worse than horrible. It was like some kind of creepy albeit pretentious *Candid Camera* episode. I mean, the *dance*, Sarah. I wish you could understand what I'm talking about here."

Sarah applied the last bit of pink polish to her toes while she balanced the phone up against her ear and sympathized. "I think you're doing a pretty good job of describing it."

"I'm sorry if it's too late to call. As soon as they left, I had to find someone to talk to who would completely counterbalance the whole experience."

Sarah smiled at the phone. "I'm happy you called. I was wondering how things went." At first, Sarah was a little hurt that Emory hadn't invited her to meet Vanessa, but hearing how the evening played out, it seemed to make sense. "Has there ever been a time when the two of you were close?"

"Um, let's see, no. The answer is most definitely no. That has never happened. The earth has revolved around Vanessa since I was old enough to remember, and I was merely meant to live happily in her self-proclaimed greatness."

"Did you have the chance to talk at all about your mother or how you're each coping with the loss? If nothing else, you have that in common."

"Other than to settle the remaining details of Mother's estate, no, not a whole lot. I did tell her about the journals though and suggested she might want to read them, but she brushed that idea off rather quickly. Like I said, we were never a warm, cuddly family, and that's not likely to change."

Sarah struggled to identify in some way, but she simply couldn't. Her family was everything to her, and she couldn't imagine life any other way.

"Enough about Vanessa and my horrible night. How was your day?"

"Productive. I've hired a designer and booked my first two jobs just via word of mouth from our staff in the field."

"You're kidding? That was fast."

"I'm ready to get this show on the road. Our official marketing materials should arrive from the printer next week. And I might be interested in taking you up on that press release sometime soon. If the offer is still on the table, that is."

"Oh, it's most definitely still on the table, among other offers."

Sarah drew a breath, her mind drifting dreamily to said offers, wishing Emory were there in that very moment.

"When can I see you again?" Emory asked.

"Well, I have to stop off at my parents' house tomorrow evening for a brief planning session for Robert's birthday. We've all been given jobs, and mine is cake and ice cream. Usually, there's some sort of theme we plan around, so we'll be making those kinds of decisions. After that, my cousin is taking Grace and the rest of my little cousins, I have five by the way, home with her own daughters for a sleepover. I'll have the rest of the night free just as soon as I can slip away."

"Oh, I have an idea!" Emory enthused. "You could spend that time with me."

"You think? I don't know. I guess that might be fun."

"The funnest. I'm thinking you, me, and a picnic on the beach."

"I do love a good picnic, but you know, it's supposed to rain."

"No way. Not on my picnic."

"You're right, you're right," Sarah laughed. "I forgot who I was dealing with here, She-who-always-gets-her-way, my mistake."

## Chapter Eleven

By the next afternoon, the chirping of a thunderstorm warning crawled along the bottom of Sarah's television screen, and by eight o'clock that night, when she pulled into Emory's driveway, a severe storm had moved into the area with several more behind it. She was lucky her cousin lived an hour east and would only catch a tad of what San Diego would get. It made her feel at least somewhat better about Grace being away from her in bad weather.

As she killed her ignition, she could barely make out Emory's house just a few feet in front of her in the downpour. She had a hunch the picnic was off.

Her umbrella hadn't done her much good that afternoon due to the gusty winds that had eventually flipped the thing inside out entirely. Deciding just to make a run for it, Sarah covered the short distance from the car to Emory's front door in record time. She was damp, admittedly, but happy to be where she was.

Emory answered the door almost instantly at the sound of the bell and pulled Sarah in quickly by the hand. "You're a little wet," she proclaimed happily, rubbing the sides of Sarah's shoulders with vigor. "But you're cute when you're wet, so there's that." Emory stepped into her, and placed a delicate hello kiss on her lips. Instantly, Sarah recognized that familiar thrum of her heart.

She grinned. "So I'm here."

"You are." Then, seeming to snap herself out of the daze with a smile and little shake of her head, Emory gestured toward the living room. "I started a fire once the chill moved in. Why don't you go have a seat, warm up, and dry off while I check on the food? Be right back."

Sarah sat in front of the beautifully sculpted fireplace, wrapping her arms around herself and enjoying the heat it put out. Her eyes widened in surprise as a friendly looking dog entered the room and licked her face in celebration. "Well, hi there."

The dog laid a paw on Sarah's knee and looked up at her soulfully. "Okay, that's pretty adorable."

"Sarah, meet Walter," Emory said, following not far behind. At the sound of his name, Walter seemed to spring into action, turning in a circle and wagging his tail eagerly. "He already knows his name because he's apparently the smartest dog on the planet." He blinked back at her in total adoration. "Yes, you are."

"All right. You just used a doggy voice. You must really like him."

"Walter's okay, aren't you, buddy?"

He whined softly and nuzzled close.

"Grace will be pleased at the newly forged friendship. She's mentioned him several times this past week and takes full credit for your union, by the way."

"You'll have to bring her by so they can play. He's pretty good with a tennis ball. Come on, Walter, dinner time for you."

Walter obediently bounded behind Emory into the kitchen where she put up a small pet gate for him in the laundry room. Beyond its confines, Sarah glimpsed an overly fluffy doggy bed and several brand new dog toys. *Someone's been shopping.* "Sorry about your picnic plans," she called into the kitchen. "I was looking forward to it."

"What are you talking about? The picnic is still happening."

Sarah laughed. "No way are you getting me on that beach. It's torrential out there."

"Who said anything about the beach?" Emory returned to the living room with a blue and red plaid blanket, which she fluffed and spread out neatly onto the carpet. "Tada, carpet picnic. Be right back."

"You never cease to amaze me."

"I'm an amazer."

"*And* you coin new terms. Impressive." Sarah laughed and watched her hurry back into the kitchen. "Can I help?"

"Sure, grab the bubbly and glasses off the counter and meet me on the picnic grounds in twenty seconds with an appetite."

As they sat across from each other, Sarah's eyes moved appreciatively over the plate of food she was handed. "You made all of this yourself?"

"Guilty. Would you like the rundown?"

"Oh, I think I need to hear the rundown."

"Okay, here goes. For your dining pleasure, we have pecan crusted fried chicken, tomato and bean salad with a blue cheese chive dressing, and that on the left is a warm apple tart. All the great picnic foods represented." Emory smiled and there were those damn dimples. Sarah loved seeing the excitement she clearly took in this "excursion." It was a side of Emory she'd only glimpsed up until that point. She wanted to reach across the blanket and pinch her adorably sexy cheek.

"Why are you so good at everything? It's a little frustrating. I can't believe you made fancy fried chicken. Who even knew it *could* be fancy? It's one of my favorite foods, by the way."

Emory seemed to sit a little taller with that information. "Really? I had no idea. I took a shot."

Sarah ate the meal slowly because it honestly tasted just as good as it looked.

"So let's talk more about what you do when you're not playing the role of high-powered business executive. I know a little already. Cooking, running, *no* painting, which is a travesty. But there's bound to be more."

Emory contemplated the question. "There isn't. I work a lot. Not a ton of down time."

"Okay, got it. But what do you *like* to do? If there were all the time in the world."

"That's a hard one. I like to read. I wish I had more time for that."

"What's your favorite book?"

"It's juvenile. You'll laugh."

"I will not. Tell me."

"Louisa May Alcott. *Little Women*."

Sarah covered her mouth. "I love that book. I must have read it seventeen times."

"When I read it as a kid, I used to imagine I was one of the sisters and Marmie was my mother. She would oversee my homework and tuck me into bed at night, and I can't believe I just told you that." Emory shook her head in wonder and stared down at her plate, her cheeks reddening.

"I love that you just told me that."

"What about you? What's yours?"

"I like all the great romances. *Wuthering Heights, Jane Eyre,* and oh, *Gone With the Wind.* Love that one. Then there's the movie version. The scene when Scarlett enters the birthday party in that red gown looking anxious but defiant, I'm so right there."

"That is a great scene."

"I dressed up as her once for Halloween. I was a hit."

"I'm sure you were. How old were you?"

"Twenty-eight."

Emory laughed and Sarah reveled in the sound of it.

"So what else do you partake in, Emory? Quail hunting, international espionage, synchronized swimming?"

"Nope. I'm utterly boring."

"You're not, and believe me, I keep waiting for the moment you are."

"Well, there's plenty of time for that, right?"

Sarah looked up from her champagne and grinned. Her tone softened noticeably. "Yeah, I guess there is."

Sarah loved how easy it was to talk to Emory. They'd developed a quick cadence between them that was comfortable and fun. She enjoyed the humor they shared and even appreciated their different perspectives on things. Emory knew aspects of life she never had a clue about and vice versa. It was enthralling.

The wind picked up considerably during the meal and Sarah felt the house shake periodically from the strength of the gusts. As they cleared the dishes, she gazed out at the darkness of the angry looking surf. "Are you at all concerned about your windows?" she finally asked. "This house is made of a lot of glass."

"Not to worry. It's all been reinforced many times over, a necessity for living where I do. I did tether down the patio furniture before it started to rain though. I hope I did a good enough job or you might see one of the deck chairs fly away to Oz. Other than that, the house is completely secure. Do storms scare you?"

"Not usually. I've always thought they were kind of cool, but then I've never actually been right on the water for one." At that, a very loud, ominous clap of thunder struck causing Emory to jump noticeably.

Sarah raised a speculative eyebrow. "Do they scare *you*?"

"Not a chance." Emory shrugged quickly and went about busily tidying up the kitchen. Sarah observed for a moment before moving to her and resting her hands on Emory's waist from behind. "Fess up. Do storms freak you out?"

Emory turned in Sarah's arms and blew out a breath. "A little. But don't tell anyone. A CEO who's afraid of a little thunder could inspire a few jokes at the office."

"Luckily, I like it when you and I share secrets and would never jeopardize that."

Emory gently fluffed Sarah's hair. "In all fairness, you should have to tell me a secret now."

"Is that right? That would even things out for you?"

Emory smiled and nodded decisively. "It would."

"Okay. What if I told you that I was nervous?"

"Nervous about what?" Emory took a step back to see her better.

"Nervous about us...tonight."

Emory nodded, took Sarah's hand, and kissed the back of it. "Tonight doesn't have to be anything you don't want it to be, and I mean that. I just want to spend time with you, Sarah, and be with you in whatever way makes you comfortable. I have Scrabble in the closet, and I don't want to brag, but I'm really good. We could play until two a.m. and I would have the best time in the world because it would be us, together."

Sarah was touched. The truth was that she hadn't been nervous until somewhere in the midst of dinner. She knew she wanted Emory, but the logistics had her head spinning a tad. It had been a while since she'd been with anyone, and it was possible she was suffering from a little stage fright. But now, hearing the gentle tone in Emory's voice was enough to cause a physical ache in her throat, and it was all the reassurance she needed.

She moved into Emory's arms and stayed there, wondering how she'd gone so long without Emory in her life. She pulled back and met Emory's eyes with a very serious stare. "While Scrabble sounds like a blast, I think I'll take a rain check." A long pause. "Did you catch that? Rain...check?" At Emory's burst of laughter and subsequent poke in the ribs, Sarah scampered away gleefully to sit by the fire, snatching up her champagne glass as she went.

Emory refilled her own glass and joined Sarah on the floor in front of the fireplace a short time later. "Speaking of rain, I'm not sure you ever completely dried out." She ran a hand across the back of Sarah's damp green button up shirt. "I guess I should have offered earlier, but would you like to borrow some clothes?"

"I'm not sure we wear the same size, but I'll take a shirt from you if you've got one."

Emory returned from her upstairs bedroom with a Stanford sweatshirt in hand. She hadn't hit the bottom step when a clap of thunder hit and the lights went out. Silence. "Well, that makes things a little ominous."

"It's okay. Don't worry, you're safe. Head back over to the fire. All is well over here."

Emory made her way back to Sarah through the now darkened living room and handed her the sweatshirt. It was impossible to not watch Sarah unbutton the damp blouse she wore and let it fall loosely from her shoulders. Emory couldn't have turned away if she'd wanted to. The firelight danced across the smooth expanse of olive skin as Sarah lifted her arms and pulled the sweatshirt over her head. The red bra Emory glimpsed and tops of full breasts just about did her in. Swallowing hard in an attempt to control her body's visceral reaction to the sight, she excused herself into the kitchen to dig up a few candles.

Sarah waited patiently for Emory to return, very much enjoying the warm, comfortable sweatshirt that smelled exactly like Emory did. Hugging it to her, she was already plotting a way to keep it. When Emory did return, she took a moment to light a few votive candles and place them at different spots throughout the room. Their warm, gentle glow gave the space a very romantic look and feel that Sarah simply could not let go to waste.

"Come sit with me. Let's watch the fire." She reached out and took Emory's hand, pulling her gently onto the floor and scooting herself in front, so she could rest her back against Emory's chest. Emory's arms wrapped around her snuggly from behind and she sighed with contentment. They sat in silence, watching the fire's unpredictable dance and listening to the sound of the rain pelt the shingles. Sarah couldn't imagine anywhere she'd rather be. "How's Walter?"

"Amazingly enough, sound asleep. I think he's just happy not to be out in this. You should see him. He's doing his Super Dog pose. Sleeping on his back with all four paws in the air. It's impressive."

"He has so much personality. It's a nice thing you did, taking him in. So I guess you're going to keep him?"

"If no one comes forward to claim him. I took a photo and had my assistant post it on a few lost dog websites as well as the homeowner's association page. I never thought I'd be a dog owner."

"You're more of a softy than you let on, you know."

"Don't tell anyone."

"I would never. It's kind of nice though. Seeing you branch out a bit. You're hanging out with kids, adopting dogs, watching mindless movies." Her tone slid into sincerity then. "One day, I hope you paint again."

They watched the fire.

"Sarah, I need to tell you something."

"Okay."

Emory felt noticeable tension creep into Sarah's body, prompting her to rub back and forth with her hands across her forearms in reassurance.

"Everything you just said is true. My life has been noticeably different since you've been a part of it, and it's wonderful in a way I never could have imagined. What I need to tell you is that the more we're together, the more I feel for you, and I don't really see that pattern ending anytime soon, if ever, if we're being perfectly honest. That's a little overwhelming when I think about it. I look at you and Grace and I can see my possible future. And that's a little overwhelming too." She paused, as if looking for that best way to ask for what she needed to. These things didn't come easy to her. "So, please, if you don't see this as a very real possibility in your life, I need you to tell me."

She finally loosened her arms and Sarah turned around in them. "Thank you for telling me that. Like you, I don't take these kinds of things lightly. I think there are some things to work out between us still. I don't know the people in your world and you don't know the people in mine, but what I've found in you is so surprisingly good that I want to find a way to bring those worlds together. It may not happen overnight, but I do think it can happen." She reached out and gently stroked Emory's cheek, breaking into an adorable smile. "Let me amend that, I want it to happen and will do everything I can to make sure it does."

It took a moment for the words to reach Emory's heart, but when they did she heard a roaring in her ears that could not be attributed to the storm outside but to the soaring within her.

Sarah kissed her then, good and kissed her, moving in until she was straddling Emory's lap where she continued to kiss her with slow and sexy determination. For several minutes, they did nothing but kiss while powerful gusts of wind rocked the darkened windows and the movement of the fire cast large shadows on the wall next to them.

Emory was amazed at how well they fit, as if their sole purpose on earth was to kiss each other. In one regard, that would have been enough and just fine with her, but in another she felt a fire within that more than rivaled the one just feet away. While loving the closeness of Sarah in her lap, she had to order her adventurous hands to obey and stay settled on Sarah's waist. But she was craving more, and in just a few more moments, she wasn't sure she would be in full control. Left with no choice, she pulled her mouth away from Sarah and somehow found her voice. It was higher than usual, but still there. "Scrabble?"

Sarah's eyes, now dark with desire, met hers questioningly. "Is that what you want?"

Emory answered honestly. "No."

"Me neither," she whispered. She stroked Emory's hair. "You may have to show me a few things."

"Sarah, we can wait. I want you to—"

Emory's answer was a kiss, a searing kiss that communicated everything she needed to know. She dipped her hands, now free and determined, beneath the sweatshirt Sarah wore and moved up the expanse of her back. She pulled her lips away and kissed up the column of Sarah's neck, earning a soft moan of pleasure. Feeling herself moving entirely too fast but unable to help herself, Emory grasped at the hem of Sarah's sweatshirt and pulled it quickly over Sarah's head. The red bra that had so mercilessly tortured her earlier greeted her now, and she kissed all around its expanse. Sarah tossed her head back and squeezed Emory's shoulders tightly in response. Emory traced the outline of the bra with her tongue, and scraped her fingernails on the material in its center.

Sarah was dying, absolutely dying. Her heart thudded in her chest as if she'd run a mile. The sensations flying through her body were entirely new and unexpected. The insistence of her arousal made itself known as her body ached and her hips automatically began to move against Emory's stomach. She'd never considered her breasts sensitive before, but with skilled attention, Emory was eliciting a tidal wave of response without even fully undressing her. Sarah was staggered and she was in need.

As if reading her thoughts, Emory reached behind and unclasped Sarah's bra, freeing her breasts and catching first one nipple and then the other in her mouth. "My God," she murmured. At Sarah's intake of breath, she raised her head, meeting her eyes. "Okay?"

Sarah nodded, moving her hands into Emory's hair, pulling her back in, encouraging her, needing her not to stop.

In response, Emory aggressively surged forward from where they sat, carrying Sarah with her, and laid her down gently on the large flokati rug in front of the fireplace. As the rain pelted and splashed, she tenderly removed Sarah's jeans, then looped her thumbs through the outside band of the red bikini underwear, the only thing left in her way. Sarah sat up and clasped her wrists.

"Wait a sec. Please."

Emory sat back on her heels obediently and swallowed.

"I need to do this first." Sarah reached out and slowly unbuttoned Emory's short sleeve white shirt and removed it, moving on to each new piece of clothing. Emory began to help.

When she was finally devoid of all her clothes, Sarah sat back and marveled at Emory's body. It was more beautiful than even she had imagined, and her mouth went dry at the exquisite site. She wrapped her arms around Emory's neck and her gaze settled easily on her gentle, beautiful mouth. As she leaned in to capture it, she felt Emory's bare skin on hers for the first time and her pulse accelerated at the wondrous sensation. And so she kissed Emory, and kissed her, and kissed her, almost undone as she felt Emory's heart beating rapidly against her own. Emory pressed her forehead to hers and said her name in a jagged whisper. Sarah'd never felt more aroused or more wanted in her whole life. She was overcome with physical yearning, throbbing to the point of desperation. "Now," she breathed, laying herself back down onto the rug, tugging Emory with her gently.

Hovering just above, Emory finished the task she'd started and slowly pulled the bikinis down Sarah's bare legs. She then crawled forward and braced herself on her elbows and forearms, catching Sarah's mouth and allowing their tongues to dance sensuously. She lowered her body fully onto Sarah's as they kissed, savoring the feeling of total connection. So worth the wait. She boldly inserted a thigh between Sarah's legs and held it firmly up against her, feeling for the first time just how aroused Sarah truly was. "God," she moaned quietly. She closed her eyes at the revelation and steadied herself once again. Finally, her eyes found Sarah's and she began to rock softly against her. She didn't shudder at the next bolt of lightning, but instead rolled with the thunder outside. Sarah kissed her neck, stopping only when her accelerated breathing didn't allow for it any longer. As Emory moved faster against Sarah, the pain of pressed fingernails on her back signaled her that Sarah was close. She moved downward, parting her thighs gently. She swiped at Sarah with her tongue once, twice, and on the third time, felt hands holding her head in place as Sarah called out loudly, throwing her head to the side. Emory continued to apply steady pressure until Sarah's body relaxed and finally collapsed into a heap on the rug.

Sarah stared at the ceiling helplessly, grasping for a way to explain to herself what had just happened. Emory, she thought, Emory had happened. She'd been prepared for the desire she knew she'd feel when Emory touched her, but there had been no way to prepare, no frame of reference for the pleasure she'd just received. "Em?" she said softly, finding her voice.

"I'm right here," Emory answered tenderly from alongside her. Sarah turned and moved into Emory's arms, nestling herself in the crook of her shoulder. "I don't know what to say."

"You don't have to say anything."

Sarah nodded and kissed Emory's shoulder, needing a few moments with her thoughts.

They lay there quietly for several minutes, Emory gently stroking Sarah's hair, only the sound of the fire crackling nearby. Finally, she tilted Sarah's face upward, searching her eyes. "What are you thinking?"

"I'm thinking that I'm not able to think…in a really good way. I don't even know if that sentence made sense."

Emory grinned. "A positive review?"

Sarah shook her head. "The word positive would be left in the dust by what that just was." Sarah pushed herself up onto her forearm, looked down at Emory and, for the first time in a while, registered that it was still storming outside. She loved the glow from the fire just beyond Emory and the way it haloed her golden hair. "You look so, I don't know. Like some sort of beautiful painting."

"I do?"

"You do. It's like nothing I've ever seen." Sarah couldn't resist any longer. She tenderly brushed Emory's hair back from her forehead and allowed her mouth to descend slowly to Emory's. It was time for the tables to turn, and Sarah couldn't have been more ready. She slid on top, hearing the small hitch in Emory's breathing when their breasts touched once again. Pulling her mouth from Emory's, she moved it to her ear, sucking gently on the lobe, taking her time. She reached down between them and trailed her fingertips across the inside of one thigh. Emory inhaled sharply. "Tell me what you want," she whispered.

"Just touch me. It's that simple."

"Like this?" She touched along the inside of the other thigh, teasing. But this time her touch was more firm.

"Yes," Emory hissed. "God."

Sarah answered with a firm stroke through liquid heat, a feeling she would never forget as long as she lived. She looked up in surprised response and met Emory's eyes. The vulnerability looking back at her was almost her undoing. Nothing she had experienced had ever felt so right.

Emory gasped as the fingers returned to where she needed them and she threw her head back against the rug in utter submission. It was the most wonderful torture, but she didn't know how much more she could take. Sarah's touch increased in intensity and she rocked her hips harder in response. Somehow, Sarah seemed to innately know what she needed, insistent strokes that brought her just to the brink and then lighter ones that held her there. At long last, and with one final thrust of her hips, she surrendered to Sarah's touch with a moan of ultimate pleasure. She tossed her head back and felt the intensity of orgasm wash over her in a tidal wave of feeling. She closed her eyes and rode out the last remaining waves. Finding herself once again able to process cognizant thought, she opened her eyes. "Sara," she whispered, using the original pronunciation of her name. "How did you know?"

Sarah looked down at her reverently. "It felt right."

"Then you're the most intuitive person I've ever met."

Sarah grinned proudly and leaned down for one more nip. "I think we just have good chemistry."

"Off the charts."

Emory placed her hands on Sarah's hips and pulled her down so that she rested more fully on top. While usually preferring the top herself, she couldn't deny how much she loved the feel of Sarah's weight on her body. "Has anyone ever told you that you're sexy as hell?" She traced the outline of Sarah's hips. "Your body has the most amazing curves."

"That's funny because my whole life, I always wanted a body just like yours."

"That would have been a travesty."

"You really feel that way?"

"I really do."

"Thank you," Sarah answered shyly.

"Will you stay tonight? It's rough out there so you can't say no."

Sarah rolled to the other side of Emory and considered the question. "On one condition."

"Anything."

She stole a kiss. "I seem to remember you promising me a game."

Emory laughed and gathered Sarah into her arms. "Are you serious? Okay, but I told you I'm good."

"You'll have to prove it." Sarah grinned back wickedly and captured her mouth yet again. "But maybe we could do some more of this after?"

"Hard bargain."

Outside, the storm raged and the waves crashed violently against the shore, but inside, they sat together, wrapped in blankets in front of the fire, engrossed in a lively game of Scrabble. In the midst of her laughter, Emory regarded Sarah across the board of letters and marveled at how her life had taken such a fortuitous turn.

Later, their bodies would find each other once more, this time in the warm expanse of Emory's bed. As slumber at last crept over her, Emory dreamily listened to the sounds of diminishing rainfall. She sighed into Sarah's soft embrace and knew inherently, that no matter what happened between them, no one could ever take this night away from her. And because of that, her life would never again feel the same.

Sarah cruised the 805 the following morning and smiled at the gorgeous day before her. Even the weather seemed happy. The morning after the big storm was shaping up to be quite a contrast to the past twelve hours. The sun shone warm and the sky shimmered its signature San Diego blue. She was headed home where she had plans to rendezvous with her cousin who'd drop off Grace sometime within the next hour.

Admittedly, she hadn't gotten much sleep the night prior, but as thoughts of her evening clouded her consciousness, she knew she wouldn't trade a moment.

She'd woken first that morning and spent the initial twenty minutes of her day watching Emory sleep while being serenaded by sounds of the sea. Awake, she was the most beautiful woman on the planet; asleep, she was an angel. Unable to resist the urge, Sarah reached out and traced her cheek delicately, moving on to her slightly swollen lips, then placed a soft kiss on her temple.

Emory stirred then, her eyes fluttering open, before a slow grin took shape on her face. "You're here," she whispered. "Hi."

Sarah slid down so they were face-to-face on the pillow. "I didn't mean to wake you. You were so peaceful."

Emory wrapped an arm around her waist and pulled Sarah in. "Just so we're clear, you can wake me anytime you want, for anything you want."

Sarah traced the outside of Emory's breast, causing her to hitch in a breath. "Dangerous declaration."

"I'm a risk taker."

They hadn't had much time to spend together that morning, but a quick breakfast with Walter followed by an impromptu make-out session against the kitchen counter had gotten the day off to a promising start.

Emory was off for a run, and Sarah looked forward to spending the rest of the day with Grace. They would first go school supply shopping and then head to the mall so Grace could pick out an agreed upon three new outfits for the first week of school. Sarah knew she needed to broach the subject of Emory with Grace soon, especially since she'd already hinted at an early understanding. It wouldn't be the easiest conversation to have, and admittedly, she was nervous, but it needed to happen.

"So how was the slumber party?" she asked Grace, who twirled her straw around her cup to thin out the consistency of her milkshake. They sat at a table nestled in the bustling mall's food court, on short hiatus in their day of shopping.

Grace took a swig of her shake. "Kind of lame. Millie made us all play Chutes and Ladders for two hours and cried whenever anyone wanted to quit. We had fun once she fell asleep though."

"Oh yeah, what did you do then?"

"Truth or Dare."

Sarah raised an eyebrow. "Uh-oh. Aren't you a little young for that?"

"All we did was dare each other to prank call Uncle Danny until Millie's mom made us stop. What about you? Did you have fun with Emory?"

"Yeah, I did. It stormed a lot, so we didn't get to go down to the beach, but we had a good time anyway."

Grace beamed. "That's great, Mom."

"So what do you think about Emory?"

"I like her. She's sofixicated and smart. Plus, her house rocks."

"Sophisticated, and yeah, she is smart." Sarah paused, searching for the right words. "I like her a lot too."

"I know. I think that's cool."

"You know, in the past, I've always gone on dates with men."

"I know."

"But I wanted to talk to you about something kind of important and get your opinion because what you think matters to me a lot."

"Okay."

"Well, lately, I've started going on dates with Emory too."

Grace looked back at her confused. "I know. I told you already, I think that's cool."

"Wait. So you knew that we were…dating?"

"You guys make it kind of obvious the way you stare at each other all the time." Grace was still smiling.

"What are you talking about? We do not."

"Mom, please." Grace rolled her eyes and scanned the food court for more interesting pastures. "Can we go to A'Gaci next?"

"So this doesn't bother you at all?"

Grace offered a small sigh and turned back to Sarah. "Have you ever read a book called *Heather has Two Mommies*?"

Sarah squinted, shaking her head.

"Well, they have it in our library at school, and I read it during lunch recess last year. You should read it too."

Sarah was reeling. Her eight-year-old not only knew all about her incognito personal life, but was now offering her advice about coping with adversity. Ordering her head clear, she pressed forward. "I haven't talked to your grandparents about this yet, but I plan to. Hopefully soon. I would never ask you to keep a secret from them, and I'm not asking you to do that now either. I'm just not sure I'm ready for them to know about Emory yet."

"I think it's better if you tell them, not me."

Sarah's shoulders slumped in relief. "Thank you. But if you change your mind and feel like you need to talk to them about any of this, I won't be upset."

"Okay. Ready to finish shopping? I have one whole outfit left to pick out."

Sarah grinned at her, so proud of the person she already was and the one she would someday be. She had the best kid. "Let's do it."

At nine o'clock on Thursday morning, Lucy stuck her head around the corner of Emory's office and playfully fanned herself with a document of some sort. Emory stared at her momentarily, but then returned to the pile of work on her desk. Lucy took it one step further, holding the document up to the light and studying the words before hugging it to her heart with a smoldering gaze.

"Is there something you'd like to say, Luce, or is this a new mime routine you're developing?"

"Oh hey, Em. Strange. Didn't see you there. Listen, I was just perusing this totally random press release I saw hit the wire. Turns out, it's about Immaculate Home and its newest division headed up by one Sarah Matamoros. This, by chance, wouldn't be *the* Sarah Matamoros, would it?"

Emory shook her head at Lucy's performance, hating to admit that her overly excited tone of voice was actually amusing. "Yes, they are one and the same."

"So interesting. I'm going to take the fact that we're now running pro bono press releases for this little upstart-that-could as a good sign for your love life. Please confirm. Minds are inquiring."

"I offered them a couple free releases to see if they liked what the exposure could do for them. If Sarah and her company receive a good response, it's my hope that they'll open an account with us and voilà, we'll have a new client. A very basic sales strategy."

Lucy's response was a big thumbs down sign. "Lame and businesslike. That isn't what I asked you. I did like how you worked in a voilà though. You don't hear that one much."

"Thank you. And if you must know, things are good," Emory answered sincerely. "I'm meeting her family this weekend, and…she stayed over on Saturday."

Lucy balled up the press release and pelted it at Emory. "And you're just now telling me? This is big news. Huge! She has located the horse, ladies and gentlemen, and she's climbing back on."

Emory laughed and threw the ball of paper at Lucy's now retreating form. "Very funny, Luce. Hysterical."

"I'll be here all night." And then from her office next door, "Tip your waitress!"

# CHAPTER TWELVE

Sarah was consistently amazed at the number of people her parents were able to cram into their backyard and feed. Friends, neighbors, and relatives milled around the large outdoor area, snacking at picnic tables or competing in games of badminton or touch football. Platters of burgers, chicken, and roasted pork abounded and a large cooler of beer sat proudly on the patio, all in celebration of her older brother's thirty-fifth birthday.

Her mother slid her hands onto Sarah's shoulders and kissed her cheek roughly. "Why are you bustling around like a loco person? Go get yourself a beer from the cooler and enjoy your brother's party. Everything here is good to go."

Sarah obediently set down the extra plates she'd brought outside, just in case, and covered her mother's hands with her own. "If you say so, boss lady."

"At least you know I'm in charge. You can help me clean up later, I promise, but in the meantime, mingle por favor. Entertain these people for me, and I may have a surprise for you later." Sarah raised a curious eyebrow, but her mother drifted away, turning an invisible key in front of her lips to emphasize the secrecy of her statement. Cryptic.

Sarah walked through streamers and colorful balloons to survey the fun. In the corner, her father held court as he grilled fresh fajitas, sporting his "Kiss the Cook" apron and tall, billowing chef's hat. Grace stood alongside him chatting animatedly, always his trusty sidekick.

Sarah had looked forward to the party for the entire week prior. But now that the day was here, the excitement she felt about Emory meeting her family had more than tripled and moved steadily into the nervous category. Things could go wrong, she admitted to herself, and this was, after all, a big deal. Even if her parents wouldn't be aware of just how big a deal when they met her.

"There's my baby sister," Robert called out as she approached. He pulled her into a loose headlock and ruffled the top of her hair just as he'd done since they were kids.

She wrestled herself free and punched him hard in the arm. "No abuse today, birthday boy. Try to act your age." She smoothed her hair back into place.

Her sister-in-law, Cristina, grinned and rolled her eyes. "Tall order." She held their son, Lucas, in her arms, and Sarah couldn't resist scooping the little guy up and peppering his tiny baby cheeks with several hundred kisses.

"My nephew is the handsomest baby boy in baby land. Little girl babies across California better watch out for this one."

"You don't have to tell me." Cristina shook her head. "He already flirts with women mercilessly—like his father." She smacked Robert playfully in the stomach for good measure.

He doubled over. "Man, I'm getting beat today."

Sarah laughed and checked her watch and then the door for the four hundredth time that afternoon, bracing against the parade of butterflies in her stomach before moving on to say hello to the next-door neighbors.

It was approximately seven and a half minutes later when she heard the distant chime of the doorbell and excused herself quickly into the house. Damn it, she was too late. Her younger brother, Danny, had already answered the door and stood staring wordlessly at Emory. In fairness, Sarah couldn't blame him. Emory wore off-white denim Capris and a turquoise top that Sarah could have easily predicted brought out the vibrant blue in her eyes. As she entered the room, Emory turned and smiled (was that shyly?) in her direction.

Sarah beamed back. "You found us."

"I did. Your directions were perfect. I only got lost three times, which is good for me."

Sarah turned to Danny who was still blatantly staring at Emory. She resisted the urge to pop him in the back of his head. "Danny, meet my friend Emory Owen. Emory, this is my pesky little brother, Danny."

"Daniel," he amended, extending his hand. His voice was suspiciously an octave lower than she was used to. She turned to him curiously and elbowed him in the ribs. "Stop it. Come on, Emory. Let's go outside and I can introduce you around."

"Maybe we can talk later, Emory," Danny called after them.

She smiled. "Definitely."

Sarah turned around and shot him one last "what's gotten into you" glare before pulling Emory into the yard. Once on the vacant patio, they had a brief moment alone, several yards from the nearest guests. Someone had put on a CD, and Tejano music now blared throughout the yard louder than Sarah would have liked. She planned to fix that problem shortly. In the meantime, her interests were elsewhere. "I'm glad you're here."

"Me too." Emory was smiling.

"Sorry about my stupid brother."

"Don't be. He seems sweet. He also looks a lot like you, and that's a big plus. You're a sight for sore eyes, by the way. It's been a long week." Sarah couldn't agree more and resisted the urge to touch Emory's cheek. God, how she wanted to.

"Maybe we could steal some time after this."

"That would—"

"Sarah Rose, who is this nice person you have with you? Introduce your mother."

Sarah turned and found her mother standing five feet behind her, hands on her hips. She took a noticeable step away from Emory, who seemed to register the move behind her eyes. Sarah felt the guilt right away.

"Mama, this is the friend I told you about, Emory Owen. She was also a recent client of ours. That's where we met."

Emory stepped forward, instantly on. "It's nice to meet you, Mrs. Matamoros. Sarah speaks very highly of you, and I have nothing but rave reviews from the services Immaculate Home provided me."

Sarah smiled sweetly. If only her mother knew the extent of that statement.

"Emory Owen! Of course." Not missing a beat, she pulled Emory into a full-on embrace, probably gripping her tighter than Emory had ever been gripped. "Sarah's told me all about what a wonderful experience she had working for you. I was so happy to hear that you two have grown to be good friends. And you know, Sarah's phone has been ringing off the hook after that press release you sent out. She'll have to tell you all about it. We're so pleased you came to the party. Have you met Robert yet? He's the birthday boy, you know, right over there. Oh, and, Sarah, introduce her to your cousin, Martin, next. He's single, Emory, and very, very handsome."

Sarah suppressed an eye roll and instead smiled obediently. "Will do, Mama."

"Emory, can I get you a drink?"

"Sure, um, maybe a glass of white?"

Her mother frowned and turned to Sarah. "Do we still have that bottle your Aunt Mariana gave us?"

"How about a beer, Em?" Sarah knew full well the bottle in question was covered in dust and well past its ten-dollar prime.

"Yes! Of course. I would love a beer. Any kind you have."

Her mother smiled gregariously once again. "Miller Lite?"

"Perfect."

"Coming right up!"

As her mother scurried happily to the cooler, Emory closed her eyes and sighed. "Sorry. Strike one."

"We're just more of a chips and beer kind of a family is all."

Emory lifted one shoulder. "I love chips and beer."

"Sure you do. Come on, I'll introduce you to all the key players. Try to look somewhat attractive, okay?"

Emory couldn't help a short burst of laughter as Sarah tugged her into the yard. She met several of Sarah's aunts, uncles, and cousins, who were all very friendly and maybe even a little tipsy. Next, she met Robert and Cristina and their baby. Robert looked like a bulkier, he-man version of Danny with thinning hair. It was fascinating to meet so many people who resembled Sarah and Grace. As if on cue, Grace appeared out of nowhere and threw her arms around Emory's waist. She looked down at her affectionately. "Hiya, kiddo. How's your life?"

"Great. How's your life?"

"Can't complain. Ready for school?"

"I can't wait. Only two more days. We did all of our shopping this week. Mindy and I are in the same class this year."

"Well, that's a plus. And George?"

Immediately blushing, Grace tugged on Emory's arm, prompting her to lean down so she could whisper in her ear. "He asked me to go to SeaWorld with his family. I haven't asked Mom yet. I wanted to get your advice. I'll tell you about it later."

"Deal," she whispered and nodded, taking the situation as seriously as Grace seemed to be. With that, Grace scampered away to play freeze tag with her rather boisterous group of cousins.

Sarah surveyed the action from a few feet away. "Why do you get all the juicy information?"

"Because you're the mom and are thereby deemed ineligible." Sarah frowned and Emory laughed. "Cheer up, Charlie. I'll tell you everything she said if you want me to."

Sarah was thoughtful. "No. As long as it's not life threatening or morally threatening, I can handle not knowing every little detail of her life the second it comes off the presses. I want her to know that she can trust you."

"Well, it's neither of those two things, rest assured. Now, when do I get to meet your dad?"

And here we go. "How about now? Come on. He's on grill duty, his favorite pastime in all of life. He's going to love you, by the way." Sarah knew this was a big introduction. Her father was the most important man in her life, and she needed for him to see how wonderful Emory was.

There was a spring in her step that took a shuddering leave of absence the moment she took in the scene ahead. Carmen and Roman stood next to the grill laughing. Alongside them, complete with her smiling father's arm on his shoulder, stood James. Sarah froze, and her mind scrambled to piece together the probable series of events.

"Surprise," her mother whispered in her ear from behind. Sarah's fears were confirmed. Unable to form a complete sentence, she felt herself ushered by her mother over to the group, Emory lagging somewhere behind.

"Hey there, beautiful," James leaned in and kissed her cheek.

She was still in somewhat of a state of shock and answered evenly. "Hi."

"I hope you don't mind me popping in on you. Your father invited me when I stopped by the job site earlier this week."

"I told him to!" Her mother grinned like the cat that swallowed the canary. "I knew you'd be thrilled to see James, and this gives him a chance to meet the rest of the family."

James wrapped his arm around her mother's shoulders. "Well, then it's you I have to thank, Mrs. Matamoros."

"Call me, Yolanda," her mother answered dreamily.

Sarah couldn't believe this was happening, but was determined to keep a cool head. "You're always welcome, James. It's nice to see you." She looked to Carmen, whose eyes widened as if to say "I had no Godforsaken idea this was going to happen. Please don't kill me." She offered a tiny helpless shrug to punctuate.

Deciding to stay the course, Sarah pressed forward. "Papa, I wanted to introduce you to someone. This is my friend, Emory Owen. Emory's the CEO of her own company and went to Stanford." A few bonus points couldn't hurt, right?

Roberto Matamoros turned to Emory and extended his hand warmly. "Are you the artist Graciela was telling me about?"

Emory smiled and took his hand. "I suppose so, though I don't actually paint anymore."

"My granddaughter thinks the world of you. Welcome to our home." He patted her hand and bowed his head. But his attention shifted back to James and Roman, the men clearly taking precedent with him in this moment. "So, James, do you have any other big projects lined up?"

"Several actually. It's hard to juggle them all, but if I want to make partner someday, I have to burn the midnight oil."

"The corporate world can be cutthroat, that's for sure," Emory interjected.

"I do okay." James turned to her.

"I'm sure you do."

James eyed Emory and Emory eyed James until finally Sarah couldn't take it anymore. Clearly picking up on the tension, Carmen swooped in and saved the day. "Emory, we haven't met yet. I'm Carmen, Sarah's best friend and, might I add, closest confidant," she said, emphasizing the words. "She tells me everything. I'm thrilled to finally meet you."

Emory beamed. "Thank you. I've been anxious to meet you too. Sarah tells me that you two have quite a history."

"You can't even imagine."

"Sarah," her mother interrupted. "Why don't you introduce James to your brothers, and maybe later he can meet Grace." She shot her a not so subtle wink, which Sarah refused to return. Sarah looked apologetically at Emory, who stared back at her blankly. Feeling caught and unsure how to proceed, she begrudgingly gave in to the pressure.

"Sure. Follow me, James." She walked James across the yard, and when they were out of earshot, tugged on his sleeve bringing them to a halt. Yes, they were in the middle of the yard, and yes, people were watching them, Emory included, but she had to figure out this situation and quick. "James, I just need to be clear. I'm seeing someone else. I thought you understood that."

"I do and I respect it entirely, but it doesn't mean I've completely given up on you forever. We're still friends, right?"

Sarah softened. "Yes, but that's all it can be. I just want to be sure we're on the same page."

"We are, beautiful."

She closed her eyes momentarily in frustration. "See, right there, that's what I'm talking about."

"The fact that I called you beautiful?"

"Yes."

"I'm sorry. If it makes you uncomfortable, it will never happen again."

"I appreciate that."

"Unless you want it to."

"James."

Over the next ten minutes, she introduced him to all the same people she'd introduced Emory to. There seemed to be a markedly different reaction to James. At the mention of his name, her friends and loved ones lit up, a sign that they'd been prepped by her mother well in advance about who he was and his potential place in Sarah's life. In response, he was universally given the careful attention she'd hoped they'd show Emory. It was disheartening and entirely counterproductive to what she'd hoped to accomplish that day.

Leaving James to continue his in-depth discussion on drafting techniques with Robert, Sarah located Emory across the yard, who much to her horror was standing with her mother and cousin Martin, the creepy funeral director. Realizing that her mother was already in matchmaker mode and a rescue mission was now necessary, she wasted no time. Sliding up next to Emory, she briefly squeezed her hand. She needed to explain things, and now was as good a time as any. "Can I borrow you for a sec?"

Emory turned to her with immense amounts of gratitude in her eyes. "Sure. Excuse me, Martin. Maybe we can finish the uh, embalming story later."

Sarah led Emory back into the house and down the short hallway. "Where are we going?" Emory asked.

"Shhh." She quickly pulled Emory into the small hallway bathroom, closed the door, and locked it. As she turned around, Emory offered a plastic smile and it didn't escape Sarah that she stood about as far away as the tiny bathroom would allow.

"Let me explain."

"There's no need. I know you didn't invite him."

Sarah closed the distance between them and tucked a strand of hair behind Emory's ear. "All the same, I'm sorry."

"I know." But Emory didn't seem convinced.

"It bothers you. I can tell."

Emory stared past Sarah at a stack of decorative hand towels. "It's just been a while since I've had to hide who I was. I don't like how it feels. Your parents are very excited about the prospect of you and James, and I get to watch that play out. It's…less than fun."

"I know, trust me, I know. I guess I just wanted to finesse this for them a little bit. Parcel out information slowly. I know my family, and it will be better if I can ease them into the idea of you and me." She let her hands drop from Emory's shoulders where they'd rested. "I'm sorry. I feel like I'm screwing this whole thing up."

Emory tilted her head and met Sarah's eyes. It was clear she was softening. "Sarah, look at me."

She did.

"So it's not the easiest of days. Let's just try and get through it. The fact that James is here just caught me off guard and complicated an already touchy situation for me. But I'd rather not focus on that. I'd rather focus on you, which is all I tend to do lately anyway."

Sarah let the comment settle and took a step in. She slid her hands onto Emory's hips and rubbed her abdomen with her thumbs. "In that case, I should probably confess that I've wanted to kiss you ever since you walked in the door."

A shy smile crept across Emory's face. "You have?"

"Mhmm. You have the most kissable mouth I've ever seen." Sarah placed a hand behind Emory's head and guided her in. The kiss was just as electric as Sarah knew it would be, hungry and fast with no buildup required. Easing Emory's body up against the door, Sarah melded against it, moaning quietly into Emory's mouth as their tongues danced. In a stroke of fantastic timing, there was a knock on the door. Damn it all.

They froze.

Sarah pulled her mouth away and listened. Please God, let them leave.

"Hello in there? Everything okay?" Oh no, it was her elderly aunt Sofia. Sarah felt like a deer in front of an eighteen-wheeler as Emory tried unsuccessfully to suppress a laugh. She placed a much-needed hand over Emory's mouth but couldn't help smiling herself as she leaned into Emory's ear. "That's my great-aunt Sofia. She's eighty-nine years old. We're going to have to make a break for it, but I think we can take her. Follow my lead." Emory nodded wordlessly and followed Sarah out of the bathroom. As they emerged, Aunt Sofia's eyes drifted suspiciously from one of them to the other.

"Sara, is everything okay? You were inside of the bathroom for a long time."

"My friend was just helping me…with a problem."

"Are you all right, mija? Should I get your mama?"

"I'm fine. I just needed Emory's uh, expertise for a minute. She was able to help a lot." Emory smiled and nodded emphatically. They made their way silently through the living room and then exploded into laughter once they landed outside.

Her mother smiled along with them. "What's so funny, you two?"

Sarah deadpanned. "Long story."

"Well, you're just in time for dinner. Sarah, I have a seat for you down here with me, and, Emory, Martin has saved a seat for you next to him." She offered her second conspiratorial wink of the afternoon, this time at Emory.

Sarah looked down the long table and the expanse of distance between her predetermined seat and Emory's. And then there was the fact that her chair was coincidentally next to James's. *Just perfect.* "Mama, I think Emory and I would rather sit—"

"It's fine, Sarah, really," Emory interjected, feeling the need to smooth things over. It wasn't entirely fine, but she didn't want to make waves on her first meeting with Sarah's family. She could hold her own against Martin and his grisly tales from the crypt for an hour or so. Luckily, Carmen was seated across the table from her, which might give her some reprieve.

Unfortunately, dinner was nonetheless excruciating. She watched from afar as James flirted mercilessly with Sarah while her parents made over him like he was their long-lost son. By the end of it all, she was mentally exhausted and ready to make a quick exit. She thanked Mr. and Mrs. Matamoros, wished Robert a happy birthday, offered Sarah's shoulder a squeeze, and headed for the door.

She needed to get out of there.

She needed to find her head.

And she needed to figure just what exactly she'd gotten herself into. So she was acting like a coward, and retreating when things got rough. She was actually okay with that. As she turned the knob, she was stopped by the sound of a small voice. "Emory, wait."

She turned and Grace appeared, breathless. "Are you coming over later? Mom said you might."

Emory hesitated. She wasn't in the best of moods, and maybe a night on her own would help her decompress a little. "I don't think so, Grace. Maybe another night."

Sarah appeared in the entryway and wrapped her arms around Grace from behind. "Please?" she chimed in. It was clear from her clouded expression that the events of the day had taken their toll on her as well. "We can eat raw cookie dough out of the tube." Sarah's eyes held hope.

Emory stared at them and felt her resolve crumble as it often did when she was sucked into their vortex. How could she resist such an odd and wonderful offer? "Well, only if there's raw cookie dough," she said quietly.

"There is!" Grace practically shouted.

"All right then, it's a plan. I'm going to go for a run with Walter first. See you two later tonight." And she was gone. Sarah stared at the door, wishing the day had turned out differently.

She decided a talk with her mother was in order.

An hour later, most of the guests had headed home and only a few of the more rowdy partygoers remained in the backyard drinking beer with Robert and her father. Sarah took the opportunity to steal some alone time with her mother as they cleared the remaining plates. "So, Mama," she began as they loaded the dishwasher. "What do you think of Emory?"

"I think she's wonderful, mija." She smiled warmly at Sarah. "Very pretty and with a good head on her shoulders. She's done a lot of nice things for you, and that makes me like her all the more. Did she say anything about Martin? I saw them flirting a bit at dinner."

Sarah couldn't prevent a sigh. "You know, I'm not sure he's her type. But I really like spending time with her, and then there's the fact that Grace simply adores her. I just wanted you and Papa—"

"Not those glasses, sweetie, we have to hand wash those. So James looked very handsome today, didn't you think? He would be quite the catch for you, Sarah." In response to Sarah's eye roll, her voice moved into that cautionary mom tone Sarah knew so well. "You need to listen to me on this, Sarah. Sometimes a mother knows what's best."

"Sometimes, maybe. But I can tell you, Mama, that James is not for me. It's just not going to work out."

"But he's so well spoken and funny too."

"I know, but—"

"Nothing wooden in the dishwasher." She took the wooden handled serving spoon from Sarah's hands and started to wash it. "Once the newness wears off, it's important that you and your husband have something in common, something to talk about."

"Is that the case with you and Papa?"

"Oh yes," she answered quickly. "And we still have a lot of fun. That's what I want for you." She turned to Sarah earnestly. "I want you to find that important someone to share your life with. You've been on your own too long, mija."

"That's what I want too, Mama, and I believe now that it's possible. I want what you and Papa have, I do. You just have to trust me."

Her mother nodded as she dried. "I can do that. Just don't give up on James so quickly, and give me those little plates. They always flop around in the machine." Sarah handed over the plate she was holding and wondered why they had the damn appliance in the first place.

❖

"I can't do it like you." Grace sighed. "My hand won't stay steady."

"Yeah, you can. Keep your eye just a little bit ahead of your pencil." Emory pointed to the white space in front of the point and laid out the path while snagging a bite of cookie dough from the nearby tube. "There. That's more like it. See how nice that edge looks? You're a natural."

Grace looked up from the page in wonder. "I did it, Mom. I finished the outline of the vase. Look!"

Sarah had to admit, it wasn't bad. It looked quite like a vase would. It was a nice vase, as far as vases went. "I'm impressed, Graciela. I think you're my favorite child."

Grace giggled. "I'm your only child."

"Details." Sarah stood behind Emory's chair and placed her hands on her shoulders, squeezing gently. "Have you ever thought of offering lessons?"

"For spare cash?"

"Would you turn around so I can roll my eyes?" Sarah swatted her playfully. "No, smart aleck, for the intrinsic value. For art. You're a very patient teacher, and I don't know if you've noticed, but when you draw, you become completely entranced in what you're doing. It gets you going."

Emory exhaled, conceding. "It always has."

"Then you should do it more. Create something original."

"Yeah," Grace said. "If you like something, you should stick with it."

"Thanks for the sage advice, short person." Emory ruffled Grace's curls in jest and began to put away the pencils, clearly ready to move on from the subject.

But Grace wasn't finished and moved until she stood directly in front of Emory. "Will you paint something for me? Please? It can be anything."

Emory didn't know what to say. Grace looked so full of hope, and damn it, utterly adorable with those big brown eyes looking up at her.

But she couldn't.

She hadn't painted anything in years and it somehow felt like opening up a can of worms she'd rather not get into. She'd made decisions for her life and it was too late now to turn back. "I'm not sure I can do that, Grace. I'm sorry."

"Why not? If you're good at it and you like it—"

"Grace, Emory gave you an answer and she's a grown-up." There was the mom voice.

Grace closed her mouth and nodded obediently. "Yes, ma'am."

"Now, it's already thirty minutes past your bedtime. Why don't you go get dressed for bed? I'll be right behind you to tuck you in."

"All right, I'm exhausted anyway. Good night, Emory. Thanks for drawing with me."

"Anytime, kiddo."

Grace moved to Emory with arms outstretched, prompting her to lean down to accept the hug fully. She held Grace in her arms, smiled at the kiss that was placed on her cheek, and watched as she scampered away to her bedroom. Emory was beginning to think she might be the sweetest kid ever.

"Be right back," Sarah said, scratching Emory's stomach as she passed.

It was fifteen minutes later when Sarah reappeared, and Emory tried unsuccessfully to suppress a yawn. It had been a long day, but she was anything but ready to say good night. She had to admit, there was something to be said for Sarah's worn in, comfy couch.

"You're not falling asleep on me, are you?" Sarah stood in front of the couch with her hands on her hips.

"What? You're forgetting who you're talking to. I pull all-nighters on a weekly basis. I don't require sleep to live like the rest of you mortals."

"Is that right? Did you work today?"

"A little this morning, and then before my run…and some after the run."

"I see." She sat next to Emory and tugged her arm, urging her to lie with her head in Sarah's lap. "Question. Do you ever take the day off?"

"Answer. Once in a while, but there's a lot on my plate." Sarah played softly with Emory's hair, moving her fingers between the thick strands and letting them drop.

"Mmm. That feels nice. Never stop doing this."

"Do you like what you do?"

"Yeah, I guess so."

"But does it excite you? Do you wake up in the morning thrilled to get to work?"

"Um, not exactly. But I don't mind it either. It's just what I do."

"Don't freak out at this question, but what if you had a family one day? You know, people who were waiting for you to come home for dinner at a reasonable hour, or you know, attend their Little League game?"

"Are you proposing to me?" Emory squeezed her knee with playful enthusiasm. She was evading.

"Not exactly."

"How embarrassing."

"Answer the question and stop stalling. I know your tactics."

Faced with no other option, Emory pushed herself up on her arm and studied Sarah. "Well, the scenario you just described would change things for me quite a bit. If I'm answering honestly, I think I'd rather be at the Little League game."

"But are you capable of that? Your whole life seems to be motivated by success and striving to be the best. It was instilled in you from a very young age." There was doubt etched on Sarah's face and it stung, because her own self-doubt was almost all she could shoulder.

"And that worries you?" Emory asked, sobering.

"Yes, it does."

It worried her too. More than she wanted to express to Sarah in that moment. She'd known all along that she could crash and burn if she tried to settle down and play house, but she wasn't ready to acknowledge that fact fully. Being with Sarah brought too much good into her life for her to ruin it with over analysis. "Maybe that's not who I want to be anymore. I like who I am when we're together." It was the truth.

"So…the Little League game?"

Emory grinned as if it were the most obvious answer in the world. "How could I miss it?" But Sarah's question played on repeat in the back of her mind. *Are you capable of that?* The last thing in the world she wanted was to hurt Sarah and Grace. She had to do what was right for them. She made a silent promise to herself that that's what she would do from this point forward.

No matter what that meant for her.

She would look out for them.

Sarah smiled and dipped her head so that their lips were just a breath apart and hovered. "I love how much I look forward to kissing you in the briefest second before it's about to happen," she murmured quietly. "It's like my insides do this little backflip in anticipation of your mouth. It's crazy."

Emory tilted her head, closing in a tad more. She felt it too. "So that's why you're teasing me like this. You like the buildup."

"Mmhmm. A lot."

Emory raised her hand and cupped Sarah's cheek, caressing it softly. Somehow, Sarah always managed to smell of lilac and cinnamon. Her new favorite aroma. It was intoxicating. She let the hand drift down her neck slowly, lingering on the very soft skin there, before continuing on its path downward. She let the tips of her fingers skim Sarah's breast, outlining the dip of her bra. Sarah's breath, which she could feel on her face, hitched noticeably. Emory palmed the breast and applied direct pressure. Sarah's eyes shut tightly and as if on cue, she crushed her mouth to Emory's and they were off.

It was only moments before Emory was flat on her back with a throbbing between her legs. They kissed, groped, and slid together with absolute perfection. She'd never had a woman excite her the way Sarah did. Passion was too common a term for what she felt. Desire too basic. Grasping for some sort of control, Emory rolled them over and pushed Sarah's shirt up, needing the access desperately as their lips clung. Sarah moaned quietly and alarm bells went off in Emory's head. She bolted upright, still straddling Sarah's body. Concerned, Sarah sat up too.

"Hey, hey. What's wrong? You look like you've just seen a ghost."

Emory shook her head, her eyes wide. "We can't do this here. Your daughter is sleeping just down that hall. This is her house. What if she wanted a glass of water?"

Sarah looked at her puzzled, doing her best to suppress the smile she felt forming at the corners of her mouth. "You weren't worried when she was asleep upstairs at your house."

"Well, I should have been." Emory removed her hands from Sarah's shoulders as if she couldn't be trusted. "Plus, I've spent a lot more time around the two of you since then and I know her better now. I—"

"Care about her?"

Emory stared at the wall and nodded mutely.

Sarah's heart soared at the admission and she cradled Emory's face in her hands, pulling it down for a very soft kiss, which Emory was nice enough to begrudge her even in her state of epiphany.

"While I love the Hallmark moment we're having, I think I need to explain something here, Em. If nothing else, one thing we can count on is that there is *always* going to be an eight-year-old girl sleeping nearby. She doesn't ever go away, I can promise you that. That's just part of being a mom. If you're afraid to touch me with her in the house, well, then we may be headed for a very polite friendship. Do you think your parents never had sex with you in the house?"

"Yikes, really? You cannot say things like that to me."

"Think about it."

"Okay. Not helping."

Sarah grinned at her patiently. "My point is that we have to live out our lives too. Just like anyone with kids."

"And if she wakes up?"

"We listen for her and stop. I can always hear when she's up. It's like a sixth mommy sense. Though, I should concede that the couch is probably not the best location. Bedrooms have doors and locks we can use...if we wanted to."

Silence.

Emory raised her gaze. "Do we want to?"

She slipped her hands under the back of Emory's shirt, moving them up the warm skin of her back while she slowly began to kiss her neck, conveniently at the perfect height for her mouth. "I don't know, do we?"

"Yes," Emory breathed. "We really do."

When they found each other that night, Sarah was more nervous the second time around. She did more thinking this time, wondering if she was doing everything correctly. She felt adventurous but too hesitant to give in to all her impulses. She knew one thing, however. She could never get enough of Emory's body. It was a wondrous thing. And when Emory touched her in return, all bets were off. She lost track of everything, including her own name. Sex, she decided, was more than deserving of all the attention the world paid to it and then some.

As she awoke, Sarah heard the water in her master shower running. She raised her head and stared at the clock. Just after seven a.m. She pulled on a T-shirt and walked down the hall, peeking in on Grace, who was curled up and happily dozing. *As it should be.*

It was Grace's last day of summer vacation and Sarah planned to let her enjoy a leisurely morning free of chores or errands. Maybe she would make her pancakes. Knowing Grace wouldn't rise for at least another hour, giving Emory plenty of time to get ready for the day, she made her way back to her own room and knocked quietly on the bathroom door. When she didn't receive an answer, she poked her head in. "Em?"

"Morning, sleepyhead." Emory pulled the shower curtain back. "I was wondering when you were going to wake up." Standing under the stream of water, Emory's near perfect body glistened, prompting Sarah to remind herself to play it cool, which was easier said than done. True, Sarah had seen Emory in a state of undress before, but never all at once like this when her head was clear. It was a sight to behold. "Come in here with me? We could save water. It's important to be conscientious."

"Um, tempting, very tempting but…"

As Sarah trailed off, Emory tilted her head. "But? Tell me."

"I don't know why I'm shy all of a sudden. It's not like you haven't seen me naked before and then some."

"And then some," Emory reemphasized, smiling wickedly at her. "Get in here, so I can show you how amazing you look without clothes on."

Sarah nodded silently, but still didn't feel entirely sure of herself. She knew she was decent enough looking. A solid six. Maybe a seven on a good day. Lucy, from the restaurant, now she was a ten. Emory was a seventy-nine.

Sarah gathered her confidence. Time to turn off her overactive brain. She could feel Emory's eyes on her as she slipped the T-shirt over her head. She stepped into the shower and underneath the stream of hot water, feeling a little bit better once Emory's arms encircled her waist.

"Do you realize that I'm more attracted to you than I have been to anyone in my entire life?"

Sarah blinked at the lunacy of the comment. "That can't be true."

"By a long shot, actually. You're a mystery to me, Sarah Matamoros. There are times when you seem like the most self-assured woman on the planet, and others when you seem to doubt yourself for reasons I can't fathom. I'd give anything for you to understand how wonderful you are across the board and sexy for days."

"Sexy too?" Sarah was starting to get into this. She cupped Emory's ass and nipped lightly at her chin.

"Very sexy," she said through hazy eyes. "In fact, I'm scheduled to meet Lucy in twenty minutes at the office for a work session. And because I can't seem to keep my hands off of you, I'm going to be good and late."

"First time?"

"Actually, yes."

"Do you think the sun will still rise?"

"I'm finding I really don't care." Emory offered Sarah a smile that would keep her heart soaring for the remainder of the day and then some.

# CHAPTER THIRTEEN

It was the week after Labor Day and Sarah loved life. School had started, and there was that new sense of purpose in the air that always came with it. The weather was turning colder, and she could hardly wait for full-fledged, leaves-falling-from-the-trees autumn to finally arrive. It was definitely her favorite season and always managed to get her blood pumping. Maybe she would purchase a new leather jacket for the occasion, something a little more cutting edge than her green cotton windbreaker. Who knew?

Grace seemed to be enjoying her first week in the fourth grade and had taken up with a whole new crop of kids. Emory still got first dibs on all the latest developments in her social life, but Sarah comforted herself in the fact that Grace still seemed to choose her for almost everything else.

Shaking herself from her thoughts, Sarah focused instead on the visitor in her office.

"One last question and I think we'll have all we need for the article."

Sarah nodded and smiled politely at the friendly looking young man who sat across the desk from her. In actuality, she was thrilled to be getting a feature article in the *Union-Tribune* about Immaculate Home's expansion and would sit and talk to this reporter until the cows not only came home, but took off again. The exposure from the write-up could give the business an incredible shot in the arm, and she knew she had Emory and her press release of wonder to thank for it. It turned out there really was something to this newswire business.

The young reporter pushed his glasses up on his nose and scribbled a few notes before continuing. "So just to wrap things up, what makes Immaculate Organization different from say California Closets or The Container Store? You offer very similar services."

"That's true, we do." Sarah came around and perched on the corner of her desk. She loved this question because the answer was the lynchpin in what made her mother's parent company successful. "There's a certain amount of hands-on, personal attention that our clients have grown to expect and depend on. It's this component that's kept our company growing each of the twenty-six years we've been in business. That one-on-one relationship transfers to this branch of the company as well."

The reporter reached across the desk and switched off his travel-sized voice recorder. "I think that just about does it. Thank you so much for your time, Ms. Matamoros. The article should run next week." He picked up his attaché case and headed for the door. "I think we'll approach your story as the little engine that could and then did. Hometown little guys making good always seem to do well with our readership, and it doesn't hurt that you're as passionate and likable as you are. Get ready. Sometimes these feature stories can attract more attention than you realize. I hope you have the manpower lined up once that phone starts ringing."

"Oh wow, you know, I hadn't quite thought of that." She jotted a note to herself on her Post-it cube. "Thanks for the tip."

But when the article came out a week later, she couldn't have been happier. She'd raced to the phone and called Emory first thing that morning after finding the write-up in the Life section. When she arrived at the apartment twenty minutes later, Sarah tugged her inside all the while grinning like a maniac. She was too excited to try to act anything but foolish and had absolutely no problem with that. "Read it. Read it. Hurry. Read it."

Emory laughed when Sarah practically pushed her onto the couch. "Okay, but you have to stop grinning at me like an adorable person so I can concentrate."

"Got it. No grinning. Not at all adorable. See?" Using the extra energy, she paced very seriously instead, killing time so Emory could read the article. The article all about *her* family's business, with quotes from *her* directly. Super stoked was an understatement.

It was only a couple of excruciating minutes later when Emory dropped the paper and shot her one of her more radiant Emory smiles. The one that caused her whole face to light up and made Sarah all tingly. "So?"

"So, you, in addition to being incredibly cute right now, which was against the rules I might add, are also incredibly famous. This is an awesome article, Sarah. I'm so excited for you."

Sarah practically tackled Emory in appreciation, threw her arms around her, and eventually settled quite happily into her lap. Emory knew more about these kinds of things, and getting her vote of confidence made everything that much more real.

"It's so strange to see my name in the paper." She picked up the page to look again. "I'm nobody. But look," she held her photo up to her face and grinned alongside it, "there I am in black and white."

"There you are. And I love this photo, by the way. Who do I have to sleep with to get a copy?"

Sarah slid her arms around Emory's neck and looked skyward. "It's possible I can set something up for you."

"Oh good, then I came to the right place." She kissed Sarah's neck at the open collar of her shirt. "Grace home?"

"Nope. Headed out with Mindy's family on a picnic."

Emory lifted her head. "So just us? Maybe we can hang out." She unbuttoned Sarah's top button and kissed her collarbone.

Sarah's mind slid to all the things they could do to each other alone in the apartment, but damn it, it would have to wait. "I wish we could, and we will soon. It just can't be right now. I have to shower."

Emory stilled. "No? 'Cause I'm really good in the shower."

Heat infused her at the memory. "You can't say things like that to me right now. I'm running late."

"You have big plans today?"

"I have to work."

She looked up at Sarah. "It's Saturday. Even I take an occasional break on Saturday. Let's take a break together. I kinda like you."

Sarah feathered her hands through Emory's hair and leaned in for a light kiss. "I like you too, but Mama picked up a last-minute job and no one else is available. I should have told you when I called. Maybe you can join us for dinner tonight? I promise I won't make you cook it."

Emory frowned, trying to piece it all together. "Wait, so you're not going in to the office?"

"Nope. A house. Real work." Her eyes flashed as she grinned. "Don't worry. I didn't forget how."

"No, I wouldn't imagine." She attempted a smile, but could feel it didn't quite reach her eyes. She didn't know why exactly, but she didn't like the idea. Emory slid Sarah off her gently and crossed to the window, trying to work it out.

"Okay. What just happened in that head of yours? What's wrong?"

"I don't know. I just—"

"Hey, look at me."

Emory did. "I feel like you shouldn't work directly for the clients anymore. In their homes. You're heading up the new division. That's your job."

Sarah raised her eyebrows. "Yeah, but I don't mind helping out. Especially if there's no one to—"

"That's just it. You need to hire more people. Delegate this kind of thing out to someone else now. You're the boss. It's your picture that is in the paper. It's better business to keep that persona intact. So find someone else for today. Threaten their job. Do what you have to do to make things happen." She decided to assert herself a little. "I just don't want you cleaning houses."

Sarah's eyes narrowed but her voice remained calm. "*You* don't want me to clean houses?"

"You're beyond that now."

Sarah had no clue what to say. She didn't understand where this was coming from, but she certainly didn't like what it was implying. "I do what I have to do to keep the business running smoothly. If my mother needs my help, I'm going to be there for her. I have bills to pay, Emory. I have a child to support."

"Then I can pay your bills."

Sarah steadied herself against the blow, closing her eyes until the urge to snap passed. "You're serious right now?"

"Dead serious."

"I can take care of myself. I don't need or want your money, Em. I never did."

"Fine, but that doesn't mean you have to go back three steps, career-wise."

"What are you talking about right now?" She was staggered by how out of touch Emory was with the realities of her life. "I work for a *family-run* business. There's no such thing as a vertical pathway. It takes a village." But there was an angle to this whole thing that bothered Sarah more, and she had to get to the root of it. "You didn't mind my working for you at your mother's house."

"That's entirely different."

"Why? Tell me why that was different." Her voice was noticeably louder now, but she couldn't help it.

"Because—"

"Why? Say it, Emory."

"Because we weren't together then. It didn't matter."

Sarah stared, her voice now calm, even. "And now that we are, I have to be worthy of you, the great Emory Owen?"

Emory looked exasperated, offended even. "What? No. That's not what I said and you know it. This is about what's right for you, not me."

Sarah stared hard at Emory and Emory stared back, crystal blue eyes cool as ice. Emory wasn't going to give in, Sarah realized, but damn it, neither was she. She wasn't committing a crime. She wasn't hurting anyone. This was her job, her life, and she'd live it as she saw fit. "I think we're going to just have to disagree on this one. You should probably go now. I have to get ready for work." Sarah didn't wait for an answer and left Emory standing in her living room as she went in to change.

Once she was alone in her bedroom, Sarah replayed the conversation again in her head. She was angry, yes, but also wildly off-balance by the fact that they'd fought.

It didn't feel good.

In fact, it felt downright horrible.

She sat on the edge of the bed and allowed her emotions to settle. Once they had, she attempted to see things from Emory's perspective.

In her defense, this was new territory for Emory. Rather than lashing out in anger, maybe she could have taken time to rationally explain to her how things had to work when you weren't made of money. True, it wasn't Emory's place to make decisions for her, but Emory was used to calling the shots in most every aspect of her adult life. Maybe she was in automatic pilot mode. It's possible that her heart had been in the right place.

She decided that she'd call Emory as soon as she had a spare moment and fix things so the nagging ache in the center of her chest would go away. She grabbed her keys and bag and headed for the door to her apartment. She'd just have to find a way to get through the afternoon.

"Please wait." She turned at the sound of the voice. Emory sat on the couch looking up at her helplessly, lost. "I don't want to fight."

Sarah let her bag fall, a spark of relief flaring in her chest. "God, I don't either."

"If you're happy, I should be happy. Sometimes, I try to micromanage and I shouldn't have done that today. I just want things to be easier for you, and instead I made them harder. Ignore me."

Sarah sighed and sat on the arm of the sofa next to Emory, offering a tired smile. "I could never ignore you, even if I wanted to. You're stuck with my attention, I'm afraid."

"Even when I'm overbearing?"

"Can you imagine how much I must like you?"

"Wow."

"I know."

Emory took her hand and squeezed. "So go to work and forget I was a headstrong idiot. Maybe, if I'm lucky, you'll call me later and let me know when I can see you again because I really want to see you again soon. You know, redeem my good name?"

She leaned down and kissed Emory's temple. "I will most definitely call you. I can think of all sorts of ways you can make it up to me. Creative ways." That earned a smile and Sarah's heart did a little backflip.

Back on track, she thought to herself, back on track.

❖

It was a slow day at Global Newswire, but then mid-quarter Tuesdays always were. Trevor was busy with client mail outs and most of the account execs were out on presentations. Emory picked up the phone, seizing the slower pace of the afternoon.

"Wanna come over and see how a press release makes its journey?"

Sarah paused on the other end of the line. "Are you offering me a tour of your office?"

"That's exactly what I'm doing. Can you swing it? How are you ever going to understand how to properly market that up-and-coming business of yours without a little hands-on coaching in PR? Plus, that means I'd get to lay eyes on you, which, you know, is kind of the whole point of this phone call."

Sarah checked her afternoon appointments while Emory waited. "I have to meet my designer, Samantha, at the Miller house at four o'clock. But I have time before. I can be there in a half hour."

"Perfect. Give your name to the receptionist and she'll call me when you get here."

An hour later, as the elevator opened onto the forty-fourth floor, Sarah found herself in a rather impressive looking lobby. It became clear to her that Global Newswire inhabited the entire floor of the office building. Three elegant couches were arranged in the center of the large room with a marble coffee table in the middle. In the corners, towering vases of fresh flowers were each showcased with dedicated accent lighting. A coffee station stood to the right with a stainless steel carafe and every kind of flavored creamer you could imagine. Near the far wall stood a dark oak reception desk complete with a beautiful looking woman behind it.

"Welcome to Global Newswire," she said in the most soothing voice Sarah could imagine. She was smiling but carried an elegance befitting the rather impressive room. She couldn't help but smile at the sharp contrast to her mother's elderly receptionist, Marjorie.

"Sarah Matamoros to see Emory Owen." The young woman eyed her for a moment, the smile never leaving her face.

"Do you have an appointment with Ms. Owen?" She turned to her computer screen and began tick-tacking away on her keyboard.

"Yes and no. She knows I'm coming, but I don't think you're going to see it on your calendar there."

"I'm afraid you'll need an appointment. Ms. Owen is very busy and hasn't made any note of your meeting."

"Would you mind giving her a call?"

"If you'll be so kind as to take a seat, I'll see what I can do." The smile was no longer quite as warm. Sarah did as she was told, but took out her phone in the process and shot off a quick text message. "Your receptionist thinks I'm trying to infiltrate Fort Knox. Help?"

It was only a moment before her phone buzzed in response. "Well trained, that one. On my way." Emory appeared shortly and whisked Sarah through the thick oak doors that led into the world of Global Newswire. The receptionist, whose name turned out to be Leslie, apologized profusely, much to Sarah's guilty pleasure.

"I'm glad you could make it," Emory said.

"Are you kidding? And miss the chance to see the empire you spend day and night constructing?"

Once inside, Sarah was surprised to see that the posh elegance of the lobby was reserved for essentially that, the lobby. The inner office of the company looked more like a working newsroom with few frills.

A series of several dozen workstations dotted the large open space with private offices flanking its perimeter. "These are the editors," Emory said, gesturing to the rather bookish looking individuals at the workstations. They stared, entranced, at a series of codes on their computer screens. "Once a press release has been sent to us with instructions on who's to receive it, the editors code the transmission before sending it over the wire through our satellite links. The codes tell the press release where to go. It's also up to the editors to proof the release. If it's transmitted with an error, we have to issue a correction, which is a huge strike against us in the industry. We try to avoid it at all costs. This office is currently error free. I can't say the same for the Dallas office, however."

"What happened in Dallas?" Sarah was incredibly intrigued by the process.

"Five errors in six months. I'm travelling down there next week to implement a new training program with one of my editorial managers. I'll be letting two of the editors go while I'm there."

"Wow. Doesn't that upset you to have to tell them they no longer have a job?"

"It's just business, and a necessary part of running a company. Haven't you ever had to fire anyone from Immaculate Home?"

"Once for stealing, but that seemed unavoidable. When someone underperforms, we always try to make them better."

"And if that doesn't work?"

Sarah considered this. "We find ways to compensate for the weak link, I guess. I just can't shake the knowledge that they have families to support and kids to put through college."

"I can't consider those kinds of things. In fact, I never have."

"I guess I'm a softie then. Now show me your office so I can ooh and ah at how important you are."

"I like the sound of that. Right this way." They strolled down the hallway to Emory's corner office and paused outside next to the desk of a very serious looking young man with flaming red hair. "This is my assistant, Trevor. I think you've spoken to him on the phone once or twice." Trevor stood and extended his hand politely. "Trevor, this is Sarah, my girlfriend."

Trevor's eyes widened in delight. "Well, in that case." He reached out and pulled Sarah into a warm hug.

"All right, all right, that's enough. Let the girl go."

"It was nice to meet you, Trevor." Sarah laughed, following Emory into the office. Once inside, she took only a brief moment to scan the spacious room before turning back to face Emory. "Do you think we could close the door for a minute?"

"Okay." Sarah had an indiscernible look on her face that made Emory uneasy. "Is everything all right?"

Once the door clicked into place, Sarah closed the distance between them until she stood in front of Emory. "You just called me your girlfriend."

It had seemed second nature to Emory and she realized now that it shouldn't have. "Oh, I'm sorry. I guess I should have asked if it was okay. I just figured because you didn't know Trevor—"

"Shhh." Sarah placed a finger across Emory's lips. "I loved it."

"You did?"

"I did. Do you know what I also love? You in this business suit." She slipped her hand inside the jacket and ran her palm from the center of Emory's chest up along the side of her collarbone. "You were wearing something similar the day we met, remember?"

"And did you like it then?"

Sarah considered the question. "No, I found it intimidating. But now that I know the woman inside it, it's just plain hot."

Emory grabbed Sarah by the hips and pulled her closer, kissing her soundly. Sarah reciprocated hungrily, sliding her arms up and around Emory's neck. Then a thought hit and she pulled back just enough to meet Emory's eyes. "Are you sure we should be kissing at the office? You are at work, after all."

Emory inclined her head. "The door is closed. We can do anything we want. No one will come in without knocking. One of the perks of being in charge."

"Okay then, maybe just a little more of the sexy kissing." Sarah grinned and dipped her head.

Emory loved kissing Sarah. She felt it all the way down to her toes and it left her in the most wonderful fog. Somewhere in the back of her consciousness, she registered that hands were tugging vaguely on shirts, moving down arms, shifting all the while closer, and she could vaguely hear the humming sounds people made while making out. It was like hovering just above heaven for her.

"Hey, Em, will you take a look—holy shit. Sorry. Oh my God."

At Lucy's highly unexpected entrance, they froze. No one spoke for several seconds, ratcheting up the awkward factor several notches. It was Emory who laughed first, followed shortly by Lucy. Sarah smiled until the tension seemed to evaporate from the room.

Once under control again, Emory turned to Sarah wryly. "I should amend that earlier statement to 'no one will come in if the door is closed except for Lucy, who does whatever the hell she wants.'"

"Wow. Again, so sorry." Lucy gestured at the door. "Sometimes I'm oblivious. What can I say? But please don't kick me out for more kissing. I'm here now, so can I please meet Sarah?" The cartoonish hope in Lucy's eyes made Sarah smile. She liked this woman already.

Emory sighed playfully. "Why not? Lucy Danaher, meet Sarah Matamoros." And then meeting Sarah's eyes and smiling, "My girlfriend."

"A pleasure." Lucy extended her hand. "And I do mean that. I've been waiting ever so patiently to make your acquaintance and I do emphasize *patiently*."

"It's nice to meet you too, Lucy. Emory's told me an awful lot about you."

"Well, she lies, so discriminate accordingly."

Sarah laughed. "Will do." She checked her watch. "I don't mean to run out on you two, but I have a four o'clock consultation across town, and if I don't leave now, traffic will triumph. The office is amazing," she said, turning to Emory. "Thank you for the brief tour."

"Yeah, sorry it got cut short with all that smooching," Lucy interjected.

Emory crossed her arms and gave Lucy the full power of the Arctic stare before focusing her attention on Sarah. "I'll call you later and we can make plans for the zoo on Saturday."

Sarah nodded, met her eyes knowingly, and then turned. "Good-bye, Lucy. I hope we see each other again soon."

"Count on it. If we both work on her, she'll actually let us be friends."

"Deal." Sarah waved and rounded the corner smiling.

Lucy shook her head in mock disapproval. "You are such a dog," she muttered to Emory. "At the office, really?"

"Shut up."

❖

The weather was wonderful on Saturday, and in Emory's opinion, the zoo was the perfect place to spend the afternoon.

If only she had gotten to go.

"We can wait, push the trip back until late afternoon so you can make it," Sarah had said over the phone, several hours earlier.

"I don't know how long this will take. I'm really sorry, but I think you should go ahead without me."

Silence. Emory could sense the disappointment emanating through the phone, but she was at a loss for how to fix the situation. She felt horrible about having to bow out of what would have been a great time with Sarah and Grace, but truth be told, she saw no other way. An hour before they were supposed to head out for their zoo trip, she'd been sideswiped with a call from the IT department that three separate offices were offline. Dead in the water. While there weren't many releases scheduled to go out on a weekend, there were a few key clients that would be upset at the drop. She'd have to spend the afternoon smoothing things over personally if they were to have any hope of holding on to the accounts.

"Sarah, say something."

When she spoke her voice was quiet, excruciatingly polite. "I hope it all works out."

Damn it. Not that. "Can I come by later and try and make it up to Grace?"

"Sure. I think that would help." But there was a distance between them that she didn't quite know what to do with. She briefly considered putting the clients off for a couple of days, but the repercussions would be big. Too big.

And now, some eight hours later, as she stood on Sarah's doorstep preparing to knock, she didn't feel much better about things. In fact, she felt worse. She had done the only thing she knew how to do and that was to act. To fix the situation at hand. But each action has a consequence. And her life seemed to have a whole new set of consequences lately.

"Hey," Sarah said upon opening the door. She leaned against its side and met Emory's eyes. Her hair was up, but as usual, strands had escaped. She seemed settled in for the night, cozy in the best kind of way. She didn't offer entrance, which spoke volumes.

"Hi. For what it's worth, I'm sorry today didn't work out. I was looking forward to it."

"I know. I accept your apology."

Emory shifted. She felt nervous, off-kilter. "Can I explain to Grace?"

"She's asleep. It's past ten, Emory. She goes to bed at nine on weekends."

Emory glanced at her watch as a million more self-recriminations warred inside her head. "Oh, I didn't realize how late it had gotten."

Sarah seemed to soften then, and stepped out onto the porch. "She was pretty disappointed you cancelled, but I explained the situation. She'll be fine."

"Will you?"

Sarah offered a weak smile that didn't quite reach her eyes and moved into Emory, wrapping her arms around her. "You were doing your job today. I get that. I just wish it had played out differently."

Emory didn't say anything because she didn't know what to say. Sarah should be angry at her. She should be frustrated. She had been ready for both of those things. But the quiet sadness she was met with was a whole new kind of guilt that Emory felt right in the center of her chest. She'd let them both down and they were accepting it.

How had she let it get to this?

"Everything okay, Sar?" Danny stood in the open doorway of the apartment and regarded them curiously.

Sarah took a step back and turned to him, brightening. "Yes, just fine. Danny, you remember my friend, Emory?"

He smiled. "Definitely. Hi. Good to see you again."

"You too, Danny."

He looked to Sarah as if a thought had just occurred to him. "Hey, I can find somewhere else to crash other than the couch if you guys want to hang out."

"What? No. Emory was just dropping off some paperwork." Danny looked from Sarah's empty hands to Emory's. "But she forgot it in the car."

What should have been an easy situation to navigate seemed to have thrown Sarah into panic mode. Emory reluctantly took her cue. "I did. I left it. I don't know where my head's at lately." She hated the lie.

Sarah met her gaze appreciatively. "I'll walk out with you. Back in a sec, Dan."

Emory walked a few paces ahead, lost in her thoughts, the stresses of the day, and what had just happened on the porch. So many things seemed wildly out of her control, her own emotions included, and it angered her. She wasn't a weak person and she hated how vulnerable her relationship to Sarah made her feel.

"Em, wait. Please." She did, but took a moment before turning fully to Sarah. "I didn't know he was coming over tonight. His roommate invited over a bunch of friends and he was looking for a quiet place to crash."

"He's your brother. That makes perfect sense."

"But?"

Here it goes. "When are you going to talk to your family?"

Sarah sighed, her eyes finding the ground as she seemed to gather her thoughts. "That's not a step I'm ready to take quite yet."

Somewhere deep, Emory needed to know more. "Will it ever be?" she asked quietly.

"I don't know."

And there it was. *I'm not sure about us* was easy enough to read in Sarah's guarded response. She didn't blame her. She couldn't.

Emory nodded, resolute. She felt herself failing at what she'd known from the beginning would be an impossible scenario. "I better get going. Here." She reached into the passenger's seat and handed Sarah a few odd papers from her junk mail pile. "For authenticity." She turned to her car, but Sarah's hand on her arm caught her attention. She looked as if she wanted to say something, but instead, leaned in and she kissed her softly. As she pulled away, Emory could see the heavy emotion in her eyes.

"Tonight was rough. But don't leave without saying good-bye. Never that."

Emory felt a wall come down at the words. Such a simple request that managed to touch something in her. "Never that," she agreed and stole a final kiss before driving off into the summer night.

If only everything between them could be as simple.

"Hot or cold weather?" They were lying in bed a week later. It was three a.m., but Sarah wasn't missing sleep a bit. She loved it when Emory stayed over. They'd spent the earlier part of the night lost in each other and welcomed the morning hours talking about anything and everything. With her fingertips, she absently traced circles across Emory's abdomen as she awaited her response.

"Hot. You?"

"Oh, most definitely cold. Lots of hot chocolate and cuddling when it's cold. I mean c'mon." Sarah lifted her head from where it rested on Emory's shoulder and shook it slightly, grinning like it was a no brainer.

Emory tightened her arms around her. "Sounds cozy. I could be swayed to your side with that kind of thinking. Favorite color?"

"Blue."

"Me too, but aqua."

Sarah smiled to herself. "Because you love the ocean. Favorite food?"

"That's hard. Mahi Mahi, if it's cooked right. What about you?"

"Nope. You'll laugh."

Emory slid down on the pillow so they were face to face. "Oh, then you definitely have to tell me."

Sarah scrunched one eye. "Whopper with cheese."

Emory's mouth fell open in playful surprise. "As in Burger King? From all the foods in the world, you choose Burger King?"

They were laughing now. "After a long day, there's nothing like it. I could go for one right now if I'm being honest."

Emory pushed herself up. "Then I'll be right back."

Sarah pulled her back to bed and crawled on top. "No way. You're not going anywhere." She kissed her. "Too cute to leave."

"You know your accent comes out when you're playful."

"It does not." She sank further into the kiss.

"Okay. Except it does," Emory murmured, as her hands drifted down Sarah's body.

They were both a lot less interested in conversation after that.

Dallas was hot. It was September and still pushing ninety degrees outside, a cherry atop the already difficult sundae that had been Emory's day from hell. She decided to cool off with refreshment at the hotel bar before heading up to her room for the night. In the forty-five minutes she'd been there, she'd refused drink offers from two different men and one woman, all the while desperately wanting the chance to sort through her own head for five damn minutes.

Her workday at the Dallas office had not gone the way she'd planned at all, and she was pissed off. She thought back on the series of events and bristled all over again, knowing full well who was to blame. She'd had two Kentucky mules by the time her cell phone notified her of an incoming call. She rolled her eyes at the readout but answered anyway. "I shouldn't be talking to you. I should be lying on a highway hoping to get run over."

"Wow. Kinda drastic. Bad day?" Sarah asked.

"Bingo." She stirred her drink with the annoying shamrock swizzle stick. This wasn't even an Irish bar, for God's sake.

"Do you want to talk about it?"

Emory exhaled, softening. "I didn't, but now that I hear your voice, maybe. I don't know."

"Okay, I can work with that." Sarah switched the phone from her left ear to her right so she could flip the pancakes she was making Grace for dinner. "Let's try it out and see how it goes. Tell me what happened."

"Today, I had to fire the two editors I told you about."

"Right, I remember. Did they not take it well?"

"No, they took it fine, because I couldn't do it."

"What do you mean? You never got the chance to speak to them?"

"No, I got the chance, but the moment I was face-to-face with them, all I could think about was what *you* said about them having families to feed and kids to put through college, and I'm dead in the water. Next thing I know, I'm flashing on an eighteen-year-old kid flipping burgers instead of growing up to be president of the United States and I'm the reason."

Sarah grinned broadly, still attempting to keep her voice entirely neutral. "So what will happen to them now?"

"I enrolled them in the new training with the rest of the Dallas editors, but I told Sheila to devote extra time to them. More one-on-one attention. I hate that I'm suddenly ineffective. This sucks."

"You're not ineffective, you're sympathetic. You took steps to make them better at what they do. If it doesn't work out, you can fire them later. Doesn't that sound like fun?"

"I want to fire them now," Emory answered.

"I get that and I'm sorry you're upset. If you were here, I'd take all sorts of care of you."

"I can't hang out with you anymore. You're warm and fuzzy and it's rubbing off."

Sarah could hear the slightest hint of teasing in Emory's voice and took the opening.

"So I should make other plans for Friday night?"

"Don't you dare."

"All right, all right." She chuckled. "I'll pick you up at the airport at six thirty. There might be kissing. I can't be sure."

Emory sighed audibly into the phone. "Now I'm going to think about the kissing all night."

"Good. Now sleep tight and try not to be too mad at me."

"S'okay. I still like you."

"Wait, before you go, someone would like to say hello."

"Emory, it's Grace! What's Texas like? Seen any horses?"

Emory sat up a little straighter at the sound of the exuberant young voice. "Hiya, kiddo! Dallas is hot. Negative on the horses. Lots of concrete and tall buildings though."

"Oh, that's too bad. Hey, we're having pancakes for dinner. Isn't that insane? Mom and I have decided to have breakfast for dinner once a month. You should come over next time."

"I would love to. I make a pretty mean Denver omelet."

"I don't know what that is, but I'll check Wikipedia later. Night!"

"Good night, Grace."

❖

"I didn't imagine she would be as hot as she is," Carmen mused, stirring her peach tea. "That's for sure." They'd come for their weekly get-together at Sabro's and dined over a plate of sell-your-mother-for guacamole nachos. "Even Roman mentioned her undeniable beauty. Though out of respect, I'll spare you his exact words."

"Thank you, but I have two brothers and I can imagine. So what exactly *did* you expect? Details."

"I don't know. Someone a little more delicate and uptight with a severe hairstyle that says 'I've got more money than God.' Real-life Emory, while well dressed, was actually kind of fun."

Sarah smiled and relaxed into her seat. "I love that you saw that. She doesn't always show that side of herself and she should."

"So what's the update on that front?"

"The update is that I miss her like crazy. She's been out of town on business all week and won't be back until Friday, which also, cue the ominous music, happens to be her birthday."

"Ohhh, the birthday. That's a lot of pressure, Sar. Any big plans?"

"I'm picking her up at the airport, taking her to dinner where I'll lose myself in those baby blues that I haven't seen in forever, and then hopefully taking her home and having my way with her shortly thereafter. Speaking of which, would you be willing to keep Grace that night? She absolutely loves staying with you."

"You're sucking up. I like it. I'm sure we can work out some sort of exchange. My anniversary is next month and my rugrats simply adore staying with you as well."

"Yikes."

"You'll be fine. I'll draft you a survivor's guide. But if they get hold of the scissors, you're on your own."

Sarah sighed. "It's a deal."

"So," Carmen managed through a bite of her nacho, "sounds like we're enjoying our newfound sex life."

Sarah smiled shyly at the tablecloth. "More than I ever would have dreamed possible."

Carmen scooted her chair in eagerly. "Specifics are definitely required. Are we talking gentle and easy or wild and crazy?"

"I think we've managed both. And maybe a few other combinations."

Carmen shook her head in envy and glared. "Bragging is the instrument of the small and petty."

Sarah grinned. "You did ask."

"I did. And everything else is peaches and cream?"

"Um, yeah, for the most part."

"Uh oh."

"Don't say uh oh, and don't take that last nacho. It's mine." Sarah snagged the last of the nachos and slid down into her chair at its wonder.

Carmen eyed her knowingly. "Don't use the nachos as a distraction. I know you, and there's something else on your mind. Tell me now or I'm getting up and walking out of here. And you know I don't make idle threats, so start talking. Five, four, three, two—"

"All right, all right. A little extra aggressive with the mommy mode today, aren't we? Geez." Sarah shifted in her seat. "It's minor. It's so minor in the scheme of everything good that I shouldn't even say it out loud. But there are times when I feel like I'm…I don't know, out of my league with Emory. Like I'm treading water or something."

"Out of your league? First of all, that's crazy. And second of all, what are you even talking about?"

Sarah took a moment and searched for the best way to articulate the nagging feeling she couldn't seem to shake lately. "Emory travels all over the world. I've never even been out of California. She's practically a world-class chef, and I peak at chicken and rice casserole. She knows everything there is to know about classic art and I watch *Monday Night Football*. Do you see where I'm going with this?"

"No, I don't. I adore your chicken and rice casserole."

"Work with me here. Focus."

"Got it. Continue."

"It's almost as if *we* fit together, and I know we do, but our worlds don't. She's used to being on her own, nothing to tie her down, and then out of nowhere there's this woman and her kid, who has these heart issues, and all sorts of ideas of family, and staying home nights. I'm worried it's too much. That we're too much and in the end, she's going to realize that.

"All right. I'm going to put it to you plain and simple. Are you ready? And please pay attention because this is good."

"So ready."

"Okay, here goes…you're a catch." Carmen sat back in her chair as if she'd just uttered the most brilliant words anyone had ever spoken and was now letting them marinate in the universe.

"I'm a catch," Sarah finally repeated with little conviction.

"Yes, you are, in fact, a catch. And so is your adorably smart daughter. You see, I've done the math. I've met virtually every kind of person, and you two are simply the best out of all of them, and I'm not just saying that because we're friends. I mean, if it weren't true, I still might say it, but in this instance, it just happens to be the truest thing on the planet. Are you with me?"

Sarah rested her chin in her hand and squinted. "I'm doing my best."

"What I'm saying is that Emory is ridiculously lucky, and if she doesn't see that, then you need to move on and quickly."

Sarah's eyes widened. "No, I'm not saying she doesn't. It's just this little voice inside my head that gets my attention every so often."

"A little voice that you need to beat the hell out of until it submits to reason."

Sarah laughed, her mood already lighter after talking with Carmen. "So you think I'm pretty great?"

Carmen rolled her eyes. "Whatever. You know I think you're freaking adorable, all right? Do you feel better now?"

"As a matter of fact, I do." Sarah grinned triumphantly and grabbed the check. "On me."

"Did I also mention that you're beautiful and smart too? Because Mama could use a new pair of boots. Just sayin'."

## Chapter Fourteen

It was finally Friday, and Emory was in high spirits. It was the first birthday in a long time that she was genuinely excited to celebrate. All she wanted in the world was a nice meal and the company of a very beautiful woman, one in particular.

The year had contained its fair share of ups and downs, but she was feeling hopeful, and that was worthy of some celebration. She couldn't have been more excited to get off that plane and see Sarah and Grace, whom she'd not seen in six full days, a torturous eternity. She didn't know how she was going to maintain the usual stream of business trips her job often called for. Things needed to be different now, and some sort of Plan B might be in order. She'd talk with Lucy about it soon.

As Emory made her way down the long corridor to baggage claim, she searched the faces of the eager family members waiting to greet their loved ones. When her eyes at long-last landed on Sarah's, it was all she could do to maintain her steady pace and not close the distance between them in a less dignified manner, like an out-and-out jog. Instead, she shook her head, chuckling at the small sign Sarah held that read "Wanda," and then took in the gorgeous black dress she wore for their evening out.

"You look amazing," she said in Sarah's ear as she pulled her into her arms.

"You're sweet, and have been sorely missed." Sarah held on to Emory for several long moments. Pulling back, she grinned, her eyes shining brightly. "Happy birthday."

"Thank you." Emory took her hand and led them to the baggage terminal. As they walked, her heart soared. She'd found her balance in the world again.

"Can you not go away anymore?" Sarah asked as they stared at each other lazily a few minutes later, waiting on Emory's bag to make its way around on the carousel.

"Already working on it. But in more pressing matters, what should we do tonight?" Emory asked with delicious anticipation of the evening. "And where's Grace? I thought for sure she'd have talked her way into making announcements over the PA by now."

"Grace is being well cared for. You see, it's somewhat of an important day I'm told, so I took the liberty of making reservations for the adults to celebrate at Donovan's Downtown. My treat. I hope that's okay. I know you said no party, but I wanted the night to be special. Thoughts?" Sarah looked nervous that she'd made the right call. But in all honesty, Emory didn't care what they did as long as they did it together. But now that she thought about it, Donovan's would actually make for a really nice evening.

"That sounds like the best offer I've had in a long time. You, me, and some amazing food." Emory pulled Sarah's hand to her lips and kissed the back of it. "Are you sure you don't want Grace to come with us? She's welcome."

"Nope. She's blissfully happy roughhousing with Carmen and her boys tonight, her idea of a walk on the wild side. She did send a gift for you, however, which I will give you later."

"Now?" Emory asked hopefully, her right eyebrow arched.

"Later." Sarah shook her head at Emory's attempt to appear disappointed. "So incredibly demanding."

Thirty minutes later, they pulled into the drive of Emory's house. The idea was to make just a brief stop so Emory could change into something more appropriate for dinner and say a quick hello to Walter, who'd been tended to daily by Lucy in her absence. By the time they actually arrived, however, Emory was beginning to have other ideas. A passion had been lit when she'd first laid eyes on Sarah at the airport and that slow building fire was now going strong. She'd stolen glances at Sarah throughout their time in the car and just couldn't get past how wonderful she looked in that dress. The occasional placement of Sarah's hand on her thigh as they drove hadn't helped her plight all that much either. "What time is our reservation?" she asked nonchalantly as they made their way up the walk.

Sarah glanced over at her suspiciously. "Why?"

"Just wondering how much time we had."

A knowing smile took shape on Sarah's face and she brought them to a stop on Emory's front porch. "I know that look."

"I have a look?"

"You have the best look. There's this hunger that shades your eyes and every time I see it, it floods me with…"

"Floods you with?"

"All kinds of thoughts about you, us, together." Sarah took a step into Emory's space, her gaze taking on the heat Emory already felt. She slipped her hands under the front of Emory's shirt and delicately moved her thumbs in circles across the planes of her stomach, not once breaking eye contact. "The reservations aren't until eight o'clock. We have a little time, if you want to, you know, explore those thoughts I mentioned. God, you're so warm."

"Mhmm," Emory murmured absently in response. "A lot of time between now and eight. A practical lifetime." Emory closed her eyes, unable to take much more of Sarah's teasing thumbs and the tidal wave of arousal they were unleashing. There was need coursing through her body and she had to act on it. She reached blindly for Sarah, catching her by the waist and pulling her in tightly until their bodies met. Sarah gasped and captured Emory's mouth aggressively with her own.

Emory slid into the kiss.

Into lilac and cinnamon.

It had been too long, she thought, too long since she'd held Sarah this way, felt her all over like this. Emory took control, deepening the kiss all the while fumbling with her keys to get them inside quicker. "Damn it," she whispered when her coordination continued to fail her over and over again.

"I've got it." Sarah took the keys and easily let them in.

Emory followed her into the darkened house, and after only a few steps, wrapped her arms around Sarah's waist, and she kissed her neck from behind. She snaked one hand up to cover Sarah's breast, and with her other hand moved her hair to the side for better access to that neck.

"Baby," Sarah breathed.

Stifled laughter emanated from somewhere across the darkened room. Emory froze. Sarah froze. The lights above them flashed to full illumination and a house full of seventy-five smiling faces screamed in unison, "Surprise!"

"Fuck," Emory whispered.

"Oh wow," Sarah echoed.

Emory took a moment to process the scene, pulling her hands from their blatant placement on Sarah's body. There was a "Happy Birthday, Emory" banner across the mantle and a large, gourmet birthday cake on a table in the corner. Her closest friends and co-workers stood smiling in celebration of her, along with a few faces she was only vaguely familiar with. She managed to smile back at her unexpected guests and whisper to Sarah at the same time, "Did you know about this?"

"Not a clue," Sarah whispered back, doing her best to straighten her dress.

What an embarrassing entrance they'd just made.

Lucy emerged from the crowd grinning. "Sorry to interrupt, lovebirds, but we have some celebrating to do." That earned a collective chuckle from the crowd. Emory registered that music was now playing from her stereo system.

"Surprised?" Lucy asked. She pulled Emory into an energetic hug.

"You have no concept of how much. Was this your idea?" she murmured in Lucy's ear.

"Guilty." Lucy pulled Sarah into a similar embrace. "This dress is beautiful on you, Sarah."

"Thanks." Sarah smiled but still looked a bit off balance.

"And about the party, I would have called to warn you, but I didn't have your number. Plus, Emory informed me last we spoke that she'd be home to feed Walter before going anywhere tonight. I knew she'd also want to freshen up after the flight. If nothing else, that part was a sure thing."

"That's okay." Sarah decided it wasn't necessary to point out to Lucy that she could have easily called over to Immaculate Home if she were serious about getting in touch with her, or that the press release she'd sent out with the Global Newswire listed her name, phone number, and e-mail address under the contact information. Instead, she decided to look on the bright side of things and take advantage of this opportunity to get to know Emory's friends. So this wasn't what she had planned for the evening, big deal, but she could still make the night into something special. And she would.

"Speaking of freshening up," Emory said uneasily, "I think I'll head upstairs and get changed. Will you be okay?"

"Of course."

Emory met her eyes apologetically and squeezed her hand once before heading further into the house and up the stairs.

"I laid out an outfit for you that I thought you'd like," Lucy called after her. "And there's a handsome someone up there who's dying to say hi, but hurry back." Emory shot a wary glance at Lucy as she ascended the stairs.

Lucy then turned to Sarah. "Come on, let me introduce you to some women you're bound to spend lots of time with in the future. Most of these girls Emory went to school with. We sort of hang out in a group, but don't let that intimidate you. Stick with me."

Sarah smiled at Lucy gratefully and followed her across the room. She really did like Lucy, despite her audacious tendencies when it came to Emory.

After preliminary introductions were made and a few niceties exchanged, the redhead in the group turned to Sarah. While she was overly pleasant, confusion was written all over her face. "So are you and Emory an item?"

Lucy laughed out loud. "Geez, Mia, you know how to get to the point."

"I'm sorry, was that bad? Sometimes I forget myself. It's just that Emory hasn't mentioned you. At all."

"But we haven't seen Emory much lately," the woman named Barrett, chimed in. "That's probably why."

Sarah nodded politely and addressed Mia. "We've been seeing each other for a couple of months now. I've been anxious to meet you all." That wasn't exactly true. Emory hadn't talked too much about her friends, a detail Sarah now found interesting.

Mia sipped from her glass and regarded her. "You have the slightest accent, am I wrong?"

A waiter whisked past with a tray full of white wine glasses. An actual waiter? Lucy snagged two and handed a glass to Sarah. "You may need it," she whispered.

She accepted the drink and turned to Mia. "No, you're not wrong. English is my second language, and sometimes, especially when I'm nervous, my accent peeks through."

"Where are you from originally?" the blonde, Christi Ann, asked. She seemed to be examining Sarah as if she were a bug under a microscope. Sarah found this somewhat unnerving and chose instead to focus on Barrett and the warmth of her smile. Within the small group, she definitely seemed the most easygoing. "I spent the first part of my childhood in Mexico, and then my family immigrated to California."

"How wonderful," Christi Ann answered a little too enthusiastically. "I love this dress. Is it a de la Renta?"

Sarah glanced down at her outfit. "No. I wish it were."

"Well, it's very flattering. Who designed it?" Mia lifted the fabric delicately.

"Uh, I don't know. I saw it at a department store in the mall."

"Oh, fabulous," Mia said brightly and exchanged glances with Christi Ann. Sarah felt her confidence flutter beneath her.

Barrett rolled her eyes at the exchange and that was something. Sarah was pretty sure she wasn't the type to get caught up in fashion. She wore dark jeans, boots, and a sleek black shirt. Sarah could tell Barrett was a lesbian, but she wasn't as sure about Mia or Christi Ann. She would ask Emory later. Emory, who was taking an awfully long time getting dressed. She glanced wistfully to the second level.

Upstairs, Emory surveyed her reflection in the mirror but wasn't really looking. She was annoyed. Annoyed the night with Sarah had been so abruptly derailed, annoyed that Lucy hadn't included Sarah in the party plans, and annoyed that she now had to go play nice with a house full of people she hadn't invited over. Walter pulled her from her mental rant, whining softly from atop her bed. When she'd first entered the room, he'd greeted her with the enthusiasm usually reserved for a prisoner returning from war. Emory knelt next to him and scratched his fur, happy to be in his company after her weeklong absence. Lucy had dressed him in a smart red bow tie that he seemed to completely enjoy. "You look so handsome, buddy." He licked her face in agreement. Emory was grateful for Walter's recent presence in her life and kissed his soft nose now to tell him so. "Here goes nothing," she whispered to him. "Wish me luck."

As Emory descended the stairs, the room broke into spontaneous applause, and Sarah happily joined in. Sarah looked on with pride, taking in Emory's graceful transformation into guest of honor. She'd swept her hair up into a simple twist and wore a royal blue cocktail dress that hugged her just so. Now *that* might be a de la Renta, she thought to herself, still not really knowing.

"She looks gorgeous," Mia said to their small group, "but then she always does."

Sarah turned back to Lucy, intent on asking what she could do to help with the party, but discovered she was gone. She scanned the room and located her easily at the bottom of the stairs standing next to Emory. With a spoon to her glass, Lucy dinged until she had the full attention of everyone in the room.

"I hope everyone has a glass," she stated, once a hush fell over the party, "because I plan to offer a toast to this beautiful woman next to me. You know her as Emory Owen. I know her as my savvy business partner and best friend. Thirty-three years ago, this firecracker entered the world, and it has never been the same since. She's amazing, smart, stubborn, funny, and confident. Unfortunately, in addition to all of those things, she's now old as well." The room erupted into laughter, and Emory turned to Lucy, looking appropriately offended. Finally, Lucy lifted her glass. "A toast to you, my friend, for your energy, strength, and the many ways you continue to inspire us all. We love you. Cheers." They clinked glasses as Sarah watched, smiling.

Christi Ann shook her head as she looked on. "Tell me again why those two broke up?" Sarah felt as if she'd been punched in the stomach. Out of the corner of her eye, she saw Barrett nudge Christi Ann subtly. "Sorry," Christi Ann said to Sarah. "I didn't mean that the way it sounded. Just a habit I need to break. They're ancient history, trust me."

"I do," Sarah said as politely as she could manage. "If you'll excuse me, I should go find Emory." But it had been hard to hear. She struggled with the fact that Emory had once been with someone like Lucy. Lucy of the sleek, straight brown hair. Lucy of the sexy legs that went on for days. Lucy of the rich and successful. It was a lot to compete with. Hell, she knew who she'd pick between the two of them. No contest.

With a shake of her head, she pushed the intrusive thoughts from her mind and focused on the task at hand. Unfortunately, finding Emory proved more difficult than she'd anticipated. There was an expansive receiving line of people blocking her path, all waiting to wish Emory a happy birthday. Rather than interrupt, she decided to wait it out. Taking a seat in one of the accent chairs across from the sectional, she made small talk with Emory's attorney and his wife while she waited.

When she found herself alone again just a short time later, Sarah couldn't help but notice how unaware these guests seemed to be about the mess they were making of Emory's home. Small appetizer plates had been discarded in a pile on the coffee table. One had overturned and dripped some sort of sauce onto the hardwood floor. Knowing Emory and her stringently ordered house, she decided to help matters rather than waiting for the caterers to get around to it. She gingerly stacked the small plates and carried them into the kitchen along with an empty champagne flute. At least she could make herself useful and help Lucy with the gathering she'd known nothing about.

Emory took in the state of things. Thirty minutes had passed since the toast, and she realized she was going to have to take drastic measures to get out of the endless receiving line. Who even did receiving lines anymore? Spotting Trevor next in line to speak with her, she seized the opportunity and whispered in his ear as they hugged. "You have to get me out of this thing."

He didn't miss a beat. "Ms. Owen, you're needed in the kitchen," he said in an overly loud voice. "And right away. Catering emergency." Emory feigned surprise and took Trevor's offered arm as he whisked her away. She smiled and said hello to her guests as she passed, all the while scanning the room for her wayward date. "I saw her head this way," Trevor whispered as he steered them behind the bar and into the kitchen.

Sure enough, there she was, dutifully stacking dishes. "What are you doing hiding out in here?" Emory said, though there was a smile on her face. She took Sarah's hand. "We can do those later, or someone can. Maybe Lucy. She owes me for this. Have you eaten?"

"Just a glass of wine," Sarah said and covered Emory's hand with her own. "It's hard chasing down those waiters. They're super fast." And then, "I met your friends."

"You did? Which ones?"

"Mia, Barrett, and Christi Ann. Lucy introduced us."

The thought made Emory a little queasy. She'd wanted to control the flow of that conversation, as she knew how Mia and Christi Ann could come off. Plus, she felt so far removed from them lately that she now wondered what had brought them together as friends in the first place. Our parents, she reminded herself, our parents had been friends. "They have their good and bad moments," she said neutrally.

"I thought they were nice."

"Really? Sometimes they can be…I don't know, hard to read." Judgmental bitches. That's what she wanted to say. Sometimes they could be judgmental bitches, and she wanted to keep Sarah as far away from them as possible. "I have an idea."

Sarah eyed her. "I'm listening."

"There's a tray of hors d'oeuvres over there with our name on it. Why don't we hit that up and have a nice little dinner in the laundry room, just the two of us, like we planned? Then afterward we can face the music and mingle with these people who have taken over my house."

"Me and my crazy appetite like this plan of yours. Are you sure we won't get in trouble? You know, for playing hooky from your party? You are the guest of honor."

"It's possible. This is a risky endeavor. Are you in?"

"I'll take my chances." Sarah moved lightning quick to the covered tray. Emory heard someone in the living room crank the stereo up another ten decibels. They were entering phase two of the party, which meant the more respectable types would head for the door, and the alcohol would flow more freely among the fun seekers. This was going to be a long night.

Alone in the laundry room, they dined on the floor facing each other, Emory enjoying their impromptu picnic.

Sarah grabbed for a napkin and raised a questioning eyebrow. "Why is it we eat on the floor so much when I visit?"

"Excellent question. Maybe it's just our thing."

She considered this. "I could be okay with that. It's kind of fun. No one else invites me to eat on their floor."

"I'm special then."

"I've often thought so." Sarah surveyed the plate of white bean and caper crostini, stuffed mushrooms, and jumbo shrimp cocktail. It was an eclectic dinner, but one she wouldn't soon forget. Tasty too.

"I hate that we were interrupted earlier," Emory said. Her eyes were dancing as she lightly dabbed a crumb from the corner of Sarah's mouth.

"Me too."

"I was thinking, maybe we can find our way back there later tonight."

"Well, in my experience, when it's someone's birthday, they get pretty much anything they want."

"Oh good, because I really, really want you." Emory looked into her eyes. "In case you haven't noticed, you make me happy." Sarah placed a gentle hand on her cheek as she listened. "And I haven't felt—"

"There you two are," Lucy announced. She sauntered into the laundry room with her hand on her hip. "I hate to break things up yet again, I feel like I'm always doing that, but the birthday girl is sorely missed. Come on, woman, you're in high demand out there. Step to it. You can make eyes at each other later, I promise."

Emory took Sarah's hand from where it rested on her cheek and squeezed it. "Guess our time is up. Join me?"

"Right behind you. I just want to freshen up a little first."

"Okay, you can use my room. Oh, and maybe bring Walter back with you? He's bound to be antsy up there all alone. He'll enjoy getting to meet everyone."

"Will do."

"I'll meet you on the front lines."

Sarah grinned and offered a mock salute.

The party was boisterous, Emory noticed upon her return, but nothing seemed to be broken or in danger, the main reason she didn't often give parties, so she decided to just let the night run its course. Someone had opened up the room to the outside, and many of the guests had taken up residence on the deck. A comfortable breeze moved through the living space, and everyone seemed to be enjoying themselves. She made a quick lap around the downstairs, saying a great many "hellos" and "thank you for comings," before settling in with Barrett, who was generally a good person to stick by.

Barrett looked at her apologetically. "I told Lucy you wouldn't be wild about a surprise party, but you seem to be handling it rather well."

"Thanks, Bar. You're right, it's not exactly my thing, but I am happy to see you. I miss hanging out, the talks we used to have."

"Me too. We should make time to get together more, though you seem to have more on your plate than usual. She's gorgeous, by the way, and incredibly sweet."

"She is." Emory beamed. "Among other things. I think you're really going to like her."

"Like who? The mystery woman?" Mia sidled up next to Emory with Christi Ann not far behind.

"She's not a mystery woman, Mia."

"Then why haven't you mentioned her before?"

"It didn't come up." Emory tossed away the comment as if it was the most casual thing in the world, but Mia didn't seem convinced.

On the second floor, Sarah took a few moments to run a brush through her hair and greet Walter properly. After her cheek had been thoroughly covered with kisses, she ushered him down the stairs to the party. His loyalty was fleeting, however, as he made a beeline for the outdoors, clearly looking for a good frolic by the water. Such a beach dog, she thought, amused at his never-ending enthusiasm.

She easily located Emory, engrossed in conversation with Mia and her set. She stood off to the side a moment and watched, proud of the confident manner in which Emory carried herself, complete with the dazzling smile that never failed to make Sarah's knees go weak.

She was lucky, she thought, very lucky to be with such an amazing, intelligent woman.

"So where exactly did you meet Sarah, if you don't mind my asking?"

"She's a client," Emory offered, refusing to give Mia too much information. Flashbacks of her sister's pretentious comments about Sarah raced through her mind in rapid succession. She wouldn't allow that kind of judgment at Sarah's expense to happen again, especially not from Mia.

"Well, that's not exactly true," Sarah said. She joined the group and handed Emory one of the glasses of wine she'd snagged on her way over. "You were my client first, remember? Don't forget that part." Sarah shot her a questioning look, clearly not understanding the omission.

"Really?" Christi Ann chimed in. "In what regard? As you can see, Emory never tells us anything anymore."

"With good reason," Emory answered icily, a plastic smile in place.

"Unfortunately, it was shortly after Emory's mother passed away," Sarah began. "I was hired to help prepare the house to be sold."

"She impressed me to no end and the rest is history. I'm keeping her. What about you, Barrett, I heard you were also seeing someone. How's that going?"

Sarah was again puzzled. She looked at Emory, who seemed incredibly eager to move on from the conversation, and it slowly began to make sense to her. Emory didn't want her friends to know that Sarah worked for a cleaning company.

She felt the blood drain from her face and she stared, lost, into the depths of her glass.

Before Barrett could answer, Christi Ann held up a hand. "Wait, so Sarah was your realtor?"

"No," Sarah answered, raising her head confidently. "I was her cleaning woman." She faced Emory fully.

Emory practically flinched at the words. "Organization mainly." She turned quickly to the group in explanation. "Sarah actually runs the reorganization branch of Immaculate Home. They do some amazing closet designs. It's revolutionary what she's accomplished in such a short time."

"But back then, I worked for you, cleaning and packing up that house." Sarah emphasized each word.

"Right. I know." The smile slowly faded from Emory's face and she nodded. "You're great at everything you do."

Silence followed and Emory felt all eyes boring into her, but her focus was elsewhere. It was clear that the way she handled the situation had upset Sarah, hurt her even, which was the opposite of what she had intended. Her instincts had failed her again.

Barrett graciously picked up the conversation and moved everyone into a teasing discussion about Emory's new dog that Sarah only half participated in. Eventually, she excused herself to call over to Carmen's and check on Grace.

Emory found Sarah on the deck a short time later and waited briefly for her to finish her phone call. As she clicked off, she turned to Emory. "I'm so sorry to have to do this, but Grace is allergic to cats, and I forgot to send her allergy medication that lets her be around them. I think it'd be best if I just picked her up from Carmen's and took her home."

"I understand. I'd go with you, but—"

Sarah looked around. "You have a house full of people."

"Right."

"It's okay."

Emory placed her hand on Sarah's forearm. "Can we talk before you go? About in there." She inclined her head in the direction of the party.

With the breeze from the beach lifting Sarah's hair gently, she looked breathtaking and a little sad. "Sure."

Because there were people nearby, Emory walked them a short distance away from the house to the water's edge. The sunset was all but gone, but lights from the deck allowed her to see Sarah's eyes. They seemed to be silently searching hers for some sort of answer.

"I'm sorry. About the conversation back there and how I handled it. You don't know these girls, but I do and I just didn't want them to rush to judgment. Mia's the type of woman who enjoys making other people feel small and I wasn't going to let her do that to you."

Sarah seemed to ruminate over the information. She looked skyward before settling her gaze back on Emory with purpose. "Can I let you in on a secret?"

Emory nodded.

"I don't think I care what people like Mia think of me anymore. Which is new, because I've more than cared my entire life. But I no longer feel like that kid in junior high, who just wanted to fit in, and would go to ridiculous lengths to do it. Because since you've come into my life, I feel like I've learned so much about myself. And for the first time ever, I fit."

Emory felt that wistful lump rise up in her throat because what Sarah was saying to her was wonderful and terrifying at the same time.

"So I guess what I'm saying is that I don't need you to take care of me. But it would be nice if you could be proud to have me at your side."

"I am proud, Sarah. You're the best person I know. Please don't doubt that."

Sarah showed a touch of a smile. "See? Then that's all I care about. And it's time for me to start being honest about exactly who I am. With your friends. With my family."

"Your family?"

"Uh-huh."

"I don't know what to say. That's wonderful."

Emory felt tears touch her eyes because she *was* so very proud of Sarah and the strength she saw taking shape within her. Proud and so much more. The well of emotion rushing through her after listening to Sarah was unique, foreign, and undeniable on every level.

Love.

And while the realization should make her want to pull Sarah into her arms and never let her go, instead it made her hesitate. It brought to the forefront everything she knew about herself and all the ways she'd fall short of what Sarah needed. So when she did finally open her mouth to speak, what she said was not at all a reflection of what she felt so firmly within her.

Because it couldn't be.

"It's getting late. I'll walk you out." She took Sarah's hand in hers and walked her to the front.

The night hadn't gone as planned. But Sarah, in her unwavering goodness, had rolled with each and every punch. It was yet another testament to her character. Back when she'd made decisions about her life, she'd never planned on a Sarah. Someone who would make her redefine her definition of just about everything. But here she was, standing in her driveway, looking back at Emory with sparkling hazel eyes. And then a dark reminder flared of the promise she'd made to herself not so very long ago.

Sarah touched her cheek. "I'll call you tomorrow, birthday girl."

Emory attempted a smile.

Sarah tilted her head to the side and studied her with concern. "You okay? I can see if my father's free to pick up Grace. I was just worried that she might—"

"I'm fine. Go take care of your daughter."

Sarah nodded and leaned in to kiss her good-bye. Emory wrapped her arms around Sarah's waist and kissed her back for all she was worth, memorizing the moment.

Late that night, long after all the partygoers had finally vacated her home, Emory tossed and turned, but sleep eluded her. Frustrated and looking for something to distract her overly active brain, she crawled out of bed and fumbled through her bedside table. She came across the small canvas book, the last journal. She settled in and let her mother's words take over.

Normally, Sarah loved a free afternoon. She could take hold of the opportunity to organize the chaos that life as a single mother brought with it. And she did, stacking art supplies, unloading the dishwasher, sorting through all the clothes Grace had recently outgrown—all while keeping one eye on her phone.

It'd been two days since Emory's birthday party and the four text messages and a voice mail she'd left for her had been answered with only one clipped reply.

"Busy week. Will call soon."

But Emory hadn't called. And something felt off.

She'd give her one more day before taking matters into her own hands. It was possible that things at the office had truly picked up, and if that was the case she wanted to show Emory she was capable of giving her space to get her job done. She wasn't a needy person, but she did feel she was owed at least a phone call in response to her messages.

But late the next day when she still hadn't heard anything from Emory, she arranged for her parents to keep Grace an extra hour after work.

The sun slanted low in the sky as Emory set out for a walk along the shoreline to clear her head. She'd come home earlier than usual from the office, as the ever doubling pile of work on her desk couldn't seem to hold her attention. There was too much on her mind. Once home, she'd swapped her business suit for a pair of cutoffs and a T-shirt. As she put on her shoes, Walter watched from a few feet away and panted hopefully as if his dream might actually come to fruition. "Come on, buddy," she said, inspiring vertical leaping and all sorts of celebratory whining.

It was a clear September evening on the beach, and Emory was relieved to find she had it mostly to herself. The setting sun caught the water's surface, and seagulls soared on the breeze overhead. Walter had tons of energy to burn and panted happily as they walked, but Emory couldn't identify. She'd been ineffective at work all week and had carefully avoided contact with Sarah, no matter how bad she felt about that.

She'd needed the time. Her life over the past few months had been nearly unrecognizable. She'd let herself get carried away into a place she had no business inhabiting. It had been selfish of her. Sarah deserved someone who was capable of giving everything of herself and then some, and Emory just wasn't equipped. Her mother's words had reminded her of that just the other night.

*"I was studying a photo of my father this afternoon and remarked how similar my brother looks to him now. Genetics is the most*

*intriguing thing. My own daughters are the perfect example. Vanessa
is an outgoing girl, the type who surrounds herself with the kind of
people who can take her places. She takes joy in life, sometimes at
the expense of others. In essence, she's her father's daughter to a tee.*

*Emory, on the other hand, is like me. She keeps people at a
distance and always has. While incredibly talented and articulate,
she's a hard person to know and always has been. She seems to have
discovered what I never did and has chosen a life on her own, thereby
leaving less damage in her wake. Sometimes, it's like looking in a
mirror."*

It had been hard to read.

And while her mother was certainly not the foremost authority
on her life, she had to hand it to her. Her points were valid. Emory
came from a long line of emotionally stunted women. Her mother
was distant and unavailable. Her sister was an irresponsible parent
who had raised a pair of morally bankrupt elitists. And while she had
opened herself up more to Sarah and Grace than anyone else in her
life, what would happen in the long term? What hope did she really
have? Who was she destined to become? She'd crashed and burned
after two years with Lucy. She couldn't take Sarah down that road.

She wouldn't.

She started for home and didn't argue when Walter ran on ahead.
When she arrived, she found him flopped gleefully on the deck in
front of Sarah, his fur sandy and wet from the run. Sarah stroked his
blatantly exposed stomach with affectionate vigor, before lifting her
eyes to Emory. "I thought I might find you out here. Car was in the
driveway, but no answer." She was smiling and Emory tried to smile
back.

She lifted a shoulder and let it drop. "You found me."

Sarah studied her as she continued to pet Walter. "You've pulled
quite a disappearing act lately. New hobby?" Sarah was attempting to
be lighthearted, but Emory could sense her unease.

She sat on the steps next to her. "I've been busy. It's been crazy
at the office."

"And yet..." Sarah checked her watch. "It's five twenty and
you're already home and changed." There was no hint of accusation
in her voice, just a quiet observation. They stared out at the tide as the

palpable silence grew and grew. Finally, "What's up, Em? Don't you think it's time you told me? Communicated in some way?"

She nodded, knowing it was. "I can't do this anymore, Sarah. I knew going in that it would be too difficult to combine our lives and it is." It was a lie. Or at the very least, an oversimplification of the facts.

Sarah didn't say anything. And then finally, "So that's it? Just like that, huh?" She nodded, seeming to let the words settle.

Emory couldn't look at her. If she did, she would lose her resolve. "My lifestyle is fast-paced, unpredictable, and that's what I need it to be. And that doesn't work—"

"With an eight-year-old?"

She hated the way it sounded and swallowed hard. "Yeah. I can't be a parent, Sarah. I'm not the kind of person who does well tied down."

Sarah shook her head. "Emory, this isn't you."

"But it is. That's what I'm finally trying to explain. I warned you from the beginning this wouldn't work between us. We burned hard and bright these past couple of months, but that can only last so long." She forgot herself then, and allowed her eyes to settle on Sarah's. A mistake. The clarity of emotion looking back at her was almost enough to make her take it all back. Almost. Her voice, full of apology, began to tremble as she continued because it was the hardest thing she'd ever had to do. "I care about you, Sarah. I just can't see you anymore. Please explain to Grace."

"Don't do this."

Emory stood and took a few steps off the deck, hoping the distance would help. "Please try to understand. Our lives don't fit together the way they should." Because if she told her the truth, if she had told Sarah she loved her but would be a horrible mother, Sarah would disagree. Want her to try.

"Em, look at me." She did, but it was hard because Sarah's eyes were brimming. "Finding you has been like a dream come true for me in more ways than one. Before I met you, I had no idea I was capable of feeling what you make me feel. So I guess that makes you my impossible fantasy, Emory. But I need you to want us too."

"I just can't," Emory whispered.

"Then you've broken my heart." With that, she turned to go, and in a moment of panic for what she was giving up, Emory felt herself waver.

"Sarah, wait." But she didn't. She kept walking. "Wait. Where are you going?"

She turned back briefly. "I'm walking away. You should recognize what that looks like." Those hazel eyes that had once smiled so magically were now guarded, closed to her, and the understanding slashed through her like a razor blade.

Emory stood alone, staring blankly at her cold, sterile house with new eyes. Finally, she slid down onto the steps where she sat alone and numb for several hours.

It wasn't until the next morning that she found the two neatly wrapped green and white striped birthday presents that were left for her on her front porch.

# Chapter Fifteen

A ll right, that's it. It's been six weeks and it's time for you to talk." Carmen broke the silence as they sat on the bench at the small playground across from Sabro's. "You asked for time to process, and I've given you that and then some. But enough is enough. Sarah, you've been a walking zombie for well over a month now. Did she cheat on you? Is she a drug addict? Did she rob a convenience store? What?" She studied Sarah's face like a super sleuth of all things relationship. "She *did* cheat on you, didn't she? If I ever run into her, I swear I'll break—"

"She didn't cheat on me, Carmen." Sarah placed a calming hand on her knee. She didn't want to talk about Emory because when she did, it was a hard place to come back from. "Grace, not so high," she called. Grace was clearly enjoying herself on the swings with Carmen's boys. "She's such a little daredevil lately. It's like she's testing me."

Carmen looked at her hard. "Don't you dare try to divert my attention. I'm not five. It took me forever to even get you out here and in the realm of semi-social, so start talking."

It was true. Sarah had pretty much gone off the grid, needed to. Driving home from Emory's the day of the breakup without turning back was one of the hardest things she'd ever done. She'd tried a million times to rationalize the series of events. Going in, she knew something was wrong. And she'd known all along that Emory didn't trust herself in the relationship, but she'd hoped over time she'd find the same confidence Sarah had begun to find.

But she had to look out for more than just herself.

There was Grace to consider, and she wasn't going to talk Emory into wanting to be a part of her life. Grace deserved more. And while deep inside, Sarah knew Emory's rejection stemmed from fear, she couldn't put her child in the middle.

She spent the first two weeks after the breakup in the land of victimhood, feeling sorry for herself and needing to be alone. She went to work each day and came straight home, really only spending time with Grace. She'd wanted to call Emory a number of times, but she resisted as a method of self-preservation. She knew if she heard Emory's voice, she'd be back to square one and that couldn't happen. Thank God for Grace. Even though it felt like her world had been flipped on its end, as long as she and Grace had each other, they would be okay. They had spent a lot of time cuddled up on the couch watching movies, but it wasn't long before Grace started questioning Emory's whereabouts and why she wasn't watching the movies with them any longer. Eventually, she had to level with her.

"Monster, I don't think Emory's going to be spending so much time with us anymore."

Grace frowned. "Why not? I miss her. She was going to teach me about color theory next."

Sarah tried to explain delicately. "I'm sure she wanted to, Grace. It's just that some things have changed between us, she and I."

"You're not dating anymore?"

Sarah decided honesty was probably the best way to go. "Not anymore, no."

Grace looked up at her, clearly crestfallen. "But I really liked Emory."

Hearing those words was like pressing on a bruise, and she steadied herself from the pain. "I did too, Grace, but it didn't work out for us."

Grace considered this before coming to a very resolute conclusion. "Don't worry, Mama. You two will make up, like Mindy and me. Probably soon." She seemed so very hopeful that Sarah didn't have the heart to correct her.

It was in week three that the hardcore reality hit her. Not knowing what else to do, she threw herself into her work full force, anything to keep her mind busy. The article in the *Union-Trib* certainly did a number on her client list. She'd had to hire her own receptionist just to keep up with her side of Immaculate Home and the huge volume of calls that were now tumbling in.

By week four, the strange, numb, workaholic version of herself started to slide away, and underneath, she found that she still very much missed Emory. And not just Emory her girlfriend, she missed Emory the person. She'd come to be a lot of things to Sarah over the months they'd spent together. Her friend, her business advisor, her partner in crime, and then of course, her lover. God, how she missed those intimate moments with Emory. The smooth, warm perfection of her mouth and the scorching feel of her skin against Sarah's. But there was still more. They'd laughed so much together. How was she going to make it through the rest of her days without that smile, those crazy dimples? For all her seriousness, when Emory smiled, it was like the sun coming out from behind the clouds, and Sarah could think of nothing else that compared.

And here she sat in week five, trying to get herself back on track a little at a time, and there was now a glimmer of hope that all would eventually be okay. Of course nothing had the same shine to it, but she was getting by. She could see that the life ahead of her would be clean and smooth, not exactly the place she longed to be, but not horrible either.

It felt good to be out with Carmen, and deciding there was no time like the present, Sarah turned to her and sighed, laying out the series of events that led up to the moment they now inhabited. Knowing that Carmen would have a million questions, she did her best to spare no detail. Once everything was out on the table, she turned to her expectantly and waited.

Carmen looked thoughtful, maybe even a little confused. "And what did you say?"

Sarah shrugged. "There wasn't a lot to say at that point. She made her feelings clear. She didn't see a future."

"And so you—"

"Walked away. Cried a lot. And here we sit."

"Yeah, but is it possible that something freaked her out and she's scared?"

Sarah took a deep breath. "Maybe. But that's not the point. In the end, she has to want to be with us. Grace shouldn't be a liability to anyone."

Carmen nodded, mulling this over. "I'm sure you're doing the right thing, but there must be a part of you that wants to know what changed her mind. Michael, if you don't stop hitting your brother with that stick, you are going to lose all bike riding privileges for fifteen days." Michael, wide-eyed, obliged and dropped the stick mid wallop, and instead picked up a handful of dirt and dumped it over his brother's head. "That's better," Carmen muttered to herself.

"Do you really think so?"

"Well, I'm going to have to give him a bath now, but—"

"No, about letting her walk away. Do you really think I'm doing the right thing?"

"Quite honestly, no. I was just trying to be nice. I miss the spark I saw in your eyes after Emory hit the scene. It was like this breath of fresh air to see you so happy all the time. I understand why you're upset, I do, but in the scheme of life, sometimes you have to fight where love is concerned. God knows Roman isn't perfect, and some of the things he does make me want to shake him violently, but I love him. Do you love her, Sarah?"

"That's not what we're talking about here. What's love got to do with it?"

"A lot, Tina Turner, it has a lot to do with it. Everything, in fact. Love doesn't come in a nice neat little package. It's rough and it's messy and there are always going to be issues. But if it's real, you don't give up."

"Can we not do this? Emory is a part of my past, and I have to do what I can to focus on the future."

Carmen sighed and stood up. "I love you and I'm here for you, but sometimes you frustrate the hell out of me. I just want to see you happy."

"Happy seems a bit lofty at the moment. I think I'll settle for just getting by."

Carmen looked at her squarely. "Make sure you're doing the right thing."

"I am," Sarah murmured. "I am."

Emory stepped back from the large canvas and studied the blend of blues. The texture wasn't quite right, but she knew how to resolve the problem. She reached for a brush a tad thicker in diameter and set to work emphasizing the rounded edge of the saxophone key until the shape filled in just as she saw it in her head.

She'd been painting for three hours, and her neck was starting to tug. Arguably, this was edgier work than she'd ever attempted before, but she acted with the kind of abandon germane to someone with very little to lose, and that's exactly how she felt.

Her phone had been vibrating incessantly from the nearby stool it rested on throughout the day, but she'd paid little attention. It beckoned her once again, and she decided to finally take her sister's fifteenth thousandth call or it was possible she would never go away. "Hi, Vanessa."

"Well, it's about damn time. Do you know I've been trying to get you to answer this phone for a week now? Have you gotten my messages?"

"I've gotten them. I've just had other things on my plate."

"Like what? We're family. I called your office and they said you were indisposed. When I pestered them further, they gave me Lucy who told me you'd taken a leave of absence from the company. Is this true?"

"It's true." Emory sipped from her cup of coffee. "I'm in Napa, taking a little time for myself. Surely that's something you would understand."

"It's just not like you, Emory, you're a workaholic. Is this about Mother?" Emory thought she detected a hint of compassion, a rare commodity where Vanessa was concerned.

"Nope. Just about me."

"What are you doing up there? Are you with someone?" she practically whispered. "I forget her name. Susan, or is it someone new by now?"

"I'm by myself," Emory bit out. Which was precisely how she wanted it. She'd been in Napa, more specifically Calistoga, for several weeks now. The slower pace was exactly what she needed to gain some perspective and lick her self-inflicted wounds. She spent her days painting and reading books, either at the small house she'd rented or on the property of some of her favorite wineries. She kept mostly to herself, but enjoyed the anonymity the small tourist town offered.

The nights were admittedly more difficult. It was in the later hours that her thoughts drifted to Sarah and Grace and the future she'd grown to hope for. It had been idealistic of her, she knew, and in the end, where had it left her? In the midst of a—what exactly was this? A mid-life crisis? A re-examination of her place in this world? Who the hell knew?

"Why don't I come out and spend some time with you?" Vanessa offered as if talking to a not so intelligent child.

"I'd rather drive a dagger into my skull." *Whoops. Too honest?*

"Excuse me?" Vanessa sputtered. Her enthusiasm deflated like a popped balloon.

"Just a joke." A lie. "But I don't know how much longer I'm going to be here, plus you have the girls. I'd hate to take you from them. Stay right where you are. All the way in Colorado."

"You're acting strange."

Emory had to agree. All of a sudden, she was quite comfortable saying anything and everything on her mind, and that had the makings of a perfect storm. "Hey, Vanessa, someone's at the door. Better run. Door people hate waiting." She ended the call just in time. Another minute and she might not have been so nice.

She looked to Walter who sat dutifully at her feet. "That did not go well," she said. "I think it got five degrees colder in here when she called. What do you think?" His tail thumped wildly in support.

She carried the brushes she'd been working with over to the small sink in the kitchen and set about cleaning them thoroughly. She'd gotten paint all over her cutoff overalls, but it wasn't like she minded. It had been a productive session.

The brushes had been her birthday gift from Grace, and she handled them with the care she would a newborn child. She knew from the brand name that they had been fairly expensive, and the gesture was not lost on her. There had been a small note attached to the wrapped package, and despite her heart's protests, her mind thought it a good idea to play the words back in her head several times a day as some form of sick torture. "Happy Birthday, Emory. I hope your dreams come true. Maybe one day, you'll want to use these again. Love, Grace." Along with them had come a canvas from Sarah, another expensive purchase.

She thought a lot about Sarah and the hole she'd left and wasn't sure how to get her old life back on track, hence her sabbatical. She needed new surroundings, a different routine, and some space from the people she knew if she was ever going to allow herself to heal. However, she couldn't deny that the existence of Sarah and Grace in her life had kindled something within her, a renewed outlook on what her life could potentially be. And even if she couldn't have them, she refused to discount what they had done for her soul.

Since she'd been in Calistoga, she'd fallen down the rabbit hole and rediscovered her love of painting, and it was not lost on her that this never would have happened had she not met Sarah. There was something that felt so very right about picking up a brush again, almost like coming home. Emory lost herself in her creations for hours at a time, shocked when she glanced up at the clock.

Her work, now that she was older, seemed heavier, soulful. She thought back to her first night in town and the moment she'd set to painting for the first time in years. The result of that night's effort sat unassumingly against the wall in her bedroom. She'd stared at it, transfixed, for hours the following day with virtually no memory of painting it. It was like her hands had taken over, needing desperately to re-create the face that had the ability to make her feel so much.

Having had time to think, she'd resolved herself to the fact that all had worked out how it was supposed to. Sarah was from a place of warmth and was incredibly likable, representative of all things good. Her family was tight-knit and loving. Emory had been out of her depth.

But no more.

If nothing else, she could at least learn from Sarah. Emory vowed to herself that she would continue to grow and explore who she was and had the potential to be. The first step had been to take a step back from Global Newswire and gather her bearings. She'd lost perspective, she understood that now, and her life was becoming the Owen cliché. Fortunately, Lucy had been more than understanding and even applauded her decision when they'd met about it over coffee.

"I think this is a good move. This place can run without you for a few months. And I promise I won't run the company to wrack and ruin. Everything will be waiting for you when you return."

Emory smiled at her and set down her mug. "Thanks, Luce. I have nothing but faith in your ability to handle everything."

Lucy reached across the small table that separated them and covered Emory's hand with her own. "You can still call her, Em. This doesn't have to be the end."

She pulled her hand back. "Even if I wanted to, you didn't see the look in her eyes when she walked off. I'd rather she shot me than looked at me that way. Plus, my mind's made up, Lucy, and it's up to me to figure out what to do with myself now."

Lucy studied her. "Things are different, aren't they? You're different now."

Emory nodded, knowing that important changes had and would continue to take place in her life. "The last few months—Mother dying so suddenly, meeting Sarah and Grace, growing to love them and then losing them both too—these months have given me new perspective. Before Sarah, I wasn't living, Lucy, not the way I should have been. I need to do that now. It may have to be on my own, but I have to find a way to do more than just stay ahead at the office. Life is too short."

"Now this is the kind of thing I've been dying to hear you say for years now." Lucy came around the table and folded her into a tight hug. "I'm proud of you, Em, and grateful to Sarah for her role in this."

Emory finished cleaning the brushes, stored her paints away for a future session, and took a long, hot bath. The water felt amazing against her already sore muscles and she took her time, allowing the unwinding process to have its full effect. She would never have allowed herself so much down time just four short weeks ago. Her days and nights had been scheduled to the minute, and even if she did have an evening at home, it was with a stack of work in hand.

She snuggled into bed for the night, Walter curled up at her feet, her always-loyal companion. She reached down and stroked his thick fur, earning an appreciative sigh.

After switching off the small lamp by her bed, Emory took a deep breath and made a cognitive decision to close off her mind. Beautiful hazel eyes had a tendency of creeping their way into her subconscious, and once that happened, sleep was a lost cause.

Tomorrow is a new day, she reminded herself, and she would find a way to somehow make it a good one.

❖

November was definitely no October, Sarah decided. Not even close. The golden, glorious blue sky of October had been replaced by November's bleak, daylight savings-induced darkness. The tree branches were bare and skeletal against the depressing pale sky. The temperatures had dropped considerably and she never did purchase herself that new jacket. Sarah hated November. It couldn't win as far as she was concerned.

Halloween came and went—Grace had gone as Vincent Van Gogh, sans the ear. They'd attended her fourth grade Halloween parade and then gone trick-or-treating with Carmen and her boys. She'd spent the following Sunday, as always, at her parents' house screaming her lungs out for the Chargers and avoiding any and all questions about her love life.

As she walked Grace to the bus stop that morning, Sarah listened intently as she rattled off the details of the papier-mâché turkey they'd be making in art class later that day. This was maybe the fifth time in twenty-four hours Grace had explained the process, but Sarah made sure to smile and nod accordingly.

"Do you think there's a way to make the turkey actually gobble?" Grace asked. Her excitement was insatiable. "Maybe a speaker inside its body would work."

"Slow down, mija. I think you might be dreaming a bit big. One step at a time."

"Okay. We can talk about the speaker later."

Sarah shook her head in amazement. The kid was tenacious. They'd gone shopping at the hobby store the night before for some extra supplies. Grace was so incredibly anxious to get to work on her turkey, already affectionately named Leonard, that she scampered in short spurts ahead of Sarah on the sidewalk and then meandered her way back to add in extra needed details on her planned masterpiece.

"Probably, I'll make his feathers a mixture of different colors, but I want them to be as realistic as possible. Our classroom computer has Google, so I'll see if Mrs. Henry will let me print out some photos for accuracy." Grace walked backward facing her.

Sarah reached out and smoothed Grace's hair. "Sounds like a good plan."

"Do you think he would make a good centerpiece for our table when I'm done? We don't have any Thanksgiving decorations up, and our place needs some spirit."

"I think that could be arranged. Now give me a kiss. Your bus is pulling up."

Grace obliged, planting a quick kiss on Sarah's cheek and heading off. Feeling the buzz of her phone in her pocket, Sarah glanced down to read the text message from her assistant informing her that she now had a ten a.m. consultation with a prospective client. *Damn it.* It was going to be a tight morning, but she hated to turn away good business. It was Grace's voice that pulled her from her thoughts.

"Mom," she yelled, sticking her head out of the door to the school bus. "Have a great day!" Sarah's heart swelled and just as she opened her mouth to call back to Grace, she watched her body go limp and crumple like a ragdoll, falling from the top step of the school bus onto the pavement below with a horrifying thud. The action of the world seemed to slow down around her as she looked on in shock. Sarah reached out helplessly, a silent scream of horror bringing her stumbling forward onto her knees. Grace wasn't moving; she could see that much from her vantage point. There appeared to be a small pool of blood forming beneath her head. *Oh God, no.* In the midst of Grace's stillness, pandemonium broke out all around her. Children on the bus were calling out, another parent at the bus stop rushed to Grace's side, and the bus driver, dialing his phone, descended the stairs rapidly. In the midst of it all, Grace still had not moved.

All sound disappeared then and Sarah could hear only an intense roaring in her ears. She needed to get to Grace badly, but her body was not cooperating.

She couldn't move.

Grass. There was the cool, damp feel of grass beneath her cheek and that was okay, she thought, as the world faded to black, because at least now she wouldn't have to watch her child taken from her. She wouldn't have to watch Grace die.

## Chapter Sixteen

By the time Sarah came to, Grace had been transported to the hospital by ambulance. The other parent had ridden with Sarah in a police car, though her memory of the ride was almost entirely nonexistent. Except for the siren. She could still hear that shrill, horrible siren.

Once she arrived at the hospital, Sarah was placed in a small exam room, and though the hospital staff assured her repeatedly that Grace was awake, she couldn't seem to stop calling out her name in a voice so wracked with fear that she no longer recognized it as her own. She was asked a lot of questions, that part she remembered, about her name, address, and what year it was. All she could think about, however, was Grace's lifeless body as she'd last seen it on the cement below the school bus. The other mother, Trish somebody, stood at her shoulder, looking through Sarah's cell phone for someone to contact.

"I'm going to call your mother," Trish said. She pointed to the contact scroll in the phone. "Is that okay? Should I call your mother?"

Sarah nodded numbly. "Where's Grace?" she asked the doctor who was shining a small light into her eye. Her voice sounded hoarse from screaming, and she noticed that her hands were still trembling.

"Another doctor is in charge of your daughter's case, Ms. Matamoros. She's just a few doors down, and I promise they're taking good care of her. Now, can you tell me where you are?"

"The emergency room. Please let me see my daughter."

"Soon. We have to make sure you're all right first. You took a bit of a fall yourself."

"I'm fine," Sarah insisted harshly. She stood and moved deliberately into the hallway. "I need to see my daughter. *Now.*"

Seeming to finally understand her urgency, the doctor led her down the short hallway to a nearby hospital room. There were several people bustling about the bed, but there Grace was, alive, awake, and looking more than a little afraid.

Sarah forced a smile and kept her voice low so as not to disturb the medical staff. "Hi, sweetheart. Everything's okay. Don't worry. How are you feeling?" Grace looked pale and not so great. She could see that there were traces of blood still matted in her hair.

Grace blinked up at her, tears in her eyes. "My head hurts. What happened? I don't feel well."

"You fell down and bumped your head, baby. The doctors need to make sure you're okay."

A petite brunette referencing something on a clipboard stepped forward. "Ms. Matamoros, I'm Dr. Riggs. May we speak outside?"

Sarah nodded and kissed Grace's forehead. "I'll be back in just a minute. You rest. Everything is going to be okay."

Once they were in the hallway, Dr. Riggs didn't waste any time. "The good news is that we got Grace here in very good time following her accident, and with head trauma, every second counts. At this point, it's encouraging that she's awake and conversing with us. However, she did sustain a significant blow and she seems a little bit fuzzy, disoriented on-and-off. It's highly likely that she's suffering from a concussion, and I'd like to run an immediate CT just to rule out any complications. This is the kind of injury we have to take very seriously."

Sarah blinked. "Of course. Can I go with her?" Sarah's heart raced as a myriad of terrifying scenarios played themselves out in her head.

"Certainly."

❖

It had been over an hour since the CT, and Sarah paced the hospital room anxiously, waiting for word. Grace continued to move in and out of lucidity and had recently grown more and more quiet. She's probably just exhausted from the ordeal, Sarah reasoned, anything to keep herself from imagining something worse.

Now it felt like a waiting game.

Her mother and father had arrived and they all waited, along with Carmen, in the common waiting room. "Why haven't they come back, Mama?" Sarah whispered.

"They're reading the tests, mija. She's going to be just fine. I know it." But when Dr. Riggs emerged fifteen minutes later, the words she imparted to Sarah were not at all reassuring.

She'd sat down with Sarah in the plastic chairs just outside the nurse's station. "So here's what we know. The CT showed significant signs of elevated intracranial pressure, which is a swelling of Grace's brain due to the fall. I have to be frank, Ms. Matamoros, this is a big cause for concern and something we have to closely monitor. It's important that we do everything we can to stop the swelling and alleviate the pressure."

"What does that mean?" Her hands were shaking in her lap, so she clenched them into fists.

"The next twenty-four hours will be critical." Sarah felt her breath catch as the blood drained from her face. The doctor took her hand. "What that means is that we need to give Grace's brain a chance to rest so it can heal, and we need to put her into a deep sleep so that can happen. She'll be unconscious for the next day or so, but if we can get the swelling down in the next twenty-four hours, her chance of a full recovery is high."

Sarah couldn't think clearly. This wasn't part of the plan. When she spoke, her voice was barely a whisper. "And if the swelling doesn't go down? What then?"

"That's harder." The doctor squeezed her hand. "If the pressure doesn't go down, or worse, it goes up, Grace could face the effects of brain damage or—"

"She could die?"

"She could. It's a worst-case scenario, but I need to be honest with you. Let's just focus on these next twenty-four hours and getting her well."

❖

Sarah sat mutely in the waiting room. Her mind kept replaying the sequence of events on some unstoppable loop. Her memory of the accident alternated between horrifyingly vivid and frustratingly blank. The small window across the room that offered a peak at the real world, the world Sarah could hardly believe still existed, showed signs of dusk falling. The clock couldn't turn quickly enough.

Her brothers checked in hourly, but at her insistence stayed home with their families awaiting word. Carmen offered her encouragement, clearly doing everything a best friend should do, but Sarah couldn't find it within herself to say much back. Because really there was nothing to say. Instead, she stared at the sterile double doors that led to Grace.

Visiting hours in the intensive care unit were monitored strictly, and Sarah was allowed inside Grace's hospital room for twenty minutes each hour. She sat with Grace, who was covered with blankets and tubes, and looking so incredibly small that it about broke her heart in half.

"You're going to be okay, baby," she'd whispered, "I'm right here with you. I'm here, Graciela," as she held her lifeless hand.

In the hallway, the doctors murmured in somber tones to one another, but inside, Sarah stroked Grace's cheek softly, telling her one of her favorite stories, the tortoise and the hare. In the deep recesses of her mind, Sarah recognized with shocking horror, that her beautiful, sweet, witty child might never return to who she once was or…worse. God, she couldn't acknowledge worse, but it hung over her in this endless nightmare.

"Sarah, you need to eat something," Carmen prodded her once she returned to the hellish waiting room. "You've been here all day. Did you even eat breakfast this morning before…?"

Sarah cut her eyes to Carmen and shook her head. "It doesn't matter. Don't worry about me. I'm fine. I'm not in a hospital bed."

"Still, I think—"

"I said I'm fine."

Carmen nodded resolutely.

Time crawled by.

Coffee cups came and went.

The fluorescent lighting in the grim waiting room spared no detail of her family's fear-stricken faces. Her mother thumbed through a battered magazine from the rickety coffee table. Carmen scanned her phone. All the while Sarah watched the hours tick by with excruciating delay.

Finally, her father stood. "Why don't I go pick up dinner for everyone?"

"Nothing for me," Sarah said. "You guys go ahead." Her eyes settled resolutely back on the set of double doors.

Carmen joined him. "I should update your brothers. Can I use your phone, Sarah? My battery is all but gone."

Sarah nodded and handed her the phone. Carmen exited the waiting room with her father, leaving Sarah alone with her mother. She took advantage of the private moment. "Mama, why did this happen? She doesn't deserve this."

"Of course she doesn't," her mother said. "You don't either. No one does. God doesn't work that way. But here we are and we have to be strong for that little fighter in there, do you understand me? She needs you now."

"I'm trying, Mama, but I feel like I'm about to cave in. I can't seem to find the strength. I feel like crying, but I can't do that either. I don't think I can handle this on my own. I need help, but I don't know where to get it."

Her mother scooted in closer and wrapped her arm tightly around Sarah and spoke to her quietly. "This may surprise you, but do you know what helps me in dark times? Prayer. I haven't raised you in the church because that's not how I was raised, but in difficult moments, I turn to a higher power. There's a chapel down the hall. Do you want me to go with you?"

"No. If I do decide to go, I think it's something I need to do on my own."

By midnight, there was no real change in Grace's condition, but at least the swelling hadn't increased. She found herself in a difficult place and thought hard on it. Her mother was right. She wasn't a very religious person. She'd only been to church a handful of times in her life, mostly on Christmas, and even then it was kind of a formality. But she believed in God. She did.

The hospital chapel was surprisingly small with only four pews and a center aisle leading up to a modest altar. Above the altar hung a large stained-glass window depicting two white doves in flight. Sarah took in the image before her, struck by its beauty. There was something about the quiet of the room that she found comforting.

She glanced around, feeling unsure and not knowing exactly how to proceed. Finally, she decided to do what felt natural. She knelt before the altar, bowed her head, and took a deep breath. *Here goes nothing.* "So I know I haven't been in touch in a while, and I'm so sorry about that. I don't know how else to say this, but I really need you today and so does my daughter, Grace." She felt her voice catch and choked back emotion. "She's only eight years old and not doing so well. Please help her through this. I don't think I'd survive if anything were to happen to her. She's my life. And lastly, God, I ask you to send me the strength I need to get through this and to give my daughter the support she needs right now. Please send me the strength and I will receive it. Amen."

Sarah raised her eyes and stared silently at the white doves for another few moments when a feeling of calm slowly and inexplicably crept over her. She couldn't identify precisely its source, but she could detect a noticeable change in her resolve. She stood slowly and turned. The figure standing at the entrance to the chapel was dimly lit but unmistakable. Sarah didn't hesitate. She moved to Emory and fell into her arms as a burst of tears sprang from somewhere deep within her. Emory held her for several long moments as she cried.

"I would have been here sooner, but I had a long drive. I came as soon as I heard."

"How did you—"

"Carmen called me from your phone a few hours ago. Grace is going to come through. Know that."

Sarah nodded, the tears falling freely now, as she clung to Emory and buried her face in her neck. Emory was here and she would help her through this. Emory would be her strength. No matter what had transpired between them, that much she knew.

They walked slowly back to the intensive care, Sarah filling Emory in on all that had happened. Emory greeted her parents and accepted a hug from Carmen. She sat next to Sarah and held her hand, not saying much of anything, seeming to know that was exactly what Sarah needed.

❖

It was four a.m. and time for another visiting session. Thus far, Emory had stayed back in the waiting area with Carmen while Sarah and her parents cycled in and out sitting with Grace. She would never want to intrude upon the family's space in any way, but when Sarah stood and held out her hand to Emory, she hesitated, glancing around the room, her throat tight. "Are you sure? I don't want to take any time away from anyone."

"She'd want you here," Sarah said simply.

Emory nodded and allowed herself to be led through the doors and down the hall. The sounds of machines hit her first. The steady sighs and beeps of the various devices hooked up to Grace took her back to the last time she'd been at the hospital, when her mother had passed. She measured her emotional response, determined not to upset Sarah in any way and willed herself to hold it together.

Pushing past that initial hesitation, she entered the room behind Sarah, who moved to the far side of the bed and looked back at her encouragingly. "You can sit with her if you like."

Emory nodded, sitting in the small chair next to Grace and taking her hand in hers. It was so much smaller in comparison.

There was so much she wanted to say to Grace, and while it felt strange to talk to her this way, she knew this wasn't the time to hold back. "Hey there, kiddo, I've missed you. Looks like you've taken creativity to new heights finding ways to get out of school." She glanced up nervously at Sarah before refocusing her efforts. "Listen, I wanted to tell you something. I've been using those brushes you gave me…a lot actually…and I think you'd really like some of the painting I've done. Surprisingly, it's not half bad. But you know what the interesting thing is, Grace? If I hadn't met you, I don't think I ever would have painted again, one of the things I love most in this world. That makes you very, very special to me. So this is what I need from you. Are you listening?" She moved closer so that she was very close to Grace's ear. "I need you to rest up and get lots better so that I can show you my work, the work that you made happen. Maybe we can even paint together sometime if your mom says it's okay. Sound good?" Emory looked up just in time to see Sarah who was staring at her so intently, with such emotion, that she almost couldn't breathe.

"She's missed you too," Sarah whispered. "You should know that."

Emory nodded, fighting against the lump in the back of her throat. She'd allowed herself to believe that Sarah and Grace had easily returned to their life without her, but sitting here now and looking into Sarah's eyes, she knew that wasn't true. She had been important to them, and even though that hadn't felt like enough a short time ago, it was everything now. "I'll let you guys have some time." She leaned down and kissed Grace's cheek ever so gently and gave Sarah's hand a supportive squeeze across the bed.

Sunlight dipped its glow through the window of the intensive care waiting room three hours later. Sarah sat next to Emory, who still held her hand loosely. They hadn't spoken many words to each other, but Sarah knew it was Emory's presence alone that kept her from climbing the walls of the hospital in utter insanity.

It was then that Dr. Riggs arrived in the waiting room, bringing everyone to full attention in anticipation of any sort of news. Sarah stood and moved to the doctor, who wasted no time informing them of what she knew.

"The news is good. The swelling is down, and all is looking very encouraging. That is one very lucky girl you have in there."

"She's going to be okay?" Sarah's heart hammered away in her chest.

"We'll want to keep her here for a couple of days to make sure there are no complications, but if we stay the course, I anticipate a full recovery. Dr. Thorpe will want to take this opportunity to implant a pacemaker to prevent any further fallout from her heart block, but I'll let him discuss that with you in more detail. Our plan is to keep her sedated until this evening just to be cautious. In the meantime, take advantage of this time. Go home and get a nap and a change of clothes. You've been awake for close to two days straight, and pretty soon you're not going to be much good to anyone. You'll want to be refreshed when she wakes up tonight."

Sarah couldn't imagine leaving Grace alone at the hospital. She shook her head to protest, but her mother placed a gentle hand on her arm. "Listen to the doctor, mija. I'll stay with her and call with any change. We can take turns. Do you want your father to drive you?"

Sarah turned to Emory, questioning.

Emory nodded once. "I'll take her."

❖

The apartment felt different to Sarah once they were inside, hollow and lonely somehow without Grace. Not really her own. Emory was in the kitchen now, she registered, but she hadn't been able to move past the entryway. She just stood there, not knowing what to do with herself.

"Sarah?"

"Hmm?" She glanced absently at Emory.

"Why don't you go grab a quick shower and I'll make you something to eat?"

"I don't think I can—"

Emory shook her head, but her voice was gentle. "Not up for discussion."

Sarah nodded wordlessly, grateful for the direction.

She practically groaned with relief just minutes later when the healing hot water hit her body. She lathered her hair and closed her eyes, allowing the water's soft caress to work its magic. They'd all been right. She wouldn't have made it much longer without some sort of reinforcement. She would do this and get right back to the hospital.

When she emerged from the bathroom in her towel, there was a set of clothes laid out for her on the bed. She sent up a silent thank-you for another decision she didn't have to make. She dressed quickly, taking note of the sizzles and sighs emanating from the kitchen. Her stomach, despite her mind's protestations, growled in response to the wonderful aroma of frying bacon.

With her hair still wet, Sarah padded into the kitchen and sat at the table. She didn't fully imagine she could eat, but Emory went to the trouble so the least she could do was act appreciative. "What do you have going in here?"

"Order up." Emory placed a BLT in front of Sarah, complete with a side of cantaloupe. Sarah contemplated the sandwich for a moment, which prompted Emory to nudge the plate just a tad bit closer. "Eat."

She looked up at Emory and dutifully took a small bite, which just about prompted her collapse. "Wow."

"I took the liberty of raiding your fridge. Bacon is happy food, and we were given some happy news this morning, remember? Grace is going to be okay. I know it's been a rough time, but I need you to remind yourself of that."

Sarah nodded and exhaled. "She's going to be okay. And that is good news, it's just, I feel like I haven't quite woken up from it all yet. Not until she's home and herself again am I going to be able to breathe."

Emory smoothed the back of Sarah's hair. "She will be soon. But the first step is a little nourishment followed by some rest. Trust me, please?"

Sarah looked up at her solemnly. "I do trust you, Emory. Know that."

Emory nodded, took a seat next to Sarah, and together they ate in companionable silence. Once Sarah had gulped down the last bite, Emory cleared their plates and put the dishes away. "Think you could try to get in a little nap?"

"Nope. I'd like to go back to the hospital now."

"Don't you think it will be better for everyone in the long run if you're firing on all cylinders and capable of rational thought? How about ninety minutes?"

Sarah exhaled deeply. "I need to be with Grace."

"And you will be. Forty-five minutes."

"Fine." She was annoyed now and it showed. "I'll try if it will shut everyone up."

"It will. We will all shut up. I promise." Emory walked with her to the bedroom, pulled the sheets back, and fluffed the pillow.

Sarah climbed into the bed, still shaking her head in frustration.

"Do this for Grace. She's a talkative kid and will need your full attention later when she wakes up."

Sarah offered her a reluctant smile. Emory tucked her in snugly and placed a reassuring kiss on her forehead.

"Em?" Sarah said as she turned to go.

"Yeah."

"Thank you. For helping me through this."

"How could I not?"

Her eyes met Emory's and something important passed between them. Regardless of everything, it was understood that they mattered to each other. Finally, Sarah nodded and turned onto her side.

In the living room, Emory stretched out on the couch, not having slept in some time herself. The apartment was small, however, and the unmistakable sound of Sarah tossing and turning in the other room had hold of her attention. It wasn't long before she heard footsteps in the hallway. She sat up and there was Sarah, eyes haunted. "I don't want to be alone right now. Do you think you could lay in there with me?"

Emory hated seeing Sarah so crumpled in, so afraid. "Of course I will." She took Sarah's hand and led her gently back to her room. Hesitating only for a moment, she climbed into the bed next to Sarah, who snuggled into her automatically. With Sarah's head on her shoulder, Emory acted on instinct, wrapped her arms tightly around her, and whispered in her ear. "I've got you. Try to sleep now."

Sarah clung tightly to her and it was less than five minutes before Emory recognized the even breathing. She stared at the ceiling and silently asked God to watch over Sarah and give Grace the opportunity to live a normal, healthy life from here on out. For that, she'd do absolutely anything.

❖

Back at the hospital, Sarah was in slightly better spirits. She could think rationally and process the world around her more effectively. The short nap had made all the difference in the world.

Her mother, who'd stayed with Grace when they'd left, had agreed to take a similar trip to her own house. That left her alone in the waiting room with Emory. She looked over at her. "If I haven't said it, I'm glad you came. You put me back on track when I was just about to lose it. I was snapping at everyone. I didn't know how else to cope."

"Given the circumstances, I think you're doing just fine. I remember the day my mother was brought in and the way that I felt. Helpless, angry, lonely, sad."

The idea of Emory dealing with that loss alone made Sarah's heart ache. She wished she'd been there for her, wished she'd known.

"I didn't handle it so well. I beat the hell out of a vending machine when it wouldn't take my dollar."

Something sparked in Sarah's memory.

She sat forward in her chair and turned to Emory. "Grace was admitted to this hospital on May seventeenth when she first fainted in her classroom."

Emory tilted her head curiously. "That's the day my mother died. May seventeenth. It was at this hospital too."

Sarah nodded as the understanding overtook her. "I think I bought you a Diet Coke that day."

Emory held her gaze for a long moment. "No. That was you? That day at the machine?"

Sarah nodded. "I didn't know it until just now, but yeah."

Emory nodded, her eyes glistened. "I guess we've been there for each other longer than we realized."

"Emory," Sarah whispered achingly. She picked up her hand, needing the closeness. "Tell me that you were just scared that last day on the beach."

Emory met her eyes and nodded. "For you."

Sarah's stomach muscles tightened reflexively. "And now?"

"I think—"

It was then that a nurse burst into the room. "Matamoros family, come with me right now!"

Sarah felt the blood drain from her face as terror infused her. She exchanged a glance with Emory and stood, staggering, but Emory caught her and practically carried her down the hallway after the nurse. Each step seemed to take a lifetime, each sound of her tennis shoe punctuated with a desperate prayer. As they passed, the sounds from the nurses' station seemed way too loud. What was wrong? What had happened? *Please, God, not this.*

When she rounded the corner into the room, her daughter, her everything, smiled up weakly at her. "Grace?" she managed. Her knees threatened to buckle again, but Emory steadied her from behind.

Grace held out her hand and Sarah didn't hesitate, moving to her side and kissing her adorable little face. "Hiya, kiddo."

"Hi, Mama." They were the most wonderful words in the history of words.

As she explained to a slightly disoriented Grace why she was in the hospital, Sarah could simultaneously hear Emory in the hallway quietly dealing with the nurse who'd taken ten years off their lives. Sarah looked up and smiled as she rejoined them, listening quietly from the doorway as Grace chatted away.

Later the next afternoon, Dr. Riggs had Grace transferred from ICU to a regular room two halls over. Visiting hours were relaxed and Sarah was able to spend more time with Grace, a welcome contrast to the hellish isolation of the waiting room. But the morning had tired Grace out and she dozed soundly in her hospital bed, as always immune to the sounds around her as visitors came and went.

Emory had excused herself to the hallway to make a few calls, which left Sarah alone with her mother. "It's nice that Emory is here with you."

Sarah regarded her mother, taking stock of the situation. "I don't know what I would have done otherwise."

Her mother hesitated a moment, seeming to decide what she wanted to say next. "Carmen mentioned something yesterday. About Emory meaning a lot to you."

Sarah didn't hesitate. It was time to put all her cards on the table and speak from the heart. "More than a lot, Mama. I'm in love with her."

The declaration was met with silence, but she'd prepared herself for that and worse months ago. It didn't scare her in the same way anymore.

"I'm sorry if that upsets you or shakes up your idea of what my life should be, but it's the truth and I wouldn't change it."

Her mother sighed and Sarah waited to hear what she would say. "This may surprise you, but I suspected."

It more than surprised her. Sarah was floored. "You did?"

"At the birthday party. It was the way you looked at her. Like she'd hung the moon. The way your father used to look at me. That kind of look is hard to miss."

"Why didn't you say anything?"

"I don't think it was something I was ready to think about. This old lady needed some time. But after a while, you just seemed so happy, in a way I had never seen you before, and that made *me* happy. There was a light in your eyes, mija, the light I'd always hoped you'd have one day. But that light is gone now. Am I right?"

Sarah nodded, a stab of remembered hurt hit her hard and deep. "We stopped seeing each other."

"I see. And is that what you want?" Sarah could tell this wasn't easy for her mother, but she was trying, and the least she could do was be forthright. She shook her head.

Her mother took a deep breath and kissed her on the cheek. "Then get the light back, mija."

Emory didn't want to interrupt. Sarah was having what looked to be a serious conversation with her mother. She watched through the small window in the hospital room door for just a moment before backing away to give them privacy.

There would be a lot to handle in the next couple of days to get Grace home and recuperated fully. Once word of her recovery got out, the cavalry had showed up in full force. Her family and friends crowded the waiting room, dropping off gifts and food. There wasn't a ton she could do, and Sarah did have an amazing support system in her family, she reminded herself. So she took a last glance through the window as she pulled her car keys from her pocket. She watched for a moment as Sarah and her mother talked. Sarah was smiling, and she couldn't help but smile too as something within her clicked into place.

All was well.

Finally, she forced herself to look away and headed off resolutely down the hallway. Because there was something she could do for Sarah. So she found the elevator that would take her down to the lobby, and out of the hospital.

❖

Sarah checked the nurse's station, the waiting room, even the women's restroom for Emory. She was nowhere. The talk with her mother had only confirmed what she already knew and set her on her way. Her heart was beating rapidly in anticipation of everything she was ready to say.

It was time to put it all on the line.

The elevator chime snagged her attention and she turned as Carmen emerged carrying a giant balloon bouquet. When her eyes settled on Sarah, her face shifted to one of concern. "Hey, you. What's up?"

Sarah nodded her head a few times too many with all the nervous energy that rushed through her. "Remember what we talked about in the park, about Emory?"

Carmen shifted her bag to the other shoulder and studied Sarah in confusion. "Yeah."

"I think I'm ready to do that fighting thing you talked about."

An extra wide smile broke out across Carmen's face. "Now that's what I'm talking about."

"Any last-minute advice?"

"Say what's in your heart. You can do this. I know you can. One of my all-time favorite quotes says 'Life is like a movie. Write your own ending.' And that's what you're going to do today."

Sarah thought on this and brightened. "Who said that? I like it."

"Kermit the Frog." Carmen held up her hands in defense. "What can I say? I spend a lot of time with people under the age of ten. It still applies."

Sarah laughed. "Now I just have to find her."

Carmen gestured behind her. "She got off the elevator just as I got on. She had her keys in her hand."

"Keys? But she didn't even say good—" That's when the horrible realization hit. "I have to go." She took the stairs because elevators were unpredictable. Bad idea. After racing down the six flights, she was wildly out of breath and the parking lot was huge. She stood on a cement bench and scanned the rows of cars. There she was.

Not too late.

*Write your own ending.*

Encouraged by Kermit and the surefire fact that she loved Emory more than anything, she covered the distance to the car just as Emory was about to slide in.

"Em, wait. Don't go. There's something I need to say."

Emory turned curiously and pointed at the hospital, tilting her head in question. "Did you just—"

"Yes, but that's not important. Please just let me say what I need to say."

Emory opened her mouth and then closed it again, seeming to honor the request.

"You can't leave. I get why you walked away before, but I shouldn't have let you. I should have told you that I love you. Because I do, love you, I mean. And I'm asking you to build a life with us, Emory, and to give me what I never knew I needed. I want to make plans with you and change them as we go. I want the fights and the day-to-day and the milestones and the make-up sex and all the snarls and tribulations that come with being together. It's going to take work, and things are not always going to be perfect. But we'll work on it. We'll figure it out as a family."

A soft smile appeared on Emory's face as tears touched her eyes. "A family?"

Sarah nodded and took a step in. "Yeah. You, Grace, and me. We're a team. So don't go."

Emory paused and slid a glance to her car and then back to Sarah. "So you don't want the Whopper?"

"What?"

"Lunch. I was going to pick us up something to eat. A certain someone favors Burger King if I remember correctly."

Sarah stared at Emory in confusion until the happy understanding settled. "You're not fleeing the scene," she breathed.

Emory covered the short distance that separated them, pulled Sarah in, and kissed her the way she'd imagined kissing her for the past six weeks. She sighed into perfection. "Nope."

Sarah was cradling her face, and as much as she wanted to kiss her again, there were things she needed to address. "But there have to be terms."

"Terms?" Sarah's eyes widened. "Okay, what are the terms?"

"I love you."

Sarah smiled, taking it in. "I think I can live with that one."

"And you have to believe that I don't fall in love with just anybody. In fact, I have very high standards and always have." She picked up Sarah's hand and threaded their fingers. "I happen to think that you are the most wonderfully smart, funny, and beautiful woman I have ever encountered. And I need you to accept that about yourself."

It was Sarah's eyes that filled then and her voice was meek. "I can do that. I can try and do that."

They held each other's gaze, the electricity between them already in full force. Emory's voice was quiet and a small smile tentatively took shape on her face. "So we're agreed?"

"We are."

"One last thing."

"All right."

Emory took a breath and tilted her head sideways. "Can you say it again?"

Sarah smiled. "Emory, I love you. I don't know why I thought it would be hard to say, because it's not. I love who we are when we're together and I love who I think we're capable of becoming."

"God, I love you too." Emory squeezed Sarah's hand. "And I'm so glad I thought to get the damn cheeseburgers." They both laughed and there was only one thing left to do. Her eyes dropped languidly to Sarah's lips as she moved in ever so slightly. "We should probably shake on it or something."

Sarah leaned in and hovered just shy of Emory's mouth, her voice a near whisper. "Or something. But once we do this, it's binding. No going back. Got it?"

"Only forward." As their lips met, Emory felt her world right itself and she sank into the kiss. What they were embarking upon was scary. But she couldn't let that take precedence anymore. This, right here in her arms, was what mattered. The last few days had shown her that. Connection to another person, in a life where nothing was guaranteed, was more precious than anything. The details all seemed so much smaller in comparison.

As they stood there in the parking lot, the early afternoon continued all around them. Pedestrians bustled, and cars whizzed past, the midday rush hour in full effect. But Emory barely noticed. She was too busy dreamily kissing the woman she loved.

It was a moment. It was *the* moment.

## Chapter Seventeen

It was the first week of December and as tradition dictated, Sarah had spent the entire Saturday baking cookies with the kids at her parents' house. Carmen had helped and in good news, her boys had been less than destructive, only starting two food fights this year. Needless to say, it had been a day.

The kids had long since retreated to the backyard for marshmallow roasting with their Uncle Danny, a part of the cookie baking tradition Grace always looked forward to. A Johnny Mathis Christmas carol drifted in from the living room. Sarah looked around the kitchen at their masterful work and offered Carmen an exhausted high five. "I'd say we conquered cookieland."

"Cookieland had no hope." Next to them on the counter sat a stack of coconut macaroons, next to a platter of peanut butter reindeer, alongside colorfully decorated sugar cookies in the shapes of bells, stars, and remarkably accurate cutouts of Santa Claus himself. "Prisoners of war," Carmen mused. "I think we've earned a hot toddy."

"Sounds good. I'll make them," her mother called out as she walked into the kitchen.

"Not for me. Emory will be here any second. How do I look?" She'd changed from her jeans into black pants and a form-fitting red sweater for their date. It was the first chance they'd gotten to spend time on their own together since Grace's release and she'd been counting the hours.

"Smokin' hot, Sar."

"That's all I can ask for." She grinned, switching gears. "Everything all right outside, Mama?"

"The kids are having a ball out there. Danny's taught them his super slow roasting method and they're transfixed."

"How's Grace?"

"Very energetic. I think her strength is back in full force."

"Clearly," Sarah said as Grace sped into the room and came to a stop in front of her.

"Can I have ice cream later?" Grace asked, wiggling her eyebrows.

"If you're grandparents say it's okay. But do me a favor and take it easy. Maybe don't run everywhere you go. Let's give that new pacemaker a chance to settle in."

"The doctor said it's fine to run now."

Sarah sighed. "That he did." She kissed the top of Grace's head and watched her speed back into the yard to join her cousins. "She just seems so much lighter, carefree. It's nice. The cardiologist says that with the new pacemaker, she shouldn't see the inside of a hospital room until she delivers her first child."

Her mother placed her hand on Sarah's shoulder as she passed. "And now that Grace is back on track, it's your turn."

As if on cue, the doorbell rang and Sarah broke out into a smile. "I think that's my date."

❖

The beach house was dark and quiet when they entered, but the moonlight reflecting off the water just yards away illuminated much of the room. Dinner with an adult had been just what the doctor ordered, and the fact that it was with Emory was delicious icing on the cake. Throughout dinner, Sarah had enjoyed the conversation, the laughs, the flirting, but she couldn't help letting her mind drift to the promise of things to come. It didn't help that Emory was looking both gorgeous and sophisticated in the pale blue dress she'd worn to dinner. Her favorite combination.

Now that they were alone, Sarah led the way in and wordlessly moved to the glass, staring out at the endless ocean. She wrapped her arms around herself and shook her head ever so slightly. "The water seems so calm tonight."

Emory settled in behind her and gently kissed one shoulder. "It's chilly out, but we could walk down to the beach, if you want."

Sarah turned. "I don't think so. I like it right here." She studied Emory's face, taking it in. "What are you feeling right now?"

Emory smiled. "You have no idea."

"Trust me, I do." She ran a finger gently across Emory's bottom lip and moved in, unable to resist her another moment. She brushed her mouth with a featherlight kiss and ran her hands gently up Emory's arms, the most tender of caresses. "You were there for me. When life couldn't get any worse, when I was at my lowest and didn't know where to turn, you were there and you got me through it somehow. I didn't know what I needed, but you knew."

"I didn't do anything that you haven't done for me. How is she today? Grace."

"Feisty, just like always. Only she can stay feisty longer now, so we're all in trouble."

Emory laughed. "I can't wait to see her."

"Tomorrow. Tonight, I get you all to myself."

Emory felt a shiver move through her body. She took Sarah's hand and kissed the back of it. "Can I get you anything? Are you thirsty?"

Sarah shook her head slowly, her eyes never moving from Emory's, communicating so much. Emory nodded wordlessly and they walked together up the stairs, hand in hand.

Once inside her bedroom, Emory moved to Sarah and pulled her close, her gaze unguarded, focused. "I can't believe you're here."

Sarah reached out and brushed a strand of hair off her forehead. "We have all night, you know."

Emory kissed her gently. "Best sentence ever."

The kiss that began delicately, transformed rather quickly to a mechanism of need. Sarah moved her hands to Emory's waist and up. As they grazed the outsides of her breasts, Emory hissed in a breath and increased the pressure of the kiss until the meeting of lips and tongues vibrated through her entire body.

As Sarah pulled off her sweater, Emory stepped back. "I got it." She moved behind Sarah, pulling the zipper of her slacks slowly downward. Emory assisted the lightweight fabric to the floor, bringing her to her knees and refocusing her attention. She closed her eyes and placed a solitary kiss on the small of Sarah's back, then moved her attention ever so slowly upward to her shoulders, the back of her neck, and around. Sarah's eyes were closed, her lips parted slightly at the sensation in a breathtaking display that caused Emory only a minor pause to take in the image before needing to taste that mouth once again.

As their lips met, it was Sarah who took control at this point, kissing Emory hungrily and backing her up until the back of her knees bumped the bed. She slid the straps of Emory's dress down her shoulders, and it fell effortlessly to the floor. She stopped and looked at her, really looked at her, as her heart filled with something so familiar, yet so exciting that she felt a shiver move through her.

She pushed Emory softly onto her back and took her time pulling off the rest of her clothing piece by piece. She willed herself to move slowly, to let the moonlight shift over Emory's skin as she revealed more of it. She descended to Emory's breast first, kissing it, taking time to linger, savor the taste, the moment, the sensation that was so all consuming. She moved to the other breast then, licking, tracing lazy circles with her tongue. As Sarah raised her head, her eyes slid to Emory's and the yearning she saw there sent a staggering shot of arousal through her. "Em," she whispered reverently in response, kissing up her neck, her chin, her forehead before finally settling back on her lips for another sensuous go-round. She settled herself more firmly on top this time, "Em, look at me." Emory threaded her fingers through Sarah's hair, pulling her face back just enough to lock onto her eyes. "I love you. So desperately, I do."

Emory's stomach fluttered as she heard the words again in such a vulnerable moment. She nodded as she looked up at Sarah and wanted to respond, to tell her of the strength of her own feelings, but her voice was strangled in her throat, the emotion too powerful. She opened her mouth to try again and closed it in defeat.

"I already know." Sarah smiled as she tucked a strand of Emory's hair behind her ear. "I know how you feel, and it's everything good in this world. I'm so lucky."

Unable to resist any longer, Emory pulled Sarah's face back down and caught her lips for another feverish kiss. She tried to turn them for better access to Sarah, to her body, but the once quiet, reserved woman she'd met those several months before was not willing to relinquish control just yet, and it was tantalizing. Instead, she pushed her thigh firmly between Emory's legs and began to move against her. Emory gasped and felt as if an electric current of yearning had just slammed her system. She arched in response and pushed back forcefully, grabbing Sarah by the hips and pulling her closer still, needing, wanting more of her.

"Not so fast there," Sarah mumbled between kisses, shaking her hair back, grasping Emory's wrists, and holding them in place above her head. She picked up the rhythm gradually, and Emory could hardly maintain a coherent thought against the onslaught of overwhelming sensation. With her breathing ragged and her body erupting, she turned her head into the pillow and moaned quietly. Taking the cue, Sarah increased her speed, the pins that held her hair in place loosening and eventually falling out entirely. Her hair cascaded wildly down around her shoulders and the sight alone sent Emory toppling over the edge in a rush of sharp pleasure. Her body stilled and she called out as the orgasm ripped through her. In that moment, she reached up and touched Sarah's face, holding fast to the connection she felt so deeply until all she saw was her. All she felt was her.

Sarah collapsed into Emory and they lay there, tangled, smiling together.

As her shallow breaths evened out once again, Emory gently stroked Sarah's hair and her ability to think crept slowly back. "You've destroyed me. I'm feeling strangely speechless."

Sarah raised her head and grinned. "I told you I'd missed you."

But it was more than just that. Sarah exuded a quiet confidence that was new, surprising, and beyond sexy. Emory turned to face her more fully. "You're a complex woman."

Sarah looked skyward in jest. "You noticed."

"I more than notice you." She gently shifted Sarah onto her back and a new surge of heat surfaced in her as her eyes met generous curves and golden skin glistening in the moonlight. She ached at the sight of Sarah. She'd always thought her beautiful, but tonight she simply radiated. She descended first to Sarah's lips and then set out to explore. Kissing, tasting, licking, Emory savored every luscious moment with Sarah's body.

Sarah was on fire. She had been ever since she'd first touched Emory and her desire had only grown exponentially. She'd been turned on before, but this was a whole new level of yearning and she didn't know how much longer she could hang on. Emory's mouth was storming her system and sensation drenched her. As Emory kissed the inside of her thigh, she tunneled her hands into Emory's hair in an attempt to guide her to what she so desperately needed. Sarah's breath exploded in a loud gasp when Emory's hand finally found her, eased through slickness, and began to move at an agonizingly slow pace. Moving her hips in response, Sarah arched upward in desperate search of purchase, of release. When Emory's hand was replaced shortly thereafter with her mouth, Sarah let control snap. With her eyes closed, she felt the shock of pleasure overtake her, and the past six months flashed behind her eyes like a movie in her mind. As she rode out the glorious release, she remembered the moments, the journey that brought them here, and her heart and her body collided.

With her heart still thudding in her chest like a jackhammer, her body still singing, and Emory's arms around her, Sarah knew she was home.

Seagulls and the sounds of the early tide woke Sarah the next morning, and it only took a moment for her to feel the happiness moving through her in big, warm waves. She sat up groggily in bed and looked around for Emory. The door to the terrace was open and the sheer curtains fluttered in the chilly breeze, a clue to her whereabouts. She crossed the room, shrugging into a T-shirt from the dresser as she went, when something caught her eye. To her right, there stood a canvas propped against the wall. She hadn't noticed it the night before, but then again, she'd been wonderfully preoccupied. She moved closer, stunned at the beauty, the simplicity of the image, and took a moment to let her feelings settle. She studied the lines, her own features so familiar, yet so new. Was this really the way Emory saw her? She picked up the painting, captivated by the window it offered into the artist's soul.

"It was the first thing I wanted to paint. I was a little out of practice, but in the end, it came out just the way I wanted." Sarah turned to Emory, who stood in the doorway to the terrace. She wore a light blue silk robe and looked sated and beautiful after the night they'd shared.

Sarah shook her head slightly in wonder. "I don't know quite what to say. It's stunning." And she meant it. She'd seen Emory's work in subtle manifestations, but nothing like this. Nothing so complete. It was true. Emory was beyond gifted.

"Have you seen the subject? How could it not be?"

Sarah met her eyes in all seriousness. "That's not what I meant. How did you do it, capture me this way?"

"Well, I happen to love your face, your hands." Emory pressed a delicate kiss into her palm. "The way you move. I had dozens of images of you sliding through my head, moments of you attached to my heart, so I just picked one."

Sarah looked back at the painting, for the first time noticing the glow on her cheek. "This is from our first night together, isn't it? In front of the fire."

Emory nodded. "That was the night my life changed."

Sarah nodded and caressed her cheek. "Mine too."

Emory looked down at the painting "I'd say you could have it, but I don't think I'm willing to let it go."

"That's okay. I was kind of hoping for joint custody." And giving in to the temptation that had been with her since she awoke, she slid her fingers into Emory's sun-streaked hair and pulled her in for a kiss that left them both breathless and stumbling back to the bed.

## Epilogue

*Six months later*

The gallery was still bustling as they approached the last hour of the showing. Intense-looking people dressed to the nines perused the various pieces that lined the walls as waiters moved about the room with trays of champagne and canapés.

Emory felt the butterflies in her stomach enter into a last dance and sighed in relief that she'd almost made it through. It was one thing to head up a multimillion dollar company, but quite another to have your art, your innermost expression, on display for the world to see and critique at will. She'd be lying, however, if she said it wasn't exciting at the same time. Because it really, really was. As she sipped her champagne in the corner of the room, she heard a patron's voice behind her.

"I can't stop looking at it," the male voice said. "On each reexamination, I see something I hadn't noticed before, but by far, the most intriguing aspect of the piece is the way the artist juxtaposes nature against the urban landscape. I mean, look at that and tell me it's not thought provoking."

"Find the gallery owner," his female companion said. "Let's see what it's listed at."

Emory hadn't been able to contain the small smile that grew steadily on her lips as the evening went on. She knew the opening's success would hinge on how many of the pieces actually sold, but for her, it was enough to hear that others appreciated her work, saw value in something she'd created. It came with a certain kind of gratification unlike anything else she'd experienced. The rush was palpable, indescribable, and immediate. She realized very quickly that she could get used to this.

"There's the famous artist now!" Emory smiled in recognition of the familiar voice and turned just in time to feel the arms of Yolanda Matamoros envelop her in an all-consuming embrace. Yolanda, Emory had come to discover in recent months, gave the best hugs in the history of the world.

She felt herself light up. "I'm so happy you both came. You didn't have to, you know."

"Are you kidding? And miss all this? Never. It's an important night for you."

Roberto placed a hand on her arm. "Your work is beautiful, Emory."

Yolanda thrust a camera at him. "Take our picture, Berto. I'll say I knew her when." Emory wrapped an arm around Yolanda and smiled warmly into the lens.

"We'll let you get back to your show," Roberto said. "We're off to see the rest of the paintings. See you Sunday for dinner?"

"I wouldn't miss it." And she wouldn't. She smiled after the people who had become her surrogate parents, still surprised at how much they'd come to mean to her in such a short time. She made her way into the next room, where most of the work was displayed. The lights were dim, and mellow music emanated from the classical guitarist in the corner. She hadn't made it but ten feet into the room before Grace was at her side like a rocket. "Emory, only two paintings are left."

She smoothed the back of Grace's hair and looked down at her. "That can't be right. Who told you that?"

"The gallery owner, Melody. She said I'm her assistant. See? Here's the inventory."

She thrust the clipboard upward for Emory to see. Emory scanned the page in mystification. "I didn't think too many would actually sell," she mumbled to herself as Grace scampered away.

"I did," her favorite voice in all of history said in her ear. Emory turned around to Sarah's sparkling eyes. "You're a hit. It's confirmed.

I just finished talking to a reporter from *CityBeat*. She's in love with your work and said to look for her review on Monday. How does that sit?"

Emory shook her head. Something about being in Sarah's presence made her incredibly honest with her feelings and emotion was now bubbling to the surface in rapid waves. "It all feels so surreal, in a good way, but still surreal." This was the kind of night she had imagined growing up when she was young and the world seemed to have endless possibilities. She'd long ago stuffed those idealistic daydreams aside and now, to actually have one come true struck a chord. "I don't know what to say, other than, thank you."

Sarah quirked an eyebrow. "For what?"

Emory took Sarah's hand and pulled her into the corner of the room, outside the earshot of the meandering guests. "For this. If I'd never met you, Sarah, I'd be sitting behind a desk at the office up to my elbows in paperwork, alone and unaware of how much of life I was actually missing out on." Her voice softened. "So, yes, thank you for coming into my life."

Sarah didn't answer. Instead, she kissed her simply. "I love you, you know that?"

Emory smiled. "I do. It's awesome."

"Don't let me interrupt," Melody said, approaching. "But I wanted to break it to you myself." She looked somber and Emory didn't like that.

"Okay. What's up? Is there a problem?"

"Unfortunately. I'm afraid you're going to have to part with every last piece we've displayed at this little showing of yours." Melody broke into a triumphant grin.

"Wait. So that means…"

"Sold out. Entirely. And we're still getting inquiries. How fast can you paint exactly?"

Emory laughed out loud. "I don't believe it."

"It's pretty impressive, actually. I don't recall another artist I've worked with doing this well their first time out."

Sarah squeezed her hand. "Of course not."

Melody checked her watch. "We should be wrapping up soon. Shall we get drinks and discuss the future?"

"Ah, can't tonight." She glanced at Sarah. "We kind of have plans."

Sarah nudged her shoulder. "It's fine. Go."

"No way. I've been looking forward to this. Melody, can we do it Tuesday?"

"Tuesday's great, actually. I'll call you. And congratulations, Emory, you deserve it."

Emory watched her walk away and turned back expectantly to Sarah. "How quick can you wrangle the kiddo and meet me in the car?"

"Time me, superstar."

❖

An hour and a half later, the kitchen table at the beach house was covered with blueberry French toast, hash brown potatoes, maple bacon, and Emory's contribution, "Hobo Scramble," which consisted of eggs, cream cheese, scallions, and ham. Sarah had to admit, it all tasted amazing.

Grace helped herself to a second spoonful of hash browns. "I think I adore breakfast for dinner."

"Not more than me," Emory echoed. She sliced excitedly into her French toast.

Sarah watched them, amused by their matching kid-like expressions. Over the past few months, she'd watched Emory slowly relax into life. She went into the office a couple of days a week to consult on any pressing issues, but for the most part spent her time in the spare room they'd converted into her art studio or painted on the beach. Her eyes shone brighter and she seemed so carefree, unencumbered. It was wonderful to see her so full of life.

"Mom, can I give Walter a piece of bacon?"

Sarah glanced over at Walter, who sat obediently back from the table watching each and every move they made as if his life depended on it. "Sure. Make his day." Walter accepted the offered piece of bacon with lightning speed and then licked his lips in gratitude. He collapsed comfortably back into his spot on the floor and rested his chin atop his toy raccoon, his best friend in the world next to Grace, whom he followed throughout the house religiously.

"That's a good buddy boy, Walter," Emory said affectionately. "You're the cutest of the cute, you know that?"

His tail wagged in seeming appreciation.

When dinner was done, Sarah and Grace worked together to clear the table, as Emory started the dishes. "Go get your pajamas on, monster, if you want to watch the movie. I'll finish up." Grace scampered up the stairs to her room and Sarah brought the last dish to the sink. In doing so, she couldn't help but let her eyes drift down Emory's body in appreciation of her in those yoga pants. Her mouth went dry, as it always did where Emory was concerned.

"Mom, it's your turn to pick the movie!" Grace's voice from upstairs brought her back from where she'd drifted, but not before Emory caught the stare.

Emory was smiling as she shook her head. "You cannot look at me like that. Not when our daughter will be back down here any second to watch a two-hour movie."

Sarah feigned complete mystification. "I have no idea what you're talking about. I'm trying to clear the table. Could you focus, please, on the dishes?"

Emory moved in and stole a playful kiss. "You're a bad liar. I will deal with you later."

Sarah grinned. "Then my plan has worked." Hearing Grace in the living room, she headed that way.

"Did you pick a movie, Mom?"

"I'm in the mood for a classic. How about *To Kill a Mockingbird*?"

"Oh, that gets my vote." Emory snuggled in next to Grace on the comfy couch, a Matamoros contribution to the beach house when they'd moved in. "You'll like it too, kiddo. It's right up your alley."

"Okay, cool." Walter wedged himself tightly on the other side of Grace, placing his head in her lap as Sarah set up the DVD. She then settled in next to Emory and took her hand just as the opening credits appeared on the screen. Sarah looked across at Grace and exchanged a private smile, her mind drifting to how far they'd come in just a year's time. So much had changed. So much had fallen into place.

But now they were home.

Her family was complete.

And she was so very lucky.

# About the Author

Melissa Brayden currently works as a theater director at the performing arts center of one of the largest high schools in the state of Texas, a job she completely enjoys. Recently, she's fallen down the rabbit hole and rediscovered her love for creative writing. Her first novel, Waiting in the Wings, was honored with two 2012 Goldie Awards for Best Debut Author and Best Traditional Contemporary Romance.

Melissa is married and working really hard at remembering to do the dishes. For personal enjoyment, she spends time with her Jack Russell terriers and checks out the NYC theater scene several times a year. She considers herself a reluctant patron of the treadmill, but enjoys hitting a tennis ball around in nice weather. Coffee is her very best friend. www.melissabrayden.com

# Books Available from Bold Strokes Books

**Crossroads** by Radclyffe. Dr. Hollis Monroe specializes in short-term relationships but when she meets pregnant mother-to-be Annie Colfax, fate brings them together at a crossroads that will change their lives forever. (978-1-60282-756-1)

**Beyond Innocence** by Carsen Taite. When a life is on the line, love has to wait. Doesn't it? (978-1-60282-757-8)

**Heart Block** by Melissa Brayden. Socialite Emory Owen and struggling single mom Sarah Matamoros are perfectly suited for each other but face a difficult time when trying to merge their contrasting worlds and the people in them. If love truly exists, can it find a way? (978-1-60282-758-5)

**Pride and Joy** by M.L. Rice. Perfect Bryce Montgomery is her parents' pride and joy, but when they discover that their daughter is a lesbian her world changes forever. (978-1-60282-759-2)

**Timothy** by Greg Herren. *Timothy* is a romantic suspense thriller from award-winning mystery writer Greg Herren set in the fabulous Hamptons. (978-1-60282-760-8)

**In Stone: A Grotesque Faerie Tale** by Jeremy Jordan King. A young New Yorker is rescued from a hate crime by a mysterious someone who turns out to be more of a *something*. (978-1-60282-761-5)

**The Jesus Injection** by Eric Andrews-Katz. Murderous statues, demented drag queens, political bombings, ex-gay ministries, espionage, and romance are all in a day's work for a top-secret agent. But the gloves are off when Agent Buck 98 comes up against The Jesus Injection. (978-1-60282-762-2)

**Combustion** by Daniel W. Kelly. Bearish detective Deck Waxer comes to the city of Kremfort Cove to investigate why the hottest men in town are bursting into flames in broad daylight. (978-1-60282-763-9)

**Ladyfish** by Andrea Bramhill. Finn's escape to the Florida Keys leads her straight into the arms of scuba diving instructor Oz as she fights for her freedom, their blossoming love...and her life! (978-1-60282-747-9)

**Spanish Heart** by Rachel Spangler. While on a mission to find herself in Spain, Ren Molson runs the risk of losing her heart to her tour guide, Lina Montero. (978-1-60282-748-6)

**Love Match** by Ali Vali. When Parker "Kong" King, the number one tennis player in the world, meets commercial pilot Captain Sydney Parish, sparks fly but not from attraction. They have the summer to see if they have a love match. (978-1-60282-749-3)

**One Touch** by L.T. Marie. A romance writer and a travel agent come together at their high school reunion, only to find out that the memory of that one touch never fades. (978-1-60282-750-9)

**Night Shadows: Queer Horror** edited by Greg Herren and J.M. Redmann. *Night Shadows* features delightfully wicked stories by some of the biggest names in queer publishing. (978-1-60282-751-6)

**Secret Societies** by William Holden. An outcast hustler, his unlikely "mother," his faithless lovers, and his religious persecutors—all in 1726. (978-1-60282-752-3)

**The Raid** by Lee Lynch. Before Stonewall, having a drink with friends or your girl could mean jail. Would these women and men still have family, a job, a place to live after...The Raid? (978-1-60282-753-0)

**The You Know Who Girls: Freshman Year** by Annameekee Hesik. As they begin freshman year, Abbey Brooks and her best friend, Kate, pinky swear they'll keep away from the lesbians in Gila High, but Abbey already suspects she's one of those you-know-who girls herself and slowly learns who her true friends really are. (978-1-60282-754-7)

**Wyatt: Doc Holliday's Account of an Intimate Friendship** by Dale Chase. Erotica writer Dale Chase takes the remarkable friendship between Wyatt Earp, upright lawman, and Doc Holliday, southern gentlemen turned gambler and killer, to an entirely new level: hot! (978-1-60282-755-4)

**Month of Sundays** by Yolanda Wallace. Love doesn't always happen overnight; sometimes it takes a month of Sundays. (978-1-60282-739-4)

**Jacob's War** by C.P. Rowlands. ATF Special Agent Allison Jacob's task force is in the middle of an all-out war, from the streets to the boardrooms of America. Small business owner Katie Blackburn is the latest victim who accidentally breaks it wide open but may break AJ's heart at the same time. (978-1-60282-740-0)

**The Pyramid Waltz** by Barbara Ann Wright. Princess Katya Nar Umbriel wants a perfect romance, but her Fiendish nature and duties to the crown mean she can never tell the truth—until she meets Starbride, a woman who gets to the heart of every secret, even if it will be the death of her. (978-1-60282-741-7)

**The Secret of Othello** by Sam Cameron. Florida teen detectives Steven and Denny risk their lives to search for a sunken NASA satellite—but under the waves, no one can hear you scream . . . (978-1-60282-742-4)

**Dreaming of Her** by Maggie Morton. Isa has begun to dream of the most amazing woman—a woman named Lilith with a gorgeous face, an amazing body, and the ability to turn Isa on like no other. But Lilith is just a dream…isn't she? (978-1-60282-847-6)

**Andy Squared** by Jennifer Lavoie. Andrew never thought anyone could come between him and his twin sister, Andrea...until Ryder rode into town. (978-1-60282-743-1)

**Finding Bluefield** by Elan Barnehama. Set in the backdrop of Virginia and New York and spanning the years 1960-1982, Finding Bluefield chronicles the lives of Nicky Stewart, Barbara Philips, and their son, Paul, as they struggle to define themselves as a family. (978-1-60282-744-8)

**The Jetsetters** by David-Matthew Barnes. As rock band The Jetsetters skyrocket from obscurity to super stardom, Justin Holt, a lonely barista, and Diego Delgado, the band's guitarist, fight with everything they have to stay together, despite the chaos and fame. (978-1-60282-745-5)

**Strange Bedfellows** by Rob Byrnes. Partners in life and crime, Grant Lambert and Chase LaMarca, are hired to make a politician's compromising photo disappear, but what should be an easy job quickly spins out of control. (978-1-60282-746-2)

**Speed Demons** by Gun Brooke. When NASCAR star Evangeline Marshall returns to the race track after a close brush with death, will famous photographer Blythe Pierce document her triumph and reciprocate her love—or will they succumb to their respective demons and fail? (978-1-60282-678-6)

**Summoning Shadows: A Rosso Lussuria Vampire Novel** by Winter Pennington. The Rosso Lussuria vampires face enemies both old and new, and to prevail they must call on even more strange alliances, unite as a clan, and draw on every weapon within their reach—but with a clan of vampires, that's easier said than done. (978-1-60282-679-3)

**Sometime Yesterday** by Yvonne Heidt. When Natalie Chambers learns her Victorian house is haunted by a pair of lovers and a Dark Man, can she and her lover Van Easton solve the mystery that will set the ghosts free and banish the evil presence in the house? Or will they have to run to survive as well? (978-1-60282-680-9)

**Into the Flames** by Mel Bossa. In order to save one of his patients, psychiatrist Jamie Scarborough will have to confront his own monsters—including those he unknowingly helped create. (978-1-60282-681-6)

**Coming Attractions: Author's Edition** by Bobbi Marolt. For Helen Townsend, chasing turns to caring, and caring turns to loving, but will love take five steps back and turn to leaving? (978-1-60282-732-5)

**OMGqueer**, edited by Radclyffe and Katherine E. Lynch. Through stories imagined and told by youth across America, this anthology provides a snapshot of queerness at the dawn of the new millennium. (978-1-60282-682-3)

**Oath of Honor** by Radclyffe. A First Responders novel. First do no harm…First Physician of the United States Wes Masters discovers that being the president's doctor demands more than brains and personal sacrifice—especially when politics is the order of the day. (978-1-60282-671-7)

**A Question of Ghosts** by Cate Culpepper. Becca Healy hopes Dr. Joanne Call can help her learn if her mother really committed suicide—but she's not sure she can handle her mother's ghost, a decades-old mystery, and lusting after the difficult Dr. Call without some serious chocolate consumption. (978-1-60282-672-4)